"Full of romance, dilemmas, and C follows the Weise family through th follows the star to the Perfect Light. Each story has a unique premise, intriguing characters, and a message about the true meaning of family and love. I absolutely adored this novella collection!"

SARAH SUNDIN, best-selling and Christy Award–winning author of *The Sound of Light* and *Until Leaves Fall in Paris*

"Three authors bring their individual flair to Christmas stories that resonate with holidays, depth, and heart. With superbly rendered, authentic characters, these novellas provide such a delightful escape into the Gilded Age, World War II, and a present-day career setting. Each with their own surprises and tender romances, these stories will draw you into the holiday spirit with a focus on the true King and what it means to root a love story in Him."

JOANNA DAVIDSON POLITANO, author of *The Lost Melody* and other Victorian-era novels

"Equal parts mysterious, funny, adventurous, and heartwarming, this collection ties three unique storytelling styles into an inspiring generational saga. Clever nods to the Weise—er, *wise*—men from the nativity story add to the overall theme that when all else fails, faith and family are lights not easily extinguished."

JANINE ROSCHE, author of *With Every Memory*

"A wonderful collection of stories, ranging from suspense on the high seas to stirring adventures involving Nazi art thieves to contemporary challenges with love and family. If you are a fan of Christmas, then you need this Christmas romance collection."

CAROLYN MILLER, award-winning historical and contemporary author

"*We Three Kings* is a generational Christmas compilation by three authors who will get you into the spirit of the holidays. Readers will immerse themselves in the Weise family tree and learn about German holiday traditions while members of the family fall in love during the yuletides. A must-add to your holiday reading repertoire."

SARAH MONZON, award-winning author of
the Sewing in SoCal series

We Three Kings

A

ROMANCE CHRISTMAS
COLLECTION

We Three Kings

CRYSTAL CAUDILL

CARA PUTMAN

ANGELA RUTH STRONG

KREGEL
PUBLICATIONS

Published by Kregel Publications, a division of Kregel Inc., 2450 Oak Industrial Dr. NE, Grand Rapids, MI 49505. www.kregel.com.

Crystal Caudill is represented by and "Star of Wonder" is published in association with The Steve Laube Agency, LLC. www.stevelaube.com.

Cara Putman is represented by and "Beauty Bright" is published in association with the literary agency of WordServe Literary Group, Ltd., www.wordserve literary.com.

"Perfect Light" is published in association with the Books & Such Literary Management, 52 Mission Circle, Suite 122, PMB 170, Santa Rosa, CA 95409-5370.

Cataloging-in-Publication Data is available from the Library of Congress.

ISBN 978-0-8254-4791-4, print
ISBN 978-0-8254-7058-5, epub
ISBN 978-0-8254-6972-5, Kindle

Printed in the United States of America
23 24 25 26 27 28 29 30 31 32 / 5 4 3 2 1

Star of Wonder

CRYSTAL CAUDILL

When they had heard the king, they departed;
and, lo, the star, which they saw in the east,
went before them, till it came and stood over where
the young child was. When they saw the star,
they rejoiced with exceeding great joy.
MATTHEW 2:9–10

Chapter One

December 2, 1884

THE DAY CELESTIA Isaacs met Aldrich Weise at a shareholder soirée, she knew they'd marry. Too bad the man was too thickheaded to realize it. Call her impatient, but two years was long enough for him to come around. By the end of this Christmas voyage on his family's newest steamer, marriage would be on his mind. Even if she had to propose to him herself.

The image provoked a smile she quickly squelched. It wouldn't do for her brother, Josiah, to notice and question her motives for joining the otherwise male investor tour of the New York City docks. While the operations behind the *Golden Gestirn* genuinely interested her, she would have forgone the chilly outdoor excursion if it weren't for Aldrich's presence.

At long last the carriage rolled to a stop at the end of Clarkson Street, where pier after pier extended into the North River. Celestia repositioned herself to better see through the window, and her grin escaped. She'd never traveled by ship, let alone been to a port. Overwhelming smells of salt water, fish, and machine grease saturated the damp air. Warehouse-like buildings ran the length of the piers. The black funnels and tall masts of moored ships rose to greet cornflower skies. Dockworkers, fishmongers, and wagons intermingled with the polished carriages, hired hacks, and travelers arriving to board ships destined to cross the great Atlantic. The noisy bustle of it all reverberated through their closed carriage and thrummed through her with the promise of excitement and adventure.

"You look as if you wish to jump from the carriage and sniff the area like a dog." Josiah chuckled from his reclined position opposite her.

"Not a dog, but perhaps a bird. Then I could soar about and perch on the masts to take it all in at once."

"I'm afraid you'll have to use your legs and be content with seeing the docks from your position at my side." His teasing tone turned serious. "This is no place to wander off. Pickpockets, lechers, and worse would target you in less than a minute. I promised Mother you'd be safe, and I need your word that you'll stay with me."

"I'm not three anymore. I know the dangers, and I promise to be an angel."

"I'm not sure how I feel about that answer. Devils were once angels, you know."

Celestia smacked his arm. "If anyone's devilish, it's you, Mr. I've-had-nine-engagements-in-ten-years."

"Better nine engagements than nine marriages. Losing one wife was enough for me."

Their driver opened the door, and the intensity of the noise and smells smacked her afresh. Renewed excitement scattered all her thoughts. She almost forgot to accept the driver's hand down before hopping to the ground. Josiah's easy laugh behind her indicated he hadn't missed her near faux pas, but he didn't chide her as Mother would have. He led her to the entrance of Pier 40, where a large group of men smoked and conversed.

"Good afternoon, gentlemen. It's a fine day for a tour," Josiah greeted from a distance.

Their attention skipped over him and riveted on her. A flurry of stomping out cigarettes and waving away the smoke followed.

Oh dear. She hadn't meant to infringe upon their relaxed fellowship.

Aldrich emerged from the group, and her stomach fluttered at the sight of his handsome face and the tenderness in his hazel eyes.

Whoever said absence makes the heart grow fonder trivialized the effect separation had on two people. Fondness failed to describe the magnitude of joy Aldrich's presence brought after not seeing him since last month's joint astronomy club excursion. As he drew nearer, his lips curved upward and conveyed not only he'd missed her, too, but that the subtle allusions to a future together had not faded from his mind either. Maybe it wouldn't be difficult to encourage a proposal from him after all. Emboldened, she reached for his hand.

He responded in kind, but when their fingers brushed, he dropped his hand and stiffened in reconsideration. Deep furrows formed in his high forehead, and his face became a study of disconcertion.

"Why are you here, Fräulein Isaacs?"

His callous welcome struck her dumb. Had she done something wrong?

Josiah's gentle nudge reminded her of his earlier warning. This was not an astronomy club gathering where she and Aldrich could talk and disappear into a world of their own. It was a business meeting, and business and women rarely mixed. Perhaps that was all that was amiss.

Even so, this was Aldrich, a man who openly admired his mother's participation with managing the New York office. Didn't that mean he wanted a wife who took an interest in the business as well?

Aldrich released a frustrated sigh. "Forgive me. I expected you to remain at the hotel."

"Is my presence unwelcome?"

He shifted uncomfortably and looked to Josiah.

Josiah shrugged, as if saying, *I tried to convince her to stay behind.*

All confidence in earning Aldrich's favor with her presence popped like a soap bubble.

"You are most welcome." His wan smile belied his answer. "However, I fear you will find the tour a tedious affair."

"On the contrary." She gifted him her brightest expression. "I'm eager to learn about the operations of my family's newest investment."

"Then may everything be found to your satisfaction." He dipped his head, closing their discussion, and addressed her brother. "Does this change our meeting plans for after the tour?"

"No. Celestia will wait with the driver until we're finished."

She opened her mouth to object, then clamped it shut. Obviously she'd intruded on more than a tour. Perhaps that explained his reticence.

Aldrich nodded and hesitated at her side in awkward silence. After shaking his head, he rejoined the group of men without a word.

What were Josiah and Aldrich up to? Josiah wouldn't relegate her to a carriage in an unfamiliar area without a serious reason. "What—"

"Please, Celestia. No questions. I cannot answer them."

Couldn't answer them? "Would this meeting have something to do with your profession?" She knew better than to name it in public. Even Mother and Father abided by his requirement that his position as a Secret Service operative be kept quiet, and Father rarely allowed anyone to dictate anything to him.

Josiah drew in a long-suffering breath, giving her his answer.

Why would a Secret Service operative from Philadelphia need to meet with a shipowner based in New York City?

Aldrich's voice rose from the front, where he addressed the tour group. "Before we begin, allow me to introduce *meinen Bruder*, Brenner Weise, the newest addition to Deutsch-Amerika leadership."

A young man who appeared several years Aldrich's junior stepped to his side. The family resemblance was undeniable. Brenner bore their father's high forehead like a family branding. His eyes were a far lighter shade than Aldrich's, although that probably resulted from the gaiety emanating from them. Even his smile declared him a jovial spirit.

Brenner's attention landed on her, and his lopsided grin grew impossibly wide. "Guten Tag. I look forward to making your acquaintance during our journey together."

His gaze lingered on hers, giving the distinct impression he specifically meant her. She severed eye contact and pretended to pick at her sleeve. Her behavior bordered on rude, but she wanted to send a clear message that his was not the attention she desired.

Aldrich cleared his throat.

Was that jealousy she detected? He need not be concerned with where her affections lay. They were—and always would be—with him. Before she could reassure him with a smile, he redirected his attention to Brenner's continued speech.

"After eighteen months of promises for a victor in the competitive market of ocean travel, we present to you *der Golden Gestirn*." Brenner gestured to the enormous ship behind him.

Celestia craned her neck to read the gold lettering of the ship's name against the black hull. Three masts capable of bearing sails flanked the two red-and-black funnels near the ship's center. White lifeboats capable of carrying dozens of people hung from rails along the top deck. How such a behemoth moved at anything more than a snail's pace was beyond comprehension.

Aldrich continued where Brenner left off. "Today, passengers desire a combination of speed, safety, and luxury. The *Golden Gestirn* provides the best of all three. Three-crank compressed engines give her the potential to reach a designed speed of 19.5 knots. The hull is divided into ten watertight compartments, and the bulkheads are carried to the upper deck and are fitted with fireproof and waterproof doors. Saloon passengers will experience luxury that exceeds the exquisiteness of Europe's finest palaces. Already the public tours have generated sales beyond expectation and suggest a payoff on your investment well in advance of the promised timeline."

A rumble of approval arose at his last statement.

They followed Aldrich down the pier as he identified the various features engineered by the genius of ship designers, William Pearce. Not that she could make out much of what he said. Josiah held her captive at the back of the group. With great effort, she eventually escaped his overbearing hold and slipped to the front beside Aldrich. Certainly no danger awaited her here. All of their party were respected shareholders and Aldrich a perfect gentleman.

While Aldrich didn't take her arm, he did adjust his position to provide a protective boundary between her and the edge of the pier. Probably a wise decision, given the sound of his voice mesmerized her. As a second-generation immigrant, Aldrich mostly spoke German with his family, giving his speech an accent that never ceased to fascinate her. His enthusiastic hope in breaking the *Oregon*'s Blue Riband speed record with the *Golden Gestirn*'s maiden voyage brought out a thicker tinge to his speech, and she adored it.

Midway through the tour, Brenner came alongside her and offered his arm. Etiquette demanded she accept, especially given who he was, but she'd have much preferred Aldrich to extend the courtesy. Brenner was a gentleman by all means, but he slowed his steps, forcing the space between her and Aldrich to grow. When they fell into step with Josiah, she suspected her brother had arranged her subtle return.

She sent Josiah an accusing scowl, which he deftly ignored.

"Do not hold it against him," Brenner whispered. "This meeting is important to Aldrich, and there were several men who appeared distracted."

By her.

Her shoulders sank. She hadn't meant to disrupt Aldrich's meeting. "I suppose Josiah was right. I shouldn't have come."

"I disagree. Your interest is admirable. In fact"—he bestowed his smile and sparkling eyes upon her—"I am rather pleased by it."

How to respond? She didn't want to encourage his flirtations, but she was thankful for his soothing over her mistake. "Please accept my apologies and extend them to your brother as well."

"Apology accepted." He winked. "Might you consider promenading on the dock with me while our *Brüder* meet instead of waiting alone in the carriage?"

"I'll have to ask Josiah. He's exceedingly protective of me."

"As he should be."

Much to her surprise, when the tour ended and Brenner asked, Josiah consented. "So long as you stay within view."

Aldrich didn't seem pleased, but he and Josiah moved to a more secluded area.

"Shall we?" Brenner offered his arm and led them along the boundary of the loading area.

They paused to watch as a crane attached to the front of the ship lifted one of a dozen crates from the pier to the deck far above them.

Once unloaded, the net lowered over the side once more to claim its next cargo.

"What do the crates hold?" she asked.

"Most are supplies for the journey, although that is not even a quarter of it. A sailing of more than a week with five hundred crew members and nearly eight hundred passengers requires a great deal of preparation."

"So many people?"

"It will be more on the return trip. Thirteen hundred passengers, in addition to the crew. The vast majority of those in steerage are immigrants, so more travel west than east."

"Is it profitable to sail a ship with more than five hundred empty berths?"

That lopsided grin appeared again. "Very astute. Our eastbound sailings are not as profitable as our westbound. However, we fill the unused steerage with cargo and recover the majority of the deficit."

Raised voices near the crates stacked at the pier's edge halted their conversation. The words sounded foreign. Not German—she'd spent the last year and a half studying it in hopes of impressing Aldrich and his family—but the language was familiar. She tugged Brenner past crates toward the ruckus.

Two men with olive complexions and dark hair lobbed their foreign conversation back and forth. Their hands spoke as much as, if not louder than, their words. Palms smacked against chests, and they parried one another until they were dangerously close to the edge.

The lankier one shoved a few banknotes in the stockier one's face. *"Non va bene."*

A romantic language. While not French like she'd studied before meeting Aldrich, the languages were similar enough to garner a basic understanding. *No good.* Did Lanky mean he wanted more? Or that the money he waved in Stocky's face was spurious?

Stocky replied too fast for a translation attempt, but his return shove was clear enough.

Someone was bound to get hurt. "We should do something."

"Not *we*." Brenner frowned. "I will return you to your carriage and then intervene."

That might be the wisest choice for her safety, but an imprudent one for the men. She glanced back at the fight, undecided if she should comply or force the issue.

Stocky held a roll of money out of reach, and Lanky lunged.

Bills scattered across the pier and into the water.

With a furious growl, Stocky delivered a punch that sent Lanky flying over the edge.

"You have to help him now!" Celestia pushed Brenner toward the fight and then screamed for help.

Stocky's attention snapped from collecting the money to her. Eyes equal parts brown and green locked onto hers, icy as the Delaware River in January. A shiver coursed through her even as her heart beat with wild fury.

He shot to his feet. With a speed she didn't expect, he slugged Brenner in the gut, shoved him aside, and sprinted straight toward her.

She tried to step out of the way, but her heel met air.

Stocky slammed into her, and her body sailed backward.

By the time she pushed through the shock of impact, she was falling with nothing to grab. The bright world above the pier disappeared, and a shadowy underbelly replaced it. She opened her mouth to scream or pray—or something—but the river rushed in to greet her with its frigid embrace.

Chapter Two

For the hundredth time since he and Herr Isaacs had started their discussion, Aldrich's gaze flicked to Brenner and Celestia. They made a handsome pair in every way. Although, anyone who stood next to her looked the better for it.

Celestia was one of those rare creatures whose inner beauty radiated outward so intensely that her appearance had no choice but to match. Hair yellow enough to make gold jealous haloed her head, and expressive eyes that shone brighter than Sirius itself enticed a man to dream of a future with her. Especially when a starry night hung as a backdrop and the warmth of her hand rested beneath his on a shared telescope.

Aldrich blinked to dispel the image. So much had changed since that evening a month ago. Had the letter not arrived sparking his need to move to Germany, it might be him promenading with Celestia now. He focused on their retreating forms, and all the bitterness at what God was calling him to sacrifice resurfaced. It was only right he allow Brenner the opportunity to pursue Celestia, given his own change of plans.

But that did not mean he liked it.

"And you have no idea who is using your ships to import counterfeits?" Herr Isaacs's question jarred Aldrich's attention back to the matter at hand.

"*Nein.*" He took a deep breath to calm the rising frustration.

This voyage was supposed to instill shareholder confidence in their company and Brenner's ability to take over the New York offices in June. Now to prevent a possible scandal, Aldrich needed to convince the Secret Service that Deutsch-Amerika did not willingly or knowingly import counterfeit money. At least there was the fact that as the son of one of their largest shareholders, Herr Isaacs had promised to conduct a discreet investigation.

"How can you be certain these counterfeits are coming from our ships?"

"A large number of immigrants traced through Castle Garden claim to have exchanged their foreign currency for American banknotes with your money changer only to discover later those notes were counterfeit."

"But we do not have a money changer. It is a requirement of Castle Garden that none but approved banks perform such a task. We even transport immigrants directly from our ships to Castle Garden in order to prevent unscrupulous people from taking advantage of them."

"Unfortunately, Mr. Weise, every one of these immigrants—and we're talking hundreds—have sworn under oath that their money was exchanged by a member of your company before disembarking."

The scrutiny with which Herr Isaacs watched Aldrich's reaction made Aldrich want to squirm, but he was innocent of wrongdoing. "Someone is acting outside of our authority. We seek to help immigrants, not harm them. I will cooperate in any way necessary, but we have a fleet of five ships with over five hundred employees each. How can we know who is responsible?"

"Of all the counterfeiters the Secret Service arrests, Italians are the most likely to produce counterfeits in their home country, transport them here, and then target their sales at other immigrants unfamiliar with US currency. As we have no jurisdiction in Italy, it allows for uninterrupted production and makes apprehending them difficult. Given the method and location of distribution, we believe the culprit is most likely Italian."

"You say likely, but you are not certain?"

"No." Herr Isaacs scowled. "Where are they going?"

Aldrich followed Herr Isaacs's gaze to where Celestia and Brenner strode behind a crate. Brenner was a consummate gentleman, but Aldrich's stomach still knotted. Celestia was sweet, innocent, and enticing. More than once he'd been tempted beyond reason to kiss her himself. Most recently at the joint excursion of their respective astronomy clubs to the Warner Observatory.

Something splashed in the water beyond view, and Celestia's scream for help pierced the air.

Aldrich sprinted toward them. Within a few yards, he spotted Brenner doubled over on the dock.

Another man charged toward Celestia.

Before Aldrich could shout, the man slammed into her and barreled past.

She teetered on the edge.

Then disappeared.

"Man overboard!" Aldrich sounded the alarm.

Dockhands responded with calls of their own, abandoning their tasks to rush for the necessary equipment.

Please, Gott. Do not let her have hit her head on the hull.

He and Herr Isaacs reached the dock's edge where she'd disappeared. Half a dozen feet below, she flailed in the dark water, doing her best to grasp the dock's piling.

Good. Had she been knocked unconscious, she might have drowned before they reached her.

Josiah stripped off his coat.

"Nein." Aldrich stayed him with a hand to his arm. "She will pull you under and drown you both. Even if not, that water is under forty degrees. We cannot risk you both suffering hypothermia. We will use a Kisbee ring."

To his relief, the cork ring slapped the water near Celestia even as he spoke.

He dropped to his stomach and called down. "Fräulein Isaacs, lock your arms around that ring!"

She studied the floating circle, hesitation clear on her face. Why should she leave the security of the piling for an object out of reach?

He did not wish to scare her, but if she stayed, the cold would numb her grip and the weight of her soaked dress would drag her under before a rowboat could reach her.

"Trust me. I will soon have you safe if you do."

She nodded. Then, with a courage he admired, she pushed from the post. Her arm hooked one side, and her weight plunged the end she clasped beneath the water, taking her with it.

Gott, help her to not let go.

A moment later she bobbed back up, still holding strong.

His breath released with a prayer of thanksgiving, and he hopped to his feet. "Pull her toward the ladder!"

She sputtered as the water lapped against her face. "Save the other man!"

Only then did Aldrich realize another person treaded the surface nearer to the ship's head.

"I have him!" Brenner rushed toward the Kisbee ring on a post farther down the dock.

Brenner could be trusted with that task. Aldrich's concern was for Celestia.

As he jogged toward the ladder with Herr Isaacs on his heels, he called out orders. "Bring blankets and coffee."

But blankets and coffee would not be enough to combat hypothermia. Not while she still wore a freezing wet dress.

"Find her dry clothes! And a female to assist!"

He grabbed the rail of the ladder, swung down to the third rung, and continued downward until level with the water. The rope attached to the ring slapped against his arm as the dockhand and Herr Isaacs pulled Celestia hand over hand toward Aldrich, stopping when the ring bumped against the ladder.

"It's a f-f-fine d-d-day for a swim." Celestia's voice shook as much as her body.

Her humor imparted hope that she was not yet suffering shock. Though everything in him vibrated with the frantic need to get her out and warm, he attempted to respond in kind. "I think we should leave that for the fish. Do you not agree?"

"W-where's the f-fun in th-that?" Her wide smile failed to disguise the remnants of fear in her eyes.

He turned the ring with one hand until she was close enough to assist. "Forgive me, but I will need to grab your waist. Can you hold the rail here while I reach for you?"

She did as bidden while still clinging to the ring.

He squatted as low as possible and plunged his arm into the piercing water. He found her narrow waist and drew her toward him until she pressed against his side. "Now lock your arms around my neck."

Again she obliged, and he pushed against the ladder rung to stand. He'd expected the weight, but a strained grunt escaped as he lifted her from the river. "Put your feet on the rungs as we climb."

It was an awkward progression—both of them squeezing onto the narrow ladder and him sliding his hand up the cold metal pole to prevent a backward fall. Once their heads cleared the dock, a bevy of arms assisted them the rest of the way. They tumbled forward, and blankets draped over them. He barely gained his feet before two of his female staff and Herr Issacs whisked Celestia off to the baggage office to change out of her wet clothes.

Relief for her safety gave way to pummeling exhaustion. He staggered to the nearest crate and capitulated to the need to sit down. Man-overboard rescues were not a new experience, but Celestia's almost drowning distressed him more than any other. Her friendship was dear to him. *She* was dear to him. Losing her to time and distance was going to be hard enough, but to death? Thank Gott for that mercy.

"Are you well, sir?" a dockhand asked.

"Well enough. Did anyone detain the man who pushed Fräulein Issacs overboard?"

"No, sir. We were more concerned with her and the other man."

As they should have been, even if it frustrated him that the scoundrel escaped accountability for his actions.

Brenner appeared with concern lining his face and a fistful of money grasped in his hand. "Please find a dry set of clothes for Herr Weise." He waited until the dockhand left before continuing.

"I have spoken with the man we pulled from the water. The fight began because the one who escaped sold him counterfeit currency. The escapee was one of *our* employees."

Aldrich scrubbed a hand over his face. Just what they needed. How many shareholders still lingered and were eager for details? Any hint of scandal and at least half were likely to pull their support. Deutsch-Amerika wasn't financially unstable, but that kind of blow would cripple their ability to make the payments for the *Golden Gestirn* without sacrificing the needed maintenance for their other ships.

"Tell no one, and isolate the man in one of the offices until Herr Isaacs can interview him. We will deal with this quietly."

Brenner nodded and set off at a brisk pace. Aldrich forced himself from the ground and sought Herr Isaacs despite still being wet. If all went well, the culprit would be identified and arrested by the end of the day and this potential scandal put behind them. Then Aldrich could focus on ensuring the *Golden Gestirn* did her job breaking records and impressing their shareholders. As long as he concentrated on that, he could ignore the painful knowledge that he would soon leave Celestia behind forever.

Chapter Three

A COLD, DENSE fog hung over the North River and shrouded the upper portions of the *Golden Gestirn* from view. Celestia shivered inside her cloak, though she'd never admit it to Josiah. With the exception of his absence for the few hours after her return to the hotel last night, he'd fretted over her nonstop. He simply couldn't accept that the sole consequence of her fall was a ruined dress.

Aldrich emerged from the Pier 40 building with long strides and met Celestia and Josiah halfway to the ship. He doffed his hat and greeted them with a stiff nod and compressed lips before speaking. "I am sorry for the necessity of requesting your presence so early this morning, especially after yesterday's ordeal."

The poor man. Didn't he know she'd wake before the stars slumbered just to see him? "It's my pleasure to be of assistance to the man who so gallantly rescued me."

His shoulders relaxed, and a reserved smile eased the tension in his face. "*Danke schön.* According to the man who fell in the water, the culprit we seek is a member of my crew brought over from one of our other ships. I cannot employ someone who would willingly risk the lives of others, let alone allow him to cross the ocean and escape the consequences."

He made no mention of the counterfeiting concerns, but then again, she wasn't supposed to know about them. Josiah's assumption that she'd been asleep on the sofa by the fire when a New York operative came to discuss the case had played to her favor.

Aldrich continued. "Would you be able to identify the man if you saw him?"

"I would." Even if only by his bone-chilling eyes.

"Good. We have gathered about fifty employees who match Brenner's description of the man. Your brother and I will protect either side of you, and Captain Müeller will serve as a boundary between you and the men, so you need not fear."

"I never fear when you're around. Lead on. You have my complete trust."

Tender regard softened his face, and his arm lifted, as if he desired to escort her.

But he pivoted away.

Celestia hid her disappointment by taking Josiah's arm and followed Aldrich to the wide gangplank, where passengers would board in a few hours. Captain Müeller met them at the base, paid her the customary pleasantries, then led them to where his men stood at attention.

Officers and stewards were first, dressed in their black double-breasted suits. At Aldrich's encouragement, she studied each man's eyes. When they didn't hold an equal mix of brown and green, she smiled and attempted a *grazie*. Based on their amused countenances, she probably butchered the word, but they offered a gracious nod, and she moved on to the next. Once she reached the end of the officers and affirmed none were the man from yesterday, they were dismissed to their duties. She repeated the process with the white-frocked cooks and bakers. They too were dismissed, as were the greasers, firemen, and trimmers dressed in their everyday work clothes.

"You're certain none of them were the man we seek?" Josiah asked.

"I am. He wasn't here."

Aldrich's lines of stress reappeared at her answer.

"Perhaps he didn't show for work. Or maybe the other man was mistaken and the culprit wasn't a member of your crew, but pretended to be."

"Both are logical explanations that I will look into before our departure." Aldrich's false smile declared the likelihood of his being satisfied with those results.

"If you're truly concerned he's still here, I can walk the ship with you and evaluate the men as they work so we don't disturb the necessary preparations."

The proffered solution helped him and also provided her an opportunity to speak privately with him and encourage the suit she thought he too desired. At the very least, she could inquire why he'd suddenly stopped writing after their visit to the Warner Observatory and assigned someone else to coordinate events between their astronomy clubs.

Aldrich addressed Josiah. "Will you join the search?"

Of course he'd ask Josiah. Sometimes the fact Aldrich was a gentleman downright annoyed her. She'd much rather her paid companion, Marybeth Adams, be their chaperone, but she had remained with Mother at the hotel to oversee baggage transportation.

"I'll not allow Celestia to go anywhere unchaperoned with a man, let alone on a search for one who attacked her." Josiah dipped his chin down in the familiar big-brother threat.

"Good. I will have Brenner join you and Captain Müeller in the chart room. You can work your way down from there. Do you remember the way?"

"You mean you're not joining us?" Celestia tried but failed to keep the surprise and disappointment from her voice.

"Please accept my regrets. I have many other duties to perform before we disembark, including looking into those alternative explanations you suggested. Brenner knows this ship as well as I, and Captain Müeller will assign someone to go with you for the less familiar areas. If you will excuse me." Aldrich bowed in farewell and returned down the gangplank.

Celestia watched him the whole way, a sneaking suspicion forming with each one of his determined strides. Aldrich wasn't hastening away to do his job. He was hastening away from *her.*

⁓⊹⁓

Aldrich buttoned the top of his crisp new shirt and then reached for his gray waistcoat tossed over the armchair in his shared stateroom. Where was Brenner? The time for the ceremony to celebrate the maiden voyage of the *Golden Gestirn* drew near. It was to be a highly publicized event, and Aldrich wanted Brenner to be the face of Deutsch-Amerika's New York office. Surely he was not still with Celestia. Walking the whole ship should not take three hours.

Not unless Brenner purposely prolonged their time together.

Aldrich rolled his neck in an effort to dispel his agitation. It had been a mistake to send Brenner in his place, but each minute spent with Celestia pierced him like an iceberg to a ship's hull. If he wasn't careful, he'd sink into a sea of bitterness and lost dreams. He blew out a breath and stared at Brenner's speech waiting on the desk. They didn't need shareholders questioning why Brenner and Celestia searched the ship. Proving the cost of the *Golden Gestirn* was worth their investment was difficult enough without the cloud of scandal hovering on the horizon.

A knock interrupted his spiraling thoughts.

"Enter."

A sooty Brenner opened the door. "Forgive my tardiness. We ran into trouble in the fireroom. Coal shifted and trapped Fräulein Isaacs."

First a near drowning, and now this? "Is she hurt?"

Brenner tossed his coat to the floor and then left a trail of clothes to his berth behind the curtain. "Nein. She is as fine as they come. Instead of fussing about her dress, she was all humor and mirth." His head popped around the curtain. "I am surprised you are not courting her. She is a good match for anyone. Even you."

Aldrich gave Brenner his back and shrugged on his coat. "You know why I cannot."

The faucet handle squeaked, and water ran from the steam-heated pipes into the washbasin. "If you cannot have her as a wife, what do you think of having her as a sister?"

He stiffened, glad for the fact Brenner could not see his reaction. It was one thing to allow his and Celestia's friendship to fade, but to always have her near yet out of reach? Aldrich swallowed hard. Would Gott torture him so? Perhaps He would be merciful and Brenner would fail to capture Celestia's affections.

"Are you ready yet?" His tone came out gruff, but Brenner ignored it if he noticed.

"Nein. This soot is stubborn, and I dare not put on a white shirt until all traces are gone."

"Do not dawdle. We cannot have the newspapers and shareholders arrive before us."

The water turned off, and the rustle of Brenner dressing followed. "We did not find the man, by the way."

Right. The counterfeiter. He should have asked about that sooner.

Brenner continued. "I do not think he is aboard ship. We visited every department and could not find him. Fräulein Isaacs did acknowledge it was possible to have missed someone with all the movement occurring. Herr Isaacs suggested delaying our departure, but we have little evidence that doing so will accomplish anything other than sparking concern and rumors. I say we do not let our guard down but proceed as planned. Do you not agree?"

"I do." His brother was going to make a fine head of the New York offices come June, and by the end of this voyage, everyone would concur. "Finish preparing, and meet me on the platform for the ceremony. Your notes are on the desk."

When Aldrich arrived at the base of the gangplank, he observed the gold ribbon that stretched from rail to rail. A dockhand stood guard, shooing away children who thought it a game to duck under and race up the gangplank until either stopped by a crew member or able to touch the ship's hull. He smirked. How many times had he and Brenner played the same game, sans ribbon, while waiting to board for their annual summer trip to Germany? Would his children one day do the same when they visited America? He shook his head, refusing to allow his thoughts to wander to the bittersweet reality undergirding that image. Deutsch-Amerika must be his focus.

By the time an eager crowd of passengers, press, and curious onlookers surrounded the platform erected next to the gangplank, *Mutter* and *Vater* had arrived and claimed their seats behind the podium. Brenner sat with them, along with Herr Isaacs and several other prominent shareholders. From the corner of the platform, Aldrich watched his parents encourage Brenner and offer a quiet prayer—just as they had for Aldrich before each of his speeches. The realization that those days were coming to a close hit with a pang he was not prepared for. Seven months were going to pass too fast, and he did not want to miss a moment of what remained.

He joined his family and said his own prayer for Brenner's speech. No one commented on the choked nature of his words, but the moisture and compassion in Mutter's eyes communicated her understanding. The decision about Germany had been left to him, and after a period of prayer and wrestling, he had accepted God's calling. But the sacrifices required were a heavy burden to bear, especially today.

Vater nodded for Aldrich to begin the ceremony, and Mutter squeezed his hand before he turned away.

Though his speech instructor would be aghast, Aldrich gripped the sides of the podium to anchor himself to the moment and not the swell of emotions that threatened to cast him overboard. He waited until the crowd hushed.

"Ladies and gentlemen, it is with great pride that Deutsch-Amerika presents to you the fastest, safest, and most luxurious ocean steamer in the world, der *Golden Gestirn*. *Golden* for its luxury, and *Gestirn*, which means star, because of its power to lead its passengers to grand adventures and new lives." He swallowed past the sudden lump in his throat. "In addition to this grand ship, Deutsch-Amerika is proud to introduce meinen Bruder, Brenner Weise, as the newest leader of our American branch."

Brenner joined him at the podium, waited for the applause to die, and then claimed his position as orator and the face of the New York offices.

Aldrich crept to the back edge of the platform, separate from his family, and waited until the crowd was fully enraptured by Brenner's words before descending to the dock. Slowly, he worked his way to the center of the gathering and watched in triumph as Brenner rose to the occasion. In his three and a half years at university, he'd matured and grown. His skills at the podium would only improve with time, yet it was unlikely Aldrich would witness more than a handful of Brenner's speeches in his lifetime. One semester more and then Brenner would fully come into his own. They'd be business partners. Co-owners in a family legacy that spanned an ocean and two generations, with hopefully many more to come. It was that ocean part that held Aldrich's emotions far too close to his sleeves today.

"He's doing a fine job, Herr Weise. You should be proud."

Aldrich startled at Celestia's voice. How long had she been standing there, regarding him with an affectionate approval that matched his own for Brenner? "Forgive me, I did not realize you were there." He glanced around but failed to spot any of her family besides Herr Isaacs on the platform. "Are you alone?"

"No, my companion, Miss Adams, is behind you. Mother allowed me to join you when I saw you leave the platform. Although, I wonder why you did so. Shouldn't you be up there with your family?"

"I will join them for the ribbon cutting. I wanted to watch Brenner from the best vantage point."

Celestia squeezed his arm, almost as if she sensed the turmoil inside him. "You are a good brother. He is lucky to have you."

Though he should not, he laid his hand atop hers and kept it in place. She could not know how much her presence soothed him as the weight of his obligations hit him with their full impact. Of all the sacrifices moving permanently to Germany required, leaving his family and Celestia behind were two of the hardest.

Chapter Four

Something serious bothered Aldrich. Celestia knew it as well as her own heartbeat. It could be that he'd heard the first whispered rumors about yesterday's excitement and today's search, but somehow she doubted it. His manner was less worried and more akin to grief. He'd watched Brenner speak as if he might never do so again. Then when all four of the Weise family members used the scissors to cut the ribbon together, she could've sworn tears shimmered in his eyes. But journalists had thronged him afterward and had prevented her from speaking to him again.

Celestia sighed as she and Marybeth weaved through the crowded promenade deck of the *Golden Gestirn*. Everyone seemed determined to claim a lounge chair or a place at the rails before the ship pulled away. All *she* wanted was a spot next to Aldrich, wherever that might be.

"Do you think the ship will rock very much, miss?" Marybeth's green pallor did not bode well for the trip ahead. The ship was still moored and barely moved underfoot.

"So long as the seas are calm, you shouldn't feel too much rocking. Especially if you stay toward the middle aft of the ship, or so I've read." Not that she knew where the aft was.

"But you don't plan to stay in those parts, do you?" Concern furrowed her brow.

"No, but I will be with trusted friends and family, so I don't believe Mother would fault you for remaining in our suite."

She nodded but did not appear convinced. Mother was a sweet woman, but her biting reproval could cow a pirate. And poor Marybeth had the backbone of a jellyfish.

At the frontmost section of the promenade, a rope prevented the crowd from invading a private area of lounge chairs and refreshments next to the chart room windows. Aldrich's parents faced the bow, where the calls of crewmen indicated preparations for departure were well underway.

"Miss Isaacs, do you wish to join Herr and Frau Weise?" The steward who escorted them through the ship and then pulled her from the coal heap this morning emerged from his position at the wall.

"Thank you, but no. I don't wish to interrupt."

He nodded and returned, but their conversation must have caught Frau Weise's attention.

"It is no interruption. Come. Sit." She gestured to the two empty seats next to her.

Celestia obliged, and Marybeth claimed the chair farthest away.

"Danke schön, Frau Weise. Your hospitality is most gracious."

The woman's smile indicated she approved of Celestia's use of German. "I am told you have ruined two dresses on account of my ship. We shall replace them. Perhaps you would enjoy something made in Germany?"

"I appreciate your offer, but there is no need. They were merely dresses. Besides, I already planned on purchasing a few in Germany. So while I will indeed enjoy the craftsmanship of your home country, it will be at my own expense."

Frau Weise studied Celestia with dark-brown eyes that revealed nothing, then nodded. "You and my Aldrich are avid star watchers, no?"

Heat climbed Celestia's neck, and she dropped her gaze to the polished wooden boards. She shouldn't be embarrassed, but for some reason their shared interest seemed private. Intimate, even. Perhaps it was because stargazing with Aldrich had been some of the most romantic and cherished moments she'd shared with the man. Last month they'd held hands over a telescope and spoken of future dreams. No one could accuse him of improper behavior or speech, but she was certain he'd almost kissed her. Too bad Marybeth had chosen that moment to announce refreshments were ready.

"I do enjoy watching the stars, but your son is far more knowledgeable than I. He instructs our astronomy clubs when we meet and points out the locations of planets, nebulas, and constellations."

"He has spoken highly of you as well."

Not even the salty breeze could cool her face now. If she hoped to maintain any dignity around the woman, she needed to move the conversation away from herself or Aldrich.

"I have never been to Germany. Where are your favorite places to visit during your time home?"

Thankfully, the woman was pleased to expound upon the topic in great detail with little encouragement from Celestia. Not that Celestia minded. She was excited to hear about the country Aldrich so loved. The way the Weises spoke of their home country made Celestia wish she would have more than two weeks to explore it. According to Frau Weise, a person could spend their whole life there and it wouldn't be long enough.

"Excuse me, Miss Isaacs. I have a few questions concerning a member of the *Golden Gestirn* pushing you into the water yesterday."

Celestia turned in her seat. The interruption came from a young man in a tweed suit with a pencil set against a pad of paper and his straw hat tilted at a jaunty angle. Not him again. That reporter had been attempting to corner her all afternoon.

"How did you sneak past? Be gone. Journalists are supposed to be disembarking." Frau Weise dismissed him with her hand, but the man remained rooted beside Celestia.

Her family often dealt with reporters of this type, but Mother's reputation for humbling them and sending them on their way usually deterred them. It must be why he sought to catch Celestia without her family. Well, no more. She could handle this man on her own.

"If I may, Frau Weise?" After the woman's nod, Celestia stood and angled her head the same way her mother did in such situations. "I'm sorry—who are you again?"

"The name's Bower Johnson. I'm with the *New York Herald*."

"Would that be the same Bower Johnson whom my brother-in-law is prosecuting in a slander suit? Your third one this year, if I recall correctly."

He stiffened. "I just require the facts."

"Then that is what I expect my brother-in-law to read in anything published by your newspaper. And he *will* know if you have strayed from the facts, because he will receive a detailed note before we leave port with instructions to pursue a slander suit on the behalf of Deutsch-Amerika if your details do not match mine. Are we clear?"

He nodded, pencil annoyingly poised to write.

"First, your statement is erroneous. An as-yet-unidentified man was in an altercation with another man on the pier. During his escape from being apprehended, he knocked me into the water. *That* is the full of your story."

"But there was a search of the ship and crew for this man."

He spoke it as fact, and with the numerous witnesses, she couldn't contradict it. "Safety is of the utmost concern to Deutsch-Amerika, and as a precaution against any possibility of the man being aboard ship, a search was conducted. As I was personally involved, I can confirm that said man is nowhere to be found. Thus no connection should, or can, be made."

"But the man who also fell in the water identified the assailant as a crew member who previously exchanged him counterfeit money for genuine."

No wonder Mother hated dealing with the press. It was a constant parry of carefully spoken words. "The man you are referring to is a known counterfeiter who is throwing blame for the possession of counterfeit money on another. His words cannot be counted as fact. You can search for his records when you disembark if you need confirmation." Hopefully her insider knowledge wouldn't get her into trouble with Josiah or lead Mr. Johnson to ask for the man's name. That was one detail she couldn't claim to know.

"You have your story, Herr Johnson. Officer Henrich will escort you off the ship now." Aldrich appeared at her elbow.

With his story in hand and an intimidatingly tall and broad officer behind him, Mr. Johnson departed.

Aldrich tracked Mr. Johnson's exit with a glower that made Celestia glad she was not the intended recipient.

Frau and Herr Weise spoke in low, angry tones far too fast for Celestia to understand with her novice grasp of German. Perhaps she overstepped. "I apologize for threatening a slander suit on your behalf. Mr. Johnson has a history of crafting articles detrimental to the reputation of good people and companies. It won't stop him from writing, but my hope is it will force him to consider his words carefully."

"Your endeavor to protect our company is appreciated." Aldrich offered his arm. "Allow me to escort you to the chart room, where you can write your letter."

She said her goodbyes to Herr and Frau Weise, and Marybeth trailed behind them as Aldrich led her inside the building and into the narrow room.

"I did not know you could be so formidable." His approving smile as he held the door open warmed her like mulled cider on a snowy day.

"It's not my preferred state, but I can pull upon it when necessary." She took a seat at the indicated table and waited as he procured the required materials.

When he brought the paper, ink, and pen over, he glanced at Marybeth before leaning close to whisper, "How is it you know about the counterfeiting accusation?"

She should've known that would come up sooner rather than later. "Josiah thought I was asleep, and I overheard the details."

Aldrich nodded and frowned.

"If it's any consolation, Josiah *will* find and arrest the person. I'll help in any way I can. It isn't fair your company should suffer because someone is taking advantage of his position."

"Do you know if the other shareholders have heard the rumors?" Worry lines crinkled outward from his eyes and mouth.

She could reassure him with false platitudes, but Aldrich deserved truth. "It is likely they will, if they have not already. The entire crew knows we are hunting for him, and if Mr. Johnson is asking about a counterfeiting connection, then it will be common knowledge soon enough."

Aldrich slumped into an armed chair next to her and pinched the bridge of his nose.

How she grieved for the weight he bore. She swiveled her anchored seat toward him and clasped his free hand. "Take heart, Aldrich." His gaze shot to hers at the use of his Christian name, but she boldly pressed forward. Had she not earned the right to speak it? She'd written it on a year's worth of letters. "You are not facing this alone. We are not merely *Bekannte*. What we have is deep and enduring. We are *Freunde*. We'll prove to them that one rat cannot take down your ship."

"Where did you learn the difference between Bekannter and Freund?"

Of all the things to be concerned about, that was what he asked her? "I hired a German tutor shortly after we met because I wanted to be able to converse with you in your preferred language. I'm a slow learner, but it didn't take long for me to learn the difference between an acquaintance and a friend and the seriousness taken in declaring someone your friend." She squeezed his hand and leaned closer. "I have long declared you my friend and thought you considered the same of me. Am I wrong?"

A sort of groan escaped as he returned to pinching the bridge of his nose, but his free hand remained in hers. He sat like that for a full minute before withdrawing from her hold and rising to his feet. "Forgive me. I have responsibilities I must see to. When you are finished with your letter, give it to the steward serving Mutter and Vater. He will see that it gets delivered to your brother-in-law."

He bowed stiffly and left.

All the air heaved from her lungs as she thudded back into the seat. What just happened? Was she wrong about their friendship? And what about their future?

Chapter Five

CELESTIA FINGERED THE Christmas greenery with pine cones and red berries artfully arranged in the vase on her stateroom table and tried to force the expected merriment into her smile. The beautifully printed schedule of Christmas-themed events supplied a plethora of opportunities to discover where she and Aldrich stood—if the man ever made his presence known again.

So far the trip was a disaster in regard to spending time with him. Celestia passed the first day perched at the railing with Marybeth and Mother, watching the pier as the *Golden Gestirn* launched among cheers and great fanfare. The horn bellowed as the ship passed competitors and raced out of the Hudson Bay into the vast Atlantic. Long after Mother and the others had sought the warmth of the steam-heated indoors, Celestia remained to watch the seagulls soar under pink-and-orange-tinted clouds. It wasn't until the sun set and the stars emerged in a glorious twinkling blanket that she acknowledged her fingers and face were numb. The entire day had been exhilarating—and devastatingly disappointing without Aldrich by her side.

She'd hoped that the next day he would seek her out, but Brenner had been the only Weise to find her. When Marybeth succumbed to seasickness, he kept Celestia and Josiah company and did all the things she'd hoped to do with Aldrich. They explored the luxurious public areas, strolled the decks, watched the sun glisten over the waves, and even participated in some of the Christmas games hosted by Frau Weise in the music room. He attended her at dinner—the fourth meal without Aldrich—and saw her to her cabin suite like a beau courting his girl. Too bad he was the wrong Weise, but she wasn't sure how to discourage his suit without placing herself in a precarious position with the family.

Today proved no better than yesterday. Worse, in fact. Aldrich spotted her, Josiah, and Brenner and immediately changed course to the smoking room, where she could not follow.

Lord, I don't understand. I thought we were friends. I thought he finally wanted to be more than friends. What happened?

Josiah knocked at the open door to her stateroom. "Are you ready?"

Marybeth groaned from her berth above Celestia's. The poor dear hadn't recovered and wasn't likely to if her continued reticence to move indicated anything.

Celestia collected her gloves and closed the door behind her before checking her ivy-and-holly-embroidered evening gown. "It's not too wrinkled, is it? I didn't have the heart to ask Marybeth to press it."

"You look fine, but I am afraid it will just be you and me tonight. Mother has also decided she's not fond of sea travel."

"Oh no."

"I suppose it's a good thing the *Golden Gestirn* is so well-appointed." Josiah offered his arm as they crossed the parlor of their three-room suite. "This area should suit Mother's taste and comfort, even if she never sees the rest of the floating palace again."

Floating palace was an apt description. Plush oriental carpet cushioned footfalls, while nautical artwork and mahogany furniture provided an elegant place to entertain guests. Even gold gilded the seafoam ceiling in elaborate swirls and brightened the room. Mother would dearly appreciate those luxuries should she become confined to the space for a week.

Josiah guided her through the halls to the main stairwell, where they climbed to the dining saloon. With three rows of white-clothed tables running the entire length of the room and nearly full with diners, conversations rumbled a hair above comfortable. Celestia sought Aldrich's face among those seated at the investors' table, but elaborate

Christmas arrangements blocked her view. He probably wasn't here. Again. She swallowed hard and lifted her gaze to the railed opening in the ceiling. Passengers observed them from the music room, but it was the glass dome above them that held her interest. During the day, it provided natural light, but tonight it allowed the boldest stars to peek in on their evening and comfort Celestia's hurting heart.

"I see a couple of open chairs this way."

She followed Josiah past columns wreathed in Christmas greenery and breathed in the comforting scent of pine. Christmas and stars. If she kept her focus on those, joy would follow.

Midway down the aisle, two anchored mahogany chairs faced outward to welcome them.

As they swiveled in their seats toward the table, a server stopped them. "If you please, the Weise family wishes for you to join them."

The family wished for her and Josiah to join them? That was unexpected. When Brenner had joined her and Josiah yesterday, he'd left his family behind to do it. Were the Weises merely circulating through the shareholders? Or was there something more to the invitation? Perhaps Aldrich felt remorse for his inattention and wanted to make up for it.

When they arrived at the end of the table, Aldrich, Brenner, and Herr Weise rose from their seats, dressed in formal attire. Good heavens. If she weren't careful, she'd spend the whole dinner feasting on Aldrich's appearance like a box of chocolates instead of on her actual meal.

His gaze connected with hers, and she held her breath, willing him to say something—anything—to explain his recent absence. But it skipped away, leaving behind the ache of disappointment.

"Fräulein Isaacs, please sit." Frau Weise indicated the empty spot next to her.

Sit? Next to Aldrich's *mother*?

The instruction terrified her more than being trapped in a room with a seasick Marybeth. How could she maintain a facade of being unaffected by Aldrich in front of the woman she hoped would one day be her mother-in-law?

After she and Josiah sat, Aldrich reclaimed his seat opposite Celestia. "Will your Mutter not be joining us?"

At least he wasn't ignoring her. "I am afraid ocean travel doesn't agree with her."

Frau Weise signaled to a waiter. "See to it that Frau Isaacs in cabin 181 is sent a pot of mein tea for seasickness." After he disappeared, she continued. "Your Mutter will soon improve. We do not wish for her to miss the festivities."

"Danke schön. Mother and I treasure the fresh hope that celebrating the Christ child brings. Especially when celebrated with friends." She caught Aldrich's eye.

He immediately turned away, disguising the cut by addressing her brother about his opinion of the scheduled events.

A lump formed in her throat, and she stared at the glass of wine set before her. Was that his answer? They were merely Bekannte. Acquaintances who would fade with time and held no special meaning to the other. After all their letters, discussions, and the future he'd hinted at outside of the observatory?

Lord, have I misunderstood this whole time? I feel certain that Aldrich is the one You mean for me. What am I supposed to do?

"Will you also put out your shoes, Fräulein Isaacs?" Brenner asked.

Celestia blinked, uncertain what she missed that brought about such a question. "I beg your pardon, but I was lost in thought. Where am I to put my shoes?"

"Outside your door. Tomorrow is *Nikolaustag*. Tonight *Heilige Nikolaus*—Saint Nikolaus—and his partner *Knecht Ruprecht* will travel the halls and place candies and small gifts in the shoes of good girls and boys, and switches in the shoes of naughty children. It is a tradition we have in Germany."

"I've heard of it done elsewhere as well. Isn't it meant for children?"

"Not on this ship." He winked. "It is part of the festivities. Even Aldrich and I will put out our shoes."

An idea sparked renewed hope. "How will you know whose shoes are whose? And that they won't be stolen?"

"The stewards will monitor the halls. As for whose are whose, I will tell you a secret." He cupped his hands around his mouth, and in a whisper that no one could keep a secret with, said, "Everyone gets the same thing, so it does not matter."

That posed a challenge. She'd need to pay particular attention to the brothers' shoes before returning to her room and pray there was a noticeable difference.

The server's arm knocked against her side as he placed a bowl of split pea soup before her. "*Mi scusi.*"

She turned to assure him all was forgiven, and eyes equal parts brown and green met hers. Her breath caught. It was him, wasn't it?

He cut short her chance to scrutinize his identity and flung the tray of bowls at her.

Scalding heat splattered against her face and arms. She shot to her feet and bumped her knees against the table. Frau Weise and the men around them rushed to her aid, plying her with napkins and questions as to her health, but who cared about that?

That man was getting away. Again.

"He's the man from the pier!"

Shocked silence followed. Then exclamations erupted from the table.

Aldrich, Brenner, and Josiah rushed after the man and disappeared from view.

Well, at least one problem would be taken care of. Soup dripped from her hair onto her cheek, then onto her dress already slathered with the green goop. Celestia grimaced. There had better be no more incidents. Her wardrobe couldn't take it.

Chapter Six

A MAN COULD hide in only so many places on this ship, and yet Vito Pellegrini continued to elude them despite the all-night search. At least they now knew his name. Not that it provided a great deal of help in apprehending the man.

Aldrich staggered from his room to the nearest parlor sofa, half-ready for the day in his trousers, shirt, and slippers. Eventually he would throw on his vest, coat, and shoes, but until he had coffee in him, that was as far as he was getting. Nightmares of Pellegrini pushing Celestia overboard into a sea of pea soup had plagued his limited sleep.

Brenner joined him in a similar state of dress but with the addition of two steaming mugs of coffee.

"You are a saint." Aldrich accepted the offered cup and ignored the scalding heat of his first gulp.

"Nein. Fräulein Isaacs is." Brenner reclined against his side of the sofa and savored a long drink. "The steward said she requested it delivered to our room when she ordered coffee and tea for theirs."

Guilt niggled him. Despite going to great lengths to avoid her, she treated him with her usual thoughtfulness. Brenner was right. That woman was a saint and Aldrich a *Dummkopf* for believing avoidance would make the inevitable easier to bear.

"Herr Isaacs should join us soon, although I do not know what can be done." Brenner set aside his cup. "Now that we are underway, the worst we can do is confine him, fire him, and deposit him in South-ampton or Bremerhaven. He has committed no crime on international waters, and we cannot hold him on board for nearly a month in order to return him to the New York police. He will escape punishment for harming Fräulein Isaacs, the immigrants under our care, and our reputation as a company."

The abysmal outlook did not improve when Herr Isaacs joined them a half hour later.

"My jurisdiction ended when we left the harbor. Until we return, I am nothing more than a civilian traveling with his family for the holidays." Herr Isaacs frowned as he stretched his legs out in front of his chair. "However, if we can catch Pellegrini, he may provide information about any others involved."

"I want the man found if for no other reason than to ensure the safety of our passengers. Twice your sister has been assaulted by the man." Aldrich tugged his coat with more force than necessary to button its front. "I will not tolerate another occurrence. I cannot have her or any other passenger afraid to travel on the *Golden Gestirn*."

"The only experience Celestia fears on this ship is being trapped in our quarters with her seasick companion and our seasick mother. Celestia begged me to escort her to the ladies' drawing room before I came here so she could escape the sound of Miss Adams's retching."

"How does Fräulein Isaacs fare? Does she regret coming?" Although he had tried to remain distant even in talk about Celestia, he could not resist the natural opening.

"She is well other than needing to escape the sickroom, although she does regret not packing more dresses. She jested this morning that if she continues to dirty them at this rate, she'll be obliged to beg access to the cargo hold by Monday."

"I will see to it that she acquires whatever she needs."

"The extra chocolate left in her shoes is enough, I assure you. Between hers, Miss Adams's, and Mother's, I doubt she'll be hungry for breakfast."

Brenner rose from the sofa and retrieved their shoes from the hall. "Here, she can have ours as well."

He dumped the contents onto the low table, and in addition to the expected gold-wrapped chocolates, a tightly folded note fell out.

Herr Isaacs picked it up and arched a brow at Aldrich as he passed it over. "It appears to be for you."

No doubt the man recognized Celestia's handwriting, and the use of Aldrich's Christian name on the front would be disconcerting for any protective brother. Especially considering the near scandalous way in which it was delivered. At least with their astronomy clubs they maintained the illusion of business correspondence.

"I think we should offer a reward for whoever delivers Pellegrini to one of the officers." Brenner's redirection failed to remove the suspicion from Herr Issacs's eyes, but it succeeded in ending further commentary on the note.

Aldrich tucked it into his pocket as both the embarrassment of being caught with a personal message and the desire to read it burned within him.

"I suggest the reward be kept to the crew members and out of public knowledge," Herr Isaacs responded. "You don't want to create fear in your passengers."

"I concur. We should begin with obtaining a rendering of Pellegrini." Aldrich stood and gestured toward the door, glad for some action they could take. "One of our officers is a skilled artist and can sketch a portrait for us to show around to those unfamiliar with him."

"I will take Herr Isaacs to him. It is your turn to escort Mutter to the dining saloon." Brenner exchanged his slippers for shoes as he addressed Herr Isaacs. "Vater prefers to break his fast here, while Mutter is eager to make the acquaintance of other passengers."

It was a poor excuse to give Aldrich privacy to read his note, but he was appreciative of Brenner's support regardless. As soon as they left, Aldrich returned to his stateroom, turned the switch for the electric light, and shut his door. When he unfolded the letter, an elegant silver hairpin fell onto the floor while Celestia's writing swirled and danced across the page. He picked it up lest it be lost, and read for an explanation.

Frohen Nikolaustag, Aldrich,

I hope I've chosen the right shoe and that you will forgive my boldness. It is my understanding that small gifts are left behind by Saint Nikolaus for those who are good and switches for those who are bad. While I am not Saint Nikolaus, I have determined that you need both a switch and a gift.

As I have no switch, I give you one of my hairpins. I know I cannot have misunderstood our friendship for so long. Acquaintances do not share the conversations we have shared. They do not hold hands under the stars and speak of futures that reveal the heart and longings of a person. Longings that I had thought ran alongside each other toward a shared future. I am confused and hurt. Since arriving, you've held my hand as if you never wanted to let go and have denied that we are more than acquaintances. I don't understand, and it is unkind of you to withdraw your friendship without explaining to me why.

However, you are a good man, and I refuse to think otherwise of you. Even on your worst days, I will always consider you my dearest friend. We are told to forgive one another, as God for Christ's sake has forgiven us. And so I have two gifts for you. I forgive the wound you have inflicted upon me, and I give you my friendship—one that is enduring and deep. Whether you want it or not, you have it. For always.

Now that I have thoroughly tromped on every known etiquette rule, which would horrify my mother, I will leave you with this. So long as the stars are shining each night of this voyage, you can find me at the foremost part of the upper deck. I hope you will find me, but should you not, know that does not change my sentiments.

You are my friend, forever and always.
Celestia

Leave it to Celestia to render a man both chastised and encouraged. Aldrich rubbed his thumb over the bumpy swirls and glass jewels of the hairpin and drifted back to the night he had last seen her wear it.

A multitude of stars had twinkled against the black of night, and half a dozen brass telescopes pointed upward to explore their secrets. Although, the only secret Aldrich intended to discover was Celestia's true feelings for him. Were they acquaintances or friends, or was there the potential for something more between them?

"Look! A shooting star!" Celestia's head popped back from the telescope, and her finger traced the path of the meteor crossing the sky.

It sputtered out a moment later, and she grinned at him. "I wish you could have seen it close up. It was marvelous."

Not anywhere near as marvelous as the joy beaming from her face. He needed to contrive a reason for their astronomy clubs to meet more frequently than once a quarter. Each time they parted for their respective cities, he grieved the absence of her exuberance and conversation with more intensity. A short train ride separated New York and Philadelphia, but to call on her at all, let alone with the regularity he desired, required a reason beyond their shared love of astronomy. A very personal reason.

He returned her smile and laid his hand atop hers on the telescope. It was rather forward of him, but she did not rebuke him or pull away. "Did you make a wish?"

"I did, but I can't share."

"Surely you do not believe in such superstition?"

"Of course not, but wishes are serious things. They are whispers to God about your most treasured hopes and dreams. They cannot be shared with just anyone."

"And you consider me just anyone?" He held his breath.

"Well, no. But . . ."

It wasn't much encouragement, but it was enough to forge ahead. "What would I have to be to hear your deepest hopes and dreams?"

She tilted her head at a thoughtful angle and studied him. "A trusted friend."

"And you do not consider me a trusted friend?" His hopes for tonight struck an iceberg and sunk.

"I do"—her free hand cupped one side of his face—"and far more. It's just that, well, my wish involves"—her chin dropped, and the never-bashful Fräulein Celestia Isaacs became indeed very shy—"a certain gentleman."

"Do I know this gentleman?"

"It is possible." Coyness laced her tone and buoyed him despite her hand falling away.

He dropped his voice. "And what did you wish for with this gentleman?"

"I wished for many more nights like this."

"Is that all? I confess to having hoped for a different wish." His thumb caressed her hand, and he leaned closer so that no one might hear. "One perhaps of a more personal nature. One which might encourage a suit."

"Oh . . ." Her wide eyes flicked from his gaze to his lips and back again. "I . . . I am not opposed to amending my wish." Her words were breathless, and she leaned forward.

He hadn't expected that response, but he was more than happy to oblige. He slanted his head to better capture her lips and pulled her as close as the telescope between them allowed.

Light from a lantern flooded the area, and they bolted upright.

"Hot chocolate and coffee are ready."

Celestia's face turned a beautiful shade of crimson. "Thank you, Marybeth. We'll be there shortly." She freed her hand from his and wouldn't meet his gaze. "I'll let the others know, if you wouldn't mind packing the telescope?"

She had raced away, and they were never alone again before their groups separated. Still, it had been enough to assure him that his suit would be welcomed. The entire train ride home he had planned for his visit to Philadelphia to formally ask permission to pursue a courtship—convinced marriage would be at its end.

Then the letter from Germany arrived the next morning and destroyed his future. For days he wrestled with Gott. In the end, he submitted to the undeniable call to Germany, knowing full well the sacrifice required of him. He immediately stopped writing Celestia and withdrew from any interactions that might encourage growing affections. No wonder she felt hurt and confused. She had spoken honestly, yet gently, and she deserved the same of him. But he would not wait until the cover of stars. He would find her now and do his best to gently inform her that the whispered wishes of last month would remain that.

Wishes and dreams.

Chapter Seven

HAD CELESTIA KNOWN her brother would be present when Aldrich discovered her note, she would have reconsidered her strategy. At the very least, she wouldn't have left the comfort and protection of the ladies' drawing room, where she'd been comparing the German and English translations of the Brothers Grimm stories. The moment she'd exited, Josiah had pulled her to an empty corner of the deck and interrogated her like a criminal.

"Honestly, Josiah, you have no room to scold me. It's not as if I'm setting up a secret assignation with the man." At least, not of the romantic variety. She simply wanted an explanation.

"I should hope not, or I'll be dragging Miss Adams from her sickbed and forcing you to listen to her retching as she follows you about."

"Don't be ridiculous. I was merely participating in Saint Nikolaus Day with the only method I had—words."

"And yet he was the exclusive recipient of a note?"

An oversight on her part, but in her defense, she hadn't thought she'd need explanation. "Other than my method of communication, do you have any objection to the man himself?"

Josiah narrowed his eyes. "You're too young."

"I am twenty-two. Older than you were when you married." He scowled at her, and she softened her tone. "While you've been busy using your career to dodge fiancées, I've been growing up. Herr Weise is an honorable man who I consider a dear friend. I trust him as much as I trust you. And if the Isaacs intuition rings as true for me as it has for everyone else in our family, then you know where this leads. Do not say or do something that you will later regret."

"I'll accept that man as my brother-in-law when he's earned it."

"Then give me and him the chance to see if that is indeed what God plans."

He harrumphed but at least stopped arguing. "Mother is going to blame me. You know that, right?"

Celestia smiled. "Nonsense. She's too ill to blame anyone for anything. I promise to behave so long as *you* promise to give me the space I need to test the truth of our family legend."

Someone cleared their throat behind them, and Celestia found Aldrich waiting a few steps away with his straw hat in hand.

Josiah sent her a meaningful look before vacating the railing. "I'll be inside speaking with the captain if you need me."

What he meant was he'd invent some pretext to be in the captain's office and watch them from the window. How wonderfully annoying and reassuring it was to have a big brother who cared.

Once Josiah disappeared inside, Aldrich claimed a spot at the rail a good three feet away.

She closed the distance, leaving a respectable foot between them. "There's no need to be so far away. He's all growl and no teeth."

"Is not the saying all growl and no bite?"

"Oh, he might bite. It just won't hurt. Much."

He appeared uncertain until she elbowed his side. A reluctant smile released, then faltered. "I received your note."

Her nerves bundled together and turned queasy. "I know. Josiah made sure I knew how inappropriate it was of me."

"As I have given you no alternative method to speak with me, I found it ingenious."

The compliment did little to ease the tension between them. Her gaze drifted out to the ocean sparkling beneath the morning sun. She might as well jump right over the rail of safety and into the deep waters of uncertainty. "May I ask where we stand?"

"You may ask, but I do not know."

She drew a deep breath and prayed for wisdom as she faced his profile. His hands were clasped together over the railing, and he leaned against it as if it were his sole support for this conversation. His chin dipped nearly to his chest, and deep lines of sorrow spread across his forehead and out from his mouth. Whatever had caused this, she longed to embrace him and assure him all would be well.

"As I said in my letter, I am your friend. Forever and always, whether you accept it or not. Nothing you say will change that."

He didn't respond, and she glanced over her shoulder. If Josiah watched them, he did so out of view.

She laid a hand over Aldrich's clasped ones and waited for him to meet her gaze. "Was I wrong in thinking you wished, as I do, that a future of more than friends could be possible?"

"You like to ask the hard questions first, do you not?"

"Iron cannot sharpen iron without first scraping against each other."

He faced the horizon, and his Adam's apple bobbed. "It *was* my wish to pursue a future together."

"But it's not now?" Her throat constricted.

"I came home to a letter from *mein Onkle* who is over the German branch of Deutsch-Amerika. My cousins have chosen other careers, and there is no one to replace him when he is gone. He is in ill health and desires for me to be his successor. After much prayer, I feel it is what Gott wants for me to do. When Brenner graduates in the spring, he will take my place in New York and I will move to Germany. Permanently."

"Which means your wife would need to as well." As much as her heart screamed this was no hindrance, that she would follow him anywhere, she knew it was not that simple.

He regarded her at length before granting a single nod.

"And this is why you have pulled away? You don't think there is a chance for us."

"I do not think. I know. I have thought it over a hundred different ways, but no matter how I try, the problem remains the same. I would be ripping you from your family and friends to live among strangers in a land you do not know surrounded by a language and culture you do not understand."

These were obstacles, yes, but not insurmountable. "Friends can be made. Languages and culture learned."

"But your family. I know how much they mean to you. How you cherish being with them. Watching your *Nichten* and *Neffen*—your nieces and nephews—grow. I cannot in good conscience pursue you knowing that what I hope for means such sacrifice."

"Don't I get a say in this?"

"Listen to me, Celestia." Hearing her name on his lips thrilled her, but the pleading for her to understand wrung the joy from it. "Seeing your family is not as simple as getting on a train. Receiving news can take weeks. You would miss births, deaths, marriages, illnesses, and other important events. You would be unknown to your family except through letters. Your Nichten and Neffen will grow into adults with little memory of you. Courting leads to marriage, and marriage would lead you to a lonely life with me."

"But—"

He held up a hand. "Do not say that I am enough. Mutter left Germany for Vater. When praying over my decision, we spoke. Mutter shared how difficult it has been to live in America, away from all she loved. I will not put any woman I care for through such pain and loneliness."

"She cannot regret it though. She has you, Brenner, and your father. She has built a life in America with friends, family, and a home. It doesn't exist only in Germany."

"No, she does not regret it, but it is not an easy life for her either."

"And so you think by pulling back from our friendship, you can save us both from hardship and pain? Really, Aldrich. Have you read your Bible?"

He sputtered. "Excuse me?"

"Jesus tells us that we cannot escape difficulties. We must travel through them in obedience to His guidance. What if He is calling us *both* to a different life than what we'd imagined? Is not what He wants for us more important than what we think is best?"

"I have prayed over this."

"Without giving *me* the chance to go before God? What if you're wrong?"

He stood silent, as if unconvinced.

She drew his hands toward her until it forced him to fully face her. "What if this voyage is meant to be a gift? What if instead of pushing me away, this week is meant to give us the opportunity to get to know each other better, to seek His will together, and to come to the end knowing whether it is a treasured memory between friends or the beginning of something more? Please, Aldrich, I am begging you not to toss aside our friendship out of fear for the pain that may or may not lay in our future. Friendship is worth fighting for, and no matter if we part ways at the end of this journey or not, we will still be friends. Pen pals if we must. But not strangers. Not Bekannte."

His thumb brushed her cheek, and she realized tears traced paths all the way down her neck.

"Such passion from *meine Mäuschen*."

She wrinkled her nose. "Your little mouse?"

He chuckled. "It is a term of endearment."

If he was calling her by a term of endearment, then she would accept the small win. Even if he was calling her a small rodent. But mice could be cute. Couldn't they?

"Promise me you will pray over this with the understanding that there might be no more than friendship between us." He brushed another tear away. "We will travel as friends this week but hold the future with an open hand."

She nodded, her throat too tight for words. This wasn't what she had planned when she boarded the *Golden Gestirn*. Instead of convincing him they belonged together, she would have to seek the answer herself. Was the Isaacs intuition of knowing who they would marry from first sight really a calling from God? Or was He calling her to lay aside what she thought was her future and let go of the one man she loved?

Chapter Eight

CELESTIA WAS PARTIALLY right. This week *was* meant to be a gift—a parting gift, not the beginning of something new. Aldrich was bitterly resigned to that truth and trying to be thankful to Gott for providing the opportunity. He wanted to enjoy this voyage with Celestia. To cherish what little time they had left together—and to keep Brenner from forming an attachment with her.

Unfortunately, he still had the responsibility of wooing shareholders to contend with. Not an easy task given Pellegrini's public flight and Aldrich's inability to assure them of the man's arrest. While Celestia and his Mutter strung popcorn for a Tannenbaum in the music room with other women, Aldrich was stuck hobnobbing in the smoking room.

"Have you wagered yet?" Herr Grayson gestured to a ledger at a table near the exit, where men bet on the *Golden Gestirn*'s average speed for the day.

Yesterday's speed barely reached 18 knots, a far cry from the *Golden Gestirn*'s designed speed. However, if they broke 18.3 knots today and every day after, hope still existed for breaking the *Oregon*'s record average of 18.14 knots.

"The only gambles I make are in business, and only calculated ones at that."

"Wise man. Ha! Of course you are! You're a wise *Weise*!" He slung an arm around Aldrich's shoulders. "Tell me, do you ever get tired of the *Weise-cracks?*" He slapped his leg, obviously having imbibed too much from the offerings provided in the corner.

Aldrich forced a tolerant smile. "It is in my best interest not to."

Herr Grayson brayed with laughter, and Aldrich strained against the desire to escape.

When the man finally left with his jokes, Herr Southworth descended like a vulture for his turn at the picking. No doubt he came to vocalize his opinion on the Pellegrini matter and provide his usual threat to remove his support if Aldrich's decision did not align with his. Aldrich wished he would. It would make life easier. But if Herr Southworth—a lead investor—pulled his support, then others would follow.

"Any word on that Pellegrini fellow?" Herr Southworth blew out a cloud of cigarette smoke.

"Nein, but the crew has been instructed to apprehend and escort him to one of the officers should he be discovered."

He harrumphed. "Likely his fellow crew members are hiding him."

"It is possible, but we have offered a substantial reward for whoever delivers Pellegrini. Even his Mutter would be tempted to turn him in should she be aboard."

"Is such an expense warranted? What is the worst this man can do? Eat a bit of food and then abandon ship in Southampton? You'll spend less harboring him as a stowaway."

"Perhaps, but safety is our utmost concern."

The fact Pellegrini harbored no concern for the consequences of throwing a woman overboard or dumping scalding liquid onto her concerned Aldrich more than theft.

"I expect Deutsch-Amerika to take greater care in who they hire. A reputation once ruined cannot be repaired, and I, for one, will not support a company whose reputation is less than pristine." He flicked his ashes on Aldrich's shoes. "Do tell me when Pellegrini has been caught and if it was worth the irresponsible cost of a reward."

Aldrich drew a measured breath before responding. "Have a good afternoon, Herr Southworth, and enjoy the play this evening with your family."

He spotted Brenner at the other side of the room and sank onto the scarlet leather couch nearest the coal-burning fireplace. He leaned his head back and closed his eyes. How long until he could politely disappear and find Celestia for a few minutes of pleasurable conversation?

The sofa cushion shifted next to him as Brenner dropped into place. "Does it ever get any less tedious?"

"Nein."

Some might consider their private use of German in a room of predominantly English-only speakers to be rude, but Aldrich was too tired to care. Most of the men were distracted by cards, smoking, or drinks anyway.

"No wonder Vater avoids the smoking room. At least tonight will be diverting. Fräulein Isaacs was especially excited about the play. I intend to sit next to her and watch her delightful expressions the entire time."

Aldrich snapped his eyes open and sat up. "Nein. If anyone will sit next to her, it will be me. I am her Freund. You are merely a Bekannter."

"But *you* are leaving her for Germany, and *I* will need to know her well enough to console her when you do."

Aldrich scowled.

Brenner grinned. "Ah, so you can leave her, but I cannot try for her? Have you changed your mind about Germany then?"

Aldrich clenched his jaw.

"I thought not."

"Celestia is off-limits, Brenner."

"Celestia, is it?" His head inclined at an annoying angle. "This crossing may be more entertaining than I first suspected. What do you say to the best man wins?"

"This is not a competition, and she is not a prize."

"Oh, but I think she is. Tell me. Are you afraid that she might discover she prefers the younger Weise over the older?"

"I have had enough of the smoke room. You can handle the small talk for now." Aldrich pushed from the sofa. It was past time to abandon this ridiculous conversation and find Celestia.

"Tell Fräulein Isaacs I look forward to our evening together."

Brenner's laughter followed him out of the room, and Aldrich struggled not to slam the door. He did not need a competition over Celestia added to the stress of this voyage. He wanted to enjoy his time with her, not to fight off his brother.

When he entered the music room, the piano melody of "Silent Night" rose above the general hum of the dining saloon below. The railing blocked the view of the player but not the golden halo of hair that belonged to the woman Aldrich sought. He nodded greetings to the families he passed as they huddled together playing games or reading books from the cabinets along the wall. Before he reached a clear view of Celestia, Mutter spotted him and abandoned the group of women placing a completed popcorn string into a crate.

"Guten Tag, *mein Schatz*." She kissed him on the cheek. "Did you survive the smoking room?"

"Barely." The humor that lit her eyes eased some of the lingering frustration. "How was your morning?"

"Delightful. Fräulein Isaacs brings much humor and enthusiasm, although her spirits were dampened when she first arrived." She arched a brow in silent question. She well knew his affection for Celestia and the struggle it brought to his decision about Germany.

"I told her." The weight of loss returned, and his gaze strayed to the golden head bent over a stack of music sheets.

Mutter silently evaluated him in that way that suggested she saw more than he wanted. After a moment, she spoke in German. "And her response?"

"This voyage is a gift where we should enjoy each other's company as much as we can."

"And . . ."

"And that we should pray to see what Gott wants for us before deciding to part ways."

Her lips curled into a satisfied smile. "I see. So she was not frightened off and desires to fight for a future in Germany?"

"She said she would pray over it, Mutter. Nothing more."

"And what is prayer but a refusal to give up? It shows a spirit willing to fight but prepared to submit to whatever Gott decides."

"I will not put a woman I care for through what you endured."

"That is not for you to decide. Moving to America was hard, yes, but I would not change a day of it. Even the days it did not feel worth the hardship. Promise me you will pray over it and be open to Gott's wisdom and not your own?"

"Yes, Mutter. I will pray."

She dipped her chin. "I mean it, Aldrich. Pray with a willingness to hear what Gott wants. Not what you have already decided. Wise men seek the King, not the reasoning of their own mind. You are smart, but not smarter than Gott." After a lingering silent reprimand, she kissed his cheek again. "Now go. Spend time with Fräulein Isaacs."

That command he readily agreed with. He traced the mahogany railing until it brought him behind Celestia settling her latest selection against the music stand.

"May I join you?"

Surprise then radiant joy brightened her countenance. "I'd be delighted." She scooted to the edge of the bench and patted the vacant spot.

He took great care not to crowd her even though he could not avoid their legs brushing. Not that he minded. "So what are we playing?"

"'We Three Kings.' It's one of my favorites."

He chuckled. "I do not suppose it has anything to do with a star being the focus?"

"With a name like mine, how could I not be drawn to a song about the Christmas star? Besides, it's the perfect mix of awe, wonder, and reverent reflection. I need something to help put my heart in the right place this season." Her smile dampened, but the underlying joy remained steadfast.

"Then I can think of no better song to share with you." He held her gaze, though he ached to hold more than that. After a moment he placed his hands over the keys. "Shall we?"

Her hand brushed against his as she claimed a complementing octave. "We shall."

Sharing a piano with her for the first time thrilled him as much as the first time their hands brushed and lingered over a telescope. They shared some bumbling mishaps that resulted in giggles and outright laughter, but the sweet tenderness of her regard wrapped around him like a favorite blanket. Song after song they played and sang together. He fumbled far more than he should have, but he couldn't help but forget to read the music in favor of watching Celestia. Each time she caught him, the temptation to kiss her cheek or abandon the keys altogether gripped him like a riptide and threatened to pull him under.

Gott, how I wish there would not be an ocean between us.

But there would be, and until then he would enjoy the gift of time together.

After they'd finished "Joy to the World," Brenner tapped on his shoulder. The mischievous glint in his eyes and curve to his mouth declared his intentions. "May I cut in?"

Nein. He may not.

"I apologize, but no." Celestia saved Aldrich from finding a way to run his brother off. "If I sing another song, I'm afraid I will sound more frog than angel and my fingers might very well fall off."

"We cannot have that happen." Brenner signaled to a server waiting in the corner by a set of carafes. "After some refreshment, perhaps we could take a turn about the promenade?"

Aldrich clenched his jaw and fought against the impulse to smash the golden tray of drinks over Brenner's head. They generally got along, but his insistence on making Celestia a competition pushed the boundaries of Aldrich's patience.

Celestia claimed a glass and drank its entire contents.

"It seems my brother has been remiss in seeing to your needs. Here, have another."

Anger at Brenner's accusation and guilt for its sliver of truth fisted Aldrich's hands.

"Your brother was a perfect gentleman. I did not realize I needed a drink until we stopped."

Her defense soothed some of the tension, although it did not change Aldrich's desire to kick Brenner back to the smoking room.

Celestia continued. "However, I do thank you for the water and the invitation to walk. Unfortunately, I need to check on my mother and companion, as I have been away from them all morning."

The excuse might be genuine, but Aldrich reveled in Celestia's refusal. Brenner graciously accepted defeat, bowing and wishing her cabinmates would be much improved. Her polite but formal goodbye tasted sweeter than marzipan.

Before taking her leave, Celestia addressed Aldrich. "Thank you for playing duet with me. We should do it again soon." Then with a smile that irritatingly included Brenner, she added, "Will you be attending the play?"

Victory sparked in Brenner's eyes. "I will. Would you do me the honor of saving a seat for me?"

Celestia nodded. "I look forward to the pleasure of saving seats for both of you. Guten Tag until then."

Aldrich waited for her to leave the room before turning on Brenner. "I said she is off-limits."

"And I said may the best man win. Although I do not mind admitting that it appears you have the upper hand."

"I do."

"Do not get too comfortable with your lead. It will not last." He winked and wandered off with a laughing shake to his shoulders.

If Brenner was not careful, the insufferable rat would wake up to discover all his trousers thrown overboard. Repayment for the prank played as a youth might be delayed, but it would be the perfect timing for Aldrich's purposes. Brenner could not pursue Celestia when confined to his room.

Chapter Nine

Mother reclined on the parlor sofa with eyes closed and a pot of Frau Weise's tangy scented tea next to her. Despite the green tinge to her pallor, she did appear a few shades better than when Celestia fled the suite this morning. Given Marybeth's absence and the silence coming from their shared room, she must be asleep.

"Do you think you have improved enough to walk to the deck? One of the ladies stringing popcorn said it would do wonders for you."

"I better not. The world tilts and spins if I even move my head."

"Then perhaps a bit of fresh air might suffice for now." Celestia opened the two portholes afforded them and breathed deeply of the salty breeze that circulated the room.

"You'll let all the heat out, dear."

"It won't hurt for a few minutes. I'll close them when it becomes too nippy in here." She claimed the seat nearest her mother's head and filled a cup with the amber liquid. "Here, drink some more. Frau Weise insisted it settles queasy stomachs. I've asked the steward to bring some crackers, as suggested by another woman."

Mother moaned as she sat up and stayed motionless for several long-measured breaths before accepting the cup. "I think this time is worse than when your father and I attempted to sail on our wedding trip. I had hoped that after forty-two years, my body would not still be so opposed to it."

"If you knew that ocean travel made you so sick, why did you even agree to come?"

"Someone needed to chaperone Josiah, and with your father serving in Washington this month, I had no choice. We can't risk your brother fancying himself in love with a German and bringing her home as his wife."

"Would that really be so wrong? I mean, if he loves her, why would it matter if she's German or not? He deserves to have a second chance at love."

"Yes, he does, but the boy doesn't know what love is. He knew that Irishwoman less than a month before marrying her, and he's had nine other fiancées since her death. He needs a guiding hand where love is concerned."

"I disagree. Those other women are merely evidence of his inability to tell a woman no. I don't remember much about his wife, but I remember how happy he was with her despite your and Father's disapproval. You practically barred him from the house unless he came without her, and yet he chose to face the ostracism and struggles by her side. Isn't that love?" Celestia swallowed as her thoughts took a personal turn. "If God calls him to marry a German and move to Germany, shouldn't he do it?"

Mother evaluated Celestia with the same look she used on reporters attempting to outmaneuver her. "We're not speaking of your brother, are we?"

"I'm not saying that I *will* move to Germany, but Aldrich is. I've known from my first investors' ball that we'd marry."

"Oh, Celestia. You know how I feel about that silly Isaacs intuition myth." She abandoned the cup and lay back down with closed eyes, as if the movement, or more likely the conversation, was too much to bear. "Love is more than feelings that ignite and weave themselves into dreams. Real love is built upon the foundation of Christ. You need to test this intuition to determine if it is an ill-fated fantasy or a true calling from God. Germany is far away without any family support to help you through. I love you, dear, but you've led a sheltered life. I'm not sure you could handle the hardship. It might very well break your spirit."

Celestia studied her lap, unsure of what to say. Aldrich had spoken of the hardship involved and his desire for her not to be subjected to it, and now her own mother declared her too fragile for such an endeavor. Were these nudges from God that their futures lay in opposite directions?

Please, God, don't let it be so.

But try as she might, she couldn't dismiss the possibility.

She rose on shaky legs and kissed her mother's forehead. "I think I'll go lie down for a while myself."

Though her eyes remained closed, Mother's hand grasped Celestia's arm. "I only want what's best for you, dear."

"I know, Mother. Rest well and perhaps you will be able to join us at supper."

She moaned in response but released her hold.

After closing the portholes, Celestia slipped into her room, where the soft snores of Marybeth rose and fell. She retrieved her Bible from the cabinet above the plumbed washbasins and crawled into bed between the brass railings. It was too dark to read, but it was a small comfort to have the worn leather Bible against her chest.

Lord, I've long prayed that You would open Aldrich's heart to a future together, but now, I wonder if it was all selfish folly on my part. Are You preparing me to say goodbye? I don't want to. I feel like I love Aldrich, but I want to do Your will. To marry who You wish me to marry and to go where You send me, but I don't even know how to look for or hear Your answer. It's not as if Your Word says, "Marry Aldrich and move to Germany." So help me, Lord. Help me to know what is Your will and not my own. If You'd be so kind as to send me a star of my very own to lead me in the right direction, I'd be ever so grateful.

Sometime later a knock on her door roused her from an unintended nap. She left her Bible on the pillow and opened the door, where Josiah waited.

His wide eyes and perusal of her appearance spoke volumes. "Don't tell me you are seasick too."

"Do I look ill?" She glanced in the mirror next to the door and winced. Red lines streaked her face, and her hair tangled into what appeared to be the remnants of a mouse's nest. Although, since Aldrich called her his little mouse, maybe he'd think it cute instead of terrifying. "I'm fine. The rocking lulled me to sleep while reading in bed."

"What were you reading? Poe? You could scare the 'Tell-Tale Heart' into not beating."

"Har-har-har. What did you want?"

"We're late for supper." He glanced over her again and shook his head. "I'll give your regrets and request a plate be sent down. Do you even have any dresses left to wear?"

"Just one."

Had she not been determined to follow all the suggestions in the travel guide, she wouldn't have been so stingy in her packing of dresses. Five proved an insufficient number for the journey, especially when three were already ruined beyond repair. What few travel gowns she saved for Germany were stowed in cargo. Had she any sense, she would've changed into a nightgown before climbing into bed, or at least said her prayers from the chair.

"Give the Weises my regrets for missing the meal, but assure them I will attend the play."

Once the door shut, she turned on the light and roused Marybeth. If she was going to look anywhere near presentable, she'd need all the help she could muster.

Chapter Ten

PERHAPS ALDRICH HAD cheated in enlisting his mother to delay Brenner's arrival to the play last night, but he suffered no remorse. If anything, Celestia's delight in his surprise arrival to escort her made him regret he hadn't followed through with tossing Brenner's trousers overboard. With her silver gown, she appeared the human incarnation of an evening star. She was so ethereal, beautiful, and bright that he could make a hundred wishes on her and believe every one of them would come true. He had been right in choosing to name the *Golden Gestirn* after her, his golden-haired star. Although, should anyone suspect it, he would deny it.

By the time Brenner arrived, Aldrich sat on one side of Celestia, with her brother on the other. For the entire performance, Aldrich had the perfect view of Celestia's expressive face. He watched her so intently that he could not honestly comment on the actual performance. However, he *could* describe her reaction to every scene. She shook her head in pity at Scrooge's poor treatment of Cratchit, shivered at the appearance of Marley's ghost, and teared up as Scrooge relived his past. She smiled at the first hint of Scrooge's softening toward Tiny Tim and laughed through the nephew's Christmas party. Aldrich's favorite part was when the Ghost of Christmas Yet to Come appeared. Celestia's hand sought his and held on until the ghost disappeared. Aldrich saw to it the actor received a bonus for playing his chilling part so well. When the performance ended,

Celestia stood and applauded like it was a robust production from a renowned theater on Broadway rather than a small no-name troupe Aldrich discovered doing skits in Central Park last summer.

Brenner might have beaten Aldrich to providing Celestia refreshment, but she latched on to Aldrich's arm while she recounted her pleasure. When Brenner requested a promenade, she made an excuse of needing to be well rested for Advent services this morning and then asked Aldrich to escort her back to her cabin. There had been no good-night kiss, but they'd stayed outside her door talking until well past Brenner's return to his and Aldrich's suite three doors down.

"Wipe that grin off your face. Today is a new day, and I will yet win Fräulein Isaacs's attention." Brenner clapped Aldrich on the shoulder.

"I would not be so confident." Aldrich set aside his comb and smirked at Brenner's reflection in the mirror.

"Oh, I have every confidence. You only have this sailing with Fräulein Isaacs. I have all the time I need after you leave her behind. Unless you've changed your mind, of course."

Aldrich's smirk died at the cruel reminder. Could he not enjoy even one day without the ache of approaching loss?

Brenner's teasing smile faded. "Forgive me. I pushed too far." He opened their stateroom door with true remorse shadowing his countenance. "Come. It is time for service. Perhaps Gott will be merciful and provide a word of encouragement to soothe my blunder."

Soothe it perhaps, but the wound would endure. Aldrich's time with Celestia had become a self-inflicting double-edged sword. While he treasured the memories they created, each reminder that he would eventually say goodbye pierced him anew and left him bleeding.

Mutter's reprimand that he seek Gott's will and not his own bit into his conscience.

Gott, show me what to do. I want a future with Celestia, but the cost to her would be too great. If it is Your will that we both go to Germany, You will have to make it clear to me.

In a far soberer state than he started his morning, he shrugged on his coat and joined his family.

In the hall, Celestia's voice rang out behind him. "Guten Morgen. May we join you?"

Confronted with Celestia's buoyant joy, his own mood lifted. She released her mother's arm, bypassed her brother, and slipped her arm through Aldrich's as if it were the most natural thing in the world for her to abandon her family for him.

The unexpected comparison jolted him. Curse Brenner for bringing those thoughts so close to the surface again. All Aldrich wanted to do was enjoy his time with her, not constantly bounce between joy, pain, and uncertainty.

"It's so considerate of you to provide services aboard ship. No experience compares to gathering with others to worship. What do you hope they will sing, Frau Weise?" Celestia bubbled with chatter, including everyone in her cheerful conversation the whole way.

They proceeded to the back of the saloon dining room, where one alcove served as a pulpit and another as a home to an organ. Steerage passengers and saloon passengers already gathered at the seats closest to the pulpit alcove, where the reverend waited to address the crowd. Deutsch-Amerika could have requested a separate service for the steerage passengers, but sharing the service provided a symbolic representation of the King who saw the hearts of people and not their social standing.

At the nearest empty table, the Weise and Isaacs families sat with Aldrich and Celestia as a bridge between the two families. While the reverend selected a child from steerage to light the Advent candles, Aldrich observed his either side. It felt right to be together, the two families—separate, yet one in Christ. Yet should they become one family, he would be responsible for pulling Celestia away from both sides, and it worried him to no end what that would do to her.

Even as they sat here with more than half her family celebrating Christmas without her stateside, Celestia exuded delight at having some family with her. She held her mother's hand and bantered with her brother. Though Frau Isaacs scolded her children and reminded them that they should be preparing their hearts for service, a smile revealed similar pleasure.

Aldrich couldn't ask Celestia to give all that up. Couldn't imagine Gott calling her to do something that might end up embittering her toward him as the challenges of living in a foreign country chipped away at her spirit.

The reverend rapped his knuckles on the table with the Advent wreath and waited for the hum of conversation to end. "This second Sunday of Advent, we come having spent the last week in hopeful meditation on the promises of our Savior's coming. The promise that though we are broken and sinful, God has chosen His heir to come, do what we could not, and stand in our place for the punishment of our sins. We have been given the promise of rescue, and we look toward Christmas with hopeful anticipation of His arrival."

He gestured to a brother and sister duo whose combined ages couldn't be more than ten. They blinked at him in their Sunday best, carefully holding the lit beeswax candle. At his encouragement, the older brother wrapped his hands around his younger sister's, and they touched the flame to the wick of the purple candle.

"As we enter this second week of Advent, let us reflect upon the faith of Mary and Joseph as they journeyed to Bethlehem. Both were called to tasks which required great sacrifice. Mary to carry the child of God, knowing no one would believe that she was indeed a virgin. Joseph, in addition to the condescension of their peers, faced the challenges of protecting the mother of God and providing for a child he knew was not his.

"But in obedience they joined their lives in pursuit of serving God as God called them to serve. In faith they went, trusting that God would do all that He said He would do, and that the Messiah would come to save those who believe upon Him."

The children lit the second purple candle, and the congregation rose to their feet to worship in song.

Though he tried, Aldrich could not concentrate on the hymns. The words of the reverend's brief meditation captured his attention and shook him with power that extended beyond some long-ago story repeated year after year. And it demanded personal reflection now, before the concerns of the day crowded out his ability to do so.

An angel might not have spoken to him, but Aldrich was certain Gott called him to Germany. And like Mary and Joseph, his calling also resulted in the loss of family and friends, but not necessarily everyone. Gott had partnered Mary and Joseph together so the purposes of His plan could be accomplished. Was it possible that Gott intended to send Aldrich to Germany with a partner to accomplish His purposes there? And was Aldrich's insistence that Celestia not go a denial of faith that Gott would see them through?

Aldrich observed Celestia, whose eyes were closed and her lips still, though the voices of others indicated the hymn far from over. Was she, too, struck by the message?

Lord, I submit to Your will. I will not deny Celestia the opportunity to participate in determining what Your calling on our relationship is. But if it is Your will for us to have a future in Germany together, I ask that You make it clear to both of us beyond this sermon.

The rest of the short service passed without further revelations, and Celestia displayed no indication she had experienced any. All day long Aldrich kept his mind open to the possibility Gott was calling them both to Germany as partners. He even allowed himself the dangerous permission of imagining that future together. His extended family would welcome her for the most part, and her personality was such that she would make friends quickly. It helped that he was already established in Germany, whereas his parents had arrived in America with no connections or knowledge of the area. He could help her along. Teach her what she needed to know. The more he thought about having a home and family with Celestia, the more he hoped that was Gott's calling on their lives.

But Brenner was proving more competition than Aldrich appreciated. Celestia was warming to Brenner's flirtations—smiling more, chuckling at his jokes, and accepting one shared walk between the three of them on the promenade. This could not be Gott's answer. If Celestia belonged with any Weise, it was him.

Chapter Eleven

CELESTIA DIDN'T KNOW what to do about Brenner. He was sweet and kind, but his constant flirtation made her uncomfortable. With other persistent and undesired suitors, she'd ignored them until their regard turned elsewhere, or she outright told them she wasn't interested. But this was Brenner *Weise*. She didn't want to upset a man who could influence the opinions of his mother and father. She was reasonably sure Aldrich would be pleased if she gave Brenner the cut, but her position was more delicate than that. How was she to treat a situation where her possible future brother-in-law flirted like he desired a romantic attachment?

She peeked into the hall from the ladies' drawing room and searched for any sign that Brenner might be prepared to bump into her unexpectedly.

"Are you searching for something? Or perhaps someone?"

Her shoulders relaxed at Aldrich's teasing tone. He was one Weise she didn't mind getting caught by—especially if it was an embrace or, better yet, a kiss.

Aldrich leaned his back against the staircase railing, with his hands shoved inside his trouser pockets, forcing his gray jacket open to reveal the dark-green vest beneath. The corners of his mouth lifted into a confident smile that captured her attention in far too enticing a manner. In fact, the whole man was one temptation to forgo waiting on God's answer and insist she was ready to move to Germany.

"Doesn't someone look dashing this afternoon?" She brushed her fingers along his sleeve. "Is this a new suit?"

"Nein, but I only wear it when I wish to make an especially good impression." His tender regard reached out and caressed her face with tingling power.

"Well, you've certainly made an impression on me."

"The feeling is mutual, meine Mäuschen." He uncrossed his ankles and offered his arm. "May I escort you around the promenade?"

She buttoned her coat before accepting his arm. "So long as you don't expect me to scurry like a mouse."

His smile dropped. "Do you wish I would not call you meine Mäuschen?"

"I am happy to be your anything, Aldrich, even your Mäuschen. However, if you call me Mäuschen, you must allow me to call you *mein Käsechen*."

He chortled. "Your little cheese?"

"What else would a mouse want but her cheese?"

He laughed again, the timbre rich and full of mirth. "I consent to being your Käsechen so long as I am not *Limberger*. I would be hurt if you thought of me as a *Käse* that smells like a rotting corpse." He held the door open for her to pass through.

She paused and sniffed at his coat, trying to decipher what cologne he wore. "Nope. Definitely not limburger. Something earthy mixed with the salt of the ocean, and I think I'm rather fond of it."

Outside, the thinning gray clouds from earlier dusted the air with white powder.

"It's snowing! I never thought about snow on the ocean. I wonder if it tastes salty." She bent her head back and tried to capture a flake with her tongue.

"Snow tastes the same whether on land or sea."

"Perhaps, but I've never caught snowflakes on the ocean before." She weaved to intercept a large fluffy one. When she turned toward Aldrich in victory, his grin stretched as wide as the horizon.

"Waiting outside the ladies' drawing room for an hour was worth every minute."

"An hour? Why did you not ask for me at the door?"

"Part of me feared you would be disappointed I was not Brenner."

"Oh, Aldrich." She clasped his hand and pulled him away from where others might observe. Cupping his cheek in her hand, she held his gaze. "It is you I desire. Always you. If you were not so important to me, I wouldn't be crying out to God, begging for His will to match my own."

His hand covered hers, but doubt clouded his countenance. "And what is that?"

"A future with you. Even if it is in Germany. I will accept whatever God chooses for us, but I dearly hope it isn't an ocean standing between us."

His eyes closed, as if breathing in the reassurance of her words, then his arms wrapped around her and drew her into the embrace she'd long dreamed of. There was no kiss, just the solid, steady thump of his heart against her ear and the strength of his affection enfolding her. How bad could Germany be with these arms to run to each time the day grew difficult?

"I do not want you to suffer as my Mutter did, but I am praying, meine Mäuschen. I am praying."

After a long time standing enveloped in their unspoken thoughts and dreams, Aldrich pulled away. "Enough melancholy. Tonight I will teach you how to make paper stars for the Tannenbaum like Brenner and I did as boys."

"Well, you'll have to beat him to it. He's already promised to teach me."

He muttered something in German under his breath that she couldn't quite catch, but she suspected it was directed toward Brenner.

"Do not be vexed. There is nothing he can say or do that will steal my affections from you. If you want, I could seal that promise with—" Celestia bit her lip to keep from saying the rest of her thought.

"Seal that promise with what?"

She swallowed hard and pulled away. "Nothing. Never mind. Shall we finish our walk?" She sidestepped him, intent on putting space between them and her almost scandalous blunder.

"Oh no, you cannot escape that easily." He wrapped his arms around her again and backed her up until he trapped her between lounge chairs. The mischievous twitch to his lips suggested he suspected her. "Seal that promise how?"

"With a handshake." She lifted her chin, proud that she'd come up with a completely appropriate answer.

"I think not. A handshake would not turn you such a pretty pink."

"Well . . ." Her voice squeaked. "That might have been my second thought."

He leaned in and dropped to a whisper. "And your first thought?"

Her gaze dropped to his lips unbidden. "Might have been a kiss."

"A kiss, even though our future is uncertain?"

"This week is meant to be a gift, after all."

"So it is." His thumb brushed over her lips, and his smirk indicated he was considering claiming that gift.

Someone cleared their throat behind Aldrich, and Celestia peeked around his body.

Josiah scowled, and she understood the nervousness criminals must feel in his presence. "Do I need to go rouse Miss Adams so that you can be properly chaperoned?"

Heat blazed across her face.

Aldrich released her and scrambled back fast enough to trip over the end of the lounger.

Celestia caught his arm. "No, we were telling each other goodbye until tonight's event."

"Mm-hmm. Then may I suggest a proper goodbye be performed with words and enough distance between you for at least a piece of paper to fit?"

Red tinged Aldrich's ears and cheeks. "Until this evening, Fräulein Isaacs." He bid Josiah a good afternoon and then scuttled back inside.

"You are not to be unchaperoned with him again. That is for both your sakes. I am not so far removed from my marriage to Shauna that I've forgotten the temptations nipping on your heels." He linked his arm with hers. "Come. Mother requested we play a card game with her while she is well enough to do so."

Celestia obliged, but her mind was on whether or not Aldrich would have kissed her if Josiah had not interrupted.

Chapter Twelve

THE MUSIC ROOM hummed with the conversations of families huddled together to create paper ornaments for the Tannenbaum being assembled in the dining saloon for tomorrow's Christmas party. Mutter and Vater drifted from table to table, offering supplies or help where needed, while someone played Christmas hymns on the piano in the background. Several servers circulated the room with mulled cider and hot chocolate. The event was turning out to be the best attended yet, but it still lacked one crucial person.

Aldrich glanced at the entrance again before returning his attention to the chatter of Herr Southworth's young daughter.

She proudly displayed a white piece of paper with random bits chopped out in no discernible design. "It's an angel."

"So it is. We will have to hang it high in the tree so it appears to be flying." With the way the child beamed, he must have provided an acceptable response.

"First she needs color!" The little girl snatched a brand-new box of E. Steiger & Co. crayons from the table and extracted a yellow. "All angels have gold hair."

Perhaps not all, but Aldrich knew of at least one who matched that description. He once again glanced at the doors. This time Celestia stood observing him. The corners of his mouth inched up as he drank in her appearance. It did not matter how many times he saw her in that silver gown, it took his breath every time. He might have to start calling her his *Sternchen*—his little star—instead of Mäuschen. Although now that she'd decided on calling him her Käsechen, he doubted he could ever give up Mäuschen.

"When you finish coloring your angel, be sure to show me." He excused himself from Herr and Frau Southworth and directed his steps toward Celestia.

By the way her eyes never strayed from his, she was as happy to see him as he was her.

Unfortunately, Brenner reached her first. "Guten *Abend*, Fräulein Isaacs. Are you ready to learn how to make paper stars?"

Aldrich cut in next to Celestia and claimed her arm. "I have reserved a table for us in the corner so we will not be interrupted."

Rather than seem nettled, Brenner smirked and rushed ahead of them. He swiveled the chair on the end outward for Celestia, then claimed the lone seat next to her—forcing Aldrich to sit on the bench across from them. Were Aldrich twelve instead of twenty-four, he might have followed through with the impulse to kick Brenner beneath the table.

"Would you mind terribly if I switched to the bench seat? I hate having my back to all the festivities." Celestia's sly maneuver exhilarated Aldrich.

"By all means. I would not dare to interfere with your ability to observe what interests you." Brenner's roguish wink as Celestia rose suggested she made the excuse to observe him and not the festivities.

The pompous flirt.

"Thank you." Celestia slid onto the bench next to Aldrich, a choice that kept Brenner out of her line of vision. "Now what are all these strips of paper for?"

Before Brenner could begin instructions, Aldrich pulled two red and two white long strips from the pile on their table. "We will use these to weave and fold the stars." He placed the set before her and grabbed strips for himself. "Fold the strips in the middle lengthwise and cut them at an angle like this."

He aligned the edges of the strip so that they matched perfectly before creasing along the middle and then cut the ends at an angle.

Celestia was far less precise, leaving her with an uneven strip that would do nothing but cause problems along the way.

Brenner cut in and corrected her. "Nein, not like this. Precision is important. If you have strips like this, you will end up with a wad of paper instead of a star. Do it like this."

Her next four strips were good enough to work with, and Aldrich proceeded to show her how to hold the first strip horizontally and then hang the second strip over it. Once she mimicked that adequately, he enclosed the third strip with the fourth and then inserted the ends of the fourth strip through the eyelet of the first. From there everything fell apart as Celestia fumbled and giggled her way through the most horrendous star to ever be folded—even with his *and* Brenner's help.

When she finished, she lifted the mass in her open hand and laughed so hard tears slipped from the corners of her eyes. "Oh good heavens. It looks more like a spitball than a star. What do you say? Should we wet it and throw it at someone?"

Brenner grabbed it and tossed it into the air as if considering her suggestion. When it landed in his palm, the force knocked it into a crumpled mess of paper strips.

Even Aldrich couldn't contain his laughter.

Celestia flicked a tear from her cheek. "I am terrible at this." After her laughter subsided, she straightened her back in rigid determination. "But don't give up on me. I will learn. Can we try again?"

"We can try as many times as you like." Aldrich squeezed her hand beneath the table.

"Or at least until we run out of paper," Brenner quipped.

"That *may* happen, but an Isaacs never backs down." She grinned and then pulled out four new strips. "Show me again."

Aldrich scooted closer until their shoulders touched. This time as they worked through the folds, he physically guided her to apply the correct pressure to ensure crisp lines. Each time Celestia peered at him in victorious glee, he weighed the merits against the consequences of ducking his head for a quick peck on the lips. And each time he came close to acting, Brenner made some sort of noise or asked some question that forced Aldrich to remember that they were neither alone nor courting nor engaged. And perhaps worse, that Herr Isaacs threatened to throw him overboard if he compromised Celestia's reputation.

Brenner constructed his own star, but despite being demoted from instructor, he smirked as he worked.

Celestia's second star turned out better than the first, with points that actually looked star-ish. It held together tolerably well, but she was determined to continue making stars until hers were as good as his and Brenner's. Finally, after her seventh star, she declared it worthy of hanging on the tree.

"Which star should we call it?" Aldrich punctured a hole through one of the points with a knife and threaded a ribbon through for hanging. "Polaris, Betelgeuse, Sirius?"

Her head tilted in contemplation. "Would it be too presumptuous to call it the Christmas star? I like the inspiration it provides. It required great sacrifice and fortitude for the wise men to make such a journey." Her voice lowered, and Brenner made a show of becoming preoccupied with the construction of another star. "I think, in a way, this trip is similar for us. We travel by way of the *Golden Gestirn* in hopeful expectation of finding the answer to our prayers at the end, but much fortitude and sacrifice is needed. Especially if we discover the answer requires us to relinquish our gifts." Somber regret replaced the childlike glee of moments ago, indicating she'd reflected much since they had parted ways this afternoon.

Had she received her answer about Germany? His breath constricted. He knew indulging in careless dreams of a future with her would only cause more pain, and this afternoon he had proved a glutton for her company.

"Pardon the interruption, Herr Weise, but your presence is requested immediately." An officer stood at attention behind Brenner.

Of all the times for his responsibilities to pull him away. "Brenner, could you—"

"I am sorry, sir, but Captain Müeller specifically asked for you. It is about Pellegrini."

Of course it was. Hopefully, they caught the man, and Aldrich could return to Celestia before long. "Very well. Forgive me, Fräulein Isaacs. I will return as soon as I am able."

Disappointment tempered Celestia's acknowledgment, but Aldrich could practically hear Brenner's inner thoughts cheering.

"Have no fear, Bruder. I will see to it that Fräulein Isaacs is entertained for the remainder of her evening."

Chapter Thirteen

CELESTIA REGRETTED HER analogy of their situation to that of the wise men even before Aldrich left the table. The pain her words brought showed in the creases of his eyes and furrow of his brow. But their situations really were similar. This week had dragged her through every emotion known to man, and it took great fortitude to endure it.

Especially when both Josiah *and* Mother scolded her for the unchaperoned and rather flirtatious afternoon. When she retorted that she and Aldrich were determining what the future held for them, Mother vehemently opposed any consideration of moving to Germany. Even Josiah, of all people, cautioned her against rushing into a decision. Their blatant disapproval indicated they believed her incapable of surviving the move.

Although she longed to escape Brenner, Celestia refused to return to the quarrel waiting for her in her cabin. Instead, she attempted to stall for time by folding stars until they ran out of paper, but Aldrich never returned. With no other tolerable choice, she accepted Brenner's invitation to walk the promenade with a barely improved Marybeth trailing behind.

They strolled to the upper deck's railing, where they watched the steerage passengers on the deck below sing and dance to their fiddles under the waning gibbous moon. Their steps were nothing like the formal balls Celestia was accustomed to, but the gaiety was decidedly more entertaining than anything she'd attended. Josiah had once confessed that he straddled two entirely different worlds with his job, and he was never quite sure which one he preferred. It had struck her as an odd thing to say then, but now as she glimpsed into that other world, she understood at least in part.

"It is no wonder your Mutter and Vater named you Celestia. Tonight you look as if you belong among them." Brenner wasn't watching the people below but the now clear skies above.

Had the compliment come from Aldrich, she'd treasure it, but coming from Brenner? It was high past time she let him down gently. The only interest she had in him—would *ever* have—was as a brother-in-law. Even if at the moment that future didn't appear hopeful either.

"You are a good man, Herr Weise, and any woman would be honored to have your attention bestowed upon her so generously, but—"

"You wish I would not speak so to you." His gaze dropped from the heavens to meet hers. Instead of hurt or disappointment, all she found was humor. "Have no fear, Fräulein Isaacs. My intention is to rile Aldrich. It is obvious the way you feel for each other, and I have no intention of interfering. At least, not in the manner of competition."

"But I don't understand. Why would you wish to rile Aldrich?"

The humor died away, and his shoulders slumped. "He has told you of his decision to move to Germany, has he not?"

"He has."

"Then you should understand. This trip is not solely the maiden sailing of our newest ship. It is our last voyage together as a family for the foreseeable future. Our last chance to be fully brothers without an ocean between us." His gaze wandered to the blackened horizon where a line of moonlight danced over the waves. "We have always been close, even though I drove him mad with the pranks I pulled. When he went to university and I remained at home, that did not change. He was never more than a train trip away, and our letters were never more than a few days in between."

He swallowed and leaned heavily on the railing. "Aldrich is not the only one to give up much in his move to Germany. I am losing my brother. The ability to write to him for advice and have it in a timely manner. The ability to unexpectedly show up on his doorstep and drag him to the club or bowling lanes. Even the ability to rile him by flirting with his Mäuschen."

He looked at her and smiled. "That is why I am making the most of this trip—to annoy him, love him, and maybe help him to see what a fool he is to think you should be left behind."

"You don't think that we should part ways when this trip is over?"

"Nein, but that is not for me to decide."

"But don't you think me too sheltered and fragile to survive leaving my family for a foreign country where the only person I know is Aldrich?"

"Whoever said that does not know you. You have impressed me with your tenacity, bravery, and persistence during the last six days. That does not mean Germany will be easy for you, but no more difficult than walking away from a man you love. It is like what you said. You and Aldrich are searching for answers, and whatever Gott calls you to, it will require fortitude and sacrifice. But whatever decision you receive, God will provide what you need to follow through."

His vote of confidence soothed her insecurities and provided insight into her family's objection. Despite all their challenges, the Isaacses were as tightly woven as a silk gown. Losing one member to a life across the ocean would leave a hole that no one could ignore.

"So you are another wise Weise, huh?" She bumped his shoulder.

He grunted. "If you marry Aldrich, you will grow tired of those jokes quickly enough."

She laughed and then sobered. "I would like to marry him, but I don't know if that is what God wants from me. Or even how to discover what His desire for us is."

Brenner stared off into the distance and remained quiet. Apparently not even he had an answer to give.

The lively Christmas tunes below slowed to the lullaby hymns Mother used to sing before bed on Christmas Eve. Familiar peace settled over her, and she lifted her gaze to the endless sky.

So many stars, and yet God knew them all by name. Even the

ones invisible without the aid of a telescope. How many more were out there beyond what even the strongest magnifier could detect? He knew their births, their deaths, and everything in between. And they were stars, not men whom He'd chosen to create in His image. How many passages had she read about God's care for her? Every detail of her life, every tear she cried. He knew it all. Even if she didn't have the answers, He did.

God, I desire to do Your will. Would You make it clear to me? I know it has only been one day of praying. The wise men traveled for years before they found their answer. They even had to stop and ask for guidance from King Herod before continuing on.

She froze and looked to Brenner. Was that what God was doing? Using Brenner to direct her toward a future in Germany? But he was one man. Mother and Josiah directed her back home. Three people. Two opposing directions. Should she listen to the multitude of opinions? Or was the answer not to come from them at all?

Lord, please give me discernment. There is no clear answer. How do I know what is Your desire for us so that we can go in obedience?

"Celestia." Brenner glanced at her. "May I call you that?"

"Given what we've shared tonight, I'd say we are Freunde no matter what the outcome between Aldrich and me. So yes, you may."

He smiled. "Celestia, I know not what the answer is, but if I may provide one last bit of weighty wisdom, it would be for you and Aldrich to pray together over this. Not individually, but together."

"As in aloud?"

"Yes. My family has prayed aloud together my whole life, and I believe we are the stronger for it. This is too weighty a decision to be made in solitude. Pray together often and honestly. I know Gott will use it whether an answer is forthcoming or not."

The thought of praying aloud with Aldrich terrified her. It was one thing to bare her deepest wounds, fears, and thoughts to a God who knew every fault about her and furnished the Holy Spirit to intercede for her when she didn't know the right thing to pray. Praying aloud with Aldrich meant revealing a part of her that no one else knew.

What if it changed his opinion of her? What if she exposed her vulnerability and then they discovered their paths diverged? As much as she loved Aldrich, could she really trust him with that part of her soul?

Chapter Fourteen

ALDRICH WET HIS face with cold water and then gripped each side of the water basin. Pellegrini needed to be found before he broke into another room and stole something more valuable than someone's clothing and money. The chosen items spoke of a man intent on changing his identity and attempting to blend in with the steerage passengers, not someone dangerous. However, after discovering his uniform abandoned in an unused cabin along with the remnants of food from the pantry, Aldrich had ordered an inventory of the steerage supplies.

It was morning before an officer confirmed that several items were missing, including some cutlery and a boning knife. The cutlery could be nothing more than the unreturned dishes of actual passengers, but the missing boning knife worried him. The cooks insisted it had been returned to the knife block at the end of the last meal preparation. If Pellegrini was running around with a knife, he was no longer a harmless threat. What other things would he deem worth the risk of stealing before they docked in Southampton tomorrow? And who would get hurt if they tried to intervene?

Aldrich banged his hand on the wooden ledge. If only he had been more persistent in his search for the man earlier.

Brenner clasped Aldrich's shoulder. "It will be all right. Pellegrini will be found and everyone kept safe. It is not solely your responsibility. We have already spent the day searching for him and assigned extra crewmen to every floor and every set of stairs. Tomorrow we will reach Southampton, and hopefully the man will leave without incident." He opened their stateroom door. "Come. You do not want to miss Celestia's reaction to the unveiling of the Tannenbaum."

Aldrich stiffened. "She is Fräulein Isaacs to you."

"Not since last night. We came to an understanding that justified the use of our Christian names." The scoundrel grinned and winked at him.

"The only understanding you need is that I will not tolerate my brother flirting with the woman I love."

"Love, huh? Does this mean I should kiss the cheek of my future sister-in-law? Or perhaps claim her first dance in order to congratulate her?"

"Not unless you want to take an invigorating swim."

Brenner threw his hands up in mock surrender and walked backward out of their room. Once his feet hit the Oriental rug, he dropped them. "You will have to catch me first." Then he spun on his heels and fled the family suite.

"What was that all about?" Mutter asked.

"How do you feel about having one less son? I am going to collar him and throw him overboard before this voyage is over."

"He is just going to miss you, and you will miss his antics as well."

"I know, but can he find a different method of amusement than flirting with Celestia?"

"Is that what this is about?" Mutter laughed. "Oh, mein Schatz, that is not a worry you should concern yourself with. Go to the party. Enjoy your time with Fräulein Isaacs, and I will maneuver Brenner's attention elsewhere for a time."

When Aldrich reached the dining saloon, a large crowd waited before the closed curtain separating the back quarter of the room from the rest. The unveiling of the Tannenbaum would signal the beginning of the final Christmas celebration before their arrival in Southampton, and by the number of attendees, the saloon passengers were eager to attend. He spotted Celestia in the corner, sneaking a peek behind the curtain. By the way she pouted when Herr

Isaacs pulled her away, she had been unsuccessful. It was adorable, and Aldrich wanted nothing more than to pretend she was his and tonight theirs to enjoy without the cloud of uncertainty to dampen their spirits.

Brenner stood annoyingly close to Celestia, and the moment he noticed Aldrich, he planted a kiss on Celestia's cheek.

"Brenner!" Utter shock laced her immediate one-word reprimand.

Forget the need for Mutter to distract Brenner later. Someone needed to take him in hand now.

Herr Isaacs yanked Brenner away from his sister. "You overstep, sir."

Aldrich reached Celestia's side, took her arm, and addressed Brenner. "Is it not your duty to unveil the Tannenbaum?"

Brenner shook off Herr Isaacs's grip. "My apologies, Celestia, Herr Isaacs. If you will excuse me, Aldrich is correct." As he passed, he leaned toward Aldrich and whispered, "If I were you, I would propose tonight while you still have the upper hand."

He walked off looking entirely too pleased with himself.

"Your brother is determined to rile you in every way possible, isn't he?" Celestia shook her head, but she appeared more amused than upset.

"Did you hear what he said?" He hoped not, but by her smile, he was doomed.

"I did, but we will move forward only as God directs. Until then, remember I promised that Brenner will never steal my affections from you, even if I didn't get a chance to seal it properly."

"It's not too late, you know."

Herr Isaacs cleared his throat. "That is enough, you two. I will leave you be, but no disappearing from this room unchaperoned. I *will* be watching."

"Only until the first single woman catches your attention." Celestia's words sang with teasing melody.

Aldrich hoped she was right, because he would not mind stealing away to a private corner and having that promise sealed properly.

Her brother grunted and melted into the crowded room.

"With his earlier threats to me, I am surprised he left us alone at all."

"Josiah cannot tell a woman no, especially his baby sister." The mischievous glint to her eyes and quirk to her mouth spoke of a scheme. "I might have asked him for an early Christmas gift."

"And what was that?"

"An uninterrupted evening with you."

"I think that is a gift to us both."

"He's generous like that."

Aldrich glanced to the curtain's center, where Brenner prepared to address the gathering. Any minute the lights would turn off to allow for the full impact of the Tannenbaum's glow when the curtain opened. A moment that he would rather share privately than with the crowd.

"Give me your hands and close your eyes."

Celestia placed her hands in his but remained focused on him. "Whatever for?"

"There are benefits to being the owner of the ship. I will take you to the other side of the curtain, but you must not see the Tannenbaum until I say."

The giddiness of a child on Christmas Eve animated her countenance as she obeyed and lifted her chin in full confidence of going wherever he directed. Her trust in him was a thrill all its own, and he delighted in pulling her through the narrow gap to the other side. Staff members still worked to light the final candles on the goosefeather Tannenbaum, a short-lived treat that would be blown out for the safety of the ship once the lights were restored. He angled her so she would have the best vantage point for observing the glittering tinsel and passenger-made ornaments.

When one eye peeked open, he cupped his palm over her eyes. "Do not spoil the surprise. I promise it is worth waiting for."

"But it's taking too long."

He chuckled but kept his palm in place.

Celestia bit her lip as Brenner's muffled voice rose above the chatter of the crowd.

The lights went out, and the string quartet in the corner of the room struck up "O Tannenbaum." The candlelight of the Tannenbaum cast the room in a dance of shadows and golden flickers.

Aldrich pulled his hand away and whispered into her ear, "You may open them now." He leaned back far enough to be respectable but still see every detail of her reaction.

Her eyes opened, then widened. A soft gasp escaped as her hand flew to her mouth. For a full minute she studied the Tannenbaum from the top, where he had instructed her stars to be placed, to the wide anchored base, where several staff stood with buckets of water at the ready.

"It's beautiful," she whispered.

"Yes, you are."

"I was talking about the tree."

"And I was speaking of you. I do not see the problem."

She popped to her toes and pecked his cheek. "Thank you."

"I hope that is not the kiss to seal your promise with. I had hoped for something a little more . . . lasting."

There was a pause as she scrutinized him. "What kind of lasting? A single-lingering-kiss lasting?"

Even in the flickering light, he could see the color rise in her cheeks.

"Or do you mean lasting like a lifetime of kisses?"

Brenner's quip about a proposal seemed less preposterous in the intimate candlelight and close proximity than it had originally, even though nothing had changed. He still had no answer.

Or did he?

Mutter, Vater, and even Brenner had given their vote of confidence in Celestia, and yesterday's sermon had been encouraging as well. But Aldrich wanted one more sign. Something to ease his fears and show that this was indeed what was best for both of them.

Aldrich lifted a hand to her cheek and caressed it. "I would like a lifetime of kisses, but I am like Gideon and his fleece. I am afraid and want answers, undeniable proof that this is what we are supposed to do."

Her hand covered his, and she peered at him with the candlelight reflected in her eyes. "I love that you are as desirous of His will as I am, but I think it time for us to step out of our individual fears. Brenner suggested last night that we pray. Not individually, but together. Aloud."

"Brenner?" He scoffed. "Does he hope the answer is us parting ways?"

"Actually, no. And I better understand now why my family has encouraged me to not rush into a decision. My move to Germany would be as hard on them as me."

Someone bumped into his back, and Aldrich realized the room was filling with people. "Come. We need to finish this discussion, and it will be easier to slip out in the dark than when lights turn on."

She followed him back through the curtain and glanced around when she regained his side. "Don't you fear Josiah's wrath?"

"*Ja*, but some things—like the possibility we might come to an answer—are worth it."

The chaos of business life had taught him that if he did not purposely pursue time for reflection with Gott, his ability to discern what the Holy Spirit wanted for him would be lost. And he would not allow that to happen now, even if it meant Herr Isaacs tossed him overboard the first chance he got.

They skirted the edge of the room, slipped out the door without being spotted, and used the main stairs to reach the upper deck. The night sky, radiant with stars, greeted them upon their arrival, along with a chilling wind that reminded him Celestia wore no coat. He slid his off, wrapped it around her, and led her to a quiet spot at the front where two vent shafts met to block the majority of the gusts.

Using his own body to shield Celestia from what little wind got by, he stood before her, half in fear and half in anticipation of what this clandestine meeting might reveal. "Have you had any indication that Gott is telling you no to a future in Germany with me?"

"I've had no obvious no, but no obvious yes either."

"It is the same with me, although perhaps there have been pushes toward yes that I have been too fearful to admit." A sneaky gust of wind wound its way to Celestia and pushed a strand of hair into her face. He tucked it behind her ear and cupped her cheek. "I love you, Celestia, and all I want to do is protect you."

Her soft smile grew, and a contented sigh brushed against his wrist. "And I have loved you from the first time we met. There is no other man with whom I would want to spend the rest of my life with. Even if it requires leaving my family to join you in Germany."

"But are you certain that is what you want? What Gott wants?" He searched her gaze for any hesitation, anything that might indicate they were about to make the biggest mistake of their lives.

"I know it is what *I* want, but perhaps we should pray together, as Brenner suggested? God promised He will hear our prayers and answer them according to His will. If when we are done, we do not feel a strong sense that we should part ways, I am willing to believe that is God giving His consent."

"Your courage never ceases to inspire me, meine Mäuschen."

"It is easy to be courageous when you have a God you can trust and a godly man by your side."

He kissed her forehead. "You give me too much credit."

"And you give *me* too much credit. Can I confess that I am terrified to pray aloud with you?"

He wrapped his arms around her and tucked her against him, as much to comfort her as to steal back some of the warmth the wind was robbing from him. "You have nothing to fear. Shall we?"

When she nodded against his chest, he poured out his desires for their future together, the fears that surrounded the decision, and the request that if this was not to be Gott's will, they would walk away from this prayerful time together certain of it. Celestia's prayer followed his, shy and quiet but echoing with surprising insights into the woman he had long admired. Yes, she was courageous, but that did not mean she was without fear. Yet, she willingly surrendered those fears to Gott and spoke with the assurance that He would help her to overcome them. When she finished, she squeezed his hand, and they proclaimed a joint amen.

Though the cold seeped through his vest and shirtsleeves, Aldrich refused to suggest they go inside. Instead they stared at the stars in their little corner protected from the wind, his arms wrapped around her as her head and hand rested against his chest. The waves lapped against the ship and drowned out the low hum of the party in regular rhythms, and a strange sensation, like the knitting together of two people, formed. Peace settled over him with a certainty that yes, this was what Gott intended for them. As if confirmation of his decision, two stars shot across the sky side by side.

"Celestia?"

"Hmmm?"

"I know traditionally I should court you before asking, but will you marry me despite all it would require of you?"

She pulled back and regarded him with tears in her eyes and a grin so wide it could divide the earth in two. "Yes. God willing, yes, yes, yes!"

In the unrestrained exuberance he adored in her, she cupped the back of his neck and drew him down.

He had often imagined their first kiss, but apparently he lacked a good imagination. Nothing had prepared him for the absolute bliss and relief that finally having the freedom to show her how much he cared brought. If angelic choruses filled the sky, he would not be surprised—if he even noticed at all. This moment was like a holy promise, an assurance that no matter what the future brought or where Gott led them, they were in it together. He hugged her closer as the full realization and excitement of it all settled over him.

Celestia was going to be his. Now and forever. Germany would be theirs to share.

Chapter Fifteen

More than twelve hours after Aldrich's proposal, Celestia still couldn't stop grinning, no matter how she tried to compose herself. Once they'd rejoined the party, they'd spent the remainder of the evening dancing to the string quartet, dreaming of all the good things the future held for them and occasionally sneaking into an alcove for kisses and intimate words. Not even when someone trod on her hem as they descended the stairs and ripped a portion of the skirt away from the bodice did it dampen her mood. The damage could be repaired by a seamstress in Bremerhaven, and one dress still remained until she could access the trunk with her travel suits.

Celestia ran a hand over her wrinkled skirts and scrunched her nose. The dreadful thing looked as if it had been wadded up and tossed in a corner. Four more days of daily use wouldn't do it any favors either. She sighed and then returned to grinning. What did it matter? Aldrich wouldn't care so long as they were together, and she didn't care either.

Her mother, however, did not share the same opinion. "Absolutely not. You *cannot* be seen in that wrinkled mess. It isn't seemly."

"Don't be so dramatic, Mother." Celestia shut the door to her stateroom and joined her on the sofa. "I am sure most passengers are looking a little wrinkled at this point in the trip. Besides, it's all I have left until we can access our trunks in Bremerhaven."

"Well, you're not going to breakfast until it has been pressed. I'll not have anyone see you in such a state, even your so-called intended."

"We're betrothed whether you like it or not."

"Stop sounding like Josiah. It's not official until the man asks your father for permission."

Celestia barely kept from rolling her eyes. If worse came to worse, Mother and Father would find she was more like Josiah than anyone ever imagined. The only One she needed permission from had given it with a splendid show of shooting stars. She smiled again. Not even her mother's poor mood could steal her joy.

"Go rouse Miss Adams and have her press your dress. You will not leave this suite until you look presentable. I am serious, young lady."

Josiah exited his stateroom, shrugging on his coat. "Uh-oh. Mother's using *that* voice. You best obey whatever she's asking."

"Tell her that my dress is fine. It's the last one I have until I can access my trunk in the cargo hold."

Josiah scrutinized her appearance and shook his head. "I'm afraid I have to agree with Mother this time." When she opened her mouth to object, he lifted his hand. "Trust me—you do not want the suspicious looks and rumors that might come your way. You may be betrothed, but both of your reputations are still important."

"Fine, but tell Aldrich I will find him as soon as I'm presentable enough for Mother to release me from this prison."

"Now who's being the dramatic one, dear?" Mother asked.

"I'd offer to order a tray for you, but I think perhaps it is best to wait until after Miss Adams has pressed your dress. We can't have her ruining your last one." Josiah chuckled at his own joke as he left the suite for breakfast.

However, it was no joke when Marybeth did just that—only it was far worse than a retching that could have been cleaned.

"I'm so sorry, miss!" Tears streamed down Marybeth's face as she held up Celestia's dress with an iron-shaped hole at the front of the bodice. "The ship rocked, and I turned away for fear of getting sick on your dress."

"Well, you did avoid that." Celestia rubbed her temple.

This trip was an outright disaster for her wardrobe. She had nothing left to wear but a nightgown and a housecoat. With their arrival at Southampton not occurring until late afternoon, there was no guarantee Marybeth would be able to disembark in time to purchase a few ready-mades before the shops closed. And the ship was scheduled to leave for Bremerhaven around breakfast time, well before any shops opened. There was nothing for it. She needed to access her trunk before the crew became occupied with preparing to dock. If she wore the dress and covered up with her coat, she should at least be presentable enough to access the cargo hold. Even if she did sweat out of existence while doing so.

Mother attempted to object, but even she couldn't argue against the logic of Celestia going to her trunk. Marybeth was halfway to retching again, and Mother barely suppressed her own seasickness. Walking to the front portion of the ship where the pitching was more prominent would likely send her back into fighting Marybeth for use of the water closet. Thankfully, Steward Yates was more than willing to obtain the location of Celestia's trunk and escort her down to it.

They descended into the depths of the steamer where, like in Jules Verne's *Journey to the Center of the Earth*, another formerly unknown world existed. However, the bowels of the ship were more akin to the cavern portion of the expedition than the vibrant forest. Here, the lighting was sparser than the above decks. Lanterns swayed with the motion of the ship, casting the long halls in a dim light that partnered with hot air and the stench of unaired bedclothes to make even her stomach unsettled.

Peeks into the open cabins revealed six passengers to a room half the size she and Marybeth shared. A few passengers lay on straw mattresses, but the vast majority stretched out in canvas sleeping berths hung one above the other. In some rooms, the canvas sleeping berths were tucked into a corner and a table lowered from the ceiling. Coffee, buttered bread, and something soupy seemed to be the full provision for their morning meal. By the smell of it, and the growl from her empty stomach, it wouldn't be unpleasant, but it was a far cry from the sumptuous fare served upstairs. In fact, not one hint of the luxurious comforts she enjoyed on the saloon decks was found here. Everything was aimed toward efficiency and bare necessity.

Yet even in the stark existence, the people laughed, sang, and conversed. At least, until they noticed her. Her very presence in their world seemed an offense. A few made snide comments about the princess leaving her palace for a look at the animals, and shame heated her cheeks. That was not her intention, but with her gawking, was it any wonder that was the impression she gave? A young boy popped in front of them and waggled his rear end at her. Celestia averted her eyes and tried not to react, but another boy joined the show. Mr. Yates reprimanded them and sent them on their way. She'd never been so glad to leave an area as when they left steerage for the deck below.

As strange and uncomfortable an experience as the deck above had been, the empty darkness of this one felt straight out of a gothic novel. If she were the superstitious type, she'd swear the floor was haunted, what with all the groaning of the ship and the roar of the sea on the other side of the hull. The sparse number of lit lanterns barely pierced the darkness with their light. Eerie shadows danced along the hall like specters.

Ghosts do not exist.

She scooted closer to the steward.

"No need to fear, miss. This deck is empty of passengers."

And of apparitions too.

Even if not, Christ was more powerful than any evil spirit that *might* exist. That truth cast out her fear, and she walked taller.

Midway down the hall, the steward opened a cabin door inward. Something thumped in the back corner, and she regretted translating Grimm's "The Robber Bridegroom" this morning. When the room's lantern flamed to life, she checked each visible spot for indications of anything—or anyone—that should not be there. A collection of trunks stacked three tall in the center of the room blocked the majority of her view. The bow of the boat pitched low and then back up again, and a canvas berth barely visible in the corner slapped against the wall. Celestia released a pent-up breath. A simple explanation for a simple sound. However, the way the trunks wobbled beneath their thick ropes raised new concerns.

Mr. Yates muttered something about sloppy knots and waved for her to stay outside the door. "If you will wait here, the trunks are not tied down as tight as they ought to be. I will secure the lines and then call you back to find your trunk."

After retying the knots at the front of the cabin, he disappeared around to the back side.

The bow pitched more sharply than before. She caught the door to keep it from closing, but she could do nothing about the trunks that toppled from their precarious perch at the back.

The steward yelped, as if struck, and the trunks thudded against the ground.

"Mr. Yates, are you hurt?"

He didn't respond.

She bit her lip and eyed the remaining top of the stack. The next swell brought a similar pitch, but the line of trunks still tied down appeared stable. Her doctoring skills were poor at best, but she could at least determine if she needed to run for help or give the man a moment to gather his wits.

Celestia edged her way along the wall opposite the tied-down trunks, watching for any sign that they too might shift. When she reached the corner, she saw a dark-haired man in coarse and grimy clothing squatted over Steward Yates with his back to her. A blanket tied as a satchel on the floor next to him indicated the man was either a passenger claiming his own space or a stowaway.

Another swell shifted the man sideways, and lantern light glinted off a knife. Mr. Yates slumped against the wall beyond him with a line of blood dripping down his face from a nasty gash near his temple. One of the fallen trunks lay across his lap, and the rest of the trunks scattered behind him prevented escape from the blade.

"Tell the *signorina* to leave."

A sensible thing for her to do given he'd evidently not realized her presence. Surely the steerage steward or other passengers would come to their aid. She slid toward the cabin door, but the movement caught Mr. Yates's eye. His shift of attention was enough to alert the stowaway, and he pivoted low on his heels with the knife ready to wield.

The wild eyes of Pellegrini locked on to hers. "You."

Like a rabbit spotted by a hawk, she froze.

He lunged toward her, but the steward, despite his pinned position, managed to wrap his arms around Pellegrini's legs.

With Pellegrini's forward momentum impeded, he landed at her feet with the knife still firmly in his grasp.

"Go!" Mr. Yates's yell broke through the ice of her fear.

Chilling clarity poured over her.

She could not run. Not yet. Not with the steward unable to defend himself. Josiah wouldn't do it, and neither would she.

She lifted her foot to stomp on Pellegrini's knife hand, but he jerked onto his side.

Her whole body reverberated with the jolt from her miss.

Pellegrini grasped for her foot, but Mr. Yates wrenched his body and Pellegrini's legs the opposite direction.

With a frustrated roar, Pellegrini twisted and slashed at Mr. Yates.

Celestia didn't wait to see how he fared but rather ran for the cabin door. Another low pitch swung it closed before she reached it, and she wasted precious seconds fumbling with the handle. Once the latch released beneath her sweaty palms, she flung it open and rushed into the hall screaming for help.

Pellegrini tackled her from behind, silencing her within seconds.

They landed on the floor, and his bloodied knife entered her periphery. "You have placed me in a difficult position, signorina. Now that I kill a man, you must go with me. We will use the pilot boat to take us to Southampton. If you are *non è un problema*, I will leave you at the docks unharmed. *Capisci?*"

What choice did she have? Her moment of bravery was short-lived. All she could do was hope and pray that Aldrich would find her and that God would protect her until he did.

"I capisci."

Chapter Sixteen

So much for breaking the *Oregon*'s Blue Riband record. Now Aldrich just hoped the ship would make it through the storm without any damage. For almost an hour, giant waves had been hammering the ship like a nail, making it roll and pitch with such ferocity that Captain Müeller ordered all decks closed to passenger use. Rain streamed across the bridge's window in river-sized rivulets as the storm clouds flickered green with lightning.

Aldrich gripped the bar beneath the window as the ship lurched. Captain Müeller compensated for the movement without a need for the bar but called out orders to adjust the ship's angle. Celestia's Mutter and companion must be well beyond miserable at this point. With all this rocking, he would not be surprised if even Celestia succumbed to seasickness. As soon as the storm passed and he could assure himself the danger of severe damage was over, he would go to her suite.

Another twenty minutes passed before the clouds thinned to gray and the rain diminished to a constant drizzle. The waves remained miserable but not as treacherous as they had been during the height of the tempest. A glance at his watch informed him they should have been in Southampton by now. It was a disappointment, but safety took precedence over speed.

"How long has the storm delayed us?" Aldrich asked Captain Müeller.

"A few hours, but the pilot boat should still reach us before dark. I estimate"—he looked over some equipment and then drifted off in thought for a moment—"about two hours, give or take. The decks can be reopened, though I advise passengers traverse them with caution."

"Thank you, Captain. You did a fine job guiding the *Golden Gestirn* through troubled waters." Aldrich shook the man's hand before exiting and making his way from the forward most part of the promenade to the main building, where he could access the stairs.

Just to be certain Celestia had not fled to the ladies' drawing room, he knocked on the door. The woman who answered informed him Celestia was not there and had not been for the entire day as far as she knew.

As he turned away, Herr Isaacs appeared in the stairwell, taking the steps two at a time. "Thank God I found you. I need you to convince your crew to allow me into the cargo hold."

"Nein. It is too dangerous. The seas are still rough. The cargo could shift and fall on you. When we are settled in Southampton—"

"You don't understand. *I* don't need something from cargo—Celestia is already down there and has been for hours."

That did not make sense. No crew member would give her access during a storm. "Why would she be there and not in one of the public rooms?"

As they jogged down the stairs, Josiah explained. "Miss Adams ruined Celestia's last dress, and Mother says Celestia convinced the steward to escort her to her trunks. They left as the seas were turning rough."

"Have you talked to the steward? Perhaps she changed clothes in the ladies' boudoir and then went to one of the other public rooms to avoid their seasickness."

"The steward is still missing as well. And before you ask, yes, I've searched every public space on this ship while waiting for the storm to pass. She is not here." He emphasized each of the last four words with a tone that bit Aldrich like a rabid dog, spreading its disease of fear throughout him.

At the base of the stairs, he turned to the crewman standing guard.

"Go ask the surgeon to meet me down in steerage. We may have injuries in the cabins used as cargo."

The man jogged up the stairs to do as bidden while Aldrich led the way at a brisk pace. He paused long enough to ask his parents to pray nothing was wrong and to add Brenner to their number. When they reached steerage, a few passengers loitered in the hall, but by the moans and sounds of retching, not many had escaped the storm's wrath. Not that he could blame them. Here the pitch was more pronounced than in the bridge.

"Have any of you seen a steward with a blond woman from the saloon decks come through here?"

A craggy old woman spoke around her smoking pipe. "You mean that princess that was gawking at us like we was an exhibition? She came through alright. Went down below with that steward. Ain't seen her since though. She probably had enough of the show." The woman cackled like she'd made a joke worthy of the stage.

The others in the hall corroborated her story. Celestia and the steward had never returned this way.

Once the doctor and a couple extra crewmen joined them, they descended to the next level of steerage used solely for small cargo storage. The hall was empty and poorly lit, but a crewman who knew the location of the trunks led them directly there. Two men strained against the door until whatever blocked it moved enough to allow entrance.

Aldrich entered first, followed by Herr Isaacs with a lantern. His stomach clenched at the mess of trunks tossed about the room.

"Over there!" Herr Isaacs scrambled over the trunks in the center toward the back wall.

Aldrich's gaze followed his trajectory to where two trunks lay at odd angles, as if atop a body rather than the floor.

Please, Gott, no.

He rushed to Herr Isaacs's side and joined him in tossing the trunks to the center stack.

Steward Yates lay facedown and bloodied beneath.

"Doctor! You are needed."

If Yates was here, Celestia must be as well. He examined the tiny room, searching for any sign that another body lay hidden.

"These injuries aren't from trunks falling."

Herr Isaacs's statement drew Aldrich's attention back to where Herr Isaacs pointed out several thin, narrow puncture wounds over Yates's back.

The surgeon shoved them aside to access the man, but his rushed assessment ended in slumped shoulders and a shaking head. "It appears he was stabbed to death."

By a boning knife, no doubt.

Please, Gott, let me be wrong. "I want every trunk removed now. Celestia is still missing."

"I do not think she is in here." Brenner approached with a tied blanket in his hands and agony in his face. "It contains the items Pellegrini stole."

Aldrich slammed a fist against the wall. He should have never allowed the ship to leave port with that man aboard. Reputation or not, one action remained if there was any hope of finding Celestia and Pellegrini.

"Close all public areas on the ship. I want passengers confined to their cabins and all available crew searching. We will not dock until they are found."

Chapter Seventeen

CELESTIA'S BACK AND legs cramped from sitting on the floor in the same position for too long. Were it not for the stress of concocting possible ways to escape unharmed, being held hostage was rather boring and uncomfortable. She stretched her legs past the metal piping and twisted to stretch her back.

"Stop moving, and pull your legs in." Pellegrini prodded her with the tip of the knife but put no real force behind it.

Given how much the man still shook and sweated after his encounter with the steward, Pellegrini didn't seem to want to harm her. However, he'd proven that he wasn't afraid to do so if the situation required it. Poor Steward Yates. May God rest his soul. Perhaps if she'd run instead of trying to stop Pellegrini, he might be alive.

Pellegrini poked her again, this time with more force.

She tucked her knees beneath her chin and wrapped her arms around her legs. How was she going to escape this mess without getting skewered in the process?

Voices arose from the other side of the door before it opened.

"The pilot ship is approaching. Have all the surrounding rooms been searched?" Relief at hearing Aldrich's voice produced a sob.

"*Silenzio.*" The knife rose to her throat.

She forced the sob back until it lodged painfully in her chest.

"This is the last one."

Grunting and metallic scraping overpowered his words, and the roar of the ocean filled the space.

"I will search it." Aldrich spoke above the noise, and the door shifted, as if it changed hands. "See to the boarding preparations."

The nearly empty room left nowhere to hide from view if Aldrich did more than peek inside, something that both thrilled and terrified her.

Pellegrini must have realized their situation as well. He scooted closer and whispered into her ear, "Stand."

She rose from the ground with Pellegrini. Once or twice the knife bumped against her coat but did not slice through the material. She sent a silent "Thank You" to God and spread her stance so the roll of the ship did not throw her off balance and give the knife a chance to succeed in piercing through.

"Do what I say, and you will live."

⁓⚜⁓

Aldrich glanced at the men opening the port gangway door to allow the Southampton harbor pilot to board the *Golden Gestirn* and guide the ship into port. Time was running out, and so were the places to search. Room after empty room had yielded nothing but a growing panic that Pellegrini might evade them.

Gott, let this be the room I find her safe and whole.

He gripped the derringer Herr Isaacs insisted he carry and steeled himself to find another empty room. He opened the door as far as it would go and used it as a shield while he peered around.

"Step inside and away from the door."

Aldrich pivoted to his left at the sound of the Italian accent. Herr Isaacs warned them that Pellegrini might use Celestia as a hostage, but Aldrich was unprepared for the ripping of his heart from his chest at seeing a knife held to her neck. He forced his gaze from the silver blade to Celestia's face. Though fear tightened her features, she appeared calm and in control of her faculties. Their eyes connected, and a brave smile curved the corners of her mouth. Whoever believed women were weak had never met Celestia. He drew from her well of courage to refresh his own before focusing on her captor.

"Let her go, Pellegrini." Aldrich projected his voice, and by the halt of movement from the officer he traded positions with, he had been heard.

"And get arrested? No. Do as I say and you will find her unharmed at the docks."

Whether left alone on a foreign dock or kept under knifepoint on a rolling ship, the danger to Celestia was similar, and at least aboard ship, Aldrich could do something to rescue her. "How do you expect to get her there?"

"The pilot boat."

Aldrich frowned. There was nothing simple about boarding a pilot boat. Even in good weather it was a precarious business. In these waves, it was downright perilous.

Celestia's eyes widened a breath before Pellegrini forced her forward. "Toss the gun and move aside."

He would not give Pellegrini the opportunity to possess another weapon, but he could not risk the man's wrath either. Aldrich skidded the gun into the hall and withdrew from the doorway.

Celestia and Pellegrini slid past, his back against the door and attention flicking between Aldrich and the crew who stood ready to act on the other side.

"Tell them to put their guns away and fall back."

Until a better plan formed, they were stuck obeying orders. "Do as he says."

Weapons disappeared, and the crew retreated. Aldrich followed Pellegrini at a safe distance to the open port gangway, where the pilot ladder had yet to be lowered. The ship listed toward the opening, and Pellegrini stumbled, yanking Celestia back with him.

Aldrich reached for Celestia's flailing arm, but someone stopped him.

"Don't. It will pull her against the blade." Herr Isaacs's pale face and white-knuckled fists declared the fear that warred with Aldrich's own desire to act.

The ladder winch stopped their fall, and Pellegrini righted them.

Celestia's eyes clenched, and her chest rose and fell in shaky heaves. A long, straight line of split material across the neck of her coat declared its part in sparing her from the blade's slice.

Thank You, Gott.

"Lower the ladder." Pellegrini pointed at the closest crew member with his chin.

"You can't climb down that in this weather! You'll both fall." Herr Issacs launched forward, and this time Aldrich detained him. The impact could send all three out the opening.

"Stay back." Pellegrini lifted the blade to the underside of Celestia's chin and forced her head up at an angle. "I will take the risk. Now lower it!"

A crewman tossed the rope ladder over the edge of the port gangway, and the wooden steps clanged against the ship's hull. As he cranked the winch to lower the ladder, no one spoke. Only the roar of the upset ocean and the thrum of the ship's engine filled the tense quiet. With each roll of the ship, Aldrich held his breath as Celestia struggled to keep her chin from bumping against the blade.

Pellegrini could not climb down the ladder without releasing her. Aldrich just needed to be patient and wait for the right moment to yank her away from the port gangway. Then his officers and Herr Isaacs could collect Pellegrini however they saw fit.

Both too soon and not fast enough, the crewman retreated.

"*Buono.* Now we wait for the boat."

Beyond them, the pilot boat—a schooner at full sail—navigated the waves with grace and speed. Within minutes it disappeared beneath the opening's view, indicating it was preparing to brush against the *Golden Gestirn* so the pilot could board.

"Start climbing, signorina. If you or anyone else attempts to stop me, I will kick you off."

The same fear that pulsed through Aldrich whitened Celestia's face. She was not supposed to get on the ladder at all, let alone be the one to go first. Her skirts were certain to tangle in her legs, and her fancy boots were not meant to handle the ocean-slicked wooden rungs.

Pellegrini removed his arm from her waist but kept the knife near her face as he prodded her toward the handrails at the ladder's head.

Aldrich could not allow her to go without saying something. He spoke slow and loud, praying that her German was good enough to understand him. "*Halt fest*, meine Mäuschen. *Ich liebe dich.*"

Hold tight, my little mouse. I love you.

She blinked. Then her brow furrowed.

"Do not speak!" Pellegrini pushed Celestia toward the ladder.

She stumbled but caught herself on the handrail. With a white-knuckled grip, she descended several rungs as her gaze sought Aldrich's with no indication that she understood his words.

Lord, may she live so that I can spend the rest of our lives teaching her the full and deep meaning of "ich liebe dich" over and over again.

"*Datti una mossa!*" When Celestia didn't respond, Pellegrini waved the knife in her face. "I said hurry up."

Some of the color returned to Celestia's cheeks, apparently with a good dose of spunk to go with it. "Perhaps *you* would like to try descending a ladder in skirts. They're catching enough wind to sail the *Golden Gestirn* themselves."

Aldrich had not considered how the wind would affect her climb. His throat and chest constricted to suffocating proportions. What if a gust yanked her feet from the steps and she fell?

Foot by foot Celestia lowered from view, with Pellegrini standing close enough to follow through with his threat. Before her head cleared the bulkhead, Pellegrini bit down on the boning knife's handle and began his descent.

Celestia was too close to Pellegrini to yank him forward, and that knife made grabbing him tricky too.

While Pellegrini looked down to check his footing, Aldrich inched closer. Herr Isaacs slid alongside him, and the Colt revolver at the man's waist caught his attention. That would solve their problem in a hurry.

"Can you not shoot him?" Aldrich whispered.

Herr Isaacs glared. "He'd fall on Celestia."

And knock her off right along with him.

Gott, give me clear direction. There has to be a way.

Pellegrini descended another rung and then stopped. He glowered downward, and his body jerked, like he prodded Celestia with his foot.

Aldrich's heart beat a chaotic rhythm as he took long sliding steps toward Pellegrini.

Celestia's voice yelled above the ocean's noise, "Grab him!"

Aldrich launched forward.

Pellegrini's face swung toward him, bringing with it the knife.

The blade collided with the side of Aldrich's chest, but the force of impact knocked it from Pellegrini's mouth. It bounced against the watershed's lip and fell overboard.

Aldrich and Herr Isaacs grasped the back of Pellegrini's coat and yanked him forward.

Pellegrini fought against their pull with his arms and legs.

A high-pitched scream cut through the turmoil.

He stilled and turned widened eyes on them. *"Dio mi perdoni!* I hit her."

The scream stopped, and so did Aldrich's heart.

Chapter Eighteen

CELESTIA'S BODY BOUNCED against the side of the ship and cut her scream short. The rope she'd coiled around her left arm tightened as it bore the weight of her body, and her shoulder strained against the pressure. At least she'd had the good sense to knot her legs around the side of the ladder before yelling for them to grab Pellegrini. Instead of dangling straight down, her rear end and upper body hung in an L over the waves crashing against the ship. If her arms failed her, perhaps her legs would keep her from plunging.

She glanced below and wished she hadn't. More feet than she cared to guess stretched between her and the pilot boat that bobbed up and down against the ship. If she fell and managed to hit the deck, she'd probably break something. Likely her neck. And if she hit the water? There were no dock posts to grab for this time. She drew in a shuddered breath and clenched her eyes.

God, this is either the stupidest plan I've ever made or absolutely brilliant. However, I didn't think ahead to the next steps. So if You could be so kind as to help me along?

She peered up, hoping that someone would be climbing down to reach her. Pellegrini's legs flailed above her. If Aldrich's crew could hurry up with the grabbing, she would greatly appreciate it.

The dampness of the mist and waves slicked her grip, and her arms tremored with the weight they held. Soon she'd either be hanging upside down by her legs, shattered over the deck below, or discovering if mermaids really existed.

"Celestia!" Aldrich's agonized cry wrenched her chest.

His head stuck out over the ledge. Momentary relief washed his face until a mix of determination and fear crowded it out. He swung onto the ladder with the same smoothness he had on the docks, although his descent was far less steady. Between her off-balanced weight, his movements, and the ship's rolling through the waves, the ladder shifted and bounced with unnerving force.

Her fingers tingled, and her grip on the rope slackened without permission by the time he reached where her legs wrapped around the ladder's side. "I've decided I don't envy monkeys."

A reluctant-sounding chuckle escaped, and he shook his head. "A joke at this moment?"

"Are not jokes better than tears, especially when hanging over an ocean?"

"Indeed." The love communicated in his eyes bolstered her as he reached around her waist and swung her back onto the ladder. "This will work differently than when we were in New York. Hold this rope with your free hand. I am going to stand one step below you, but keep my hands above yours. If you slip, I will be here to bear you up."

His last words coupled with the warmth of his body against her back was enough to prompt the tears she'd been avoiding. *Thank You, God, for Aldrich. Help us climb without incident and without me blubbering like a whale.*

It was a struggle to shift from her knotted position to standing, and when she unwound her arm from the coiled rope, knifelike tingles made maintaining a tight hold difficult. Even so, Aldrich's presence wrapped around her and steadied her. They paused at each rung while Celestia lifted her skirts for the next step so she didn't trip and knock them both loose. When her head cleared the lip of the opening and her hands shifted from the rough rope to the smooth metal handles, Josiah swooped in and pulled her inside.

Rather than releasing her, he crushed her in an embrace. "I thought we were going to lose you."

His tears mingled with hers as the rush of all she'd endured crashed over her. Her eternal future was certain no matter what, but the thought of her family being left behind to mourn her was too much. She sobbed against him as prayers of gratitude for her safety sang from her soul.

After her crying subsided, Josiah drew back, and his gaze shifted beyond her shoulder. His heavy exhale caused her to glance back to see what elicited such a response.

Aldrich waited, wringing his hands and watching them with a face as wrinkled as her dress. Even at a distance, seeing him relaxed her body and prompted a smile that couldn't be contained. How she loved that dear man. It was obvious he wanted to come to her but restrained himself out of respect to Josiah.

"I suppose I will be losing you after all, won't I? And not just to him, but to Germany." The heaviness of Josiah's voice brought her attention back to him.

Though she could not miss the mourning in his gaze, neither could she mistake his love for her or the understanding of a man who knew the sacrifices love sometimes required. It was enough to bring tears to her eyes again. Their family might have its struggles and conflicts, but they loved fiercely. Saying goodbye would be one of the hardest trials of her life.

She hugged him tightly. "I may be an ocean away, but you will never lose me."

He released her. "You better go to him before he wears his hands down to nubs. But don't linger here too long. Mother is beside herself. I'm going to personally see to it that Pellegrini is locked in a room and guarded until he's handed over to the Southampton police."

"Thank you, Josiah." Celestia squeezed his hand and turned toward the man who not only had rescued her twice now but held her heart in ways no man ever had or would again.

Aldrich opened his arms in invitation, and she launched once again into a crushing embrace. As she nestled into his hold, contentment and the sense of home settled over her. Not that hugs from Josiah and Father hadn't once provided that, but there was something to be said about the difference between embracing family and embracing the man you loved. Her entire body sighed as if relieved to be reunited with the other part of her whole.

After a lingering kiss to her forehead, Aldrich whispered in her ear, "I think I lost half my life when you screamed."

"I should hope not. I expect nothing short of a hundred years with you."

He laughed as he brushed a wet strand of hair from her face and studied her like she was a masterpiece of art. "Ich liebe dich."

"Ich liebe dich *auch*."

"I did not think you understood when I said it earlier."

"I understood that immediately. 'I love you' was one of the first phrases I made my tutor teach me." A blush heated her cheeks at the admission. "It was the 'hold tight' that took me a minute, but I did figure it out, and hold tight I did."

"Praise Gott for that." He released her and offered his arm.

Her disappointment must have shown on her face.

He brushed her bunched lips, and an amused smile smoothed away his lingering worry lines. "Come. You need some dry clothes." He guided her away from the room still full of people contending with the pilot boat and Pellegrini.

"I concede that I'm wet, but everything I have left to wear will preclude us from seeing each other. I'm not ready to be away from you again."

"Neither am I." After they turned the corner, he led her to the main stairway. To the crewman standing guard at its base, he said, "Please find a spare female uniform for Fräulein Isaacs and have it delivered to cabin 181."

To her surprise, Aldrich did not lead her upstairs once the man disappeared. Instead he took her to the hallway on the other side of the stairwell and a few doors down.

The agony returned to his expression, and he rested his hands on her shoulders. "Are you certain you still wish to marry me? I will not hold you to our understanding if you see what has happened as an indication that we have made the wrong decision."

She blinked. "Did you hit your head or something? I told you I love you."

"And I love you, but—"

"Then don't be foolish. The actions of a deranged man do not speak for God. We prayed over it, obtained our answer, and even in this He has protected us both." She fingered the slice in the material over his chest and realized exactly how true that last bit was. "I am certain that this"—she wagged her finger between them—"is what God has called me to. Even if we experienced a dozen more life-and-death adventures, it would not change my answer."

"I pray He doesn't call us to even one more life-and-death adventure."

"I agree. Although I pray we have plenty of life adventures together, starting with this one."

"This one?"

She cupped either side of his face and popped to her toes. Their lips met, and his face relaxed beneath her touch as his arms slid low on her back. They drew close, and a most pleasant adventure began. One she hoped would be repeated many times over. Wherever God sent them, whatever He asked them to endure, they would follow, just as the wise men before them had followed the star of wonder to find the Light of the World.

Chapter Nineteen

It was not until Pellegrini had been handed over to the police that Aldrich finally breathed easier. It took well into the night before their business with the police concluded, but Celestia proved her courage once again in identifying Pellegrini and describing what had occurred over the course of her interactions with the man. Steward Yates and his family would receive justice, and Aldrich would see to it that Yates's family was provided for. A paltry consolation in light of his death, but it was all Aldrich could offer. He well understood how nothing could fill that loss. He had almost experienced it himself.

His gaze drifted to Celestia as she took in the surroundings of her first *Weihnachtsmarkt* in Frankfurt with childlike wonder. Fluffy clumps of snow drifted and danced in the air, landing in growing piles on the walkway and in between the rustic timber booths. Draped with fragrant evergreen boughs and lit with the warm glow of lanterns, it resembled a fairy-tale village. Wursts sizzled over grated fires, roasted candied nuts sweetened the air, and the customary mulled wine, *Glühwein*, promised to tickle the tongue with its spices and warm the body. Aldrich could not have asked for a better show of the annual tradition.

Even Frau Isaacs and Herr Isaacs seemed to delight in the experience as they ambled from stall to stall admiring blown-glass ornaments, hand-carved toys, and pottery. Knowing that Celestia's future lay here, they'd decided to forgo the group tour of Germany provided to the investors. Instead they traveled from Bremerhaven to Wiesbaden to spend Christmas with Aldrich's extended family and get to know the people with whom Celestia would soon live. It was a bittersweet trip but one that seemed to ease their concerns.

Celestia picked up a chimney-sweep figurine with walnuts for a body and dried plums for appendages. "What are these strange little men?"

"*Quetschemännchen.* A suitor is supposed to give it to his sweetheart, and if she keeps it, it means he has secured her affections."

She scrunched her nose and put it back. "I think I'd prefer another one of those marzipan treats. If you keep me supplied in those, you'll always have my affection."

"Is that so? What if I were to keep you supplied in something else sweet?"

"Like what?"

"Like longer versions of this." He swept his hat from his head and shielded their faces from view as he stole a kiss that lingered long enough to tease but not forget where he was.

Celestia gave a long-suffering sigh and shook her head, although she could not quite suppress her smile. "I suppose if that is the best you can do, it will suffice."

"Best? Hardly."

"Then I guess you will have to prove that to me later."

"Oh, I plan to."

Her laughter accompanied her nestling against his side as they strolled to the next stall of carved wooden ornaments.

Aldrich watched as she cooed over the workmanship of each creation displayed. Mäuschen was going to have to give way to something brighter and more meaningful. She had become his *Sternchen der Wunder.* Much like the Bethlehem star had guided the wise men to the Christ child, Celestia had led him to become a better man of faith. Not one who stands in his own wisdom but one who seeks and follows Gott through prayer. She was a gift that he looked forward to spending the rest of his life cherishing.

"Oh, Aldrich! Look! It's perfect! We have to get it. Please?"

As if he would deny Celestia any trinket this market had to offer.

Celestia lifted a wooden star with three intricately designed wise men carved into the center. "Not only is it our song, it has a star too!"

Their song. He smiled. For so many reasons, that seemed an apt choice for their lives. Aldrich paid the vendor and then cradled her hand so that they both held it aloft. "I think it should be the first ornament we hang each year as a reminder of whom we seek and follow."

Celestia leaned back into him. "Yes. Wherever He sends us, no matter what fortitude and sacrifice it requires, we'll do it together."

He squeezed her waist and dipped his head for a quick kiss. With a promise of more to come later, they joined their families at the base of the lit Tannenbaum. As they gazed at the clearing sky, the stars peeked out, and the brightest one of all rested atop the tree as if announcing they had arrived where God had called them to serve and worship Him. In Germany for now, but ready to follow Him wherever for always.

Historical Notes

The Golden Gestirn

The steamer ships of the *Golden Gestirn*'s generation were the predecessors to ships like the *Titanic*. By the mid-1880s, travel for entertainment had taken hold and the expectation of luxury developed. Companies all over the world competed to be the best, and those who made the fastest trek across the Atlantic from New York to England became the coveted Blue Riband record-holder.

Nikolaustag—St. Nikolaus Day

All over the world, December 6 is known as St. Nikolaus Day and is a celebration of Saint Nikolaus, the Bishop of Myra and the patron saint of seafarers and children. Children leave shoes outside their door in order for Saint Nikolaus to deposit a sweet treat for their year of good behavior. However, in Germany, Saint Nikolaus is accompanied by a more sinister figure who carries a sack and switch. Children who were bad could be given a switch or taken away in the sack. This assistant has various names based on the region, the two most familiar being *Krampus* and *Knecht Ruprecht*. I chose to use *Knecht Ruprecht*, as he first appeared in a seventeenth-century Nuremburg Christmas procession and *Krampus* appears to be used more often in the Alpine Region.

Weihnachtsmarkt—German Christmas Markets

These open-air markets are a German Christmas tradition that signal the beginning of the Advent season and date back to the Middle Ages. Traditionally, the stalls are made from timber, and everything sold must be locally produced and handmade. Twinkling lights, music, and the scent of traditional German foods mixed with the scent of a hot mulled wine called *Glühwein* set the atmosphere for this unique experience. If you ever get the chance to go, be sure to check out the hand-carved ornaments, Advent calendar wreaths, and my favorite, *Quetschemännchen*—the little figurines made from dried fruit and walnuts.

Beauty Bright

CARA PUTMAN

Chapter One

Early June 1945

His prewar dreams marched through his mind as Lieutenant Charles Weise placed his hat under his arm and then opened the door and stepped into the hotel room he'd been directed to. The crammed twin bed had a desk thrust against it, and a man about his age, or maybe five years older, sat behind it, typewriter balanced to the side and a stack of paper at his other elbow. The man didn't bother looking up from whatever he scribbled. Dressed in civilian clothes, he didn't fit as military, and uncertainty flashed through Charles. If he wasn't certain he'd memorized the correct address, he'd disappear before the man noticed him. Instead, he cleared his throat. Too much demanded his time to waste it with a man who didn't respect the scope of work in postwar Germany.

When he'd received his draft notice, Charles hadn't expected to put his family connections or education in fine arts to work. Instead he'd taken the opportunity his education gave him to move into the officer ranks. Days spent hunched over maps applying his knowledge of geography and culture hadn't seemed like much but had been enough to get him noticed by someone.

The question was who.

He cleared his throat again.

The man slowly focused on Charles, as if evaluating him, so he returned the favor. The man's slacks held a crease that must have been a challenge to create in this war context. He'd rolled his shirtsleeves to the elbows, and sweat stains marred the fabric under his armpits. "You are?"

"Lieutenant Charles Weise, sir. I received orders to report here."

The man pinched the bridge of his nose and sighed. "Yes, you did." He gestured to a rickety chair crammed against the wall. "Have a seat."

"Thank you." He edged down to ensure the spindly-legged chair would hold his weight. It had survived the war, so it should outlast him. Then he set his cap in his lap and waited, his knees practically smashed into the edge of the mattress.

"I've reviewed your file." The man slid a paper in front of him. "It says you're educated in the arts."

"Yes. A bachelor's and master's in fine arts."

"Sculpture?"

"Yes." Where was this going? No one in the military appreciated his art background, yet he hadn't had a chance to create much of a civilian career.

"And you speak both French and German fluently?"

"Yes. My father's business had an office in France, and extended family lived in Germany."

The man steepled his fingers and peered at Charles. "And their loyalties?"

"Opa Aldrich owned a shipping company based in Germany and New York. Oma Celestia was born in the States but moved with him when my grandfather took over the German side of the business. After he built it into a thriving shipping company, the Allies took it as reparations after the Great War. The family shifted to art and antiquities, and my father expanded the family's art dealership in Paris and New York City. My grandparents escaped Europe in 1938 as things were getting bad. They came to live with us in New York. My grandparents were too old to work but have often told me how much they hate what happened to the old country. They say the Nazis stole treasure beyond understanding." He stopped talking before he told this stranger how much his grandparents left behind when they'd fled. If even half the stories were true, a treasure had disappeared, stolen in exchange for the freedom to move.

"Spend time in Germany?"

"Other than the war?" Charles shook his head. "No, sir. I planned to spend a year here learning the art business, but . . ." He examined the hat he held. "Sir, why am I here?"

The man tapped a finger on the desk once, twice, three times, then nodded to some unseen adviser. "I need your services for a few weeks."

"I'm sorry, but who are you?"

"John Trout with the OSS."

The name was fake, but what caught Charles's attention were the initials. "OSS? What would you want with me?"

"One of our missions is the Art Looting Investigation Unit. Created in November, it's new, but important for the reclamation of the looted art, jewelry, and furniture that's hidden around Germany and other occupied areas." The man tapped the paper in front of him. "We need your skills."

"Sir, I'm attached to the navy."

"And now you'll work with the ALIU. We'll start with a few weeks. See how things go."

"What will I do?"

"Escort and interrogate men who played a critical role in the looting and relocation of art and other antiquities. We need a good process to manage the return of the items, and that means locating the caches and systematically identifying and returning the recovered items."

Charles's mind spun with the implications. "Where will I be located?"

"Altaussee."

The location was one he'd heard before. "The salt mine in Austria?"

"The town adjacent. That's where we've located an interrogation center for the men involved in developing and implementing the looting plan." He steepled his fingers and leaned back. "If we do this right, we will each play a critical role in reversing the damage done by the Nazis. We've compiled a preliminary list of two thousand individuals believed to have participated in the greatest art theft in history."

"Two thousand?" The number was baffling. "We're supposed to interrogate all of them?"

"Well, we'll unlikely find them all, but those we do will be worth the time and effort." He shifted the folder to the side and opened it. "You'll no longer work as naval attaché to Spain. If all goes well, you'll permanently work with this unit. It's small, but we expect you to accomplish a lot. Are you up to the task?"

"Yes, sir."

"No sir for me, I'm afraid. Just go out there and help us find what the Nazis and collaborators stole." A small smile twitched the corner of the man's mouth. "You'll need this so you can report to Austria." Trout handed over a sheet of paper with a seal that, with a quick glimpse, showed Charles now worked with the OSS.

Nearly two months later, life had fallen into a routine. One that meant days interrogating men like Karl Haberstock, a respected German art dealer; Walter Hofer, the director of the Goering Collection; and Bruno Lohse, an executive officer for the Einsatzastab Richsleiter Rosenberg (ERR) in Paris. Some men cooperated more than others, and on occasion Charles accompanied a particularly important painting or other item as a sort of security on its journey back to its homeland.

The work had meaning, but the challenge and scale could easily overwhelm him. It took him about a week on the job to learn to take one day at a time. Charles reviewed his orders for the next few days. He'd just delivered a crate of paintings to their rightful owner and boarded a return flight from Paris to Wiesbaden, Germany. From there he would reclaim his jeep or requisition a new one for the drive back to Altaussee in Austria.

He'd received instructions to wrap up his interrogation, which had proceeded more like an interview, of Lohse. It was time to decide what would happen to the man. Trial in Germany or sent to France to face charges there. Either way the man had played a role, and Charles needed to document it in a way that those above his pay grade could reach the correct decision.

Charles shook his head in a failed attempt to dislodge the creeping overwhelm. *Focus on today.*

Just as the thought crossed his mind, a young woman with shoulder-length dark hair claimed the seat in the row across from him. She clipped the belt across her lap, laid her officer's cap on her lap, and peeked up. Their gazes connected, and she raised an eyebrow before turning away. He'd been dismissed, which had the side effect of diverting his attention from his notes and ever-present work.

As the flight continued, he found his attention returning to her. She had the long, graceful fingers of an artist or musician. Connect that to their destination and he wondered if she was the new officer rumor whispered was on the way to assist at the Wiesbaden Central Collecting Point. If so, he both pitied and envied her. Wiesbaden was to be the collection and distribution point for all paintings and antiques the Nazis had stolen. The volume of paintings and other art pieces the army moved from Frankfurt and other locations would stagger a bystander and was unlikely to shrink based on the interviews coming out of Altaussee.

While the woman in uniform intrigued him and he'd like to meet her, he doubted she'd be interested in even a conversation when so many men stood ready and waiting for a beautiful distraction.

Better to keep his head down and do the work Trout had assigned him. That was always a better option than unnecessary distractions a woman could create, a lesson he'd learned the hard way in grad school. He'd focus on the job, even if his gaze tracked back to her. That he could correct.

⁓⁂⁓

Monday, July 30, 1945

When she looked through the plane's tiny window, Lillian couldn't articulate what she'd expected, but something more than what she had seen in her view through the tiny window. The plane had landed at the army airfield on the outskirts of Wiesbaden, but she'd seen how desolate the surrounding area lay as the plane approached the landing strip. The piles of rubble interlaced along the runways left her feeling fortunate to have landed safely.

So much devastation.

From the sky, she'd watched destroyed buildings and homes pass in a never-ending diorama beneath her, some horrible small-sized rendering of the evil men could commit against each other. It had shaken her, and now she stood in the middle of the devastation.

She would call this home until the army decided it no longer needed her service. In other words, she would live in Germany for the foreseeable future. It sent a shiver up her spine. Was she prepared to cope with the need and depravation she'd seen from above? While life in the United States hadn't been easy, it had been nothing like this. That realization hit her anew, with guilt mixed in, now that she stood here in the middle of it all.

She'd never imagined when she'd earned her bachelor's in fine arts that she'd be scooped up by the Women's Army Corps and assigned to Germany for continued service after the end of hostilities in Europe, but here she was. The specifics were still fuzzy, but she'd learned the army often operated on filling in details at the last moment. She straightened the skirt of her navy uniform and then collected her satchel and suitcase. Someone would show up to escort her.

When it was her turn to exit the plane, she instinctively ducked and then stood with a hand to her face to shield her eyes from the sun. No one appeared to pay her the least amount of attention.

She didn't need or expect everyone to notice her.

She did need one somebody to see her though.

The sun slid behind a cloud, and she shivered at the loss. She shifted her satchel over her shoulder and turned up the collar of her uniform coat. With the sun gone, the day had turned cold and gray.

A throat cleared behind her, and she startled. "Sorry."

She stepped forward and started to slide down the stair. She gasped as she tilted to the side, and then a steady hand grasped her elbow, steadying her.

"All right, ma'am?" The deep voice didn't quite calm her sudden adrenaline, but she wouldn't let him know.

She set her feet firmly on the step and then turned to glance over her shoulder. The small smile she intended to give the man froze when she noted his movie star mien. "Thank you for the assist."

"It's what we do." He dipped his chin, but there was an air of—could that be interest?—in his eyes.

"Are you arriving as well?" What an inane thing to say.

"Well, I flew with you, but it's a return flight. I had to deliver a painting to Paris."

"To Paris?" She'd always wanted to visit that city, but the war had interrupted her dreams.

He grinned, and the dimple gave him a boyish air, though nothing boyish lurked in his physique. He had the Germanic appearance that Hitler had highlighted as perfection . . . despite Hitler's own traits. Some things failed to make sense no matter how many times you considered them. And now that odious man had caused the reason she stood in Europe for the first time. It should have been a dream, but watching the landscape as the plane had sunk from the sky had prohibited anything but horror.

The man must have seen something shift in her expression, because he shook his head. "It's not all awful here. We have to find the good or we'd give up."

She pondered his words, then acknowledged them and continued down the stairs. In the short time they'd talked, the light had weakened further, giving the surroundings a gray tinge as she considered where to go next. She shivered but kept moving. Always forward, as no other options presented themselves.

The man moved around her and spoke over his shoulder. "Follow me to the hangar. Someone there should direct you where to go next."

"Thank you." It was more help than anyone else offered. She regripped the suitcase and followed him across the cement.

Activity buzzed all around them on the tarmac, but no one paused to give her a second look. She quickened her pace to follow the man, noting his lieutenant's stripes. They reached the large metal building that resembled an expanded Quonset hut, and he paused to hold the door for her.

"Say, what's your name?" She sidled past him, set her suitcase down, and unslung her satchel. She'd packed light, but it didn't feel that way now.

"Lieutenant Charles Weise at your service." He gave her a sweeping bow before moving around her to create space for the soldiers hustling back and forth along the hallway.

"Is it always this busy?"

"Maybe, but you owe me something."

She scrunched her nose as she considered him. "What do you mean?"

"Your name."

The way the words rolled off his tongue tasted more intimate than it should. What was wrong with her? He cleared his throat, and she realized she hadn't answered. She forced a quick smile that she prayed covered the exceeding awkwardness. "Lillian. Captain Lillian Thorson, Women's Army Corps."

He extended his hand, and she reluctantly reached out to shake it.

"See, that wasn't so bad." His rakish grin reminded her entirely too much of a blond Rhett Butler as played by Clark Gable, when he was watching Scarlett O'Hara.

She pushed the thought aside and squared her shoulders. "Thank you for the assist. I'll find my way from here." She picked up her suitcase despite her muscles telling her they'd already carried the item farther than warranted.

⚜

Charles watched the spitfire try to hide her fatigue. He knew well how the long flight from the States took time to overcome. This gal seemed to want to fight, but the reality was the fatigue weighed her down.

"Let me take that." He reached for her suitcase, and he could see the moment she wanted to fight back before she acquiesced.

"Thank you." She shivered again, and he knew he needed to move her out of the hallway.

"It's a drafty spot." Though if she thought this was cold, winter's arrival would surprise her. "You'll find the weather tends toward cold and wet. Probably more so than you're used to back home."

"I'm sure it's better earlier in the day."

"Yes, but it's easy to forget how far north Germany is compared to most of the States. Carry a sweater and you'll be fine until winter hits. Part of the charm."

"Charm." She sounded unconvinced but also like she desperately wanted to believe his words. No need to tell her about how hard it would be to find things she needed. If it didn't come by military transport and the army's exchange, it would be nearly impossible to find essentials. The economy in Germany was devastated, first by being fully turned to the military for years, and then by the bombing the Allies used to bring the ultimate surrender.

"Let's find someone to help you." But twenty minutes later they still hadn't found anyone who knew where Captain Thorson belonged. "As you can see, it's a bit chaotic. Systems are good but not great. Do you know what sort of work you're supposed to do?"

"Something related to the ALIU."

"The Art Looting Investigation Unit?"

"Yes." Her brow furrowed as she frowned. "I think." She sighed. "It's a bit oblique, but I have an art degree, so that makes sense. Does the WAC work with the ALIU? And who decided everything needed letters in alphabet soup?"

"You're in luck. I'm assigned to the ALIU and will head out tomorrow to the interrogation center. You can come along."

"Are you sure I should?"

"Right now we need help in Altaussee, and you've been sent, so it's serendipitous."

"Where do I stay tonight?"

"The women all stay in an old hotel the army turned into housing. You'll be good there for the night. I'll make a few calls as well." He tried to reassure her, but answers didn't come easily. So much was fluid—not as much as before the end of the hostilities, but it still took time and process to get anything approved.

"Thank you."

An hour later he'd dropped her off with a promise to pick her up in the morning, and then he'd headed to the OSS office. Sometimes he wondered what it would be like to do real spying and hunt for the dangerous war criminals who'd disappeared at the end of hostilities or keep an eye on the ever-changing situation with the Allies. The world had changed dramatically in the last six years, and it would take time to reassemble the pieces, especially in countries like Germany, where Berlin was stitched into four sectors and the country into a mismatch of controlled segments. Everything took more effort and required patience as the countries rebuilt the infrastructure. There were cities that were barely back to medieval standards.

It had startled him when he'd arrived, and he fought the hardening of his defenses to the utter destruction that surrounded him and filled the background of his days.

When he entered the facility, it was largely empty, but he strode to Trout's office.

The man didn't surface from the paper he was signing. "You get the painting delivered?"

"Yes, sir."

Trout grimaced at the continued use of *sir*, but Charles did it as much to tweak his nose as habit instilled by the navy. "Did you run into a young woman, a WAC officer on your flight?"

"I did. Is she assigned to Altaussee?"

"Yes. She can assist with the wrap-up operations. Then you'll both transfer to the Central Collecting Point here and work with the Monuments and Fine Arts division."

"You won't need me anymore?" He tried to keep the disappointment at bay.

"No." The man shook his head and stacked some papers. "Your unique skills will be better utilized with the art you've helped us recover." He picked up the pipe he kept on his desk. "How is Bruno?"

"Lohse's the same as always."

"Recommendations?"

"Still unsure, sir."

"Well, you're running out of time."

"I know." But the thought of a pretty captain to keep him company on the drive served as a nice distraction. He'd enjoy the opportunity while it lasted.

Chapter Two

Tuesday, July 31

DARKNESS COATED THE sky somewhere between inky black and the faintest hint of dawn on the horizon when Charles—no, Lieutenant Weise—collected Lillian that morning. The relief at his arrival overwhelmed her, as she remained hypervigilant in the strange setting with people, particularly men, watching her with overt hostility. She'd stood ramrod straight and eyes up, with muscles tense as she waited. Every person who'd walked by assessed her, and she knew she did not belong, not here.

Then Charles arrived and she'd wanted to hug him, a response that shocked her normally confident self.

After stowing her suitcase and satchel, he opened the door for her and then extended his hand to help her in. If his chivalry hadn't already made her melt a little, the spark of electricity at his touch dissolved her in a puddle. Fortunately, the jeep's seat was cold enough to snap her out of the ridiculousness, and his walk around the jeep gave her a moment to pull herself together. She had to remember she was here for a job. She forced her thoughts away as he drove through the edge of Wiesbaden and stopped at the airfield.

There they hopped a ride on a cargo transport to Munich. The flight shot into the sky then back down in less time than it took to read a couple chapters in her art history book, and then they grabbed another army jeep and headed out of town.

An hour later she noticed mountains in the distance. "Are those the Alps?"

He looked at her and then directed his attention back at the road. "I guess you could call them foothills or baby Alps. If we were driving the other direction, more to the west, we'd reach Neuschwanstein, the castle on the edge of Austria. The experts are still sorting the art stored there, and it's situated at the beginning of the mountains." He kept his gaze on the road as he shifted. "Germany is hillier than most people expect."

She nodded but stayed quiet, aware of how foolish her lack of knowledge about the local geography and anything about the region made her. "I need a map."

"We can find you one. Imprinting the layout of the region on your mind could serve you well." Then he grew silent again, and she tried to ignore how that unsettled her.

In Washington she'd worked with other WACs in various capacities. This transfer to Germany had the potential of an adventure. Then she'd landed and had to absorb the reality of what war did to geography, landscapes, and people. She should have better prepared for the truth, but the silence did nothing to pull her from the dark world in which she found herself transported. The detritus of war lay scattered in the fields along the road, present monuments to all that had transpired.

How long would it take to remove the hulking shadows? Where would the remnants disappear to?

Movement caught her attention. She squinted and raised a hand to shield her eyes from the sun. The shadows shifted and slowly morphed into people. "Lieutenant Weise?"

"Refugees."

"Refugees?"

"We estimate there are millions all over Germany. People forcibly moved here by the German military. Others have fled the Russian zone. It's a geopolitical mess that impacts millions."

"Oh my." The words captured too little of the emotion but were all she could manage as the miles melted away. "How did I not see them?"

"You weren't expecting them. The army is moving many of them to various camps to receive help, but there are too many, and some prefer taking their chances in the country." A cloud crossed his face. "It's a bad situation."

As time passed the winding road made Lillian's stomach lurch, and as the refugees slowly faded, she wondered whether they'd entered the mountains yet. She kept her gaze focused straight ahead, her spinning thoughts doing nothing to ease the churning in her stomach. The drive took forever and, as far as she could tell, didn't get them any closer to wherever this town sat. "Are you sure we couldn't fly?"

While she didn't relish the idea of flying over the Alps, it would have saved her the torturous road.

"Town doesn't have an airstrip." His fingers tightened around the steering wheel as he slowed for another tight turn. "Even if it did, bombing would have destroyed it, and it's too far down the list of repairs to matter."

Maybe studying Charles was better than watching what lay ahead on the road. His dark-blond hair would curl around his ears if he didn't get it trimmed soon. Sweat beaded his forehead and colored the neck of his uniform. "So where are you from?"

"Here, there, and everywhere."

She frowned at his nonanswer. "It's a straightforward question, Lieutenant Weise. I would answer that I'm from Iowa. Then you would ask which part, and I'd say Cedar Rapids. Then I'd ask if you'd ever heard of it."

"At which point you would fill in more of the conversation. Seems you don't need me." There was a trace of an accent she couldn't quite identify in his words.

"That's what conversations are. A back and forth."

He yanked hard on the jeep's wheel, and she gasped as she clapped a hand onto her hat. "You really don't need to run off the road, sir."

"Maybe, if that's what will buy me a few minutes of quiet." She might have been offended, but she saw the ghost of a smile tip the corner of his mouth.

What could she say or do to get more of those? "Tell me about the work we'll be doing."

He glanced at her, then quickly back at the road. "There's a house in this Austrian town where we interrogate about a dozen of the men involved in stealing art for the Nazis. These men represent the high-level minds behind the looting." He steered the jeep around another series of potholes and then slowed to a stop for an old man who herded a flock of sheep across the road. "Some ran museums in Germany. Others worked for the ERR."

"ERR? Does that make *err*?"

"No, the Nazi organization that routinely rounded up and stole art and other items from European Jews. It had a take-what-you-like mentality, and these men formed the heart of it. Our interrogations could provide details about the art deposits scattered across Europe."

"How will I help?" Lillian couldn't figure out this missing piece. Yes, she had the fine arts degree and had worked as an assistant curator at a museum, but that did not mean she'd prepared to interview Hitler's art dealers. She needed to know what the brass expected so she could focus on her role rather than the disquietingly surreal remnants of war-torn Europe. "I want to make a difference." At his chuckle, she swallowed. "I didn't mean to say that out loud."

"I didn't imagine so." He chuckled again, the sound rich, mirroring the creek that flowed along the side of the road. "Don't worry. I won't share your secret." He rolled his neck and then pulled to the edge of the road.

"Everything all right?"

"Just need to stretch my legs a second. That stream appears as good a place as any to grab some water while we're at it." He slanted a look around, and she wondered what or who he searched for.

"Is it safe?"

"Should be, but we won't wander far."

It was hard to imagine that anything dangerous hid in the gentle slopes or graceful evergreens. "This is unlike anything I've seen before. It's so peaceful."

He unfolded from the jeep and stretched, arching his back. "Nothing like the bits of the Alps I've seen."

"It's so green."

"And rugged. The hikes can be hard, but they're stunning." He shielded his eyes as he scanned, as if searching for the right path.

Lillian followed his gaze and scanned up. They had passed Salzburg, and she had no mental map to place their location other than the center of beauty. Then she thought of the shadows and refugees. Would they run into desperate people when there were only the two of them? "Where are we exactly?"

Charles came to stand beside her and pointed up the slope. "A few kilometers to the west takes you to the Eagle's Nest."

"Hitler's escape?"

"Yes. Let me refill the canteens and then we'll keep driving. If all goes well, we'll make it to Altaussee before dark." He sighed, and she sensed a deep weariness in him, like he wanted to do one thing but knew he had to do the other. "The roads get worse when you can't see what you're trying to avoid."

A couple of hours later, as the sun sank behind the mountains, they drove into another quaint village. From the soaring, forested mountains to the design of the buildings, everything appeared so different from Iowa.

"We're here." Charles curved along a couple small streets and then parked in front of a home that sat alone on the edge of town. "Welcome to House 71."

"House 71?"

"They don't number the houses by street here." He turned to her. "Stay close to me. I'll find a place for you to stay nearby, but tonight you might need to stay at the house with us."

A shiver sliced through her at his words. "Am I in danger?"

"Not other than from urbane men who think they are a gift to everyone who meets them. They tend to be charming or arrogant, sometimes both." He rubbed his pointed jaw. "Maybe this wasn't a good idea."

Did he realize how his words made her more determined than ever to prove her usefulness?

What were the brass thinking to send him back with a woman in tow? If she resembled some worn-down, homely hausfrau, it might protect her, but instead she appeared like she should fill the screen at a theater as the leading lady's best friend. The brass hadn't thought through this plan, limited as it was, and he didn't know where to safely house her. The men would take to her like bees to nectar, and he needed to ensure that didn't happen.

Lillian carried an internal spark, something that hinted at a special depth. It didn't take two minutes with her to discern she was a highly intelligent yet extremely naive woman. Her years spent studying art didn't equal studying human nature through a war. His mind was permanently seared with memories he'd like to forget.

Charles didn't want to believe that the fact he'd been surrounded primarily by men for the last few years had anything to do with his fascination with Lillian.

But he couldn't discount the prospect.

Still he had an important job to do as the continent tried to imagine a way forward from a war that had literally changed the landscape of country, village, and town. Aerial bombing had turned cities he'd visited prewar into largely unidentifiable rubble. Even the lucky cities like Paris had altered. The buildings might be more intact, but the population bore the wounds of occupation.

And underneath it all, a subtle yet present overlay of those few who had returned from the concentration camps. Many survived the horrors only to die in freedom, their bodies too scarred from the years of abuse and deprivations.

It all left a mark.

One that made a moment of beauty something to grab hold of and not let go.

Lillian wouldn't understand or appreciate that sentiment. Not yet.

And he hoped she could maintain some of the wide-eyed amazement she'd brought with her. The world he walked needed more of that. Everyone's did.

"Are you still here?"

Her words jerked him from his thoughts. "Long day."

She tipped her chin in a yes, her dark waves bouncing in a fetching way. "Should I leave my bag in the jeep?"

"No. The needs are many, and there's no guarantee everything will wait here when you come back for it." He reached behind the seat and grabbed the bag. "I'll carry it for you."

"I've schlepped it across a continent."

"Then it's time you're reminded there are men who still respect women and have manners."

She rolled her eyes, but he noted the faint twitch in the corner of her mouth. "Fine. Lead the way, Mr. Post."

"Who?"

"You know. Emily Post. The etiquette expert?" She stared at him for a minute, then shook her head. "What did they teach you at Princeton anyway?"

"More important things than they taught you at Harvard."

She snorted, and he fought back a grin. Maybe this would be fun after all.

⁘

Infuriating man. She was tempted to tap the side of his head and see if a bunch of rocks rested where his brain should be. She didn't need another man telling her that she couldn't contribute in meaningful ways. What she needed, as she fought back a yawn, was a place to take a nap.

Despite her attempts to hide the fatigue, he must have noticed, because his stance softened. "Let's get you into the office while I figure out what to do with you."

She made herself as comfortable as possible, curled inside a chair. Two hours later she opened her eyes, fatigue still dragging on her. A spring pushed against her spine in a way that her muscles protested. She rubbed her cheeks and then straightened. Someone had covered her with a blanket. Scratchy army issue, but the gesture still warmed her.

A man in uniform strode into the room and startled. "Well, hello there."

She straightened further. Who was this man, and how should she respond? No one had prepared her for the protocol or what to expect, but she knew enough about being alone with a man in a strange room to be cautious. "Hello."

"You are?"

"Captain Lillian Thorson." She paused, waiting for him to reciprocate.

She arched an eyebrow, and the man startled from his gaping stupor. "Sergeant Tony Presley at your service, Captain." He practically clicked his heels together as he straightened. She opened her mouth to tell him to relax, when he gave her a subtle wink.

She laughed. "I see how it's going to be around here."

His eyebrows rose. "You stationed here?"

"Seems so, soldier. At least for the moment."

He swallowed as his gaze darted around. "Sorry about that, ma'am. Guess I've gotten a bit informal with the end of hostilities." Then he grinned at her and waggled his eyebrows. "We can have a good time while you're here. I can show you all the private spots."

"I don't know what you mean."

"You know. Find a quiet place for you and me. Private." His expression slid closer to a leer.

Lillian shifted, and hated the display of weakness. "You forget yourself, Sergeant." She considered pushing to her feet, but her height wouldn't come close to his. Maybe safety came by staying in place. "I outrank you."

"Sure, but you're a woman. It doesn't mean nothing."

Perhaps the lieutenant had been right to be so cautious even in the relative safety of an army safe house. Of course he hadn't left her with any sort of weapon or warning either. Her stomach rumbled, and she pressed a hand against it, hoping the sergeant hadn't heard.

"Sounds like you're hungry."

She tensed as he took a step closer.

"I'd be happy to escort you to a local establishment."

Oh no. She was not going anywhere alone with this soldier or any other who didn't treat her with the kind regard that Charles Weise gave her. Many soldiers, if given the slightest encouragement, would take it as an invitation to much more. Yet this sergeant didn't need any hints to go to crazy lengths with his imagination.

A throat being cleared had the man stiffening to attention again.

"I'll take it from here, Presley."

"I should have known she was with you," the sarge grumbled, but relaxed. "Need any assistance?"

"Just a place for her to stay." The sarge started to open his mouth, but Charles spoke first. "And not with us. I'm going to check with Frau Alice and see what she thinks. I bet she'll feed us at the same time." He held out his hand, gesturing toward the door.

In that moment Lillian had the thought that he was safe and she could follow him anywhere. And she knew she was in trouble.

Chapter Three

Wednesday, August 1

THE MAN IN front of Charles didn't look intimidating. He was an art lover, after all.

Yet he had contributed as a key member of the ERR in Paris. Bruno Lohse had negotiated the transfer of art collections. But were they thefts or sales? That was why the ALIU had sent Charles to interrogate Lohse and determine whether he led the ERR's efforts in some way and whether the Allies should prosecute him as part of the Nuremberg proceedings. Or should the Allies send him back to France for that country to deal with the crimes that had occurred inside its boundaries? And Lohse was just one of many the ALIU staff members interrogated.

All in the furtherance of truth.

It hadn't taken many iterations with Lohse and the others like him to realize they operated from a different interpretation of truth. That made it challenging to ascertain reality's boundaries.

But if Charles didn't establish the boundaries, survivors of the families the ERR had taken the art from might never recover their possessions.

The pressure to ascertain the truth was a heavy weight.

And he couldn't allow anything or anyone to distract him from that mission while he could make a difference for the families like Oma and Opa.

Charles settled back, arms crossed on his chest, stretching the fabric of his uniform. "Herr Lohse, how would you describe your work?"

The man didn't hurry to fill the silence that Charles allowed to stretch. Lillian kept still in the corner as her dark-green eyes took in the proceedings. The purpose of her presence was still a mystery, but she'd quickly learned to listen and fade into the background. If nothing else, she witnessed history, and that was valuable . . . maybe in ways neither of them could anticipate yet.

Charles scanned the small sitting room with its heavy oak door, thick wood trim stained a dark color, and faded red wallpaper. The furniture was old, leaning more to worn than treasured antique. The scarred table had been pulled in from the kitchen, while the emerald velvet settee was thrust against a wall next to a tall bookshelf that practically sagged with books. One window opened to a field that ended at the edge of the nearest mountain. The field lacked the carpet of flowers it had in the early summer when he'd arrived.

He let his gaze travel to where Lillian sat in a chair behind Lohse.

Her posture was erect, and she held a steno pad of paper on her lap, pen ready for notes. He could imagine Lohse would underestimate her. It was what Charles counted on. He needed something to break through with the man.

"Lohse?" The man had been quiet too long.

"*Ja?*" The man feigned indifference as he twiddled an unlit cigarette.

"Thief?" Charles leaned forward and rested his elbows on the battered kitchen table.

"Me?" Lohse's expression shifted to a glower. "I merely bought and sold art. Not a thief."

"Many people don't see it that way."

"I do not care."

"You should." He slid a folder forward and tapped it. "There's testimony about the role you played. The disconnect is you're a nice guy."

"Why would I not be? Just because I am German?"

"No. I've met plenty of wonderful Germans. What makes you different is that you participated in leadership."

"Not anymore."

Charles considered him. "That's where I'm also unsure. I've heard about your conversations with Goebbels. You haven't cut ties."

"We've been friends a long time. One does not just stop."

An hour later Lohse hadn't moved from his ongoing assurance he wasn't a thief. He had facilitated sales. That was it.

Words didn't make it so. That was where things got tricky to evaluate. A man could seem genuine and nice but be a thief and looter in practice. Time to try something new. Charles stood and stretched, and Lillian moved as if to stand, but he slightly shook his head, and she eased back into her position.

Lieutenant Weise paused at the door. "Bruno, I'm getting some water. Need any?"

The man shook his head, and Charles left the room, the door clicking firmly into its frame.

"You do not follow him?" The German's sophisticated voice with its fascinating accent filled the quiet.

Lillian ignored his words as she scanned through her notes. The man remained an enigma to her. He communicated with an urbane flair, yet underneath lurked an intellect that missed little. She sensed he weighed her now, determining her role on the chessboard. Part of her hoped he'd fill her in when he figured it out.

He blew out a breath, the smoke curling around him. "Why are you here, Fräulein?"

"Captain Thorson."

He waved his cigarette in the air, as if batting aside her title. "Why?"

"To find answers."

"That's what they all say, but they ask the same questions every time. And you sit there days at a time, never asking a single thing."

"I am here to learn."

"What do the words mean?"

She leaned forward, focus tight on the man. "You know what they mean." She smiled. "I want to understand why you participated."

"Why should I tell you? Can you promise I won't hang in Nuremberg or be shot in France?"

"You know I have no such power."

"Ah, but you are a captain in the great United States Army. You have all the power in this room." Yet his tone suggested he did not believe that. "*Nein.* If that was true, you would not be here. Nor would I." He smiled. "You need something from me. That is why you did not follow Lieutenant Weise out."

"Why am I here?" She leaned forward and waited for him to answer. After all, she was appealing to his sense of superiority. "What do I add?"

"Other than beauty? Do you need to add a thing?"

The question she couldn't answer because she longed for the answer to be yes but feared it was no. "Why did you do it?"

"Do what?"

"Work for the ERR?"

"It was that or be sent to Russia." He shivered. "Do you know how many Germans died there? If you fell out of favor, you would be on the next train to the eastern front or a camp." He gestured to himself. "How do you think I would have fared in either?"

"Probably not well."

"*Exakt.*" He inhaled again and then blew out slowly. "I had no choice if I wished to survive. Who does not wish that?"

"So you knew what you participated in?"

He gave a broad shrug, one she would have called Gallic if he'd been from France instead of a conqueror there. "I did what I must. Goring liked art, and we were friends."

Charles returned, and the conversation continued a few more minutes before a guard took Lohse back to his room.

After the German left the room, Lillian added to her notes, ignoring Charles, though she could feel his attention. Finally, she met his gaze. "What?"

"What did he say while I was gone?"

"What makes you think he said anything?"

"You're a beautiful woman, and that's one thing Bruno adores. Cold canvases and women."

"I think I'm flattered."

He growled and pushed from the table. "I have spent weeks trying to get the man to admit to what we all know Lohse was involved in. I need his words, or no rational person will believe such an educated, polished man could do the things we'd accuse him of."

"He's willing to talk in a roundabout way."

"We've engaged in that game since I arrived."

"He's still playing but slipped a bit. He said he had no options."

"Of course he had options." She raised an eyebrow, and he stopped. "What?"

"If you ask my opinion, do me the courtesy of listening." She brushed a strand of hair behind her ear as she considered how to answer Charles's question. "He's interesting."

"How?"

She took a minute before she spoke. "He seems sincere and unaffected, but it doesn't mean he's not deeply embedded in what was done. There's an undercurrent of duplicity."

He rubbed his hands over the hair on the back of his head. "The sense he's playing us won't leave me. I can't figure him out."

"Did he tell you he was Goring's friend and was told to get the man art or go to the eastern front?"

"He admitted that?"

"Yes."

"That's good and could help us." He reached for her tablet. "Did you get it down?"

"Of course." She let him take it and scan her notes. "Are they all like this?"

"What do you mean?"

"Seemingly good people who participated in an evil scheme."

"Some. Others enjoyed their roles and believed in what Hitler was selling. Being around them will give you chills."

She glanced away, thinking over the conversations she'd had with

Lohse. "We heard rumors, but in Iowa it was hard to know what was real."

"My grandparents fled Germany. They left in 1938, leaving behind a lifetime of accumulated wealth." He leaned into the table. His gaze focused on something she couldn't see. "I'll never forget that Christmas. I'd dreamed of coming to Germany, spending time with family, and exploring the museums and the art scene. Then I'd go work in the Paris office of our art business. Instead, my grandparents told us stories of how Germany was no longer the place they loved. It had changed. I'm fortunate my grandpa sensed the need to leave, although Oma may have pushed him." He swallowed, and it seemed to take a minute for him to continue. "I can't escape the parade of images of people I've seen since the end of the war. That could have been my grandparents. Despite how much they lost, I doubt they'd have survived what came."

"How does that color your interactions with Lohse?" She kept her question quiet, astute, and pointed. She couldn't let him dodge it, because it got to the crux of his dilemma with Lohse. Was he letting his grandparents' experience color his perception of Lohse? Or could he see the truth of the man's role?

"My family left everything behind. Part of me says it was a treasure . . . something that ties me to history and the people I love. But the other part, the logical part, says it's just art."

"You know it's more than that." She noted the questions in his expression and continued. "Art is part of a family's story. Someone curated the pieces with intention, even if it was as simple as they liked the colors or the subject."

"Opa talked about items they'd left behind as if they were animate objects."

"Exactly. And the disappearance of those items is a loss."

His words made her wonder if they could locate any of those Weise treasures. Was there a chance the family treasure existed somewhere the Nazis wouldn't have found it?

Chapter Four

Friday, August 17

TWO WEEKS LATER Charles read the new orders from John Trout.

His time with the OSS was ending. Now the army wanted him back in Wiesbaden, Germany, at the Central Collecting Point opening there. Knowing it was coming didn't minimize the loss. He'd liked having an unexpected role in the agency, but he understood the shift in responsibility. Now that the calendar had flipped to August, Wiesbaden would start processing recovered art. The reputation of the man running the Wiesbaden center was stellar. An architect by training, Captain Walter Farmer had spent time during the war building bridges and other items for the advancing Allied troops. Now he oversaw the Wiesbaden Collecting Point.

Charles Weise had three days to report. Monday he had to be in Wiesbaden.

That was all the information he had.

The army was emphasizing the "need to know when you need to know" nature of his work. Or wanted to make sure he knew he operated at its beck and call.

He glanced across the office to where Captain Thorson sat on a window seat. Her lips moved as she read a sheet of paper. Was she moving to Wiesbaden as well?

He shouldn't want that to happen as much as he did, but something about her intrigued him in a way that hadn't let him go yet. Instead the more time he spent with her, the more he wanted. There was a depth to her, a layer of seriousness and insight that had nothing to do with the war. He wasn't sure what to call it other than a solid stability.

After years of the world shifting beneath his feet during the war, he couldn't help but lean toward something steady and secure.

Then he studied the paper in his hand. No matter where her orders sent her, he would move to Wiesbaden . . . at least for the near future.

She sighed, and her dark gaze met his intently as she held up the paper. "I have new orders."

"Oh?" He tried to stay noncommittal even as he deeply wanted to know her orders.

"The military wants me in Wiesbaden."

He fought a smile as she pronounced the city wise-bottom. "It's vees-baa-dn."

"What?" She wrinkled her nose as she tried to understand. He had a feeling she had no idea she did that when she was thinking deeply.

"It's how you pronounce the town."

"How do you know that?"

"Family lived there for a while." Or something like that. Maybe they passed through. "It's basic German pronunciation. The *W*s become *V*s."

"Do you know why I'd be sent there?"

"There's a collection point for art and other antiquities. Beyond that I'm not sure. But we'll find out together. I'm going there too."

No matter what their assignments, he'd turn it into something that helped him prepare for life after the army. That day would arrive sometime. He'd be ready, and he couldn't help but hope that life included her.

Two and a half weeks in Altaussee had passed quickly, giving her a world-class education about the men who had been involved in various parts of the elaborate scheme to relocate art from the hands of Jewish owners and move it to the privileged few and the state. Add in the conversation with Bruno Lohse, which had given Charles and his team some insight and ammunition into Lohse's why behind the role he took. It wasn't quite a confession, but it edged them closer. Now it was up to the team in Nuremberg to decide where he went for trial.

How could she use that new knowledge at the Wiesbaden Collecting Point?

These experiences and Europe were so far removed from her days growing up in Iowa.

Altaussee was tiny, but the men she'd watched and interacted with were larger than life. European. Hidden.

Now she'd return to Germany and another set of unknowns.

The long drive back to Wiesbaden on Saturday was quiet. Charles might as well have been in another vehicle for all the words he said.

"I spy something green. Do you know what it is?" She said the words to spur something from him.

He shot her a look that suggested she was crazy, and maybe she was. She cocked an eyebrow. "What?"

"I spy?"

"It's a game."

"Really?"

"If it was good enough for people to play in Victorian England, there's no reason we can't play it." She hid a smile as she shifted toward the passenger window.

"You are something, Thorson."

"Why yes, I am." She fought to keep the grin out of her voice. "The question is, what am I?"

"What are my options?"

"Brilliant art historian. Femme fatale."

Now it was his turn to be startled, and he snorted. "Or a woman who's a long way from home riding in a jeep with a grouchy man." The car sputtered, and he drove it to the side of the road. When it stopped, he turned the key, but the vehicle only stuttered. "Hmm. Let me check under the hood."

The sun started its slide behind the trees, and Lillian fought back a shiver. "Will we get stuck out here?"

"Don't worry. I'm adept at monkeying together solutions for the vehicles. There aren't ready repair shops along the road." He hopped out and strode to the rear. He rattled a few fuel cans until he apparently found one with some liquid. "Here we go." He soon added gas to the vehicle's tank. "That should get us farther down the road."

When he climbed back into the driver's seat, the engine turned over reluctantly.

"Should we get more gas soon?" A night spent outside held no appeal.

"Keep your eyes open for any collection of our military. That will be our best bet."

She swallowed but nodded. No need to let him see how unsettled she was by the prospect of a night spent outside. Alone with him. She had fought off men who assumed she'd happily keep them company and wouldn't change her stance now. But that wasn't fair to Charles. He'd been nothing but kind and respectful to her. The fact she'd encountered a few men who weren't didn't allow her to paint him with the same brush and black paint those men deserved.

An hour later they pulled into a temporary army base. While Charles refilled the fuel tank and cans, Lillian stretched her legs and ambled toward the mess tent. She ignored a handful of soldiers who wolf whistled as she picked up her pace. She'd learned early the best thing to do in such situations was to hold her head high and ignore the sound. It would frustrate the men, and most gave up.

If Charles walked beside her, they wouldn't dare whistle.

When she sat at a table with a mug of bad coffee, she tried to anticipate what awaited her in Wiesbaden. Everything was foreign in a way that reminded her that despite her time in Boston for school, she fundamentally remained an Iowa girl wandering in a world recovering from a war that had threatened to pull life apart from the seams.

Charles sidled up to her, and she tried to ignore the way her pulse surged to life for a different reason from the men she'd passed on the way in. She could not allow herself to be sucked into some ill-fated romance. She had too much to do and prove before she headed back to the States and picked up her life curating exhibits at one of the top-tier museums. After all, that was what she was supposed to want after investing all that time in an education.

During the war, none of it had seemed to matter though. And now? How could she impact the world if she was locked up safely in a dusty museum?

The devastation made her time invested in art seem frivolous.

Being part of the Lohse interviews hadn't changed the feeling she was on the periphery and only adding moments of value. If she couldn't do it there, where could she?

"We've got enough gas to get back to Germany." Charles's quiet words pulled her from her thoughts.

Lillian forced a smile. "When would you like to leave?"

"Tomorrow."

She blinked. "Tomorrow?"

"It's already dusk, and the roads are too hit or miss to leave now and risk a blown tire from something we can't see."

He didn't mention the refugees she'd seen clustered alongside the road. "All right." Her mind spun as she thought back to whom she'd passed. "I haven't seen any other women here."

"There's a small contingent of nurses attached to a medical unit. You can crash in their housing tonight. I'm told they're in an old farmhouse on the edge of the village." He paused, his expression serious. "I'll park the jeep outside and sleep in it."

"That's not necessary." But it made her feel safer knowing he would be near and alert.

"Maybe not, but I'll rest better staying close." He took another swig of the coffee and then pulled a face. "I'm ready for real coffee. Any day now." He sighed and set the cup down. "When we get back to Wiesbaden, I'll work at the collecting point."

"Will I be assigned there too?"

"Maybe. What did your orders say?"

"CCP."

He shrugged, and there was something regal in the way he carried himself. "The army usually places people where it makes sense, but not always. What's your expertise?"

She shifted in her seat and met his blue gaze. "Do you realize after all our time together, this is the first time you've asked about that?"

"Guess I was engrossed with Lohse. His case was tricky." He focused on her. "It was a missed opportunity on my part."

"You also had the long car rides," Lillian teased, but noted how he tensed, so let it go. "My expertise is Italian High Renaissance art, but I also enjoy the Dutch masters."

"Those are quite different styles."

"Probably why I like them—keeps boredom at bay." She studied him. "What's your expertise?"

"Large-scale sculptures."

"*David*?"

"Who?"

"Michelangelo's *David*?"

He grinned, and it about blinded her. "Maybe not quite that large, but yeah. I love taking a block and carving out the image that was waiting to be released."

"Is that what you'll do when you return to the States?"

"No, I'll step into the family business."

"Oh." That wasn't what she expected to hear, based on his enthusiasm. "What's that?"

"Art galleries. My family was in shipping too, until our line was claimed as part of the war reparations after World War One."

That didn't make any sense. "How?"

"Our family heritage is German." He shrugged and stood, as if it didn't bother him. "You could say I've returned to my fatherland."

The words sounded odd combined with his American accent, even if they were true. There was more to his story, and maybe she'd be lucky enough to learn it. As he led her to the jeep, she stifled a yawn. She'd let her curiosity wait until another time when she wasn't exhausted from travel. But as he pulled into the yard of a farmhouse, she knew she wanted to understand Charles and all the elements at play in him.

Chapter Five

AFTER HOURS SPENT driving along more broken roads than she cared to remember, Lillian was ready to stay in one place.

There had been no flight to hop from Munich back to Wiesbaden, so the hours in the jeep had passed in unending sequence. Finally, Charles pulled in front of a nondescript apartment building constructed of stone. A small child—girl or boy, it was hard to tell—slipped into the shadows before the jeep came to a complete stop.

"Are you sure you don't want me to carry your suitcase? The apartment's on the third floor."

"I'll be fine." She had to prove she could do this, or he'd never trust her to do things on her own.

He frowned, but it didn't lock in place like it did when something upset him. Instead it mirrored the one he wore when he wanted to argue back when concern motivated him. "All right."

"Please, I'll be fine."

"Then I'll see you in the morning."

"I'm sure I can get where I need to on my own."

"I speak German."

"So do I." A little more now that she'd worked at Altaussee. She opened the door and pulled her bag from the back seat. "There's no chance I'll get lost. Promise." She'd lived in an apartment before and knew how to navigate one. How hard could it be to find the apartment when he'd dropped her in front of the building?

He studied her a moment, then dipped his chin. "See you in the morning." Charles pulled away even before she'd finished shutting the door, effectively ending the conversation.

She turned toward the building. Judging by the number of windows, it was four stories tall, the stone facade only suffering minor damage. However, there were piles of rubble from the damaged building next door, which had apartments on the other side with gaping holes that allowed easy entrance to the units.

A survey of the building didn't show where the child had gone. If she could find this child, maybe she could actually do something for her, unlike all the refugees they'd driven past all day.

"Hello? Guten Tag?" She waited as she scanned again. No one answered, and she couldn't spot the child. "I'll be back." The promise lingered in the air, making her wonder why she'd made it.

Well, nothing to do but head into the building. The stairwell and halls were industrial, dull yellowed paint with dirt and leaves swirling in the corners. A frayed broom that appeared handmade leaned into the corner, broken bristles listing in the dirt. No one had the energy or inclination to deal with such minor things, including Lillian as she stood there with her suitcase, staring up the stairs.

By the time she reached the second-floor landing, Lillian wished she'd let Charles heft her suitcase, especially since the second floor in European countries was the third in the United States. With a bag that was almost her size, it had been a weighty burden to haul up step by step.

After maneuvering up one more flight, she searched the doors for a large number 12, then moved to rap on the door. At one point it had likely been a lovely wooden door, but war had left it scarred and pocked. She listened for footsteps on the other side and was relieved when a young woman with hair covered by a bright-red kerchief cracked the door and then pulled it wider. Her smile welcomed Lillian. "You must be the new roommate."

"I think so." Lillian extended her hand. "Lillian Thorson."

"Angelina Corder. Nurse at the base."

"I'm an art conservationist." Or would be while she was here.

"Welcome." Angelina made a sweeping gesture. "This is now your humble abode too. Is there anything I can take for you?"

"I'm all right."

"Then follow me." Angelina waited for Lillian to follow before starting a quick tour. "There's a small sitting area and kitchen. We are lucky this building has functioning bathrooms and water. The electricity comes and goes, so we always keep candles around. And there are two small bedrooms. You and I will share one, and the other is for two more nurses. Sometimes they put a fifth in here because we live at work and rarely make it home. Fortunately, it's not like during the war."

"I imagine you're ready to go home if you experienced fighting."

"Not really. I wouldn't mind a quick trip to see family, but the men who fought should go home first." Angelina crossed her arms over her stomach. "This might sound odd, but I like Germany. I can imagine myself helping to rebuild it. What happened after the last war didn't work, but we can do things differently and create a new outcome this time." She let her hair fall forward over her face. "I need to believe that's possible." She seemed to shake herself from her thoughts. "I have the bed on the left. You can take the right. The trunk at the foot of the bed is for your things, and when your suitcase is empty, we'll find a place for it somewhere."

"Thank you." Lillian peered around, noting the way her bed was carefully made and the room neat. "I'll do my best to keep my space organized."

"We'll make it work." Angelina glanced at her watch and started. "I have to hurry to the hospital for my shift. There's food in the kitchen. Help yourself, and we'll get you to the PX soon. We're lucky we have access to necessities there. Not everyone is so blessed."

And then she was gone, leaving Lillian alone in the small apartment. She set the suitcase down and sank to the edge of the bed. The stillness settled over her, but it wasn't heavy. More a comforting moment, a pause before she met her other roommates. She might not know these women yet, but the comfort of not being alone wrapped her in warmth.

⟜⟡⟜

After dropping Lillian at her apartment, Charles made his way to the barracks. He didn't feel right about leaving her, but he'd sensed fighting her wouldn't be a winning strategy. She'd wanted to create some distance, prove her independence, so he let her. In fact the idea of an independent woman made him like her more. She didn't need a guy, and when she chose one, it would mean something rich and real. He could give her the gift of space after the drive when he knew they'd spend many of their days working together once the art arrived. For all he knew, some art might already wait for them to process.

He'd heard the stories of the Nazi art thefts firsthand. It was no rumor to him, but a large-scale seizing of what they wanted regardless of who it originally belonged to. Interrogating men like Lohse had only put a spotlight on the scope of the theft.

Now Charles might play a role identifying the rightful owners and returning the art.

He wanted that to be his role, righting the wrongs done to so many families.

The army had uncovered caches in the Merkers and Altaussee salt mines. Then they'd located a stash at Neuschwanstein Castle. The Eagle's Nest. The list went on.

Finding the art was the first step.

Before the items could be reconnected with their owners, the army and local governments had much to do. Walter Farmer would run that daunting and labor-intensive process. People's homes and dreams depended on them performing the job correctly.

Luftwaffe general command had used the former museum as its headquarters, but the US Army had transformed it into a central collecting point, a sister to the one in Munich, for housing and sorting the art caches found all over Germany and Austria. The Allies had rushed to restore the building in time for the first delivery of art from the overflowing Frankfurt location. He was ready to be part of the process to return people's priceless treasures.

When he arrived at the barracks, he found the space spare—they were left over from when the Luftwaffe operated the airfield. One building had been destroyed in the bombing, but the other had been patched together in a slapdash manner that kept a ceiling over their heads and walls up. Still, he was grateful. That protection from the elements was more than many living in town had.

He entered his room, ignoring the stained ceiling and the way the paint flecked. The simple twin bed was pushed against one wall. A desk and a chair leaned against the opposite wall. At the end of the bed was a metal box for his personal items. A couple of hooks on the wall completed the arrangement. It was basic but private. The benefit of being an officer. Something else he was grateful for.

The sound of footsteps, boots against flooring, alerted him to the return of other troops to the building. The Allies had much work to complete as they decided how to run and rebuild Germany. There were no easy answers in a country fully engaged in war for so many years. The economy was devastated, and it would take years to rebuild in any meaningful way.

The deprivation and poverty were astounding.

He clenched and unclenched his hands where he sat on the edge of the bed. So many times he drove by the children who had been impacted by the war, and he needed to do something but couldn't. The need overwhelmed the resources of the Red Cross and Allies. How did he think he could make an impact? The simple answer was he couldn't. It would be less than the blip of a pebble dropping into one of Monet's Japanese garden paintings.

When an economy and its population had lived focused on sustaining a war machine for more than six years, it left a lasting impact.

The absence of jobs.

The inability to rebuild homes.

The lack of food because farming had not prospered. Each took a toll individually and combined would keep Germany devastated for years to come, even with all the aid from the United States.

Charles was jolted from his dark thoughts when someone pounded on his door.

"You in there, Weise?"

"Nope. Move along." Charles waited, knowing the man wouldn't agree, but Charles would get a rise out of Scott Langer anyway. Scott had gone through basic with Charles, but without the degree, Scott had been relegated to private. Now he was a sergeant but outranked by Charles, something that rankled Scott at times. However, most of the time his good humor prevailed.

Yep. The door opened, and a burly Nebraska farm boy filled the doorway. "It's time for chow."

Charles made a show of studying his watch. "So it is. Is that an invitation?"

"Yep." The man might have run a washcloth over his head and arms, dark hair wet around the ears. "I've heard it's something with potatoes."

"Always the potatoes."

"It seems to be a staple."

Charles nodded, but he'd like a traditional German meal, one from the stories his grandparents told about: spaetzle, pfannkuchen, and schnitzel. The problem was, he didn't want to head out and find food that would be taken from someone who needed it. In the cities it was hard to get food straight from the farms. And even if you could get to a farm, many had suffered from a decimated workforce.

Together they walked downstairs and out to the separate mess building. It had been erected quickly and served those who lived at the airfield. Basic tables and chairs were arranged in long lines, separated from the kitchen with a serving counter. The space echoed with noise as soldiers and pilots filled it at mealtime, but the cooks kept the coffee ready, ensuring a constant small group or two nursing mugs of the thickening liquid. The later in the day, the denser the brew.

Charles filled his plate and tray with food, glad to be done with K rations for now. The slop on his plate was still mass-produced, but it tasted better than what he'd lived on when on the move. However, the food at Altaussee had been much better. The hausfrau who'd cooked for them had been an impressive creator of meals out of what was available. Of course, it helped that the OSS had brought in whatever she needed in order to keep the men they were interrogating satisfied and talking.

"Any word on your new assignment?" Scott squinted up from his pasta concoction.

"It involves the looted art."

"Sounds better than hunting for unexploded ordnance." Scott shivered dramatically, then scooped another heaping pile of pasta onto his fork. "I keep waiting for one to decide now is the time to do what it was manufactured to do."

"Cheerful thought." Compared to that, using his training to work with the art was a walk in Central Park. "Look, I know I'm fortunate."

"Nah, I wouldn't want to spend my days locked in a building evaluating canvas and paint. Though I've heard they're searching for security guards." Scott grinned, something stuck between the gap in his front teeth. "Nah, I'm a farm boy at heart and prefer the outside and wide-open spaces. Besides, someone has to do my job. Can't let just anyone discover a bomb."

"When you put it that way . . ."

Scott guffawed and slapped him on the back. However, the image of his friend approaching various munitions with little to protect him would fill Charles's nightmares. His war had been fairly quiet and routine, unlike Scott's. And now that the war had ended, it sobered him to realize how much hadn't changed. There were still dangerous jobs that had to be completed by someone. All while he stayed in his safe bubble of a world filled with art and culture.

There had to be more to his time in Germany, but Charles was at a loss as to what.

Chapter Six

Monday, August 20

WHEN THE APARTMENT building door closed behind Lillian, she glanced up and down the sidewalk. Would she see the child from the night before? She'd brought half of the apple she'd cut up for breakfast with her in case she could share it with the child, but she couldn't spot anyone in the shadows.

Then a movement caught her eye and she paused. "Hello?" She held up the apple half. "Are you hungry?" She took a step toward the shadow, suddenly seeing a larger child put an arm around the smaller one, but both backed away. She paused and then set the apple on a piece of rubble. "This is for you." She stepped back and then took another, watching the children the whole time.

Her heel caught on something and she glanced down to pick her next step. When she looked up, the children had disappeared into the shadows.

By the time she reached the airfield, she wished she'd let Charles pick her up in some borrowed jeep, because she was on sensory overload from the challenges of navigating the bus and more.

The army base was chaotic, the former Luftwaffe airfield buzzing with Allied troops since March. Over breakfast she'd heard stories of the bomber sorties, as many as forty taking off every three hours during the height of the Luftwaffe's preeminence in the air. But now she could see the results of the Allied bombing raids when as many as eighty-seven craters pocked the landing strips. Unfortunately, not all the bombs fell on military targets. Nearly one in five civilian homes had been destroyed too—something she forced herself to witness on her commute. Someone had to remember.

Now with the paperwork complete, she had arrived at the Wiesbaden Central Collecting Point. The day flew by in a rush of meeting her colleagues and setting up for the art that would arrive in short order. It turned out Lillian and Charles had arrived only two days before the first shipment was set to leave Frankfurt.

A couple mornings later the sound of Lillian's heels against the checkerboard marble floor of the former museum echoed loudly in her ears. The first floor had a regalness that bordered on formal, while each subsequent floor became less formal unless one stood in the rotunda, which gleamed with gold leaf and ornate mosaics. When there was time, she needed to find someone who could explain the meanings behind the standards and images placed along the rotunda. What she did know was that the rich colors used in the mosaics caught her eye, the brilliance telling a story she couldn't yet read.

The first shipment should arrive tomorrow, and as she reported to work, the enormity of the task settled heavily on her shoulders. There was no knowing what the condition of the art and other items would be until each arrived on-site. Lillian tried to imagine the coming work as she walked the hollow space but had no frame of reference. Her work at a couple small museums in the United States had not prepared her for postwar conditions.

Her colleagues were a mix of American servicemen and German civilians. Some of the Germans may have served in the war, but without their uniforms it was hard to know, so she ignored the questions. She'd need to earn their trust before they shared their stories, if they ever would. As she noted their threadbare clothing, carefully cleaned, and worn leather shoes, she realized just how little the Germans had. How did one restart an entire economy? Maybe she couldn't answer that question, but she could focus on how to restart the art scene.

Captain Walter Farmer strode into the room, his jacket buttoned and tie knotted at the neck to regulation even though it was the end of summer. There was a stiff formalism to him that belied his ability to get things done quickly. Over the last two days, she'd seen him convert a ragtag team into an efficient operation, cleaning out the last of the debris and creating the receiving systems. She only had to wander around the museum to see the handiwork of his ability to complete the impossible under incredibly difficult circumstances.

"Good morning, sir."

He nodded, his glasses sliding down his nose. "Good morning." He glanced around the room. "Our first delivery arrives in the morning. We have to find a fast system for processing the items as they reach us." He wiped a finger along the surface of a desk he'd created out of a board and two file cabinets. "We should also make one more sweep to see if we've cleaned enough."

"Is that something we can have the local workers help with?" They might welcome work.

"Possibly, but the key is that we're ready. Whatever it takes." He pulled his glasses off and rubbed his eyes.

She'd heard the rumors of how he had single-handedly transformed the former museum that had evolved from headquarters to a tooling factory and then a location for displaced persons into a space ready to receive art and antiquities. He was the reason it could safely store art.

"Why the move from Frankfurt?" she asked.

"The Reichsbank isn't designed to house the ten truckloads from Merkers. Then there are all the other stashes still being located and cleared." He sighed. "It's a big job to conserve art that the Germans thrust into the salt mines with insufficient packing to protect the works from looting, moisture, and other conservation issues."

"Do we have everything we need to process the items efficiently? What part of the process is keeping you up at night?"

He smiled, tired yet resolved. "We'll learn as we go. The key is to do the job as quickly as possible, but with a commitment to accuracy. The worst thing we can do is rush the process and misidentify the provenance of the items entrusted to us. Or rush past repairs we can make before forwarding them to their owners."

"Agreed, sir." Lillian tried to imagine what could smooth the process. Until she saw how receiving the art went, it was an exercise in guessing. Not grounded in any reality that would make the process better or even good.

"It was the work of men like Lieutenant Weise that has allowed us to identify so many locations where art was stashed."

"He built a good relationship with Mr. Lohse."

"And others." He sighed as another man hurried into the room.

The man snapped to attention. "Sir, we need you."

"Of course." He bowed toward Lillian. "Thank you for your assistance."

"Certainly." She watched the men leave, then pulled out her pad of paper and outlined steps she could anticipate for processing the items. She didn't shift her focus as footsteps entered the room.

"You are hard at work."

Charles Weise's deep voice pulled her head up, and she spotted him leaning against the doorframe. How did he manage to cause her heart to dance when he entered a room? No one had ever done that.

She swallowed and prayed he couldn't see his effect on her. "Trying to imagine an efficient way to manage the paintings when they arrive tomorrow."

"More than paintings will come."

"I understand." She bit her lower lip and sighed. "If I have a system for one type, it might work for the others too."

He stepped toward her. "Can I see?"

She slid the paper toward him, pleased that her fingers didn't tremble. "I need a picture of how we'll move items through in a way that allows us to process efficiently while also moving fast enough." She scrutinized the empty room. "Tomorrow this room will fill with crates. If the rumors are true about the quantity of what the army has recovered, we will have to move quickly."

He scanned the paper, his finger sliding down as he read. "The pressure will be for speed."

Lillian nodded, the responsibility weighting her shoulders. "That's what concerns me. If we aren't careful, we'll miss key details that will allow us to do a good job matching looted items with original owners."

"You're assuming everything was looted. Some of the items come from museums and other public collections." His gaze was steady as he studied her. "Not all items were forcibly taken."

She froze, the thought ricocheting through her. "You're right." She scratched a note on the next sheet of paper. "Provenance will be key." She rubbed her temple, where a pounding was beginning. "How will we do that when the country is in ruins?"

"We'll be careful and use lots of due diligence. Fortunately, the Nazis were very efficient and systematic in their record keeping. That will help."

She ignored the irony in his words. "Captain Farmer left me to make sure everything is ready."

"Then we'd better get to it."

His words filled her with warmth. We. It was a word she wasn't used to, especially in the military, where artificial lines could separate people. Yes, you had to act as a unit, but her assignments often required tasks assigned to her individually and never with the authority to make people help her—there was little more frustrating.

But as the hours melted away as she and Charles worked together to check on the rooms across the first floor of one wing, she realized it was more than that. He kept the mood light with small jokes and comments about people he'd worked with during his time in the military. There was nothing mean spirited about his words. Instead he made keen observations about human nature and those around him.

It also gave her insight into his character.

While he might appear quiet at times, he remained deeply observant. He truly saw those around him, to a level that made her nervous about what he saw in her. She almost asked but was afraid of what he might say.

⚜

The next morning Charles dressed with a tense anticipation swirling through him that only built as the first trucks arrived from Frankfurt. The state of the art was as Charles had feared. Whoever had packed the items had rushed in a slipshod and hurried fashion, making it a miracle that damage hadn't occurred. Who thought that grunts in the army would understand what they were transporting across the miles? These soldiers were weary after years fighting and living away from home. Many only wanted to return to their lives, a need he understood. He was as ready as the next to try to forget all he'd seen during the fighting and press into a future without exploding shells and the whistle of bullets.

The challenge for him came from the art student's deep desire to stop and soak in each painting and sculpture, but the soldier took over and focused on directing others to the various rooms from the map that Lillian and he had developed the previous day.

Her time working at a museum had shown up in her system of rooms dedicated to art categories. It would work exceptionally well if they had the time of a museum to organize its collection. Instead, the collections of several galleries and museums would land at the Wiesbaden Central Collecting Point for processing in a matter of days, requiring a more broad-based approach of keeping the shipments together through the first review. In the simple cases, they would quickly process which painting was whose and confirm it was duly owned with authentic provenance. In others, it would be a twisting puzzle of ownership to decipher.

They would have to resist the pressure to move quickly.

Doing the job thoroughly and right mattered more than speed.

He directed another soldier carrying a painting covered with a wool blanket to the room on the left. The organization had devolved to paintings in a couple of rooms, sculptures in another, and antiquities in still another. So far furnishings hadn't arrived, which was good since the size would consume the precious space. At the rapid pace the assigned rooms were filling, it didn't take imagination to know they would run out of space in a matter of weeks, if not days.

At the end of the first long day of processing, all Charles wanted was a good meal and a hot shower. Instead he had to settle for a sandwich and a quick rinse. Once in his quarters, he found an envelope from the United States. He studied the writing, small yet bold, a quick reminder of all the letters his father had sent throughout the war.

He carefully sliced open the thin sheet and began to read.

Charles, it has come to my attention that when your Opa fled Germany, he left family items in storage. Not just any items but the art he spent a lifetime collecting. Two items are of special significance to him as he nears the end of his days. One is a scene with the wise men that Oma commissioned an art gallery to purchase for their tenth anniversary. The other is a small statue that was used to burn frankincense by those in ancient Egypt. King Tut's tomb had recently been discovered, and he was delighted to acquire something from that era. Both represent parts of the wise men and their story, precious to him because of the play on our last name and reminder of who is worthy of our worship.

Now that hostilities have ended, we need you to reclaim what you can of it. It is his dearest dream to be reunited with the painting in particular. It's a painting of the magi worshipping the Christ. I believe it dates to the Rococo period and is by an Italian artist, though I am still investigating details from here. However, the art was left behind as your grandparents fled the growing persecution. He said he left that and more in storage in a bank in Hannover, a city near Bremerhaven. But his memory is growing fuzzy . . .

There a word was indecipherable, but Hannover was all he needed to know this hunt would be nearly impossible. That city had been heavily bombed as a result of the industry that lined its perimeter.

> *I would enclose the key, but that is not allowed with this kind of mail. Instead, here is the pass phrase that will prove you have authority to access what he stored at the bank. If it is still there. We must pray it is, as it is important to your Opa. He often mentions that and the frankincense statue. One because it was a gift from Oma, the other because it was a gift from history. Both represent times when life was still good.*
>
> *His health is failing, and finding his treasure may be what he needs to keep fighting.*

The note continued with a few sentences now in his mother's delicate writing, her quick take on details about life in New York and the urge for him to quit the military and return home. It wouldn't matter if he told his family the military didn't leave it to him to choose. One didn't quit and leave. In addition, as long as he had the opportunity to work with the art, his work would maintain importance. That was more than he could say about returning to New York and the family's art business. Would working in the art trade still be his driving goal?

After all he'd experienced, he wasn't certain.

He folded the letter and slipped it in his shirt pocket. Now wasn't the time to dig into this directive but to rest. Tomorrow another long day would unfurl, filled with unraveling the mystery behind many pieces . . . and maybe he could add locating this family treasure.

Chapter Seven

Thursday, August 30

LILLIAN STARTED DOWN the sidewalk as she left for work, her thoughts already focused on what she'd tackle first.

"Excuse me." A man stepped in front of her, blocking her path.

She tried to step around him, but he stood like a rock, clutching a child, dressed in rags, by the arm. "Let me through." She hated the way the last word quavered. Not the strong, unruffled image she needed to project.

"Give me your purse or I hurt the child."

"What kind of monster are you?" She raised her bag to hit him, but his hand shot out and grasped her wrist. She squirmed. "Let me go."

The sound of a car's engine reached her, but she didn't see a way to escape. What if the driver passed without stopping? She flailed toward the car, trying to make it clear she didn't want this man holding any part of her.

"Let me go." She pushed the words out louder and desperate.

The man tightened his grip, and now the child, a little boy, whimpered.

"Please." Lillian didn't want to beg but could do nothing else, as it felt like her wrist would snap.

The car stopped and footsteps approached, but she couldn't turn to see who neared. *Please let it be a friend.* She groaned and tried to twist free, but the man held firm.

"Mind your own matters." The German's gruff tone suggested no fear of whoever approached.

"I'd suggest you do the same."

At Charles's voice Lillian would have sagged with relief except she couldn't move.

"Let the woman go."

"I'm not some woman, Charlie."

He sputtered a laugh. "Charlie?"

"It slipped out."

"Unhand her now."

The German's eyes widened, and he thrust Lillian at Charles and then threw the child toward the rubble before taking off.

"Do you recognize him?"

Lillian shook her head, her arms wrapping around Charles as if he could keep her anchored in place, while her vision narrowed and dots formed behind her eyes. "Why are you here?"

"I was hoping for a bit more awe for my heroism."

She shook her head and then leaned back so she could see him. "Thank you. I don't know what I would have done." Before she could stop and think, she reached up and placed a kiss on his cheek. Then she pushed away, not wanting to see what emotion played on his face. She didn't regret it but feared he might. And that unsettled her even more than what had happened with the German.

"Lillian?" The question was quiet, undecipherable.

"Where's the child?" They needed to find the child and stay far away from what she'd just done, even as her lips tingled, practically begging for a real kiss.

She searched along the rubble, hunting in the shadows, but the little boy had disappeared. "There has to be something I can do to help these kids."

"Are we going to talk about what just happened?"

"No. I need to get to work." She paused long enough to remember he wasn't supposed to be here. "Why are you here? You never answered."

"To take you to work."

"I've gotten myself there all week."

"And what I pulled up to is exactly why I came."

She wanted to argue she could handle it herself, but she'd been trapped with no way to release herself from the man's grip. "Thank you."

"You're welcome." He ran a hand through his hair. "I know you can handle yourself, but not everyone is glad we're here. We are the conquerors."

A shiver shuddered through her at his words. "I know you're right."

He led her to the jeep, and she settled in. As he drove to the CP, she considered his words. Germany had a rich history, but it had been colored and altered by the last dictator. She wanted to step below the surface and learn what existed at different levels but sensed that wouldn't be easily accomplished, not when the US had arrived, as Charles put it, as one of the conquering heroes, here to punish all for what they had collectively done wrong.

Her thoughts flashed back to Bruno Lohse and the other men she had encountered at House 71 in Altaussee.

She had learned from those interactions that the easy answer suggested each man was 100 percent evil. Yet reality considered that not one could justify his actions, but neither was each the devil in disguise. Instead they represented humans who allowed their greed and opportunity to lead them to pure evil.

What about the man from this morning? How did he fit into the equation?

It all formed a cautionary tale of the highest order. But for the grace of God, would she have committed similar acts?

The thought sobered her with its weight. She couldn't easily answer it.

She peeked at her watch and noted the time. Charles pulled to a stop in front of the building. "Go ahead and hop out."

"Thank you again for coming to my rescue." She slipped from the seat and felt his gaze on her as she hurried past the protective fence and up the stairs to the main entrance.

She greeted the guards and then rushed to the gallery she'd worked in yesterday. Maybe she could disappear and avoid Charles until she had brushed the kiss from her mind. Lillian didn't know that she wanted to forget it though.

Instead, she let the relative silence that cloaked the building at this hour of the morning settle around her, very aware it would soon disappear as transports arrived with loads of art and treasures.

Lillian pushed philosophy to the side and focused on what the day would hold. Today she'd shift from processing incoming items to starting some provenance research on the trickier items. She could track some items' history easily because no surprises popped up, such as a painting that disappeared for forty years in Germany to reappear in England or another that wasn't listed in any of the catalogs for works by an author. Others took time and care she couldn't apply in the pressure of receiving more items.

In the chaos that would erupt soon, she could lose the bigger vision.

And that chaos could also lead to items disappearing.

They had to avoid that if at all possible.

Last night Captain Farmer had selected a room to start in, and when she arrived there, Charles sat at the table.

"How did you beat me in here?"

He continued to study whatever was in front of him. "Speedy, I guess."

"Thank you again."

"Glad I was there." He pivoted in her direction. She posed casually against the doorframe while he watched her. That small uptick of his mouth let her know he wasn't too annoyed with her interruption.

"I knew it was you, Captain."

"And how did you know that?"

He pointed at her shoes. "You have a unique cadence to your walk, which is punctuated by those heels. How do you stand those?"

"Army issued."

Not everything the army did made sense to her. The shoes were one in a long string of things she would change if she led. "Ready?"

"As I can be." He rubbed his chin as he studied her in that

appraising way he had that made her feel as though he saw through her every defense. He opened his mouth, then closed it, as if deciding against his words.

⁕

The art arrived in a rush of crates. Ten trucks. Three hours to unload. And a multitude of hours ahead to process and discover the history of each piece. If an academic exercise, Charles would have enjoyed the challenge. The reality of why the pieces leaned against the walls, in the specially designed racks and other configurations, warred with the relief that they were safe.

He should focus on the art.

Instead he couldn't forget the brush of her lips on his cheek. She acted like nothing happened, but his entire world had shifted. Almost like the pieces to a puzzle finally sliding into perfect place.

That didn't mean he knew what to do with the change.

Still, he shook his head to refocus just as Captain Farmer whirled through the rooms, directing traffic and inspecting each larger piece quickly as it arrived. He seemed satisfied as the privates unloaded the trucks. Charles stood next to Farmer to monitor the work.

"Pleased with how it's going, sir?"

Farmer nodded, then slipped his glasses up his nose. "The museum is ready, we have a process, and now the works will be safe."

"They seem in decent shape."

"We won't know for sure until we closely inspect each for any damage. Did you know at Montegufoni in Tuscany, the Germans left Botticelli's *Primavera* leaning against a wall? The German soldiers used Ghirlandaio's *Adoration of the Magi* as a table." The man shuddered. "They flipped it over and ate meals off it. At least here we can prevent that abuse and neglect from happening."

"Absolutely." In fact stories like that highlighted the importance of their work. "We recognize what's entrusted to us."

Farmer's gaze followed that of a soldier who banged a corner of a crate against the museum wall. "Do we?" As the young soldier did it again, Farmer straightened. "Private, you hold a priceless work of art. Take care."

The soldier didn't say anything but kept moving, this time with more care.

"He'll learn."

"Or be transferred." Farmer rubbed his forehead. "We need more trained personnel. People like you and Captain Thorson, who recognize what they handle and evaluate."

The next hours passed in a blur. In addition to Farmer, Lillian, and Charles, several Germans—former employees at the museum and others that Farmer had meticulously interviewed—worked with the art. These individuals would help with translating the Nazi documentation uncovered when men like Lohse told the Art Looting Investigation Unit where they had stored caches of documents. Lohse had decided being helpful worked in his favor, and his memory was practically photographic.

Lohse's help could speed the process, as he'd walked them through the paintings and what had happened during the war. But the man would stand trial either in Germany or France after the army moved him to a new holding location.

The documents discovered in the various salt mines and castles would help as they spent the next months painstakingly unwinding the provenance of each piece. Any idea the work would be fast had been eclipsed by the unending stacks of crates. No shortcuts existed because even the pieces from a museum did not mean the museum had properly purchased them. Nor did it mean the items were looted. Many didn't realize that the Germans had stored private and state museum collections in the salt mines alongside looted items when the bombing accelerated. Then there were the private collections of men like Goring and Hitler that had been stored at their estates and places like Neuschwanstein.

Moments like this he wished his grandparents had stayed in Germany and he'd pursued his art training here. He would have known the players intimately rather than trying to piecemeal identify who told the truth and who liked forgeries and falsehoods. He could have visited the museums prior to the war and known what hung on the walls before the systematic taking of art occurred. Such information would be a valuable boon to the work, especially when motives had to be second-guessed and checked.

As staff moved the pieces to a room, he filled card after card with notes on what they did know, leaving blank the parts that someone must research.

Before the small rectangular cards came to him, someone had to fill in preprinted blocks by assigning each piece as a painting, drawing, sculpture, woodwork, or book. Then they filled in its author or creator if known, followed by identifying properties and a description. Finally Charles or someone else filled in its material and subject before attaching a photo. Each piece was assigned a number after the three letters *WIE* to indicate it had passed through the Wiesbaden Collecting Point and what its arrival condition was. If they knew a presumed owner, they added that too. The back side contained history and ownership details for the piece along with its location in the museum, arrival date, exit date when it passed out the doors, condition, and repair record. Some cards were copiously completed, while others remained blank due to the little known about the item, its ownership, and history.

His shoulders tightened as the day ended and each room was locked.

He walked by and double-checked the doors before leaving. At the main doors Lillian waited, to his surprise. He'd managed to ignore their almost kiss for most of the day, but he couldn't avoid noting each detail from the slightly rumpled state of her uniform to the dust streak along her cheek. He had to restrain from reaching up and brushing it away. Even in the weary slope of her shoulders, she probably wouldn't welcome the indication she wasn't perfectly ordered.

"Ready?" Her soft voice wrapped around him in the silence of the building.

"Everything's locked up." He opened the door for her, but she remained in place, watching him. She should grace a portrait like one of the many lining the rooms. A beautiful frame and elegantly colored details only marred by the chaos of the last years.

Part of him wondered how she'd appear all dolled up in an evening gown, hair perfectly arranged, but he sensed that version of Lillian wouldn't appeal as much as the one he'd worked alongside. That version labored hard, not waiting for others to work for her.

Together they'd progressed through a stack of paintings, but hundreds more waited for their attention.

"We'll get the work done." The certainty in her voice seemed misplaced as he considered their day.

He bit back the sarcastic response he wanted to toss out. "Not unless we move faster. Work longer."

"We'll get faster. Now that we know the information to capture, we can create a better system." She rubbed her lower back, as if the muscles had tightened from leaning over a table all day. "It's more detail that we need. Someone to rapidly find and share the pertinent facts from the records."

Each tidbit of information aided in reconnecting the piece with its original owner. Making the calls about what constituted a valid transaction remained the hard part.

While the Germans kept meticulous records, the Allies had bombed many locations that held the archives, leading to the destruction of many documents. For those that survived, identifying where the records were stored required finding the men involved and encouraging them to share what they knew. Some did willingly, like Lohse. Others didn't.

Realizing he'd grown lost in the weight of the work, Charles refocused on Lillian. "We need more artists and historians."

She barely shook her head. "We need to trust the ones we have. Not all Germans were part of the system, Charles."

"I know." He said the words because she expected them, but he knew the truth. Too many sat by and did nothing while the country of his Oma and Opa was transformed into a ghoulish shell of itself. He hoped his grandparents never learned of half the horrors, but he knew. And it made what he did now meaningful yet not enough. It would never be enough.

Chapter Eight

As THE WEEKS passed, the collection point filled with shipments. While she spent time evaluating the art, Lillian's heart beat with a thread of mourning for the children roaming the street in packs in the early morning and evening hours.

Why did children bear the heavy cost of war?

The question confronted her each time she traveled between the small apartment and the former museum.

You couldn't destroy 20 percent of a community's homes without children losing parents and siblings. The fact Wiesbaden had not suffered the extensive bombing that left other cities in near total ruin did nothing to lower the desperation she noted in those who'd survived.

The children experienced real pain, with many wandering the streets in scraps of clothing. As the weather continued to cool into fall and the days shortened, the need for some way to help the orphans pressed against her. The words of James 1:27 pounded like a drumbeat in her ears. *Pure religion and undefiled before God and the Father is this, To visit the fatherless and widows in their affliction, and to keep himself unspotted.*

She couldn't love God and walk past unaffected by the suffering.

What could she do to help the fatherless around her, especially as a woman who'd never had children of her own?

During the day when she worked, she could bury her head and

focus on the next painting, the next sketch. But the questions lingered as the flow of days entered a rhythm. Up while it was dark and eat a quick breakfast before being picked up by Charles or another soldier for the short drive to the museum. On the nice days Charles would walk with her, warning her that bitter cold and darkness would arrive soon enough.

Things had cleared between them, her thoughts only roaming to her spontaneous kiss a few times per day. He seemed better equipped to write it off as a chance happening that meant nothing.

Eventually she would convince herself of the same thing, but each day spent near him made it challenging.

One morning as she stepped from her building, she noted a little girl squatting on the street, a patched sweater buttoned around her, a toy truck in hand. She rolled it on the cobblestones, ignoring the bombed rubble of the apartment building behind her. Her brown curls were dirty, her face streaked with dirt. Of course at five or so, the child probably didn't know anything different than what she saw.

A slightly older boy watched from the shadows. Hunger lurked in his eyes, which made Lillian wonder how much he had seen and experienced. Was it his truck the girl pushed? Was he the girl's brother?

Lillian stepped closer but hesitated as the boy pushed to his full height. It didn't match hers, but she didn't want to threaten him with her presence. "Hello. Guten Morgen."

The little girl stayed focused on the truck.

Her brother, if that was who he was, melted even deeper into the shadows and rubble.

She stilled and waited a minute.

It wasn't unusual to see children alone on the streets. But she still wanted to identify ways to help.

The boy edged his sister into the shadows, and Lillian froze. If she couldn't connect with these children, what could she do?

Lillian turned, more determined than ever to do something . . . anything. In the quiet moments, the question returned like a never-ending fresco on a wall demanding more work. Was it her burden to bear? Even in part?

She prayed with each returning thought that she'd gain clarity. The need was too big to tackle without a path forward. Yet nothing came to her. No ideas, but no lessening of the burden either. And she had no one to talk with about it.

Here she lived in a building that was in good working order. The electricity worked, the water ran where it was supposed to, and the walls were largely intact. And she invested her days immersed in art, something that grew less important every time she passed a hungry child.

Each time she remembered the child who had been held by that man the morning he'd attacked her. There were so many ways the children needed help and protection.

Just like she had.

Charles had acted as her protector, but he'd started traveling, gone many days, checking rumors of caches or document stashes. Then he'd be back for a few days or a week only to disappear again, and some of the light vanished with him. Then in October she saw a familiar person striding across the mess hall.

She watched from her seat at a table, noting the moment he saw her. Charles hesitated, then slightly changed the angle of his walk to intersect with her table. She sensed the heat that flooded her cheeks as he approached. If he noticed, she hoped he'd attribute it to the bite in the air. Winter was on the way. Yes, that was what she'd blame her red cheeks on. Better still if he didn't notice. It would be harder to explain since she sat inside.

He'd turned up the collar of his coat, and his hat rested firmly against his head, everything perfectly turned out as he sauntered toward her.

She swallowed against the realization of how much she'd missed him. Her colleagues were nice enough, but the Germans stayed largely to themselves, and the rest focused on the unending piles of work.

"So this is where you've kept yourself." He stopped in front of her, a twinkle in his eyes as he studied her.

"Every day at least twice a day for meals." She wanted to say something witty but went blank.

He didn't seem to notice as he sank onto a chair and pulled something from his pocket. "I've missed you."

The quiet words had her shoving her hands deep inside her coat pockets to keep him from seeing the nervous energy that vibrated through her. "It's good to see you, Lieutenant."

He tilted his chin as he watched her. "Ah, so you're mad I was gone." He edged the item across the table to her. "I saw this and thought of you." He opened his palm, and she noted a small wooden carving. "It's a Christmas tree ornament."

"Oh, Charles." She reached for it, then pulled back. "Is it for me?"

"It is. You can think of me each time you see the three wise men." He smiled as she took the ornament and examined it.

"It's so delicate."

"Some enterprising soul has started a small business making these for the GIs to send home. My Oma and Opa used to send something similar to us for our Christmas tree." He shrugged but didn't stop smiling. "I thought you'd like one."

"I do. Thank you." She leaned forward, then caught herself before she could do something foolish like kiss him again and sank back on her chair. "I'll treasure it." She pushed to her feet, not wanting him to see how much she'd missed him. She took a step toward him. "I need to get to the museum. Can you give me a ride, soldier?"

He frowned, as if it was suddenly hitting him where they were. "Why are you on base?"

"I came to grab a couple things at the PX." She patted the bag that hung off her shoulder. "Grabbed breakfast while I was here. But now I need to hustle."

"I'll walk with you, or better yet, grab a jeep."

"If you have time, I'd like that." She didn't want to admit how much she wanted his protection. Though she walked on her own, she couldn't stop looking over her shoulder for another attack.

Charles fell into step next to her, quiet but resolute. She didn't know what to say without letting him into how much she had missed him, so her thoughts wandered with her steps. A block from the base, she spied the same boy she'd seen the other day. She reached into her bag and pulled out a bread roll and a sugared orange slice and set them on the sidewalk. It was small, but it was something. Maybe someday he would trust her enough to let her help more.

⁓⚜⁓

"I've missed working near you." Charles hadn't expected to say those words, though they were true.

"It's routine." She almost hid her small smile as her hair fell forward over her face. "You're doing important work on your scavenger hunts."

"Maybe." What he didn't say was anyone could do it. Leaving the collection point to evaluate the items found in another cache underscored the ongoing need for more people. "We'd just found our rhythm."

"What? Feeling irreplaceable, Lieutenant Weise?" The tease in her tone kept the words from feeling as harsh as they sounded.

"Maybe." He shrugged, glad the heavy silence between them had lifted. "Two truckloads will arrive this week. Mostly paintings, but a few coin collections and some silver."

"Anything stand out?"

"Not really. We'll also receive more documentation from the National Gallery of Art Library. That should help with the research."

"We're running out of room." Her cheeks had a bright color from the wind as they walked. She stopped and pulled a roll from her bag before handing it to a little girl who couldn't be more than four or five. Another child appeared, and so did a roll. Then Lillian resumed walking.

Charles watched her from the corner of his eye. "Do you do that often?"

Now the color that filled her cheeks represented more than the brisk air. "Just when I can get here for fresh bread. It's not much, but it's something."

"To those kids, it's everything. I'm ashamed I never thought to do it." Her actions demonstrated the kindness he'd noticed before. "I'm glad to call you my friend."

"Thank you." She spoke so softly he almost didn't hear.

That made him want to stop and pull her in for a hug, but he couldn't here. "You are one impressive woman, Captain Lillian Thorson."

"I'm just trying to make a difference."

A block down the road he picked up their conversation. "I've got a few ideas for streamlining what we do at the CP."

"All right." Her words were clipped, which brought him to a halt. She groaned. "What?"

"I was going to ask you that. We're on the same team."

She sighed, and her shoulders sagged under her trench coat. "While you travel Germany exploring, I'm stuck in the museum." She held up a hand, as if to stop any words. "I'm grateful for the work with the artifacts, but the only time I'm not in the building, it's dark or twilight." She paused, then whispered, "I'm letting it all get to me."

"What do you mean?"

"Do you see what's all around us?" She gestured to the rubble-strewn sidewalk across the street. "I've been here six weeks, and nothing's improved. Me handing out rolls doesn't make a dent."

"That we can see. I bet to the children you just fed it makes an immense difference." He shoved his hands into his pockets to keep from pulling her close, her passion drawing him like the best work of art, worthy of time and study. "There's a lot happening behind the scenes."

"You hope. All I know is what I see." A lone tear slipped down her cheek, and she roughly brushed it away before he could respond to the temptation to do exactly that. "But that's not enough for me right now. These people are hurting."

Charles had watched her hand out the bread with sweets. She'd not only noticed the children but allowed their plight to grip her heart. It was the hardest part of living in the city. There were those who asked why it had taken so long for the Allies to arrive. There were those embittered by the bombings and destruction. Others waited in the shadows for the Allies to leave and fascism to rise again. And in the middle of the maelstrom, the US personnel worked. It made for a challenging quagmire to navigate.

"Then let's do what we can for those who have lost their family treasures. It might not feel like much, but for them it could be everything." He thought of his grandparents. The sorrow on their faces at all they had left behind. Keeping their lives was meaningful, but it didn't negate the loss. "My grandparents and those like them would be grateful for any part of their legacy we can return."

His father's line in the letter about his grandfather's health resurfaced. Had time already taken Opa's life? If it had, then he would have died in peace, unlike so many in Europe. Still, Charles would do his best to reclaim his grandfather's treasure, even if that was harder than searching for a needle in a Monet haystack.

Lillian studied him, her green eyes intent as they measured his words. "You're right, but part of me wants to scream, 'We're wasting our days on art when people starve all around us.' We can go to the PX and buy what we need. They can't." Her hand clutched the straps on her bag as she blinked rapidly, then turned and started moving again. "It's hard to watch and do so little."

"Then identify a way to do something." The words slipped out before he could weigh them, consider what they might instigate.

Lillian paused and searched over her shoulder. "What do you think I'm doing?"

He could defend himself, but bit back the urge as she took off at a clip that left him hurrying after her, ready to steady her if her ridiculous shoes got caught in the cobblestones.

He needed to focus on finding his family's treasure. Lillian needed someone who saw and understood the depths of her heart for this people and their suffering. And each time he left, he searched for his Opa's paintings and frankincense burner. Reichsbank branches dotted the country, and he didn't have enough clues.

However, he'd journey north to the Saxony region on the next trip.

Maybe he could find his way from there to Hannover. If that didn't work, he might need to change his strategy.

So far, he hadn't shared that he used the trips to also scout for his Opa's paintings. The details were sparse, but those paintings directed his current steps.

Only his family knew this collection had sparked his love of art. He wouldn't have pursued graduate studies in fine arts without the passion and interest that was birthed the first time he'd stood in the hallway of his grandparents' Bremerhaven home and noticed the vibrant colors on the wall. Then he'd discovered the power of marble transformed under the careful efforts of a master.

It had captivated him with an attraction that never waned.

Confirming art was returned to the correct museum or private owner it had been looted from was meaningful. But reuniting his family with even one painting or statue would carry more weight.

Chapter Nine

Tuesday, October 9

As CHARLES STRUGGLED to find a path into and then through Hannover, the devastation in and around the former city was so complete that he couldn't foresee how it would return to a functional town. The bombs' destruction had added extra layers of complexity to his attempts to reach the bank he hoped contained additional caches of art.

It was a relief to finally pull to a stop in front of the small building located within sight of the Rathaus. All around the bank, buildings stood in broken fragments, yet this one had sustained only superficial damage. The vagaries of what was destroyed and what survived in the new style of war. He strode through the scarred, heavy wooden doors into the bank's lobby and noted how the staff stood to stiff attention behind their gilded barriers.

There were hints of the old glory of this branch of the Reichsbank, but the gilding was fading, just as the marble floor had chips and missing tiles. The branch manager practically goose-stepped across the floor and stopped with a click of heels that sounded wooden as they clacked against the stone. "Sir, how may I assist?"

"I need to see your vault." Charles fingered the letter he carried with him but didn't pull it free.

"May I ask why?" He spoke the proper words, but a fire filled his eyes that suggested he didn't appreciate the request.

"I represent the Monuments and Fine Arts Division of the US Army, which has received information your bank holds works of art. Our job is to evaluate and return those to their rightful owners."

"And who says they are not held for those very individuals?"

"That is what I will confirm." He kept his arms loose at his sides while he made note of where other staff stood. "I can wait, but you will take me to the vault."

A man scurried up next to the manager and whispered in his ear, muffled and in a rapid German Charles couldn't decipher. A moment later the bank manager's frown deepened, but he gave a crisp nod. "This way."

Charles followed close on the short man's heels. While his suit coat was shiny from wear in places, the war hadn't been as hard on him as on many others, if his girth was any indication. Charles tried not to immediately dislike him, but it took effort.

When they reached the bank vault, it appeared small from the outside. Then the manager pulled out two keys, inserted them in the correct slots, and opened the door with a grunt. Inside stood a row of boxes on two walls. Along the longest wall, someone had installed a series of shelves and lined those with paintings and ceramics, a hodgepodge collected over lifetimes.

"Who deposited this here?" Charles kept his voice steady, knowing the answer at least in part. He made sure he always knew the answer so he could test the veracity of those he interacted with. It was a necessary approach he'd learned the hard way. When he led with what he knew, people often agreed rather than corrected bad information he'd received at another stage of the investigation. Worse was when he didn't know the information at all and had no way of confirming what they told him.

He wished Lillian had traveled with him, but she and the German staff back at the collection point continued the meticulous work of completing as much information as possible about each piece. While they worked, he'd evaluate this collection and ascertain whether to move it to Wiesbaden. They must have processed close to a hundred thousand items, and there was no end in sight.

"Herr Müeller."

"Can you be more precise?" At the man's blank expression, Charles firmed his stance and tone. "Which Müeller?"

"Johann."

The man might as well have claimed John Smith deposited the items.

"Come now. You are the bank manager and keep meticulous records. You'll need to grant me access to those now. Otherwise I'll requisition the contents of the vault, and you can send your Herr Müeller to Wiesbaden to collect the items when he returns with his receipt and key."

Color rose in the man's cheeks, and Charles noticed the frustration and anger rolling off him, a mirror of that building inside Charles. It didn't matter. Men like the manager had played critical roles in the looting and theft. If this man hadn't actively participated, he likely knew what had happened, and his silence now equaled participation.

Charles let the quiet stretch. It hadn't taken long to learn that silence was a powerful tool when trying to coerce self-important men to cooperate. Those active at high levels in the Nazi regime believed with certainty they were second to none.

It could be infuriating, or he could use that tendency to his advantage by reminding them they weren't in control anymore. Far from it. Now they lived and worked at the mercy of the victors, a reality that galled most.

The man licked his lips, beads of sweat forming at his temples. "This is no good."

"You're right. None of this is good." Charles crossed his arms and didn't waver.

The man ran his finger around his collar and then sagged. "The records are kept in an office. But you cannot tell anyone. If so, my life is forfeit."

"I doubt it's that dire."

"You are a fool if you think there is not still a structure and system. Those who break are punished." The man swallowed, his Adam's apple shifting up, then down.

"All I need are the records and key to this room." Then he could lock it while he identified the best strategy.

An hour later he took a sip from the pot of weak tea the manager had provided as he scanned the lists. His German was more than serviceable, but he liked to keep that knowledge to himself. Pretending he didn't understand half of what he saw and heard served him almost as well as silence. People got careless around him, but written German still tripped him up, words so long they often consisted of a series of smaller words jammed together.

He sketched out the timeline on a separate sheet of paper. The items in this vault had been deposited over a series of months. So far no records matched the time frame when his grandfather would have deposited items, but he wouldn't give up. Ownership would be cleaner if the items had arrived in one lot, clearly from one owner. Instead he couldn't know if what he saw represented multiple lots and owners. He would take the documentation to translate it with the aid of one of the native German speakers in Wiesbaden.

What to do with the paintings and other items? There were so many paintings, too many to examine here. He needed to get them to the Central Collecting Point to analyze and review, but he took a few minutes to review a couple stacks leaned against a wall. Someone had haphazardly stacked them and as flipped through them, he saw two paintings with wise men. Maybe in the time and space in Wiesbaden, one could belong to his family, even if the dates didn't line up precisely.

A catalog would provide an efficient record while he waited for a transport to relocate the items. They wouldn't fit in the too-small jeep. Yet, based on the attitude of the manager, he couldn't be sure the items would remain here. Guess he'd stay put until someone else could guard the vault.

⁓⚜⁓

Monday, October 15
Another week started, but Lillian found it hard to stay engaged in the steady effort. Yes, she understood at her core that each item was a treasure to someone, even if that entity was a museum. Lately she'd

reviewed items from the Berlin Museum that had languished in sub-optimal conditions in the Thuringian salt mine. From there the pieces had journeyed to Frankfurt, and then when Frankfurt ran short of room, the pieces were moved again to Wiesbaden.

She could only imagine the impact those moves had on the price-less pieces.

First, she needed to catalog and prepare the crates, then open them.

Tiny splinters riddled her hands from all the times she'd unpacked a crate on her own rather than wait for someone to complete that task.

Lillian arched her back and considered her next steps.

For every emptied crate, dozens more waited in this room alone. It took time to evaluate each piece and decide the right approach for restoration efforts. All she could do was identify the next and then the next, being precise and systematic in her approach. Losing even one item could mean the loss of a Monet or Rembrandt.

The idea terrified her.

Arnold Simmons, one of the American security men, poked his head into the room. "Everything all right in here, Captain?"

"Yes." She refocused with a tired smile. "I can't imagine you'd let anybody get by your station. Is Jake there now?"

"Yes, ma'am. Let us know if you need anything or see anything." He tipped his cap her direction.

She watched him leave, then took a moment to evaluate her prog-ress of the morning. Not enough. She'd forgo leaving for lunch and get another piece analyzed.

Hours slipped by as she worked, and everyone else must have left by the time she set aside the latest painting. The quiet settled in an oppressive blanket, like eyes were on her. She swallowed, pushing to her feet. A shadow in the corner shifted, and Lillian jumped, a little squeak escaping her lips. "What are you doing here?"

Charlie Weise leaned against the door, a box of documents in his hands. "Didn't want to disturb your deep thought."

"What do you have?" The box didn't appear overly heavy, but he also didn't seem eager to release it.

Charles moved into the crowded room, finding the path between the crates and set the box on the edge of the makeshift desk. "Most of the records from the Hannover Reichsbank." He rubbed the back of his neck and frowned.

Two lines formed between his brows, and she restrained herself from pressing them away. The man carried the weight of the lost stories, the lost lives, as if all taken was his personal burden.

"The manager wasn't forthcoming at first, but silence wore him down."

"Probably mixed with a well-placed threat."

He squirmed enough to confirm the truth in her words. "No violence."

She almost laughed at the idea he would use his fists to protect the art. He was more of a gentleman who used words to gain what he desired. "What do you find in a vault like that?"

"What do you mean?"

"What do you really see?" It was her turn to use silence to force his answer. It wasn't uncomfortable, just heavy in this room filled with stark canvas-and-paint witnesses.

He sighed, and there was a heavy weariness in the sound. "I see my Opa."

The words were simple, but there was a deep meaning behind them. "Did he . . . die?"

"Not that I know of . . . not yet." Charles leaned into the desk. "But each piece could represent the collection of a man who loved art. Or maybe it's an investment piece." He paused. "Or it belongs to a museum's collection, one obtained through proper channels without coercion or threats."

"That's a lot to see, to feel."

"Yes."

She wanted to lean close and wrap her arms around him, offer some comfort to this large man who took care of others and their valuables so well. She didn't know how he'd respond, so instead she stayed still, watched, felt.

"I'm supposed to find our family treasure." His words slipped into the silence, quiet yet steely.

"Treasure?"

"Opa left a large part of the family art collection when he fled with Oma. The family was quite wealthy before the end of World War One when they lost the family's shipping business." A wry grin twisted the side of his mouth. "I see so much irony in that loss through reparations. Now I'm one of the Allies making declarations about what happens."

"You're doing it carefully."

He shrugged off her words. "I think to the men and families on this side of another war, it feels the same as it did for my family."

"Did your grandparents move to the States then?"

"No." He shook his head. "They were determined to stay and help rebuild Germany. But they sent their son, my father, to the States for college and didn't let him come back. He grew the business on that side of the ocean, occasionally working out of Paris too. Sending him away ended up shielding him from the worst of the fighting in the Great War."

"And now you're here."

"With a letter asking me to find what Opa left behind. He took such pride in the collection. In the way he and Oma chose it piece by piece. It reflected their tastes and their unique combination of loves."

"I've toured homes that were filled in that way. It's beautiful."

"Yes. So when I walk into these vaults and mines, that's what I picture in my mind's eye. My grandparents, sitting in front of the fire, telling stories about their collection." He sighed, and his expression clouded. "I visited once when I was young. All I have is their notes on what they lost." He shoved his hands into his pockets. "That makes it hard to know what I'm searching for."

"The bank?" At his nod, she wanted to assure him. "Surely they've sent a list and it's still there."

"If so, it hasn't found me yet."

"Then I'd say you're on something of a fool's errand." The words sounded harsher than she'd meant. "I'm sorry."

"No, you're right. I want to find my grandparents' art, but that may be impossible."

"Tell me what you know, and I can watch for them too." She leaned closer to him, wanting to share his burden. "Let me help."

He studied her a moment, then tipped his chin. "I recently received a letter from my father with more information. One is a painting of the *Adoration of the Magi* painted by an Italian artist, Corrado Giaquinto. It's from the Rococo period and a good painting of the wise men." He relaxed and smiled briefly. "My Oma purchased it for their tenth anniversary because she loved the painting of the wise men."

The reason resonated in a moment. "Your last name."

"Yes."

"Then we will start with that one." She took notes as Charles described the painting and its provenance.

"It may have been sold if it was discovered."

"Any of the art could have been. That's why we're here." His quiet intensity made sense as she realized how personal this work was for him.

She realized that his story made it her work too.

Chapter Ten

Friday, October 19

THE HALLS WERE heavily shadowed when they exited the storage room, her heels clicking against the marble floor. Charles waited while Lillian fumbled through her pockets, searching for the key. He was about to reach for his copy when she pulled it free.

"I knew it was here." She sighed.

He imagined her eyes rolling in that way they did when she got frustrated.

"Why are you certain your family's collection landed in Hannover?"

"That's what my father thought." He shoved his hands into his pockets to keep from fidgeting. "Maybe he's wrong."

"Or you didn't find it yet."

"Maybe." But unlikely. He'd spent the days searching carefully before he left.

As they walked down the hallway to the stairs and then down to the main floor, all stayed eerily quiet. His arm brushed hers, but she didn't step away. Instead the air snapped slightly between them. He paused, and she stopped next to him.

"What?" Her question softly echoed in the large hallway.

"Nothing."

"You're acting odd."

He shook his head. "It's not that. I'm glad to be back, but I'm tired.

I keep imagining what it would be like to send a telegram home with the message I succeeded. But I can't."

"That doesn't mean you aren't a success."

"What?"

"You're engaged. You keep looking and fighting for your family. You just haven't found the right place yet."

He wished he could see her expression.

"You will. I know it."

"How can you be sure? I'm not."

"Because I know you. You don't quit, and you'll keep looking as long as you are here. That's what family does. That's what you do."

Her words plumbed the recesses of his heart. The places where he hadn't known he needed to be found. They were a gift he would cherish, and maybe he could live up to them. Words failed him, so he reached for her hand, and when she didn't tug it back, he eased it gently to his lips and kissed it. "Thank you."

Her inhale was soft, but he heard it, and it emboldened him. He tried to focus on the details of her face in the hazylight that lingered at the edges of the windows. But he could sense a sweetness in her response that nudged him closer. He ran a finger along her cheek to brush a loose strand of hair behind her ear. Her skin was as soft as he'd imagined, and he inched closer still.

Then she was reaching up on tiptoe and pulling his head down to hers. The kiss was sweet, intoxicating, everything he'd wanted to imagine but didn't allow himself to believe was possible. Why would she be interested in him? He was a man who didn't belong in the military, and he hadn't had a chance to create his civilian career yet. But all the uncertainty melted away in the light of the moment.

It wasn't until his lungs screamed for air that he eased back and placed his forehead against hers. "Wow."

He heard an answering word from her.

Then she slipped space between them, and he felt the absence of her closeness. He wanted more but realized it would push the boundaries too far. They were alone in a dark space, and he didn't want to mar the sweetness and purity of her kiss.

"I won't apologize, Lillian."

She took another step. "I'd be insulted if you did." Her words were breathless and thready. "I don't run around kissing men."

"I didn't think you did." He wanted to believe something real grew between them. But he held those words inside. If he spoke them now, he would rush the process and force unnecessary pressure into the space here between them. Instead he wanted to capture the moment, frame it with a simple yet rich wood that would seal this like a canvas between them forever.

Lillian took another step back, and he let her. Maybe this was like art where white space allowed the viewer to appreciate all the artist created. Crowd too much in and perspective disappeared because the patron didn't know where to look.

Similarly, crowding Lillian wouldn't win his case.

"We should slip out of here before Klaus hunts for us." Charles appreciated the German night-security man who usually made steady rounds. Klaus preferred the stillness of the night and the isolation from others but also didn't appreciate company in his domain. So long as nothing disappeared, all was good.

"We should." Lillian gestured down the hallway. "I'm surprised we haven't seen him."

"I am too." In fact he should have stopped by to harass them to leave. "Maybe he's delayed."

"The day shift wouldn't leave before he arrived."

"True." They walked in silence to the doors that led to the rotunda. The security personnel controlled all access to and from the building from that point. With a tall, barbed wire fence surrounding the building as well as multiple teams of security during the day, the building appeared secure. At least it did until the security guard was absent. Charles turned the knob on the door, but it didn't budge. Then he shoved against it. Nothing.

"Can't you open it?"

Charles thrust against it again, and nothing happened. "Nope."

She edged around him and tried it with no more success than he'd had. All she got for her efforts was a sore shoulder, and she rubbed it. "What should we do?"

"Wait until Klaus comes through. He must not realize we're here. Might be on rounds."

"Do they normally lock the doors?"

Charles shrugged. "I don't make a habit of staying this late without anyone knowing."

"Why wouldn't he confirm everyone had left?" She sucked in a breath, then let it out in a rush, obviously trying to calm herself. "He'll get here." She searched the lengthening shadows as less sunlight entered through the windows. "What do we do while we wait?"

"We could process a couple more paintings." Not that he wanted to, but it would keep her distracted.

She straightened. "Or we could hunt for your grandparents' painting." She spun slowly, as if taking in the rooms fanning off the hallway. "There are several collection rooms along here I haven't entered yet."

"And you think this is the time?"

"Why not?" She waggled her eyebrows as she grinned at him. "Do you have something else you'd rather do?"

Better not answer that, because he imagined a better use of their time would be a repeat of the kiss they'd shared. That sounded like an excellent way to while away however long they remained trapped. Now to convince her. "Come here."

She slid back with another grin and then walked to the first door on the left. "What's in here?"

"No idea. Crates. Paintings."

"Very funny." She opened the door. "Us."

He frowned as it sank in that the door hadn't been locked. "Wait. Did you have the key for this room?"

She froze and then stumbled to the wall where she fumbled along it for the lights. "No." She frowned and flipped the light switch. "It should have been locked."

"Yes." He entered the room and gave it a slow scan. "Nothing appears out of place."

"I agree." Lillian drifted around moving different crates as if searching for evidence someone had tampered with them. "Maybe someone was sloppy. Forgot to lock up."

"How do you forget when surrounded by all this?" He gestured to include all the items crammed into the space.

"I couldn't."

Charles knew Lillian meant it. She was as conscientious about protecting the art as anyone. "Let's check the other rooms along the corridor."

It only took a few minutes to test the doors on each side and discover no one had locked any. This moved from an accident to a serious breach in security.

"We've got to let Farmer know."

Lillian nodded. "There's no way he would approve this."

"Let's see if anything is missing."

They spent the next hours side by side moving through the rooms, attempting to determine whether anything was out of place. Finally Charles had to admit defeat. No one could tell if anything had disappeared without comparing the cards with the contents of each room. "We'll have to wait to confirm."

Lillian stifled a yawn and then pressed a hand to her stomach as it growled. "I'm surprised Klaus hasn't come by yet. Do you think something is wrong?"

"It has to be." Nothing else could explain it. Either Klaus was sick, hurt, or bribed. "We have to be more careful. We've trusted everyone when there's a fortune in art and other items here. We're surrounded by a city filled with the destitute and refugees. What did we think? No one would steal?"

Charles paced, when Lillian suddenly stepped forward and tipped up until her lips met his. Everything else he planned to say evaporated on the haze of her touch and the sweetness of her kiss.

⁓⁓⁕⁓⁓

Lillian knew the moment Charles let go of his concerns and focused on her. Funny how quickly she could pick up the nuances. His arms wrapped around her, and she found herself trapped in the best way. Still she needed to end the kiss before they lost their heads. Maybe she already had, at the rate she'd initiated a kiss.

She eased back, her hands still on either side of his face, roughened by his stubble.

Charles's gaze was dazed, and he blinked. "What was that?"

"I decided it was my turn to steal something."

He blinked again and leaned closer. "I like the way you think."

She giggled, then wiggled from his hold. "Time to focus, soldier."

"I'm not really a soldier. I just play one in this uniform."

"To this art and its owners, you're the last line of defense. They will be grateful when you reunite them with their property."

The sound of a key turning in a lock had her attempting to slip into the hallway, but Charles tugged her back into the room.

"Wait. We don't know that it's a friend on the other side."

"Why wouldn't it be?" Then her thoughts caught up with the unlocked doors. "You think someone might have gotten the keys from Klaus."

Charles shrugged, but his eyes remained focused on the door. "Maybe."

"All right." She searched around them. "Won't we be trapped if we stay in here?"

"It's a risk."

Yes, it was, but she didn't see many other options. All the rooms were like this one, with high windows but no exterior doors. It made sense since the building had been a museum. Controlled ingress and egress restricted the ways someone could steal even as it limited escape paths.

She swallowed and nodded. "What do you need me to do?"

"Stay quiet and in the shadows." His head pivoted as if assessing options. There weren't any good ones if whoever was out there wasn't a friend. "It's probably Klaus."

"True. People left and didn't realize we were here." She sensed him shift and then they were sharing the same space, breathing the same air. Her breath hitched before it took off at the pace of Monet's paint strokes. "But just in case, we need to appear innocent."

She felt more than saw him lean closer, and she couldn't move, didn't want to move. Instead she tipped up on tiptoe, and their noses collided. She giggled, embarrassed at possibly misreading the situation. Then his lips found hers again, and she forgot all about the unknown person at the hallway door, barely registered the sound of footsteps in the hall, forgot whoever it was would come straight to their room since it was the only opened door off the entryway, and then startled as a beam of light slid across the back of Charles's head and her face.

"Vat have ve here?" There was music and a touch of enjoyment in Klaus's words.

Charles eased back but didn't turn toward Klaus. "Where have you been? We were locked in here and making the best use of the time."

Klaus hit the light switch, and in the flood of light, Lillian caught Charles's slow wink.

And in that motion she wondered. Did anything that transpired between them matter to him? Or was she just a distraction while they waited for someone to come find them?

The magic of the moment evaporated like a Rembrandt stolen yet again from a wall in a castle, leaving her with a hollow feeling.

Chapter Eleven

Late October

Ever since Klaus stumbled on them in that gallery, Lillian had created distance with Charles. It took the man long enough to make his rounds, but he'd been as unapologetic as Charles, only for different reasons. While Charles had no desire to apologize for the magic of the kiss, Klaus felt no need to explain his long absence other than an outside disturbance had kept him from the inside rounds. And then he'd found the two in their embrace, something that his continued smirks hinted at each time he saw either. Lillian had seemed to appreciate the close moment until Klaus arrived. What had changed Charles couldn't identify.

Then Farmer sent him to check out more possible caches, and she'd stayed behind, the fruit of her methodical efforts visible each time he returned.

At the rate the items poured in, it would take years to process them all.

Another letter had arrived from home with more information on where Opa had deposited the Weise treasures, but Charles had yet to find anything. Nothing was located in the Hannover bank, and each additional search was more fruitless than the last. At every new location, he searched for two things: first the general items, and second his family's.

It tore him in two directions but also kept the importance of the work in front of him. Other families couldn't hunt for what others took in the chaos of a fallen government and system. But the United States government had seen fit to assign a few men and women to the important job, and he would do his utmost to do all he could.

Each night he fell into his bed in the barracks, exhausted yet unsure he'd done enough. Work would always exist, more than he could finish. The challenge came in doing his best as if he worked unto the Lord and then letting himself rest for the night before doing it all over again. He needed the sleep that came with the peace of knowing he'd done his best.

In early November he worked in a room near Lillian and a couple of their German colleagues, when he stood to arch his back. He had to open the crates remaining in this room before he could examine the contents, complete cards, and move the items to the correct staging room before the latest shipment arrived the next morning. It would require a long day of nonstop work.

Dorothea, one of the recent young German art historians hired to help process the crates more effectively, joined him with a stack of blank cards in hand. The prim woman was thin around the edges, a carryover of the rationing and shortages that remained unabated. Still, she was serious and reliably focused. "Need help?"

"Definitely." He took the crowbar and pried open the next crate. When he slid out the painting, she gasped, and he barely held one back himself.

He set the crowbar down and then eased the painting from the straw surrounding it.

"I hope it's not harmed." The words were a reverent breath from Dorothea.

"Me too." Charles carefully set the painting on the ground next to the crate and let the vibrant colors and the size of the work settle over him. "Raphael?"

"It is possible." She pointed at the gold leaf worked into the painting. "It is stunning and has his signature style. The faces match one of his."

The painting was of a Madonna with one young boy on her lap

and another leaning into her side, probably Jesus and John the Baptist. It was arranged in Raphael's typical triangle with the Madonna creating the height, Jesus at the center, and John the Baptist on one side. The colors stayed vibrant, and Charles fought the need to touch the paint, confirm it was real and not a mirage.

Lillian walked over to join them and inhaled sharply when she stopped in front of the painting. "Oh my." She stood as if frozen in a painting herself as she took in the art. "What a find. Maybe the *Alba Madonna*?" Lillian sounded sure but made the statement a question.

He considered her question. "That would certainly fit, but I think that particular painting was gifted to the Smithsonian National Gallery of Art a few years ago." A gift of the Mellon Trust out of Pittsburgh, if he was correct. "That doesn't change the fact that this painting needs our protection while it's here. No one will examine it and miss Raphael's touch."

Nothing had come of his off-the-record investigation into the night he and Lillian had been locked inside the museum. He could find nothing to confirm his suspicion someone was or planned to steal items. Without a clue, he could do little.

"It is exquisite." Dorothea reached out but kept from touching it. She seemed almost reverent as she moved closer and examined the brushstrokes.

"Was there a packing slip?" Lillian searched through the straw and other packing materials.

"No."

"I will search." Dorothea moved toward the box, her skirt swishing around her legs as she moved. "Would you like to help me?" She gestured toward Charles, ignoring Lillian.

❦

Lillian gritted her teeth against the frustration of watching Dorothea flirt with Charles. She knew the woman didn't mean anything by it, but what would Lillian do when Charles succumbed to the woman's charm? It was only a matter of time. The woman flirted with an edge born of desperation.

Somehow Charles didn't fall into the art student's arms.

Lillian would take it as a small favor as she forced her attention away from the painting. "Let's see what else we can uncover. We can mark the card as a possible Raphael for now and hunt for the painting's title and details later."

"A sound strategy." But there was something in the way Charles watched her that made her think he'd read part of her thoughts, an idea she despised.

She should be practically a mystery to him. Instead she was well aware of all the ways she wanted to know so much more about him. Why this dive into art? Why stay in Germany when he could go far away from the country that had harmed his family and its legacy?

Instead shyness overwhelmed her around him. He hadn't mentioned their shared kisses since they'd escaped the locked museum. If anything he was unaffected, while her daydreams were filled with the moments, reliving them over and over. The memories were the sweetest sort of torture.

"Should we create a more secure room for items like this?" If it proved to be a Raphael, the painting's worth could surpass her ability to calculate, especially in a country filled with desperate survivors. "If word gets out we have treasures like this . . ."

"Farmer wants to create a display of sorts. Start turning this building back into a museum. Help people remember what it's like to be part of something bigger than our immediate problems."

Dorothea wrinkled her nose. "Art does not replace the need for food in our stomachs."

"True, but there is value to acknowledging we are more than our most basic needs."

Dorothea flicked her hand, as if to dismiss his words. "Not at times like we live in."

An image of the children she still saw near her apartment flitted through Lillian's mind. "Dorothea, how can we help? Is there something we can do to change that equation of harm?"

"What do you mean?"

Lillian pictured one small girl she saw often yet who refused to draw near. "I pass the same orphans most days, and I want to do more than hand out rolls when I can. They won't let me get near them to help."

"You are the conquerors."

"I'm not."

"To them you are." The words landed heavy and harsh.

Lillian swallowed against the desire to fight, but if that was how the children saw her and the other Americans, they would stay away. "What can I do to change that?"

"The children do not understand that you have freed us in one sense. Instead they know the loss of brothers and fathers. Many mourn close family killed by the bombs. That does not make you saviors but oppressors."

"I'm so sorry."

"Wiesbaden was relatively fortunate. Bombs obliterated many cities." The words sounded so harsh in her guttural German tones, but that didn't hide the truth of what Dorothea said.

"We weren't perfect."

"It was war." It wasn't forgiveness or even an acknowledgment, but the bald truth.

"Yes, but I want to help."

"Cannot be done." There was a tightness to Dorothea's face, and she couldn't stand straighter.

Lillian blew out a hard breath. "I can't accept that. There are children on the other side of this door who need help. I can be part of that. We all can, but we need help."

Dorothea considered her but remained quiet. Lillian's gaze traveled to where Charles stood quietly watching the interaction. He raised his eyebrows as their gazes connected, but didn't say anything. She sighed and returned to the common ground of art. "Charles, where do you want the painting?"

He stepped forward, accepting the change in topic. As he did, Dorothea disappeared out the door.

Lillian sighed, and her shoulders collapsed. "That didn't go well."

"It could have been worse."

"How?"

"She could have punched you."

Lillian gave a shaky laugh. "I guess that qualifies as worse."

"I bet Dorothea will come back in a day or so with ideas. She's upset now, but she also sees what you see, only more personally." Charles slid the painting back into its crate, then studied Lillian. "Your instinct to help is good, but we have no idea what it's like for those who survived here."

"I know you're right." Lillian leaned against the wall and tried to shake off the heaviness of getting it wrong. It mattered too much not to keep trying. "They need so much that I don't know where to start."

"They also need the opportunity to help themselves."

"So we do nothing?"

"I'm not saying that." He sighed and seemed to marshal his thoughts. "As you know, my family is German. It's a proud people humbled after years of being terrorized from within. That's a dynamic you cannot understand."

"I'm tired of people telling me that." It was one thing to know it as a fact and another to have it constantly explained. "I'm up to the task and know more than you give me credit for."

"I know you do. I've worked with you the last three months."

An expression she couldn't identify swooped across his face before it disappeared. One that suggested he wanted to say more but resisted.

"Have you prayed about how to approach this?"

"No." And she should. She might not know the right way to show love and respect to the German orphans, but God knew exactly what would serve them best. "Thank you for the reminder."

"Actually, let's pray now." He wrapped his warm hand over hers. His deep voice echoed in the room as he prayed for wisdom and a heart that acted from pure motives.

When he finished, she couldn't help but smile at the peace that filled her. As much as she was concerned about the suffering of those living in postwar Germany, God saw them and loved them more deeply than she ever could.

"Thank you."

His smile warmed her before he turned back to the painting. "My pleasure. Let's get this painting to Farmer so he can decide what to do with it. I have a feeling as we work, God will give you an idea."

She hoped so. But as she returned her attention to the work in front of her, she realized she had a new dilemma. A tenuous connection to Lieutenant Weise had blossomed that had nothing to do with their kisses, and it had her racing for cover.

She shouldn't want the growing closeness. Not when she wasn't sure of his motives and within weeks or months, they'd go their separate ways. They'd have to, wouldn't they?

Chapter Twelve

THE DAYS WERE colder, daylight shorter as Charles made his way back to the Wiesbaden Collecting Point later that week. November had brought with it fewer trips to suspected caches. Instead they focused on what had already arrived. So many collections sat in banks and other locations waiting to replace what filled the CP building.

Each day required a dance of diligence and pushing back against the pressure to send works off without a thorough search.

Doing the research right took time.

Farmer felt the pressure of expiring time and transferred that pressure to Charles and his team. Lillian kept her head down working through the books to track ownership. Her speed built as she identified what information could be found in each resource. But at this rate it would take the rest of the century to process the one hundred thousand items. That didn't count all the others still spread around the country.

Dorothea and a couple other Germans worked on the superficial restoration of pieces that had been damaged in transit or where they'd been stored. Deeper work would wait for better conditions and more skilled technicians. At least they could make the simple stabilizing repairs before the pieces returned to their owners or collections.

The pounding of a hammer against wood, likely a frame that had been damaged, greeted Charles as he entered the rotunda. After a quiet greeting to Arnold and Jake on the security team, he proceeded to the hallway of rooms. They had made progress because they'd emptied one room. A second was almost sorted, and Lillian had moved on to a third. He stuck his head in each room until he located her.

She sat on the floor in front of a four-high stack of crates. It was one of many, each stamped with a *43* and another set of numbers followed by a few letters. Each helped them trace through the paperwork where the items had shipped from so they could return the works if the provenance was clean. In the process some might be placed on the empty racks that lined the walls behind the stacks. It was slow and tedious work, and she was already deep into an evaluation of a small painting that appeared Rococo.

"I see you beat me in again."

She flashed a big grin, ready to spar over their friendly competition. "What do they do on base? Keep you locked in your barracks?"

"Not normally. Guess I'll have to set my alarm earlier."

"You could try." She gestured to the painting before her. It was a piece that could have been part of a larger altarpiece, appearing to have a depiction of John the Baptist in the wilderness. "This one just needs a dusting and tightening of the frame." She held up the card. "I've made the note here."

"Which shipment?"

"The one from the Reichsbank you visited in Hannover."

Charles frowned. "That got mixed in here?"

"Looks like it."

"Hmmm." He moved farther into the room and read the labels on crates.

"Can I help you find something?" Lillian's voice held concern as she watched him.

"I don't know. I have a niggling thought I saw something when I was in the vault."

"What? I can help you search if I know what we're hunting for."

"It's probably crazy, but maybe it's one of Opa's paintings." He watched her reaction and flinched when her eyes widened and mouth opened. "Told you it was crazy."

"I'm just surprised you never mentioned that."

"I wasn't sure." He shrugged and leaned closer to another crate. "I also thought we'd sorted everything from there."

"I did too, but this one got misplaced." She watched him another moment. "Which painting did you see?"

"The *Adoration of the Magi*. The second letter from my dad gave more information, but with so many paintings on the subject it was hard to know what to look for. This latest letter gave me an additional clue."

She rolled her eyes. "There's only a zillion of those." She rubbed her forehead as she peered at the stacks. "I never understood how many people painted that configuration."

"All with a slight difference."

"Sometimes very slight." She glanced around. "So we need to pursue that painting. How will you know it's his?"

It was a good question and one he'd kept close to his vest because once others knew about it, one key to reclaiming the family collection would disappear. Still, he needed to trust someone, and why not Lillian? "My Opa snuck his initials onto the back canvas of each piece he acquired."

"He wasn't concerned it would devalue the work?"

"No, because he used a light paint that would be hard to see without knowing exactly where he applied it."

"So where do I search?"

"When you find a painting of the three magi, let me know." He wasn't ready to give the full secret away.

Her intent expression let him know she saw right through him. "Someday you'll trust me, Charles Weise."

"So we're back to first names?"

"Until you do something else to frustrate me."

"All I want to do is sweep you up and kiss you until you can't remember my name." He stilled, unsure where the words had come from and how she'd receive them. What he did know was it sounded like a great idea, one that grew on him with each second of shocked silence.

Then the corner of her lips quirked up.

After all this time and his holding her at arm's length, should she lay into Charles or play along with his words?

She would have slapped him except she'd noticed the way his eyes flared as he spoke, as if he hadn't realized those words would escape. That bought him a few moments of grace while she decided how to handle him.

"I don't think you want to do that here." She sighed. "I'm not sure I do either. What happened, Charlie? Was I a terrible date?"

"That's what you think?"

"What else could I think? Any time I kiss you, you disappear inside a shell. It's not exactly confidence boosting."

He reached for her hand, and she paused, considering whether to take it. But when he wiggled his fingers in a come-here motion, she laughed and took it. He tugged her to her feet, and then she examined him, the electricity zinging from his hand, down her arm, and straight to her heart.

"That's the opposite of what I want you to think." He tugged her closer. "If I don't mention our kisses, it's because I don't want to pressure you." He leaned nearer until his lips floated above hers. "I'd like nothing more than repeating them often."

"Really?" Her muscles relaxed, and she fought to stay standing.

"Absolutely." He closed the distance. "Like this." And then he kissed her in a way that let her know he very much appreciated her.

After a moment she pulled back to catch her breath. "How do you do that?" The words whispered from her.

He quirked an eyebrow. "Do what?"

"Make the world stop so that all that exists is us . . . and a horde of John the Baptists?"

His eyes twinkled. "Are you saying I affect you?"

She gave him what she hoped was a sultry smile. "Yes, but maybe we should step back. After all, we've got John the Baptist watching everything."

He cocked his head, as if studying the painting. "He's too pint sized to understand what we're doing."

She frowned and tried to follow what he'd found. Then she broke out laughing as she noticed the image of the Madonna with a chubby toddler Jesus and an even chubbier John the Baptist. "Not that one. I meant the one where he's coming out of the wilderness."

"There are so many, it's easy to get confused."

"Yes." She blinked in a feeble attempt to break the connection and return to some normalcy. Then she decided she didn't want to. She wanted to let herself experience this moment and each emotion. Each nerve ending zinged, so alive, and she didn't want to do anything to change that. "Don't let it go to your head."

He laughed, and the whisper of it caressed her cheek. He leaned closer but stilled as the sound of heels clicking on the marble in the hallway reached them. "Grrr. Really?"

Lillian acknowledged a moment of relief even as it swirled with disappointment. "Later."

"I'm going to hold you to that."

"All right."

Charles stepped back, and she recognized each inch of distance. She might have to strangle whoever had decided now was a good time to make their presence known. Then Dorothea entered, and her pale face made Lillian forget any frustration she'd been feeling.

"What's wrong, Dorothea?"

"Fever, maybe typhoid. It is sweeping through the street children."

Charles stilled and then focused fully on the distraught woman. "Fever?" At her nod, he continued. "Stomach issues?"

"Yes. Other cities have had similar outbreaks as the people scavenged for food."

"How many?"

She shuddered. "I do not know. Too many." She twisted her hands as her gaze darted around the space. "We must do something. They are so young."

Lillian watched him. "We have to help."

He nodded, a resolute set to his jaw. "There is help. Let me go talk to the base doctor. I've heard of some success with penicillin."

"*Was ist das?*"

"A drug that fights infections. It has saved many lives."

"Ve do not have it here."

"Maybe not. But we do." Charles adjusted his cap and headed for the door. "Should I bring him here?"

The woman dipped her head. "There are so many."

Lillian walked to the woman and placed a hand on her arm. "I'm so sorry. What can I do?"

"They are so small." A tear trickled down the woman's usually stoic face. "We have survived so much for this." Her hands waved in the air. "We cannot take more."

"I understand." Lillian tried to think about what could be done when someone was sick with typhoid fever, but it wasn't an illness anyone close to her had suffered. "What will the children need?"

"Clean clothes. Easy food and liquids."

"Good. We will work on that today. Surely we can find clothes and food."

The woman didn't appear convinced, but she followed Lillian to the rotunda. They collected the other staff as they went, and soon Dorothea spouted orders in German, leaving Lillian wishing she understood more of the language. Then the women headed to the apartment complex that housed the American women.

"My roommates will want to help."

And the nurses did. They canvassed the complex, collecting items while Lillian and Dorothea located a vehicle they could drive to the children's location. After filling it with the early collections, Lillian drove, certain she'd never locate it on her own. There were so many turns and restarts when a road was too blocked to navigate. Eventually Dorothea got them close enough to their destination, and together the women cleared the vehicle of its load of clothing, bread, and towels.

A foul smell greeted them as they neared. Children lay on ragged blankets in different corners of a half-demolished building. One wall had collapsed, but the wall had been partially rebuilt from the bricks and debris. It would provide some protection from the elements, but it was still frigid in the open-air space. A cold fire ring sat in the middle of the ruins. If wood could be obtained, the children would at least have a fire. But the conditions hurt Lillian's heart.

A disconcerted shuffling filtered through the children, and Lillian straightened, prepared to protect them. But it was Charles and another man in uniform. His insignia indicated he was part of the medical corps. Then Lillian noticed several others wearing the same insignia, but different rank, filtering in. Charles hadn't brought only one person to help. As she noted Dorothea's face, Lillian realized this could be the beginning of better relationships with the orphans. Then she rolled up her sleeves and began to help.

The days passed with twice-a-day visits to the orphans. All but one recovered. That poor little girl had been too weakened to recover even when moved to the base clinic. Lillian tried to console herself with the number of children they had helped and the fact that they now smiled when they saw Lillian or the soldiers. Many soldiers had taken on the role of helping, as if informally adopting the band of children. The building had been shored up, and new blankets appeared as well as wood to keep a fire going through the coldest nights.

Lillian rubbed her eyes as she saw all that still needed to happen to protect the children. "We should do more."

Charles shook his head. He'd been a constant presence here too. "The Germans need to care for their own. We got them through the crisis. Now we need to let them do what they can, knowing we can step in and help if needed."

"Waiting for them to do something led to this crisis. And that little girl's death." She cleared her throat against the sudden onslaught of tears.

"But now they know there's a problem." He took her hand and waited until she met his eyes. "We won't abandon the children, but you know we can't be here forever. They need to find help in their permanent community."

Of course he was right. She leaned her head into his chest, smiling through the heaviness over this soldier who loved art and children nearly as much as she did.

Chapter Thirteen

Wednesday, November 21

THE NIGHT DESCENDED quickly as the calendar turned toward the end of November. Charles was still at work sorting art the day before Thanksgiving. If he was back in the States with family, he'd enjoy turkey with all the fixings. But this year he was grateful for more time to search. He'd cleared four of the rooms filled with crates but had yet to return to the collection he'd recovered from the Reichsbank. It frustrated him to know the painting was here somewhere or had been stolen. There was no way to be sure it wasn't lounging in some corner, and that made it hard to know whether to keep searching or stop.

Another letter from his father included a short note from Opa, who was recovering from his illness. The man was determined to learn the fate of his collection, and Charles couldn't blame him. The collection had been carefully curated and was not only a legacy to be passed down but held the memories of a lifetime.

Charles dreamed of laying out the collection and hearing his grandparents tell the significance of each one.

While he had seen photos and heard some of the stories, he wished he could have seen them hanging on the walls and sitting on shelves as an adult. It would have made his current job easier.

Lillian always offered to stay late to help his personal search, but he could see the fatigue that had settled into lines around her eyes and the slouch of her shoulders. She needed the chance to get out of the dark hallways before the light faded to black. So she arrived early and he stayed late, with a quick kiss as she left for the night. That rhythm also gave him a chance to test the boundaries of security and make sure the art stayed protected as the value of it grew.

He didn't mean to be paranoid, but he didn't want anyone's collection, let alone his grandparents', walking out the door because of lax protection.

He rubbed his eyes as he entered a new room and then searched around the crates. There were so many.

At a noise, he turned.

Captain Farmer stood behind him. "Still here, Lieutenant?"

"Yes, sir."

"I've noticed you put in a lot of late nights."

"Yes, sir."

"Any particular reason?" Farmer's gaze searched his, as if trying to determine whether Weise was on the up and up.

Charles shifted his feet. "Yes, sir."

After a minute's silence, Farmer cleared his throat. "And that reason?"

Should he tell?

"Lieutenant?"

It was Charles's turn to clear his throat. "My grandparents escaped Germany in 1938. They left their art collection behind. Opa is eighty-five and wants to know if his collection is still where he can reclaim it. It's his legacy, sir."

"Understood." Farmer considered him, then swept the room with his gaze. "You'll let me know if you find it. And before you do anything about it."

It wasn't a question, but the man seemed to wait for a response. "Yes, sir."

"All right. Then we're clear." Farmer didn't turn and leave as Charles expected. Instead he stayed frozen in place by a weight of some sort.

"Everything all right, sir?"

"I'm not sure." He shook his head. "Seen anything that still bothers you about security?"

"Not since the night I was locked in." Charles shrugged. "It's one reason I stay late. It's easier to make sure everything is locked tight."

"Understood." Farmer knocked the top of a crate. "These will still be here in the morning. You should call it a night. I need you sharp and not bleary eyed. There will be plenty of work for tomorrow regardless of how long you stay."

"If it's all the same, I'd like to stay a bit longer. I have a system."

"Good night then." With a curt nod, Farmer left.

Charles watched him leave and knew he didn't want the man's job. There was such responsibility on his shoulders. It would be a lot to carry.

He picked up the crowbar and slid it against the lid of the next crate. Straw surrounded several paintings inside. He carefully pulled out the first painting, searched for his grandpa's mark, and then set it aside. When he reached the last painting, his stomach grumbled. It was time to leave and rest before starting again tomorrow. Then he saw it. He squinted. Could it really be?

⚜

The hint of dawn was streaking the sky as Lillian reached the museum. It was depressing to get to work while it was dark and leave when it was also dark. She couldn't get used to such oppressive darkness.

But the quiet hour before the others arrived allowed her to triple-check her work from the prior day and confirm that everything was ready for the new one. This morning a light glowed in the room where they were supposed to start. She frowned. Electricity wasn't stable enough, even with the generator, to leave lights on. Maybe she should go back and get a security officer. Then she peeked around the corner and stopped.

Charles stood with his back to the door, oblivious to her arrival. His hands rested on his hips, and his head was tilted to the side as he examined a row of paintings.

"Did you work all night?"

He pivoted, hand traveling to the gun she rarely noticed. She put her hands in the air.

"I'm a friend, remember? A really good friend, based on our kisses." She was proud of herself for not blushing as she tried to tease him into relaxing.

His smile was slow to build, but she experienced it to her toes as warmth spread through her. If she wasn't careful, she would fall in love with a man who had never declared any specific interest. She took a step back, needing to create a little space as the intensity in his gaze grew as it moved to her lips. Then his attention returned to her eyes.

"I found them."

She cocked her head at the change in subject. "Found what?"

"Some of our legacy."

"Really." She reversed course and focused on the paintings. "These?"

"Yes. There may be more, but these are from Opa's collection."

She studied the small paintings. "They're beautiful."

"They are." He pointed at the first one on the left, a small parklike scene with a few people in Victorian dress. "That's a small Pissaro. Oma liked the colors. She claimed it reminded her of the springtime park where they met, so Opa got it for her."

"It definitely has his pointillism style. It's so peaceful."

She could sense the energy surging through him as he bounced on his toes. "Of all the paintings, Oma will be grateful to have this one back. The next is probably a Vermeer, based on the darker colors that make it from the Dutch school. But the context and subject line up with his work."

"A milkmaid?"

"Likely. The pitcher might hold milk, and she's definitely working class."

"It's peaceful. Both have a pastoral feel to them."

He nodded. "It would make sense if that is what my grandparents were building the collection around. The last one is this." He pointed to a painting that took her breath.

"The *Adoration of the Magi.*"

"Yes. This is quite the anniversary gift, don't you think? It's one of the first works my grandparents acquired, and my dad mentioned it. Said it was something of an inside joke because of our last name and the subject matter. We were wise, but we also needed to keep our eyes fixed adoringly on the Christ, grown and risen." He smiled, as if participating in the conversation again. "I didn't think I'd ever see it."

"I love when there's intention behind the purchase."

"Opa was a key part of the family that created a massive shipping company. That takes a certain ability. The end of the prior war changed that, but he'd transitioned the family into art and other investments." He shrugged. "We might not have been the Vanderbilts or Carnegies, but we have more than enough and have created too many jobs to count."

"Is that why you turned to art?"

He frowned. "What do you mean?"

"You didn't need to generate wealth, so you could turn to passions and interests."

"Maybe. I hadn't thought of it that way, but my parents had the leisure to take me to the museums along the East Coast. I fell in love and wanted to create my own art that might reside in a museum one day. My other option is to join my uncle at his art gallery in New York City. I'm here instead." He studied the three paintings. "Now if we can find the frankincense burner."

"Any idea what that looks like?"

"Small and Egyptian? If I know Opa, he'll have marked it someway that doesn't damage it."

"Why didn't your grandparents send their art to New York?" She'd wondered, since the family had a foothold in the art world. "It should have been easy."

"The Nazis wouldn't allow it. By the time my grandparents left, they were lucky to escape with what they could carry in a suitcase. If the authorities caught someone taking valuables, they could arrest them and end any hope of escape." He took a step back, as if examining the array of paintings. "That's why Opa deposited them in a bank."

Lillian knelt to examine the paintings more closely. "I'm glad you found them. Now what will you do?"

"Farmer made me promise to show them to him before I did anything." He rubbed the back of his neck. "I'll need to prove they're ours. He won't, and shouldn't, let me take them without proving ownership. The letters and marks will have to be enough."

"Enough for what?" Farmer's voice had her turning to see him in the doorway.

<hr />

Charles didn't want to have this conversation now. He'd wanted time to marshal the facts and create a compelling case for claiming the paintings for his family. Then he'd figure out transportation.

Lillian eyed the two men, then stood and moved away from the art. "I'll leave the two of you to talk." She stopped by Charles, and he warmed under the power of her smile and the excitement in her eyes. "Congratulations. It's incredible that you located them."

And that was the crux of it. It truly was incredible that out of all the paintings he'd handled, he'd found a few of his family's.

"Your grandpa will be so excited." Then she moved past him, pausing in front of Farmer. "Sir, I'll get started in the next room unless you need me elsewhere?"

"That will be fine."

Charles was too tired and needed sleep and a meal. Then he could convince Farmer to let him ship the paintings home.

Once Lillian had left the room, Farmer sank onto the edge of a crate.

"Everything all right, sir?"

"I've gotten word we're supposed to select two hundred items to send to the United States." The man appeared exhausted. "I'm not sure how to stop this, but we have to."

"What do you mean 'send' to the US?"

"The government wants to ensure their safety."

"Isn't that looting? Sir?"

"It sure smells like it." Farmer focused on the unopened crates. "I've called a meeting of other Monuments officers so we can respond. I don't know that it will be enough."

"At least you're trying." He studied his family's treasures. "Sir, those belong to my family. When my grandparents fled Germany in 1938, they had to leave their art collection behind. I discovered those during the night. There may be more here." He wanted to take them and run so he could hide them in a safe place. "That art represents my grandparents, not some government, US or German. 'Protecting' art is what led to the theft of so many families' collections. Museums hid their collections as well." He tried to bite back the anger that crept into his words but couldn't fully rein it in. "We're no different if we send art home."

Five days later the larger contingent of Monuments officers agreed with Charles and Farmer as they drafted and signed a document, called the Wiesbaden Manifesto, urging the government to leave the works where they were.

But it wasn't enough. Even though it was signed by 32 of the 335 Monuments officers in Europe at the time, Charles and Lillian were part of the team at Wiesbaden ordered to pack up some German art for shipment to the United States. Arguments that it went against the policy of the US and other Allies didn't matter.

They'd boxed up 202 paintings for transport to the United States. The reason? Protection. After the boxes shipped, several German employees stayed away for a few days in a form of protest. All that kept morale above a zero was the hope that the government would receive enough resistance to not repeat the removal. Even if someone believed it was for the protection of the art, it felt too much like what the Nazis had done to not be looting.

That left Charles wanting to wash his hands of the whole affair and return home, but he still had art to locate and reclaim for his family. One night Lillian asked him to stop working when she did so they could have dinner together.

"All right. Let me finish this box first."

"I'll help." Lillian sifted through one end of the box while he sifted the other. She pulled out a small statue of a dancer and set it aside reverently. "Do you think this could be a Degas?"

Charles frowned as he picked up the piece. "Maybe, but that would be quite a find."

She leafed farther into the crate and pulled out another small item. She frowned at it. "Charlie?"

He shifted to look at her. "Yes?"

"Is this what you've talked about?" She held a small animal shape that looked like a rustic camel, with a slot near one of the humps. "Is that where the oil would go?"

"Probably resin." He reached for it. "May I?"

She nodded and turned it over to him. The statue felt solid yet delicate. If he was right, this was millenniums old.

"Do you think it could be . . ."

He nodded.

"Where would your grandpa have marked it?"

Charles looked inside the hold for the resin and smiled. "Here. See the initials in the residue?"

"I do. Oh my."

Dinner became a celebration until he asked what her plans were back in the States.

"I'm not ready to go back. Not yet." She took a sip of her water, then continued. "Few museums are ready to give me the chance to become a curator. Now that all the boys are returning home, I think I'll gain better experience by staying."

"If you stay, then I'll re-up if Uncle Sam will keep me."

The blush that colored her cheeks tugged at him, making him want to kiss her right there in the small café. Instead he contented himself with holding her hand. It was soft beneath his, reminding him that beauty existed in a world that still teetered out of control.

She leaned forward with a conspiratorial smile. "I think I've figured out what to do for the orphans. Something that will let them know we see them and care without moving into the place the local population needs to take."

"What's that?"

Chapter Fourteen

Monday, December 10

THERE WAS A scent that warned of imminent snow, and the air smelled that way as Lillian walked from her apartment to the CP. The clouds were gray and low, and she didn't know whether to wish for the clean covering of white or to pray it would hold off, since so many still lived in buildings that were far from weatherproof. It had taken her a while to realize how many lived in buildings that weren't completely destroyed, but neither were they safe. Her thoughts strayed to the locations they'd found the orphans when they'd battled typhoid, a foe that could come back at any time.

Such abodes were little better than being exposed to the elements without any protection.

The needs were vast and her resources small, so she'd carefully planned what she wanted to give the children at a small party. Her roommates and a few soldiers she'd gotten to know had contributed to the cause as well. That had led to a pool of funds that she had spent as if each cent could be the difference between a child surviving the winter or not.

Now she needed the PX to obtain the items she'd ordered in time for the Christmas party.

Organizing it was a nice separation from her work of hunting for the next clue about this painting or that. Captain Farmer had tasked her with confirming the provenance of the possible Weise paintings, and she was grateful to have something additional to focus on, something that didn't carry the potentially heavy cost if she had to tell Charles that he'd misidentified the paintings he'd discovered and claimed for his family.

So far nothing had disproven his theory of ownership, but she had to keep a clear head and explore everywhere she could for accurate information.

The trick was finding the correct documents when she needed them and then peeling back the layers to see which entries were accurate and which were doctored to benefit those in power.

Identifying the reality behind the veil of deception drained her.

Some days she needed anything to do other than examine another page in another book, trying to decipher the handwriting of some Nazi dignitary who fancied himself an art historian and connoisseur. There were days her head pounded after squinting at the pages. And then she had to have someone interpret them if she couldn't, all while searching for truth.

It was a lot, which led to a unique joy in planning a party for orphans.

Many children had found the basics in a new home set up on the outskirts of town, but it didn't have capacity for all in desperate need. However, the director had worked with her on the details of the celebration, helping her understand what would make the day meaningful. She hoped that would make it more likely that children would come.

They needed the socks and mittens. And they would want the candy.

They actually needed it too. The children needed to know better days were coming. That sweetness still existed in this life.

Everyone needed that reminder after the war that circled the world. Even her group at the collection point.

The German employees who had disappeared for a week in silent protest of the theft of their country's treasures were back. What more could the Monuments Men do to protest other than sign and support the Wiesbaden Manifesto? She'd watched Farmer go from intense and focused to ready to depart for home as his efforts had failed to change the orders. He'd fought hard, and what else could he do that wouldn't lead to a court-martial?

It was a hard question and one she didn't want to answer.

She kept her head down and did the work in front of her. There were many, so many, artworks that needed to be vetted and reviewed. Sometimes she had to acknowledge they only progressed backward as more flooded in than were released out. The tide would turn, but it remained on the inward rush that was exhausting and overwhelming.

Charles had been noticeably absent the past two days, and that worried her. Surely he wouldn't have been reassigned without saying goodbye. She thought she meant more to him than a quick exit, but without seeing him, she couldn't ask the question that would put her fears to rest. One conversation would be all it took to put her mind at ease.

She set her writing supplies and cards to the side and stood before stretching her back. A quick walk would clear her head and help her refocus on the details in front of her. Might as well go check on the security team. See if they needed anything.

As she passed through the hall, she spied Charles in the second-floor hallway. She changed direction from heading to the rotunda and climbed the stairs.

During her climb he must have slid to the floor, but whatever Charles was pondering had his fully engaged attention. He didn't peer at her as she approached, so she eased next to him, carefully arranging her skirt. Studying the floor below them, visible through a railing, she spied the white-and-black marble laid out in a checkerboard pattern. Above their heads the gold and jewel tones of the mosaics danced in the light.

"I should have come up here before this. The mosaics are stunning."

He blinked, as if coming out of some deep reverie, and then his gaze traced upward. He bowed his head, then popped his elbow onto his knee and leaned back against the wall, one leg stretched in front of him. "I like to come up here when I need to think."

"That happen often?" She tried to insert some teasing into her tone, but it seemed to go over his head, missing wherever he was.

Then she noted the thin sheet of airmail paper he clutched in his hand.

───※───

Charles tried to ignore the way he wanted to lash out. Lillian wasn't the issue. He knew she had come seeking him, and that made him want to tug her close and never let go. But he froze in place, unsure what to do or which way to turn.

All he knew was he was too late.

She touched his hand, and the softness and patience in that slight movement almost broke him. "Are you okay, Charles?"

He fought the emotion that wanted to tremble from inside him, pushing it out in one short two-letter word. "No."

She seemed to read all the pain he didn't know how to voice in that short phrase. "What happened?"

"Opa got pneumonia a couple weeks ago. The letter just reached me today." His fingers tightened around the paper, and he had to force himself to relax before he crushed it into a tight ball. "I'm too late. I'm always too late."

"What do you mean? You found his art."

"But he's never going to see it again."

"You can't know that for sure."

He turned to her for the first time, his gaze colliding with her intent emerald one. It was focused completely on him, and he didn't want her to see how broken he was. "I was too late to help them get out of Germany. I thought one more semester in school wouldn't matter."

"The newspapers and many elites loved Hitler. They didn't understand."

"Or didn't want to. My grandparents were telling us the truth. I should have gone to see them when I originally planned. Then I wouldn't have had to scramble all over the region trying to find the paintings. They would have been in New York with Oma and Opa."

"But you did find them."

"Not enough. The walls of their home were covered."

"You found the ones that matter most." She placed her hand on his arm, and the heat of the touch burned through the parts of him that had turned cold when he read the letter. "You can't lose sight of what a miracle that is."

"It's another time it's too late to do any real good."

"We can pack them up. Get them on the next transport out."

"I don't think the military will place a few family treasures over the need to get men home."

"You won't know if we don't ask."

He noted the way she said "we," placing herself squarely in his trouble. "It's too little. Opa could already be gone."

"If you don't buck up and try, then you're right. He will never see the paintings. But what if he is still alive? What if pushing could make it possible?" She leaned closer until he couldn't turn from her intent gaze. "You've come this far. Let's see what other miracles God can accomplish."

"Farmer hasn't released the paintings. You haven't finished your analysis. That's another reason they're still here."

"Then let's ask again, with that letter you're holding as evidence of the dire need to move now." She slipped to her feet and then held a hand down for him. "Come on. At a certain point we have to follow what we can see of the provenance trail."

Against his better judgment, he let himself be caught in her enthusiasm. She was right. He didn't have anything to lose by trying. When they located Farmer in an empty room, overseeing the placement of another shipment, he listened before scanning the letter, then led them to his office, where they held an animated conversation about what to do. A half hour later, he granted Charles permission to send the three paintings and little statue to his family in the States.

While that was happening, Lillian grabbed a phone and started hounding everyone she could find at the air base about getting the crate on the next flight to the States. When she rang off, she had a triumphant gleam in her eyes. "There's a flight leaving in two days. Telegraph your grandparents and let them know they can collect the crate at the end of the week. We'll send a telegram with the details once it's en route."

He reached out and cupped her cheek with his hand, loving the softness of her skin. "You've thought of everything."

She leaned into his touch with a smile. "I'm sure I forgot something, but I want to give your grandpa something special to live for. Reconnecting with his legacy might be the ticket."

"How do I say 'thank you'? I would have given up."

"I'd say a kiss will do." As he leaned closer, she pushed him away. "After we get the paintings crated and ready for their trip. Let the adventure begin."

Indeed. That sounded like a great idea. The thought took root, and he knew it had strong merit. Let the adventure begin. As they worked side by side carefully preparing the paintings for the long trip, he knew this was the woman he wanted by his side, solving problems and facing challenges each day for the rest of his life.

As she peeked up and warm color stained her cheeks, he thought she might feel the same way about him.

Epilogue

January 1946

THE DAYS PASSED quickly as Lillian and her friends planned the Epiphany celebration for the children. When the day finally came, Charles arrived before the sun to give Lillian and her roommates a ride to the mess hall on base. They had several hours to turn it into a space the children could enjoy.

When the Americans trooped into the building, Dorothea and other Germans waited to help.

Lillian gave her colleague a quick peck on the cheek. "Thanks for coming."

"Of course." Dorothea wore a dress Lillian hadn't seen before. The red silk was a bit faded, but she looked festive. "Thank you for seeing our children."

Angelina looked equally festive out of her nursing uniform. "I still don't understand why we didn't host this party on Christmas. Why Epiphany?"

"Dorothea, do you want to explain as we set out the decorations?" Lillian plopped the bags she carried onto a table and started pulling pine cones from it.

Dorothea nodded as she pulled out a red velvet ribbon. "This is so soft." She began unspooling it. "Epiphany is a time when we give small gifts here. You may have noticed marks are added on many doors to welcome and commemorate the wise men who traveled seeking the Christ child. In my village three men dress as the kings and travel through the community from door to door. It happens often in other places too. These men offer a blessing."

Lillian smiled at the image her mind created of that moment. "I love that image."

"Before the war children would also dress up." She tugged at the waist of her faded and worn skirt. While neat and clean, it was one more sign of the everyday hardships that lingered after the war. "One child would hold a star, and the others would follow that star, getting treats as they walked."

"I made a star for the children." Lillian dug through her bags until she found it. "I wish I had more supplies so I could have made it more special."

"It is special because you honor our traditions and history."

Lillian turned to find Charles pushing some tables against the walls with a few other soldiers. "Did you talk three of the soldiers into pretending to be the wise men?"

"Yep. We even found bathrobes we can wear. I'm not sure about crowns and all, but we'll ham it up."

Dorothea frowned. "What do you mean 'ham it up'?"

"We'll make the kids believe we're the real deal." Charles grinned at her, then pushed another table. "Arnold Simmons is one of the men."

"From the collection point?" Lillian resisted the urge to clap her hands. "Where is he?"

"Promised he'd be here shortly. He's helping round up sheets and blankets the kids can wear as robes if they want to re-create the scene of traveling wise men following the star."

"This would be good." Dorothea smiled, a gentle one laced with memories. "Maybe a few of the children could also sing for treats."

"I brought chocolates and other sweets like you suggested."

Dorothea frowned, the action marring her soft beauty. "Will there be enough? Better to have none than run out."

"I haven't stopped praying that there will be more than enough." Lillian found it sweet that the event would be focused on the children, and it encouraged her to think about the wise men in a new way. Their journey had been fraught with unknowns. They'd followed a star, after all. No road. No landmarks. They'd kept their gaze fixed on a star as it worked its way across the sky.

The faith that journey exhibited wasn't something Lillian had spent much time considering. She'd defaulted to a position of, What else would they have done? But now? She realized they'd had a choice. They could have stayed home rather than put their comfortable lives on hold as they wandered across a desert to find what the star promised. How had they known it was a star worth following? They had, and now their story and journey were known to all. It was an amazing and sobering thought.

Would she ever do something worthy of other people knowing and remembering? Maybe it didn't matter, if she could serve those God put in her path. He'd softened her heart through these months in Germany. It was a gift she didn't want to abandon too quickly.

As she watched Charles slide on the robe and a handmade crown, she knew he was another gift from this year and this experience.

Something had shifted in him when he'd received the telegram that the paintings had made it back to the States and his grandpa had lived long enough to be reunited with part of his treasure. He'd shown her the telegram and then swung her around before kissing her until she could hardly remember her name.

Even now, days later, she found her fingers trailing to her lips as heat burned her cheeks whenever she remembered that long moment that was frozen in her mind. In the cold of winter in Germany, she pulled it out when she wanted to remember there was hope for beautiful moments.

It was time. Charles, Arnold, and another man she didn't know marched out of the mess and through the neighboring streets around the base, masquerading as the wise men. Soon they had a trail of children behind them, following them back to the mess hall. Once they arrived, the children clambered to the tables that were loaded with food and small presents of candy. The wise men were the pied pipers leading the way. Later as she watched the children play simple games with the soldiers, Charles slipped up behind her and pulled her close.

She turned to study him and embraced the warmth of his smile.

This was the place she wanted to be. Safe in the shelter of his arms. Not pressured, but cherished, serving others together.

As he tugged her closer, she knew she had found her way home, just as his family's treasures had. And she was content in his love.

Author's Note

I'LL NEVER FORGET the moment I strolled past the new releases section of our library and spotted a nonfiction title with a photo of a soldier carrying a work of art. My attention was captured, and I started on the journey of learning about the Monuments Men. I was captivated by the idea that the Western Allies tasked a small group of men (and later women) with essentially saving Western civilization through its art, architecture, and special buildings. With the advent of large-scale aerial bombing, it was an important initiative but by no means guaranteed. That fascination led to my novel *Shadowed by Grace*, which focused on a Monuments Man in Italy during the war.

When I was asked to write in this novella collection, I began dreaming about how my characters would fit into the larger family legacy my coauthors and I had begun to imagine. I'd listened to another nonfiction title on one of Hitler's art dealers, and it added a layer to my knowledge. That man, Bruno Lohse, worked his way into this story.

If you're like me, you're probably wondering what's true. As much as I could identify. The German ERR was active in stealing art through outright theft and sales that may or may not have been coerced. The Monuments Men and a branch of the OSS were tasked with trying to unravel the transactions that led to the paintings, sculptures, and other art pieces being returned to their rightful owners. Men like Bruno Lohse were interviewed at House 71 in Altaussee, Austria.

The Wiesbaden Central Collecting Point was opened in August 1945 and processed hundreds of thousands of items. Walter Farmer was the Monuments Man tasked with repairing the Wiesbaden Museum buildings so that it could serve as the collection point. The US base in Wiesbaden was located at the former Luftwaffe airfield, and the number of sorties and bombs were real. The Wiesbaden Museum was the Luftwaffe General Headquarters during the war. Wiesbaden was 20 percent destroyed, while Hannover was 90 percent destroyed.

My first experience in Germany was teaching in a study-abroad program in Hannover for two months. I will never forget the first time I saw the dioramas in the Rathaus that illustrated what Hannover looked like in 1939 and then in 1945. It was eye-opening, and not in a pleasant way. Hannover holds a special place in our family's collective experience, and the families we stayed with that summer as we spent weekends around the country (Frankfurt, Regensburg, and Berlin) are like family to us.

If you have the opportunity, I highly recommend a trip to Germany. The history is rich, the people kind, and the land worth exploring. I hope you enjoyed doing so in Charles and Lillian's story.

Perfect Light

ANGELA RUTH STRONG

To Uncle Tim and Aunt Chrissie,
for always offering the gift of joy.

Chapter One

Lacey's ex-husband had apparently spent Thanksgiving on his honeymoon on Aruba while she spent her Thanksgiving alone. Well, not really alone. She'd had her unborn baby to keep her company.

Since snow closed down the pass, Mom and Dad weren't able to join her for the holiday weekend in Salt Lake. Her parents seemed more disappointed than she'd been at the change of plans. They worried about her, but she had enough work to keep her busy. She would spend Black Friday finalizing the tree-lighting ceremony for her favorite local company.

Her event-planning business was her saving grace. That, and carbs.

At least eating Thanksgiving dinner by herself meant lots of left-over mashed potatoes and apple pie. Of all the weird pregnancy cravings women spoke of, she'd never expected to crave the savory starch of potatoes or the crisp tartness of apples. She simply couldn't get enough. Or more appropriately, her little nugget couldn't get enough.

A sharp jab to her ribs reminded her that the little nugget wasn't so little anymore.

Lacey rubbed at the hard lump poking from the side of her protruding belly. While some women claimed to enjoy pregnancy, she didn't find pleasure in being nauseous and exhausted all the time. Not to mention the back pain that first alerted her to her condition. And compared to the pictures of Scott's new wife in a bikini currently pulled up on her computer screen, she felt like Mrs. Narwhal. Which only added to her shame of being a single mom.

Despite the discomfort of pregnancy and her fear of the future, babies were a gift. Expecting one of her own gave a new sense of awe to the Christmas story. Mad props to Mary. How in the world had the teenager ridden a donkey to Bethlehem when Lacey couldn't even ride the Liberty Park carousel anymore without getting dizzy?

In fact, her stomach churned just thinking about it. Or maybe it was photos of the man who'd promised to love her forever now romancing someone else that made her sick. She clicked on the X to close her laptop's web browser and checked the time in the corner of her computer screen. She had better things to do than torture herself. Especially since she was about to meet the man who'd changed her life for the better.

Brendon Wise had a few minutes before he was due to join her in the conference room of his company, Oil of Joy. She'd come to their meeting early to see how much work still had to be done for the first annual Christmas of Joy celebration.

The two of them had been emailing and video chatting ever since he'd contracted her as the event planner to coordinate his extravaganza. Tonight's Christmas tree lighting at the campus just outside the Salt Lake city limits would kick off the event. She simply needed to verify the schedule with him and get his signature on a few invoices.

Hopefully, the publicity would bring in a large crowd. She wasn't sure if the fact that Temple Square turned into Disneyland at Christmastime was a good or bad indicator. It could mean there was a strong need for family activities, or it could mean Brendon was going to have some fierce competition.

Lacey spun her leather desk chair to face the wall of windows overlooking the impressive grounds five stories below. So far snow hadn't been sticking in the valley. The brown grass would appear drab if not for the way sunshine highlighted the surrounding jagged white peaks against a crisp blue sky. Its brilliant presence also promised warmer temperatures and a night of starlight.

She nodded in approval, knowing that with such weather conditions, the modern new campus would be seen for miles, displaying the giant J-O-Y lit along the roof. That was the one thing Brendon insisted on, and she couldn't argue. It was the name of his essential oils, the beauty of the season, and the bundle she carried in her belly.

Though she didn't necessarily feel joy, being pregnant offered purpose. Even satisfaction. The kind that made her sleep well at night in spite of her loneliness and the constant need to pee. Or maybe that was just a result of being tired all the time. Either way, she'd take it. And she believed the hard work she put in now would build a solid foundation for the joyful home she wanted to create.

She watched the landscapers check the lighting on the massive Christmas tree at the center of the circular entryway. She wouldn't be putting up her own tree at home, so this one would have to do. It'd take too much work for her to lug her fake tree down the ladder from the attic. She'd have to settle for hanging a wreath on her front door. Goodness, she could hang a wreath on her tummy.

She smiled at her reflection in the window and twisted her seat back and forth a couple of times. If she looked straight at herself, her long body didn't even appear to be pregnant. It wasn't until she turned sideways that she seemed to have stuck a basketball underneath her sweater dress. She'd shocked a few unsuspecting strangers.

Her smile slipped. It was no wonder Scott hadn't believed her when she'd told him he was going to be a dad.

With that sour thought, she focused past her image and through the glass. Next to the roundabout, a patio full of iron scrollwork tables properly festooned with garlands and red bows would serve cocoa and cookies. Perfect snacks for the local high school choirs and bands she'd scheduled to perform throughout the month to create a jolly ambience and bring in supportive families as visitors.

Brendon had also asked for an ice-skating rink, and she'd wowed him with a skating "ribbon" that wove around firepits and benches. In the middle of the looping track, she'd installed a smaller rink for parents to teach their little ones how to balance on skates.

Everything she did now had her thinking about little ones. She pinched at her dress to adjust the tight spandex maternity leggings underneath her sweater and continued surveying her work on the property.

A pathway wound beside a creek filled with fun decor, ranging from penguins floating on icebergs to a snowman fishing from a canoe. Along the way, bridges and tunnels had also been covered in lights—à la Clark Griswold.

The grounds to Oil of Joy were magnificent even without the decorations, and Lacey had heard a rumor that its landscaping had won awards. She only knew that in the spring this was where all the high school students came for prom pictures, and in the summer outdoor concerts were held in the amphitheater at the end of the pathway.

For the Christmas of Joy event, the amphitheater would naturally accommodate Santa's workshop. Lacey's gaze followed the path toward the stone courtyard in the distance. The grassy terraces edged with cement bleachers were decorated to look like a winter wonderland, but the spot she'd designated for Santa's workshop remained bare.

She squinted to ensure she was looking in the right place. She hadn't made it that far on her walk through the grounds earlier because of back pain, but Mrs. Claus had assured her over the phone last night that their elves would be here first thing in the morning, setting everything up. Yet now at—she checked her smartwatch with the rose-gold band—12:15, there were no elves, no workmen, and not even a reindeer to behold.

Lacey's heart fluttered the same way her stomach had when she'd first felt the baby kick. Except this wasn't good.

She spun to face her computer and slid her index finger along the smooth touch pad. She opened her email account to double-check that the company she'd hired hadn't sent any messages.

Right at the top of her email, "Santa's Workshop" awaited her in bold font. Her toes curled inside her tall suede boots, and she offered up a quick prayer. Besides her nugget, it was just her and God these days.

Please let the elves have blown a tire. Were there any better scenarios than a blown tire? *Please let Santa have overslept, and he's almost here now, and he's going to cut his fee in half to make up for the stress he's causing me. And Brendon won't ever have to find out.*

Oh no. Brendon. The guy she owed her health to. The guy she owed her career to.

She hadn't only wanted to get this contract to coordinate Christmas of Joy, she'd wanted to bless the company in return for all the ways it had blessed her. She at least wanted to make a good impression to the brilliant, self-made millionaire who'd been friendly and encouraging all the times they'd talked through video chat. He'd be here any minute, and she dreaded having to tell him—along with all the kids who would attend the grand opening—that there was no Santa.

Please, Lord. Don't let me ruin anyone's day. She bit her lip and jabbed at the touch pad to discover if she'd be on the naughty or nice list.

Chapter Two

TODAY WAS THE day. Brendon bounded up the industrial rounded staircase lined with pine garland and through the large circular opening into the top floor of his new office building. Not only was it the day he'd launch his first annual Christmas of Joy celebration, but it was the day he'd ask out Lacey Foster.

He didn't date casually. He didn't do anything casually. So when she'd caught his attention—first as the top-selling consultant for Oil of Joy, then as the owner of the event-planning company hired by his assistant—he'd written out a list of pros and cons for inviting her to dinner.

First pro, he admired her work ethic. Though he only did business with people who had a strong work ethic, so there had to be more reason than that.

Second, she was easygoing. He usually associated such a trait with laziness, but in Lacey it came across as confidence. She'd already proved herself and could relax as a peer in his presence. Once he'd started to make money with the business his mother had inspired, women became less and less comfortable around him. They all seemed to be putting on a show or going after something. In contrast, Lacey knew she had something to offer and thus appeared to care more about giving than receiving.

Third, he couldn't stop thinking about her smile. It was natural. And captivating. And the sparkle in her brown eyes reminded him of the amber bottles he used for his company's oils. Both signified they contained something genuine inside. Something valuable. Something worth pursuing.

The only con to their dating had been the fact that she'd been contracted to work for his company, but once he'd decided to pursue Lacey, he'd done his research.

He'd checked her ring finger: bare.

He'd checked her religion on social media: Christian.

He'd checked with his lawyer and HR: It wasn't against business policy to date her since she wasn't a paid employee. Furthermore, dating her would not be frowned upon by his staff if he was up front about his intentions.

So he'd told his assistant, his lawyer, and Mom about his plan to ask the woman out. They'd all been thrilled for him—in their own ways, of course. Mom had asked a million questions before she'd approved. Joel had chuckled and patted him on the shoulder. Hallie had squealed and clapped her hands, confirming Brendon's suspicions that she was younger than she tried to appear in her business suits, glasses, and severe hairstyles. He'd think of her as a little girl playing dress-up if not for how efficiently she organized his schedule.

Though sometimes he felt the company's success could be attributed to his own youthfulness and vitality. People wanted what he had, so they bought his products. They also seemed to adore his small stature and baby face the way fans raved over the kid who played Spider-Man.

There was Hallie now. Running his direction down the hallway as best she could in high heels that were most definitely not made for running.

"Mr. Wise," Hallie called from a distance.

He sensed her excitement for his appointment with Lacey like *Coffea arabica* in a diffuser.

"Is she here?" He didn't even have to specify who he was thinking of. His assistant knew.

Hallie stopped when she reached him, except for the wobbling due to her shoes. "Yes, but . . ." She paused to catch her breath.

He'd feel really guilty if her enthusiasm for his love life caused her to trip and fall. He steadied her arm as he passed. "You're going to hurt yourself in those shoes. Be careful."

He continued striding across the slate tile, fighting a grin. This was the same thrill he'd felt when he'd first discovered the perfect lot on which to build his campus. He'd been looking forward to this moment for a while now, and life as he knew it was about to change for the better.

Hallie's heels tapped after him. "Wait, sir."

She probably wanted to straighten his tie or smooth down his hair, which always curled a little on top if he went a few extra days without a haircut. Hallie kept him looking presentable for interviews and press conferences. He would have paused to let her fuss over him if he hadn't visited his barber the night before. And if he hadn't just spotted Lacey waiting in the conference room.

Seated across the long, glossy white table, she looked both delicate and determined tapping at her keyboard. Though how well could she see said laptop with her long dark-blond hair falling over one eye? He wanted to brush it back behind an ear. Hopefully, it wouldn't take too long before their relationship progressed to such a level of intimacy.

Unable to wait another moment to meet the first woman he'd ever considered a candidate to be the future Mrs. Wise, he kept his eyes on her and waved Hallie back to her office. "We'll talk after this meeting."

His assistant's heels clicked closer, and she may have said something else, but he couldn't let himself be distracted from his goal. He took a deep breath of the refreshing evergreen air, realized he'd probably always associate the scent with this very moment, then pulled open the glass door.

"Lacey," he greeted as he stepped across the quiet carpet, arm extended for his normal handshake. Except there would be nothing normal about getting to hold her hand for the first time.

Her light-brown eyes flicked up without their usual gleam. Shiny nude lips smiled tightly. This wasn't the welcome he'd expected from their previous online interactions. Lacey raved about how his oils had helped her overcome debilitating migraines and claimed she was honored to work with him.

Was something wrong? Is this why Hallie had been trying to stop him?

Lacey planted her palms on the table and leaned forward like she was going to push herself out of her seat to shake hands. He'd rather she make herself comfortable.

"Don't get up for me." He reached across the table to offer his hand so she wouldn't have to stand.

Lacey eased back down and sent him a sincere smile. A small one but sweet enough that he knew whatever her issue was, it wasn't him.

Her fingers slid around his palm. Firm, smooth, cold. They needed mittens, or a warm mug to hold, or a fireplace.

He reluctantly let go and scanned the contemporary wall paneling for a thermostat. "Your hands are freezing. I'll turn up the heat."

"Actually . . ." She grimaced, nose scrunching. "We have bigger problems."

He gripped the back of the chair in front of him. He'd planned to sit across from Lacey, but if there was a dilemma, he needed to think on his feet. More important than sitting together was working together. In a weird way, he relished this opportunity for problem-solving as a team. Of course, he always considered problems as opportunities in disguise. "What's going on?"

"It's more like what's *not* going on." She brushed hair out of her face to make eye contact. "Santa isn't coming."

He nodded, keeping their connection. Studying her in return. Appreciating that though her slim eyebrows dipped in consternation, she remained calm.

Brendon liked to consider himself objective too, but as someone who respected diligence, he couldn't help thinking of their Santa as a slacker. The big guy only went to work in December. "He had one job . . ."

Lacey huffed out a chuckle. "Yeah, this is his Super Bowl."

With or without him, they still had to put on a show.

Brendon crossed his arms. "Is Santa on strike? Does he want more pay? Did someone offer him a better position?"

Lacey's natural-looking lashes lowered against her light cheeks, hiding her eyes. "His daughter went into premature labor. He's flying to Florida with Mrs. Claus to meet their grandbaby."

Well, then. The guy was a terrific dad. No fault there. "Good for him. I'll have Hallie send a gift."

Brendon glanced toward his assistant's office as part of making a mental note, but the young woman stood watching him through the conference room windows. From an angle where only he could see her, she motioned to her stomach, then rocked her arms like a cradle. Ah . . . so she'd known about Santa's grandchild and had been trying to warn him. Thoughtful.

If anybody deserved a raise, it was her. Definitely a Christmas bonus. He'd let the payroll department know.

Meanwhile, he waved her in to appease her fears. She could take care of sending a company gift to grandbaby Claus while he took care of filling the man's fur-trimmed boots.

Hallie stiffened at first, then wobbled her way to the door and peeked her head inside. "Yes, sir?"

"Could you put together an essential oils baby shower basket, please?"

She blinked a couple times, glanced toward Lacey, then nodded. "I'd love to."

Brendon turned toward Lacey as well. "Do you know if it's a boy or girl?"

His event planner looked up, all serene, like a painting of the Madonna. She definitely remained more cool under pressure than his assistant. "I don't know."

He nodded to Hallie. "Just make it a gender-neutral basket. Yellow rubber duckies and such."

"Yes, sir," she said, but remained in the doorway. "Are you still . . . moving forward?"

Brendon tilted his head in confusion. It wasn't like her to question his decisions or stick around for any kind of small talk after being given a task. And it definitely wouldn't be like him to cancel his plans over a baby bump in the road. Honestly, an infant was the whole reason Christmas even existed. "Of course."

Hallie's pale eyes widened from behind her tortoiseshell frames. "Okay. Let me know if you need anything else." She withdrew slowly.

Finally the door fell shut. Back to business.

He faced Lacey again, absorbing some of her peace simply by looking at her. "Any other Santas you can hire?"

She grimaced at her computer, then shrugged, as if she'd already tried. "Not this late in the game."

"Do we have access to a Santa suit?"

"I can ask to borrow the one our Santa was going to wear." She tapped at her computer. Her fingers clicked even as her gaze rose to Brendon's, a wry smile lifting one side of her lips. "Are you going to wear it?"

He rubbed his smooth jaw and couldn't keep from smiling back. "You don't think I could pull it off?"

"No offense, but—"

Not offended in the slightest, he motioned for her to continue. "This is where you say something offensive."

The corners of her eyes crinkled in amusement. "With your baby face . . ."

Baby face. Baby. The answer had been there all along. And if Santa hadn't gone rogue, Brendon never would have realized he needed it.

"That's it." He pointed to the painting on the wall his great-grandfather, Charles Weise, had recovered for their family after World War II titled *Adoration of the Magi*. "How fast can you put together a living nativity?"

Her fingers froze over the keyboard, and not only because it was still chilly in the room. "Are you serious?"

Her words might have sounded foreboding if not for the inflection of hope. As if she thought only religious institutions were daring enough to celebrate the birth of Jesus and she'd be delighted if he chose the manger over the sleigh.

"Yes." He waved his arms as he spoke, and he probably paced.

People told him he paced, but he thought of it as looking around to better visualize his ideas. And sometimes they were directly in front of him. "Why didn't I think of it before? I mean, I hung this painting here in connection to my essential oils of frankincense and myrrh, but it holds even more meaning."

She studied the piece of art depicting three kings in search of the one true King. "It also fits with your name, Wise."

He paused. He didn't want to claim to be something he wasn't. Especially not with her. "My family name actually used to be Weise with an *e*. But after the war, my great-grandparents worked with a lot of Jews, returning artwork the Nazis had stolen. Understandably, the very people my great-grandparents were trying to help had trouble trusting Great-Grandpa's German heritage. He Americanized it to put their associates at ease, and now it's a name I aspire to."

Her contemplative gaze turned from the painting to him. "With the way you work to share joy with the world, I'd say you've arrived."

His list of reasons to date her was growing. Number four wasn't that she considered him a success but that she considered sharing joy as the definition of success.

"I do want to share joy." He spun to look through the window at the terrace in the distance. "We can move the star from the top of the tree to the amphitheater."

Lacey scanned the ceiling. Perhaps her own way of visualizing. "We had a living nativity at my church last year. They decided not to host it again because there weren't enough visitors to justify the effort."

Brendon held his hands wide. "I'll bring in the visitors."

She laughed, the sound deep and real and wonderful. "Let me call my pastor. I'll see if he still has all the materials."

"Do it." Brendon pulled his own phone out of his pocket to google other living nativities and get an idea for what he was asking. He appreciated that she was already one step ahead.

This was meant to be. The two of them. The collaboration. Who else could have made it happen?

He listened in on her half of the conversation so she wouldn't have to repeat everything to him after getting off the phone. It sounded like someone in their church even had farm animals.

He scrolled through photos and stopped at one with a camel. "Is there a camel?"

She did a double take to shoot him a look that seemed to question his sanity. Fine, no camel this year. Next year he'd plan ahead. Maybe even offer camel rides if insurance allowed.

She hung up with a flourish and shot her arms overhead in victory. "We have all the actors and everything needed." But then her smile faded, and she lowered one arm to look at her watch. "Except maybe time."

Brendon loved a challenge even more than he loved the idea of camel rides. He shrugged. "Just tell me what to do. I'm all yours."

His heartbeat tripped over the double meaning in his words. Did Lacey feel it too?

She rubbed her cheek and studied her computer, as if putting together a plan. Or maybe she was hiding her own reaction to his intimation.

If he was going to ask her on a date, this was the opening he needed. "We're going to pull this off, Lacey. Then afterward I'd like to take you to dinner."

Her eyes zipped up to his. Wide, serious eyes. They held surprise and maybe a little alarm. This wasn't a look he'd seen on her before.

Did it mean she wasn't interested? They'd seemed to have a good connection. Maybe it wasn't disinterest he read in her expression. Maybe she simply hadn't thought of him as more than a client before. She was professional that way.

She hesitated. "In order to celebrate?"

"Yes." He gave his most dashing smile. The one that had grandmothers telling him if they were fifty years younger, they'd want to court him. "And because I'd like to get to know you better."

"Oh." Her lips stayed in the O shape, her eyes just as round.

Yeah, he'd wanted to take a moment to ask her out, but they still had things to do. They didn't have time for all this speechlessness. "Do you like sushi?"

"I do, but . . ." She bit her lip and flinched as if she'd bitten it too hard. "I'm not eating it right now."

"Okay." That was weird. But there were other options. "How about Mexican? Or Italian? Or German, from my own heritage. We can observe Christmas around the world. I'll take you out for something different every week."

Her eyes cleared, making them hard for him to read. He'd hoped they'd flash with excitement or shimmer with attraction. Instead they held his gaze with intent.

"I'm also not dating right now." She spoke the surprising words with the tranquility of a decided heart. Its tone made him respect her all the more. Only, he'd want her heart to be decided on him.

Was she healing from a past relationship? Was she becoming a nun? Did women do that in real life anymore or just in musicals?

She closed her laptop with a click and slid it into her bag. When she looked up again, her small smile mixed wistfulness and sadness like citrus and cinnamon. "Thank you for asking me out. It's been awhile since I've felt pretty."

Was she serious? She glowed. He opened his mouth to tell her so when she stood, and he saw the reason for her glow. She couldn't be with him because she was with child.

Chapter Three

THE AIR OF festivity whirled around Brendon like snow that didn't stick. This was his event, and its success should make him feel successful, but he'd been hoping to celebrate more than a company milestone. Besides, Lacey deserved all the credit for this crowd. He just hadn't seen her to thank her, and he could only presume she was avoiding him. The invitation he'd expected to draw them together had pushed them apart.

"The mayor wants to meet you," Hallie announced without pausing as she speed-hobbled by in boots that really shouldn't have heels.

Brendon waited for excitement to spring up at the request from Mayor Young, but his normal well of enthusiasm seemed to have run dry. He could fake it, but he preferred to build his reputation on authenticity. "Invite her to join me for the tree-lighting ceremony," he called after his assistant.

He'd never let life's setbacks stop him, but he couldn't figure out how to get around this roadblock with Lacey. There was nothing he could do. She wasn't opposed to dating him specifically, just dating in general. And with good reason, since there was obviously another man in her life.

A group of teenage boys jostled him as they passed. "Can you believe the food truck ran out of donut kabobs?"

Brendon blinked and shook his head. Good thing there was a backup plan, though nothing would sweeten the air like the donut truck's sugar and grease. He debated texting Lacey, but his mom was friends with the owner of Curbside Cupcakes, so he called the food truck operator directly. Then he double-checked messages to make sure he hadn't missed something from his event planner. Nothing.

Men's hiking boots stepped into his line of sight. "Hey, buddy. Could you take a picture of our family for us?"

Brendon glanced up to find a man wearing a buffalo-checked hunting cap. He waited a second to see if the stranger recognized him as the company's owner, but the man was too focused on making sure his huge family posed in such a way that every face could be seen. Plus, Brendon was fairly incognito in his jeans and wool peacoat.

"Sure." He pocketed his own phone and took the one offered to him. Then he used the photography trick Hallie had taught him, stepping backward while zooming in to make the surrounding campus appear bigger. Hopefully, the snapshot would become part of a social media storm that covered his event with publicity.

The family man took his phone back and scrolled through the images. "Wow, these are great. Thank you."

"You're welcome. Merry Christmas." Brendon hated how hollow the words sounded coming from his own lips. He nodded to excuse himself but couldn't help overhearing the conversation he left behind.

"Do you know who that was?"

"Who?"

"Brendon Wise."

"*The* Brendon Wise?"

"Yes. The mogul who started this company out of his mother's garage."

Brendon used to dream of becoming a mogul when he took his first job at Chick-fil-A after Dad died. He made commencement speeches about it, encouraging graduates to follow their dreams. So why didn't overhearing such an interaction cheer him?

He knew why. And it was ridiculous that he was still obsessing over her. Time for him to move on. His festival was named Christmas of Joy, and here he was acting like Scrooge. He simply needed to focus on the magic surrounding him.

The living nativity proved to be a miracle. Its stable had been raised faster than an Amish barn. But the sight of Mary holding her baby seemed to mock Brendon. For the first time, he realized how hard it must have been for Joseph to accept his fiancée's pregnancy.

He shook his head and looked toward the youth choir bundled in down jackets and scarves that threatened to muffle their music, yet their breath came out in white puffs as they sang "What Child Is This?" Brendon rolled his eyes toward the stars twinkling above. *Seriously, Lord?*

The clop of horse hooves drew his attention to the carriage rides circling the parking lot. He may not have had Santa show up, but the horse pulling the white carriage was dressed as the big guy himself, beard and hat included. Normally Brendon wasn't a fan of animals wearing clothing, but the carriage seemed like the getaway he needed at the moment.

He strode toward the line of waiting passengers, hoping there would be room for one more rider. It looked like two parents with a child and a pair of teenagers, so if the carriage held six . . .

He turned to count the passengers already aboard and rolling toward the edge of the sidewalk for the end of their trip. Six exactly with one family and an additional woman.

Something about the blond snagged Brendon's gaze. She wore a cranberry parka with fur trim, a taupe pom-pom hat, and matching gloves. Her gloved hands rubbed a protruding belly. Lacey.

Brendon had wanted to ride in the carriage to escape thoughts of her, but if she'd climbed aboard to stay away from him, then he'd bow out. Once Christmas was over, they would have no more connection. They barely had a connection now. She'd never been more than a contractor for his company, and he shouldn't let his unmet expectations damper reality. They'd both go on with their lives, and they'd both be fine.

As he took a step backward while making sure Lacey hadn't

noticed him, she jerked up from her seat and reached for the door of the carriage even though it was still moving. Her lifted hand made Brendon think she had seen him and was going to wave, but then the hand landed over her mouth. She was not fine.

The carriage driver twisted in his seat to check on her. Brendon couldn't hear what she said, but the driver pulled on the reins to stop Santa Horse. Lacey swung the little door outward and clambered down the steps.

Brendon frowned. Had she gotten a text and there was some emergency on his campus that he didn't know about? He scanned the crowds enjoying the lights, skating rink, and refreshments. All seemed normal. Next he checked the giant tree awaiting its inauguration. Still standing peacefully.

He glanced back at Lacey to see her duck behind a row of bushes twinkling white. Was she actually hiding from him?

A retching sound came from behind the bush to lyrics to "Merry Christmas, Baby," alerting him to what was actually going on. Maybe her morning sickness wasn't relegated to mornings. *Now what, God?*

With a flash of white and gold, an angel from the nativity raced past to where Lacey had ducked. The Lord worked in mysterious ways.

"Lacey? Are you okay?" the angel asked in a voice that was very befitting of her outfit. The woman with wings stood straight and made eye contact with Brendon over the bushes. He was vaguely aware of her stunning beauty that could have had her posing as an angel for Victoria's Secret rather than a Christmas pageant, but he was more appreciative of her inner beauty that had her looking after his event planner.

"Could you get us some water?" she called to him.

He nodded. So much for ridding his thoughts of Lacey, though he was actually glad for an excuse to help her. As he jogged toward the nearest food truck, he couldn't keep from wondering why the baby's father wasn't here taking care of the pregnant woman. If the man had abandoned her, she might need assistance as a single mom. Since it wasn't his place to ask, he found comfort knowing she had a good church family. Maybe God had allowed him to have feelings for her to inspire him to better support single moms in his company. He'd never really thought about it before.

With a water bottle in hand, he returned to the sick woman and her guardian angel.

Lacey wiped her mouth with a tissue while the angel rubbed her back. "I knew I shouldn't have gone for a ride, but I was trying to keep from running into Brendon because I feel awkward after his dinner invite. Ironically, the carriage ride is what caused me to puke on his property, which is even more awkward. If he finds out, he's going to be so glad he's not taking me on a date tonight."

The angel bit her lip and met Brendon's gaze behind Lacey's back.

He shrugged, then stepped next to Lacey and held out a water bottle. She couldn't avoid him anymore. "I just wouldn't have taken you on a carriage ride."

Lacey's eyes snapped to his, wide and mortified. Her cheeks stippled pink. "Mr. Wise."

He arched both eyebrows at the formal title. Only Hallie called him Mr. Wise, and that was because her dad came from the South. As for Lacey, he'd soothe the sting of her embarrassment the way lavender oil soothed chicken pox so she could stop avoiding him like a rash.

"Ms. Foster." He lifted his chin in greeting, as if they always acknowledged each other by their last names. And maybe they would now, to reestablish footing on a professional level. "The mayor is here and has experience with Christmas tree lightings, so if you aren't feeling well, she can take over the ceremony while I drive you home."

"What? No. I just . . . I didn't . . . I mean . . ." Her arms flailed in her attempt to convey what he assumed was supposed to be an apology.

The angel covered her mouth as if to hide a smile and backed away slowly.

Meanwhile he still held the water bottle extended between the two of them. "Take a sip, hon." *Hon?* Where had that come from?

She was Ms. Foster now. Or Mrs. Foster, for all he knew. Her relationship status on social media could have been outdated when he'd checked it.

She grabbed the bottle from him and guzzled until it was gone. He'd overheard women talking about how pregnancy could make one overheat, but he guessed it was more likely that she was taking time to figure out what to say rather than trying to cool off in the near-freezing temperatures. Hopefully, all that fluid stayed down this time. If not, he could grab some ginger oil to rub on her wrists.

She finished with a gulp, dropped her arm to the side, and met his gaze with new determination. "I've never been pregnant before, but I strongly suspect it has churned my emotions as well as my stomach."

He waved an arm to dismiss her discomfort. The truth was that he admired her for facing him after all that. "It's okay—"

"No, it's not. I have no excuse." She took a deep breath. "I'm flattered you asked me out. I think you are a very fine man, and I'm honored to be working with your company. I want tonight to be a success for you, and I'm not going to let you miss the tree lighting. I'm not going to miss it either. I feel better now, and I'll be staying to make sure everything else goes smoothly."

The angel waved though neither of them was looking at her, and Brendon barely noticed out of the corner of his eye. "I've got to get back to the manger scene."

Brendon studied Lacey. The reflection of Christmas lights in her shiny eyes. The rosy tip of her little nose. The way she propped her free hand against her lower back, either because of back pain or because she was top-heavy.

He appreciated how dedicated she was to her job. He appreciated how direct she was even while keeping boundaries. And he appreciated that she'd called him "a very fine man." It made him kind of sad she hadn't gotten to know him sooner before meeting some other man, but that didn't matter now. What mattered was that she'd just been vomiting and that she wanted to keep working.

Brendon clicked his tongue. "You've earned every penny I've paid you. I already had to call in the cupcake truck because the donut kabobs sold out. Half of Utah's here. Your job is done, but . . ."

The edges of her jaw softened. She dropped her defenses to meet his gaze with a sparkle of hope. She wanted to be here. "But what?"

"You could join me on stage as we light the tree."

Her lips curved up, as if she thought he was joking. "I'm not going to steal your spotlight."

"No, you're going to share it."

She took time to read his eyes. Back and forth. Double-checking his meaning. "I'm as big as a house. I'll block you from view."

He couldn't help chuckling at that. "Hardly." If she was truly as big as a house, he would have known she was pregnant from the beginning, and he would have never made things uncomfortable between them. "Besides, the view that matters is the tree. From onstage you'll have the best view of it lighting up."

She nodded slowly, considering. "Thank you for inviting me. I would pass except I want to make the most of this moment since I'm not putting up my own tree this year."

His chin tucked toward his neck in disbelief. She was so good at decorating. And this very well could be her baby's first Christmas. "Why aren't you putting up a tree? Because you're exhausted from decorating for me?"

She rubbed a hand over her face. "I'm sure I look like it, but no. I just can't climb up the ladder into my attic and bring the tree down by myself."

So there was no man to put up her tree for her. Brendon didn't need to know her story to know she deserved a helping hand during the holidays. She might not want a relationship, or she could even be better off without the father of her child in her life, but nobody should be alone at Christmas.

His company wasn't simply about making money. It was about making a difference. And though he might not be the man in Lacey's life, he was going to make sure she got her own tree this year.

Chapter Four

Lacey curled on her side, trying to get comfortable on the eggshell-colored sofa. She'd probably have to replace the light furnishings once her baby became a messy toddler, but she wouldn't think about that now. This was her time to rest—the reward for last night's successful event. It had turned out even more beautiful than she'd imagined, which made her undecorated home feel all the more drab, even with its brick wall, freshly painted white beadboard, and refurbished pine floors. Like the bright afternoon sun streaming through her shutters and painting stripes on her red fleece blanket, the holidays definitely highlighted her loneliness.

A stabbing pain to her ribs reminded her that she wasn't actually alone. Of course her nugget decided to wake up when she was ready for a long winter's nap.

She rubbed the hard bump protruding from the side of her abdomen. "Hey, kiddo. I'll decorate for you next year." Her eyes drifted closed. "This year I just don't have the energy."

Her little one moved in response, though this karate chop was accompanied by a couple of loud thuds. It took her a few blinks to wake up enough to realize someone was knocking on her door. Probably Gemma checking up on her after last night's nausea. Or coming by to get the scoop on Brendon.

Lacey's BFF from youth church camp, Gemma, was in town for the holidays to introduce her new beau to her family. Gemma's relationship seemed to make her think Lacey needed to be in a relationship as well. So far Lacey had been able to put up with Gemma's meddling because in exchange she'd gotten Gemma to play the angel in the living nativity.

She groaned and pushed herself upright. Holding her aching back, she waddled to the doorway, but she apparently wasn't moving fast enough to forestall a second knock.

"I'm coming," she called before flipping the dead bolt and swinging open the old-fashioned arched door. "Just wait until you're pregnant, and you'll understand."

A Christmas tree stood on the cement patio she'd poured when replacing the crumbling steps. It smelled fresh like the forest, and Lacey immediately forgave the other woman. In fact, she had to blink away grateful tears threatening to freeze on her face in the biting wind.

"I'm not planning on getting pregnant anytime soon." A deep chuckle drew her attention to the man half-hidden behind the blue spruce. "But I do understand that if you're going to have a tree this year, you need a little help."

Lacey's hands flew up to cover her mouth, and she stared at her own personal St. Nick. There were not words to describe her mix of gratitude and embarrassment. With the way she kept putting her foot in her mouth around Brendon, she was probably better off speechless anyway.

He was here because she'd told him she didn't have a tree. She'd have to be careful not to make herself sound needy again. Whether he was still interested in dating her or not—most likely not—she didn't want him to feel like he had to rescue her.

"I take it you didn't get my voicemail?" he asked.

She glanced toward the giant ottoman where her phone sat, silenced for her nap. "No." Unfortunately. She would have tidied up and maybe, you know, brushed her hair. She smoothed a hand over her crown to rid herself of possible bed head.

At least Brendon looked casual as well. A navy hoodie made him appear even more youthful than he did in a business suit. He had to be as opposite from Santa as one could get, except for the twinkle in his eyes. "After all you did for my tree lighting, I couldn't let you go without your own tree on what might be your baby's first Christmas. I was just going to leave this here if you didn't answer your door, but I don't mind setting it up if you want me to."

His words appeased all reservation. He wasn't here because she needed him—he was here to thank her for what she'd already done. A form of repayment. And it really did feel good not to be forgotten.

"Come in. I'll make some cocoa to warm you up." She stepped backward and swung the door wide, glancing over her shoulder to see her house through his eyes. It wasn't as impressive as her old residence in the Yalecrest neighborhood full of Tudor and Craftsman-style homes, but the Sugar House district could be described as quaint, and she was pleased by the updates she'd done to her little brick bungalow.

"This is cozy." Brendon carried the tree in front of him, set it in the middle of the room, and steadied it with one hand while looking for the best spot to display it.

"Thank you." She accepted his compliment, even though she knew he used the word *cozy* in place of *tiny*. She pushed her ottoman more toward the center of the room to create needed space, then pulled her shutters wide and blinked at the brightness. "Since I'm not decorating outside this year either, let's put the tree in front of my window. Then others can see it from the street."

"Perfect." He held out a round plastic stand that she hadn't noticed before but was glad he'd thought to bring.

They aligned the tree and screwed the trunk into place together. And by *together*, Lacey meant that she balanced the tree and inhaled its woodsy fragrance while Brendon did all the work. She'd always believed nature had healing properties, but she'd never believed it more than in that moment. She'd been tired, but now she felt both peaceful and energized enough to decorate the entire house.

Brendon stood and wiped his hands on his jeans, his eyes first taking in their handiwork, then moving to her without losing any wonder. Maybe it wasn't only the scent of evergreen that brought her joy.

Lacey cleared her throat. "I'll get some water for the tree."

She retreated to the kitchen. Once her pitcher was full, she filled a kettle of water to heat up on the stove, though she wasn't sure if that was to buy time away from Brendon or to buy time with him.

Those flutters in her belly came from a baby, not butterflies. She was too old for butterflies.

She took a deep breath, picked up the pitcher, and turned to find Brendon's frame filling the arched doorway. Funny that she'd always thought of him as a small man when he had such a huge presence. *Baby, not butterflies.*

"Where can I find your Christmas lights?"

She paused, remembering the last time she'd decorated a tree with a man. This was dangerous territory. "They're in my garage attic, but you don't have to—"

"Because you're going to climb up there?" He arched an eyebrow in challenge. He had her.

She pressed her lips together before admitting, "I'll probably buy some new ones at Smith's."

He tilted his head in admonition.

"Okay. Come on." She grabbed her parka off the hook by the back door and led him outside to her unattached garage. The cool air would do her flush good. They had to wait for the water to heat up anyway.

He followed, scanning the three different fence styles separating her little lot from the neighbors. "Are you going to finish fencing the back yard when your baby starts running around?"

She punched in the garage code, feeling like a failure for not already having considered the fencing issue. Giving birth still seemed far off, let alone having a child who could play outside alone. "Yes," she said. Because when the time came, she would.

The garage door ground open, revealing her Honda SUV. At least that would be a good vehicle for hauling around soccer equipment and science-fair exhibits. See? She could do this.

She led Brendon to the unoccupied second bay and reached for the string that pulled down the ladder to the attic. He let her tug it open, then he unfolded the ladder to reach the ground and pulled out his phone to use as a flashlight. "How long have you lived here?" he asked as he climbed into the darkness.

"Almost three years." She was thankful he was out of sight for this conversation. Otherwise he might read on her face things she wasn't sure she should say. "The lights are in the green tub."

His footsteps thumped overhead, followed by some scraping, then the tub appeared in the opening of the ceiling. He peered over. "Did you grow up in Utah?"

Lacey avoided eye contact by focusing on retrieving the tub. "I moved here for college and stayed."

"I was born here. Very family oriented and outdoorsy. It's a good place to raise kids." A silhouette of his profile revealed he was scanning the rest of her attic. "I see a box of ornaments. I assume you want these too."

"Yeah, but my parents will be out on Christmas Eve. Dad can get all that down for me." As long as they didn't get stuck on the pass again.

Brendon squatted in the ceiling's opening to look her in the eye. "Do you usually wait for Christmas Eve to decorate your tree?"

"No, but—"

"Then I got this." He didn't stop with the ornaments but grabbed three other boxes of holiday decor. By the time they made their way inside, the teakettle whistled its merry tune.

Lacey set the one box she carried onto the farmhouse table in the corner and scurried to quiet her teapot. She turned off the burner, then reached behind her regular mugs in the cupboard to grab a couple of Christmas mugs from her holiday stash. Steam whispered over her hands as she poured, sending a shiver to thaw the rest of her body. Coming in from the brisk temperatures made the water's warmth feel hotter than usual, and she suspected that in the same way her home would seem lonelier after Brendon left. But she still didn't know if she wanted to kick him out sooner or invite him to stay longer.

By the time she added the hot chocolate mix to their mugs, Brendon had taken all the boxes into the living room, leaving the tabletop clear. She set their mugs on the table, intending to sink into a chair and relax with a big sip of creamy chocolate, but for the first time, she realized which Christmas mugs she'd grabbed, and she froze in horror.

Brendon breezed through the doorway. "Perfect." He pulled a small amber vial from his pocket and tipped it over the top of his mug to dispense a drop of liquid, then paused over hers. "Peppermint oil will taste like candy canes and help your nausea. Ours is safe for pregnant women after their second trimester. Would you like to try it?"

"Uhh . . ." Her current nausea came from the fact that since he'd already added peppermint oil to his drink, it wouldn't be as easy to transfer his beverage into another mug without him noticing.

"You don't have to," he reasoned. "You raved about how much our lavender oil helped your headaches, and I thought this one could help you too."

"Right." She held her hand to her temple and closed her eyes. He was so sweet. Helpful while respectful. She could trust him with her story. The fact that she was crushing on the man didn't mean things had to get weird again. Because clearly nothing was going to happen between them. "Fine. Yes."

"Do you have a headache now?" He tapped a drop of oil into her mug, eyeballing her.

She laughed at herself, then let the sound fade into a sigh. "No." She lowered herself to the striped chair cushion. "I just realized what mug I gave you, and I was looking for a way to switch it out before you noticed."

His gaze questioned hers for a moment before sliding to his mug. He sat across from her and lifted the cup between them. The scroll-work *MR.* had a Santa hat hanging off the top of the *R*.

She smiled sweetly. "It just means you're Mr. Wise."

"We're going to start that again, are we?" He sipped his beverage and leaned back to study her. "What's your mug say?"

She twisted her lips before turning her mug to reveal the *MRS.* with the Santa hat. Last Christmas she'd kept the mugs and prayed she'd get to use them again, but she'd never imagined it this way. "I'm divorced."

His eyes stilled, offering compassion. "I'm sorry."

Even if her divorce was for the better, that only made her failed marriage sadder. "Thank you."

He studied her in the quiet. Not judging. Not prying. Just caring. "Can I ask if your ex-husband is the father of your child?"

"Yes, you may, and yes, he is." Lacey hadn't made the best choice in marrying Scott, but at least she hadn't made more poor choices on top of that one.

He took another sip but watched her over his mug. "May I ask where he is now?"

"Aruba. On his honeymoon."

Brendon's eyebrows arched. "That's fast."

Lacey agreed with a nod, but unless she was going to make Brendon keep playing twenty questions, she might as well explain. "Scott and I have actually been separated for three years now. He came over in early spring and apologized for the ways he'd hurt me. It turns out he was coming over to ask me to sign divorce papers, but I thought God was answering my prayer for reconciliation, and, well . . ." She motioned to her stomach.

Brendon leaned forward. "Noo . . ."

At least he was as appalled as she had been with her ex. Though she should have known better than to trust Scott had changed without any proof. Her own counselor had warned her not to take him back too soon. So she'd accept responsibility for her choices and would do her best to raise a child on her own.

"Is he helping out financially?" Brendon wanted to know.

Leave it to a businessman to make it all about finances. Though Gemma had asked the same thing.

Lacey shrugged. "He refuses to admit he's the father. Probably because of his girlfriend . . . I mean wife." So weird. "He can be part of this child's life if he chooses to, but I refuse to rely on him for support."

Brendon looked around, perhaps viewing her place through a new perspective. She was relieved to see his sympathy for her situation, but she didn't want him to feel like she needed rescuing.

"Yes, I used to live in a much bigger house. And yes, I'd probably receive good child support from a doctor. But . . ." How did she explain? "He left me because I didn't need him anymore, and I don't want him ever to think he can be my hero again."

Brendon's hazel eyes peered closer to better understand. "What do you mean?"

She took a sip from her cup, the peppermint oil adding just the right amount of refreshing tingle to the sweet chocolate. So ironic how the very oils that offered so many health benefits proved poisonous to her marriage. "Scott has a bit of a hero complex. It's probably why he became a doctor and probably why he married me. With my debilitating headaches, I depended on him for everything."

Brendon leaned away, awareness shadowing his expression. "Then when our oils helped you overcome the pain, not to mention become one of our top sales consultants, you weren't reliant on him anymore."

She lifted a shoulder and offered a sad smile. "But another woman was."

"Lacey. Wow." He ran his hands through his hair, then dropped them on the table. "I can't even. I never imagined my oils could hurt someone like that."

She shook her head and reached for his forearm. "Your oils didn't hurt. They helped me heal. It was Scott who couldn't keep his vow of 'for better or worse.'" Still a crazy concept to her. What bride ever worried about life improving? "The problem was that he wanted to be the better one."

Brendon stilled, and their gazes locked. "The best is yet to come."

For the first time in a long time, she believed the sentiment. It felt good to not be alone. It felt good to have someone listen to her troubles. But she couldn't help wondering what he was getting out of their exchange. He wasn't going to try to solve her problems for her, was he? She didn't need another hero.

Chapter Five

Brendon pondered in his office the next Monday. He had to make it right for Lacey. He knew he wasn't to blame for her divorce, but he couldn't help thinking that if not for Oil of Joy, Lacey's baby would have two parents.

Crazy how the oils that played a part in the end of Lacey's marriage were what saved his mom after Dad died. As for Brendon, he hadn't set out to create a multilevel marketing company. He'd simply planned to help Mom organize her little sales booth but kept coming up with advances for her business plan. She'd gotten frustrated with the growth and let him take over while she continued to peddle her handmade products at Christkindlmarkt.

The German holiday market would be opening soon, and he loved the way Salt Lake focused on putting "kind" in their Christkindl-markt. They offered service projects to bless the community, and everyone who did a good deed was invited to make a paper lantern and march in the parade, another German tradition. For his good deed, he always donated the booth's earnings to a local charity, then made lanterns with his mom. That had to be coming up. Was it on his calendar?

"Hallie?" he yelled by default.

Heels tapped, and she appeared in his office doorway. Today her long black pants hid most of her stilettos from sight except for their pointy red toes, which could not be comfortable. "Yes, Mr. Wise?"

"Do we have a theme for Mom's vendor booth this year?"

"You picked 'the joy of giving' theme, sir. The market starts today, and you have the parade tonight."

"Oh, that's right." They'd made these plans back in July. Back before he'd gotten distracted with his own holiday extravaganza, including one distraction in particular. But this distraction gave the joy of giving a whole new meaning. "Did we decide to which charity we'd donate all the proceeds?"

Hallie's head swiveled to keep her eyes on him, alerting him to the fact that he was pacing. "I compiled a list, but you wanted to discuss it with your mother first."

Mom had brought up the subject of charity at Thanksgiving dinner, but he'd been called to the campus when there were issues with the crane delivering his giant Christmas tree. "I'll go buy her some schnitzel for lunch, and we'll make a decision. Is there a foundation for single moms on the list?"

His assistant pushed her glasses up her nose. "I believe so. There's a local group that provides support by adopting single moms, but—"

"Adopting? Like personally providing community and financial support? Mom will be all over that." Maybe his mom would even get involved. He could see her adopting Lacey. He grabbed his jacket from the back of his chair.

"Sir, you can't go right now. A reporter from Channel 2 is on her way over to interview you about Christmas of Joy."

This was even better. He could announce to the whole community his plan to aid single moms. Get them on board to make donations. Then he'd be able to help more women like Lacey. She was the one who'd inspired such a desire. He'd call her and have her join him for the interview if she was available.

"Perfect. Can you get Lacey on the phone for me?"

Hallie paused. "Are you dating now?"

"What?" He froze. Hallie had known he'd planned to ask Lacey out, and he'd apparently never updated her on their relationship status. But she'd seen Lacey's baby bump before he did. In fact, she'd tried to warn him. Did she think he'd actually date a woman who was pregnant with someone else's child? Just because he'd invited her to join him on stage at the tree lighting, and he took her a tree of her own, and when she touched his arm, he'd felt the warmth of connection . . .

"I'm sorry, sir. None of my business." Hallie retreated.

"Wait." He studied her guarded expression. She was his assistant, but she was also a woman. She might better understand relationships. "You don't think dating Lacey would be inappropriate?"

Her mouth parted, but she simply stared at him. Finally she said, "I once heard that people are attracted to others who are at about the same level of emotional health. If you're both healthy, it's not inappropriate."

Brendon rubbed his chin. Could that be why Lacey's ex left her after her illness improved? The man hadn't wanted to do the work it would take for himself to grow healthy alongside her?

Lacey had been separated and living on her own for years, but she'd remained committed to the possibility of reconciliation. That showed a lot of strength. Yeah, she'd have some wounds from her husband's rejection, and perhaps that was what led to her lapse in judgment and resulting pregnancy, but she'd owned her mistake, which he admired.

He was all about health, so the fact that he'd been interested in her in the first place should mean she was healthy as well. Her pregnancy had shocked him but hadn't changed who she was. How did he feel about the possibility of inviting both her and her child into his life?

"Mr. Wise, do you still want me to get Lacey on the phone for you?"

He blinked to bring his assistant back into focus. "No. I have her number on my cell." If he was going to ask Lacey out, he'd make it personal. Though he'd wait until after they filmed the news interview. He didn't want either of them to get distracted before their business concluded.

Lacey chided herself as she pulled into the parking lot. She shouldn't be this excited to see Brendon again. Theirs was a professional relationship with a touch of friendship. She was here to be interviewed about the event she'd planned. It would help grow her business. That was all. Though she couldn't help looking up at the windows to the top-floor boardroom where Brendon had asked her out last week.

It had been a long time since she'd gone on a date, and if she hadn't been expecting, she would have said yes to his invitation. Being with him was not only easy but inspirational.

Her belly fluttered. *Baby, not butterflies.*

As much as she admired Brendon and believed he'd make an amazing dad, he wasn't the father of her child. She'd do her best not to envy whoever got to have him in her life. She had God to provide for her, and He'd given her everything she needed.

After shifting into park, she gathered her belongings and gave herself one last glance in the rearview mirror. Not because she was seeing Brendon but because she was going to be on TV. She'd specifi-cally chosen the fitted wine-colored dress with pleats over her belly to complement the holiday theme, though she couldn't bring herself to wear matching lipstick. Her nude lip gloss was much safer.

She reached for the door handle, but before she could even get out of the car, Brendon was there, opening it for her. Very kind of him, but not something she would let herself get used to.

"I'm pleased you could make it on such short notice." He took her hand, and for being a smaller man, his grip was surprisingly firm.

She did her best to push herself up so he didn't feel her full weight. She also held back the groan that normally accompanied the climb from her vehicle. "Thanks for inviting me. It will be great promotion for my business."

"Happy to help." He released her hand, and she dug in the pocket of her plaid peacoat for a glove to replace his warmth.

Normally she turned down offers of help, but this was more like networking. She was grateful for the opportunity to show off her skills.

"The cameras are set up by the nativity to interview us. I already took them on a tour of the grounds."

Lacey kept stride with Brendon as they crossed the campus, and she was glad she'd worn her bootees. They were easy to walk in and also hid her swelling ankles.

"Are you keeping busy planning Christmas events over the next month?" Brendon wondered.

Lacey chuckled. "I took December off. I didn't want to worry about my water breaking in the middle of a party. Plus, I figured I'd need a break after Christmas of Joy. This job actually gave me the financial cushion I needed in order to relax for a month."

Brendon beamed at her. She'd always seen him as direct and enthusiastic, but his smile also felt personal. Like he truly was proud of the work she'd done and thought she deserved a holiday. "If you like that, you'll love what else I have planned."

They'd reached the amphitheater, and she turned to face him fully. What could he possibly be planning? An image of them sharing a fireside dinner popped into her mind, and she wanted to shake it away, but not as much as she wanted to study the depths of his hazel eyes. They started out as brown next to his pupil but blended into a green, blue, then gray on the outside. She wondered what color he put on his driver's license.

A familiar clip-clop finally tugged her attention toward Hallie tottering their way with microphones to pin to their clothing. If the girl had that much trouble walking on a normal day, she was going to need a wheelchair once she got pregnant. Well, a wheelchair or comfortable shoes.

"Who gets the first interview?" called a reporter in bright red. It would clash with Lacey's dress, but maybe they wouldn't be in the same shot.

Brendon motioned for Lacey to step ahead of him. "Ladies first."

Was he always such a gentleman? He could simply be taking extra time for Hallie to groom him. The assistant tamed an ash-brown curl that still hung over Brendon's forehead, then straightened his wine-colored tie that matched Lacey's outfit.

Lacey took a deep breath to refocus. "How do I look?"

Brendon had already been looking at her, but now his gaze roved from her long hair down to her short boots and back. One corner of his lips curved. "Radiant."

Her cheeks burned at his compliment, but in a good way. Like the sting of a hot tub in a snowstorm.

"Alright, Lacey." The reporter looked at her clipboard. "Lacey Foster, right?"

"Yes." Lacey widened her eyes at Brendon in mock fear before taking her place in front of the camera.

"I'm Melanie McGuire. Pleased to meet you." The reporter asked a few boring questions before finally getting to the meat of her message. Then Lacey took over, sharing her passion for Oil of Joy and her delight in being able to create the first annual Christmas of Joy.

"That brings us to Gifts of Joy," Melanie announced. "Brendon, do you want to step in here? Lacey, stay put."

"Okay." Lacey didn't know what Gifts of Joy meant, but at least her part was about over, and it had been less painful than expected. She smiled at Brendon as he joined her in the stable. Add a donkey and Gemma in her angel costume, and they'd practically have a living nativity.

Though Brendon wasn't Joseph. He was simply offering gifts as a wise man. Wise man. She smirked at the meaning in his last name.

Melanie counted down for the camera to start rolling again, then turned to face Brendon and Lacey from behind the lens. "Brendon, tell us about your inspiration for Gifts of Joy."

Brendon cleared his throat and stood straighter. He wasn't much taller than Lacey. She should date him simply as an excuse to never wear high heels again.

"My mother started Oil of Joy twenty years ago out of the back of her minivan. She still oversees production of the oils, but her favorite part is selling them face-to-face at the local German holiday market, Christkindlmarkt, opening today."

Lacey knew about Brendon's mom from her experience selling the company's oils. She'd seen Mrs. Wise speak at their annual conference last year. The woman had a way of looking at twenty thousand people that made them feel seen. Now that Lacey knew Brendon, she believed it to be an accurate assumption and a trait passed down through the family.

Brendon continued. "Every year we are excited to give back to the community, and we donate one hundred percent of the earnings from the Christmas market to a worthy charity."

Lacey nodded along. She loved that about the company.

Brendon put a hand on her back. "This year I've been inspired to donate to single moms."

The puff of air Lacey had been about to exhale crystalized in her lungs. She wasn't here as a colleague. She was here as a charity. Someone who was incapable of helping herself. Someone who needed him to be her savior.

Her eyes locked on to Brendon like a target. She hoped the heat of her laser sight would warn him to back off before crossing boundaries. But he was too busy smiling at the camera.

"Both my mother, who started this company, and my event planner for Christmas of Joy are strong single mothers."

Blood surged through her veins, almost drowning out Brendon's monologue. How much more of this was she supposed to listen to? Did he expect her to simply stand there and smile so everyone watching would pity her and buy more product?

"As the son of a single mom, I know how hard it is to parent alone in our family-oriented community. So let's reach out and lend a hand."

She willed him to be done. She willed him not to say anything about how she could take the month off because of how much he'd paid her. Or about how she hadn't had the energy to put up her own Christmas tree. Or about the ex she now regretted discussing.

He turned to her proudly. Oh so proudly. Like he had just single-handedly saved the planet. Maybe all men were this way. Brendon saw himself as a knight in shining armor, but he was more like a wise man who couldn't even stay on his camel. That made him a fool. And she felt the fool for falling for him.

She'd been fighting to hold it together, but a lone tear broke free and drew an icy line down her cheek.

"She's crying," Melanie rasped. "Get a close-up."

Wouldn't that be good for sales—a pathetic single mom who got overwhelmed by help from strangers because she wasn't capable of taking care of herself? Lacey swiped the liquid emotion from her face.

Brendon rubbed her back, though it felt more like stabbing her in the back. "I thought that would touch you."

Touched? It was a gut punch. She pulled away and cradled her belly. If she had a son, she'd teach him not to think men had to rescue women.

The man continued to grin at her, as if expecting praise. Hallie tottered between them, her bulging eyes taking in what was really going on. "Mr. Wise, can I have a moment with you, please?"

Lacey huffed at the sight of a woman trying to rescue her boss— only the boss was too arrogant to realize how much trouble he'd gotten himself into.

"In a minute, Hallie." Brendon stepped past his assistant and reached for Lacey's gloved hands.

She watched him lift her fingers between them, disconnected, and wondered how she'd ever been attracted to him.

"Lacey, can I take you to lunch?"

He couldn't be asking her out again. Unless he was like Scott and needed to be needed.

She narrowed her eyes to get a better read. Why did he have to appear so genuinely eager to please? It had to be his youthful appearance that made people trust him. He was a charlatan. "Because I'm a poor single mom who can't afford to eat for two?"

"No." His eyebrows dipped down in the middle. "Because I'd like to keep getting to know you better. You said you aren't dating, but now that I'm aware of your condition, you can see I'm asking you both out."

For a brief second she wanted what he offered—interest in her mind and heart and child. It would be nice to not be alone. But as good as it would feel having him there for her, he'd just proven that once she stopped needing him, he'd go rescue someone else.

She stood taller, stretching against the constant throbbing in her lower back. "We don't need you to rescue us. Go offer your charity elsewhere."

Chapter Six

BRENDON ROCKED BACK on his heels at the sight of Lacey storming away.

"Ouch, dude," the cameraman said.

This was not how Brendon had imagined she'd respond to his invitation. She wasn't charity. She was inspiration.

Did he follow or let her cool off? Never one to give up, he took a step forward, ready to push into a run.

Hallie blocked him, palm out. He could easily topple her over to keep going, but Lacey already seemed to think he was a monster, and tackling his assistant wouldn't help his image.

"What just happened?" He'd thought he was good at communication. He'd given a keynote about it only two months ago. Did business basics not transfer to relationships?

Hallie wrinkled her face in pity. "She didn't want to be the poster child for single parents."

He closed his eyes. Is that how she'd felt? Having his assistant pity *him* offered a taste of the humble pie Lacey must have thought he'd been serving.

He opened his eyes to see how far she'd gotten. She'd only made it to the skating rink. Surely he could catch her. "I have to go explain. Why'd you stop me?"

Hallie nodded toward Melanie, packing her things. "I think you'd better rerecord your interview if you want to ever be able to smooth things over with Lacey."

He ran a hand over his coarse hair and looked after the pregnant woman. She was angry he'd talked about the needs of single moms like her on television, but it wasn't too late to keep her tears from making the evening news. He had to let her go if he was ever going to win her back.

"Melanie." He marched toward the reporter. "We need to reshoot the last part of my interview."

"Why?" She tossed her auburn bob. "It went great. We got to see Lacey's bleeding heart. If it bleeds, it leads."

Well, that was morbid. "My goal with donating to single moms is to help, not harm. Won't you please partner with me in doing so?"

"Not my job." Melanie clicked her tongue. "My job is to get ratings, which ultimately helps *you*."

Frustration simmered, threatening to boil over. Brendon kept trying to make things right, and he just kept making them worse. "I don't want Oil of Joy to profit at anyone else's expense."

Her high-pitched laugh mocked him as she swung a purse over her shoulder. "That's how this game is played, my friend."

Hallie stepped in Melanie's path, arms crossed and steadier than Brendon had ever seen her. "Ms. McGuire, are you the same Melanie McGuire who has a spring wedding scheduled on our campus?"

Brendon arched his eyebrows. If the reporter thought this was a game, she'd have to play hardball with his assistant.

Melanie paused. "Yeah, by the fountain. Why?"

"If you're going to disrespect our CEO by spinning our company's vision, I'm going to have to restrict you from the premises."

The humor drained from Melanie's face. She glanced at Brendon to see if he was on board with banishing her.

"That sounds like it could make a juicy headline too." He shrugged. "Reporter not allowed to attend her own wedding . . ."

Hallie lowered her chin. "Though it wouldn't be the first time you've been kicked off private property, would it now, Ms. McGuire?"

Brendon wasn't even going to ask about that one. He just made a mental note to double Hallie's Christmas bonus. And, you know, stay on her good side.

"Fine." Melanie marched back to her spot from earlier and gestured for the cameraman to do the same. "Are we cutting the Foster chick out entirely or just focusing more on your mother?"

He'd leave Lacey in to promote her business, and then he was going to have to go talk to Mom. She was better at this relationship stuff than he was.

"You look so pretty," Gemma gushed. "I love your dress."

Lacey grunted. After leaving Brendon, she'd immediately gone searching for her old pal. All her local friends had taken sides in her divorce, and she needed someone who could be impartial. Unfortunately, Gemma was also friends with an actor in the troupe hired to hand out candy canes at the German Christmas market. Lacey wasn't thrilled about hanging around outside with nothing but wool tights on her legs, but at least she wasn't as ill-dressed as Gemma.

"It's so cold. How are you not freezing in your dirndl?"

Her friend wore the traditional green costume over a white shirt with puffy sleeves, and her long braids wrapped around her head. Yeah, she looked silly, but also, if any screenwriters from Disney saw her, they would immediately go home and write a princess story set in Germany.

Gemma smiled her Sleeping Beauty smile and handed candy canes to two little girls who stared at her in awe. "Being cold is a good excuse for Karson to put his arms around me when he gets here."

"Way to rub it in."

"Oh, I'm sorry." Gemma held a hand to her heart. "I forget not everyone is as happily in love as I am. Here, have a candy cane."

Lacey lifted her palm to pass, then remembered Brendon saying peppermint helped alleviate nausea. She took the treat, peeled down the ends of plastic, and let the sweet zing carry her back to better days. Oh, how quickly things had changed since she'd drunk hot cocoa with the essential oils CEO. He apparently wasn't who she'd thought he was, but maybe her expectations had been too high.

She sighed at the merriment surrounding her, from the sounds of polka music to the scents of warm, yeasty pretzels and sizzling sausages. Little wooden booths with red-and-white striped awnings for roofs lined the streets from where artists peddled their wares. White lights zigzagged overhead and around trees, though their wattage seemed dim in the middle of the gray day. Normally the mountains offered a pristine backdrop, but the same clouds that hid them also evoked excitement for the possibility of snow. A far corner held metal pens for a petting zoo, and a green train engine gave rides from one end of the festival to the other.

Gemma tossed a handful of candy canes to the train passengers as they chugged by.

"Why are you giving out candy canes instead of German candy?" Lacey asked around the stick in her cheek.

Her friend bestowed her with a benevolent smile. "Germany invented the candy cane. Sugar sticks were given to kids to keep them quiet during a living crèche ceremony. In honor of the occasion, they were bent into shepherds' crooks."

"Huh." Too bad Lacey hadn't had a candy cane to keep Brendon quiet earlier.

Gemma rubbed a passing baby's cheeks and cooed. The child clapped and smiled. Lacey would have to remember Gemma's charms after her own baby was born. She could turn to this woman for more than love advice. Not that she was in love. Nor had she asked for advice. Yet.

Gemma glanced at her watch, grabbed Lacey's arm, and headed toward the shell of a building that had been decorated to serve as a *Bier Haus*. "I have half an hour before I have to help line people up for the lantern parade. So tell me why you're really here."

Lacey rolled her eyes and followed along. Sometimes Gemma seemed lost in daydreams and disengaged from reality. Other times her experience as a screenwriter gave her unexpected insight.

Once inside the barn doors, the warmth of heaters washed over Lacey, thawing her fingers and toes. Across the room a couple of men with thick accents sang along to the foreign music. As the women took a seat at the other end of the long table, the men's boisterous antics didn't prevent their eyes from following Gemma.

Gemma didn't even seem to notice. "Is this about the Oil of Joy owner?" she asked.

Lacey folded her hands together for added warmth. "He brought me a Christmas tree Saturday."

Gemma clapped. "I knew he liked you."

That wasn't the issue. Lacey shrugged. "Well, yeah. He liked me before he knew I was pregnant. That's why he asked me out. But now it feels like charity."

Gemma rested her forearms on the table and leaned closer. "Just because he brought you a tree? Perhaps he was thanking you for making his tree lighting a success."

"That's what he said, but . . ." Lacey shook her head and looked to the rafters. Admitting her humiliation would make it real. "Then he announced in a television interview that this year he's donating the proceeds from his fundraiser to help single moms like me."

Gemma gasped. But then her vibrant blue eyes widened and her hands churned between them, as if she was trying to produce some kind of excuse. She was like that with her innocence and optimism. All she could drag up was, "At least he's generous."

"Yeah, so was Scott." But it was just to make himself look and feel good.

"Did you talk to him about it? Tell him how you felt?"

Lacey shrugged. "He asked me out again, and I told him to offer his charity elsewhere."

Gemma planted her elbow on the table and her chin in her hand. "What did he say to that?"

"That's when I left." Emotion clogged Lacey's throat even now. "I was afraid to cry even more in front of the cameras. But he didn't follow. I think that's what stings the most." Yeah. Now that she thought about it, his silence said more than his words had. "He got what he wanted for his company, and it was never about me."

Gemma frowned, which was still too pretty to be fair. "But he asked you out, Lacey. He asked you out knowing you're pregnant. So maybe he does care."

"Or maybe he has a hero complex and feels powerful when dating weak, needy women."

"You're not weak. Or needy."

"Not anymore."

Gemma's hand dropped to hold Lacey's. The feel of it was still cold enough to make her shiver, but the connection brought warmth to her heart.

"You're the toughest woman I know."

"I cried in my Lamaze class."

"My sister fainted in hers."

Lacey sniffed to hold back tears but ended up laughing at the comparison between how pathetic she felt and the idea that even married women struggled with childbirth. "You know what's weird? The holidays are supposed to be merry and bright, but I feel like the struggle I'm going through with this pregnancy makes Christmas all the more real. We're celebrating the birth of Jesus, while in actuality, it had to be so scary and painful. I mean, imagine if I was going into labor and someone tried to send me over to the petting zoo to give birth."

Gemma guffawed in her cute little breathy way. "I'd never thought of a stable and manger in that light before, but you're right. That would be the least hygienic place to bring a baby into the world, let alone the Savior of humanity."

Lacey cringed a little inside at the term *Savior*. She didn't want to rely on anyone to save her ever again. She took a deep, calming breath, and squared her shoulders with resolve. "I'm going to be fine. If Mary can do it, so can I."

Chapter Seven

In the dimming light, Brendon wove his way through the crowd toward the Christmas of Joy booth at the end of the German Christmas market. Usually he enjoyed the liveliness of people playing accordion music and wearing bright costumes, but today they slowed his progress and delayed his purpose.

Finally he reached the booth where a line of customers hid his mother. He circled around them next to the red wagon trimmed with garland that had been set up beside the booth as part of their display. It held three large barrels, each stenciled with a letter on it to spell out J-O-Y. The word taunted him.

He squeezed into the shop beside Mom to help ring up sales since they were closing soon. "Hey, Mom."

She paused to kiss him on his cheek with her thin lips, which looked even thinner because of the dark lipstick she loved so much. He scrubbed off the sure imprint.

She tucked an order of oils into shredded red paper inside a raffia bag and added the wooden Christmas star with the cutout wise men. The ornament resembled one that had been passed through the Wise clan for generations, even back when they'd been known as the Weises, and Brendon loved the opportunity to continue their legacy.

"I saw you on the news," Mom said.

So the story had come out already. Hopefully, Melanie cleaned it up the way he'd asked her to. "What did you think?"

Mom handed the gift bag to the woman waiting, then took the next order. "I'm touched by your heart for single moms."

He rung up the sale. "I wish everyone was."

Mom turned to face him, her pale eyes narrowing behind rimless glasses. "Who isn't?"

He took her customer's credit card and swiped it since Mom was too busy studying him. "The single woman who decorated the campus for Christmas."

"Oh?" Mom returned to bagging orders. "Lacey Foster?"

Brendon slid his eyes sideways, his turn to study her. How much had she seen in his interview? "Yes."

"She's the one you were going to ask out before you realized she was pregnant?"

Brendon rolled his eyes. He'd been unwise to announce his intentions before even having met the woman face-to-face. "Yes."

"The one you had join you on stage for the tree lighting after she got sick in the bushes?"

"Yes, Mom." Obviously his mother knew who he was talking about.

"I like her." Mom's chin-length brown hair hid her square face from him as she focused on the amber vials in her hands. "She seemed to think highly of you in her interview."

Brendon exhaled. That was a relief. "Good." Hopefully, that meant Melanie hadn't aired the footage of Lacey crying and storming away.

Mom handed the full bag to the next man in line. "Are you staying for the lantern parade?" she asked him.

The man looked around. "What's a lantern parade?"

Mom clasped her hands in front of her heart, like she was about to tell the most beautiful story. Brendon listened, though he knew it by heart. "In Germany they celebrate St. Martin's Day with a lantern parade. Tradition says St. Martin was a soldier who had given away his last cent when he spied a man shivering in the cold. Out of compassion he took off his cloak and cut it in half with his sword to share. The whole town heard of his generosity and wanted to praise him."

Brendon returned the customer's credit card while finishing the story. "Embarrassed by the attention, St. Martin hid in a goose house, so the townsfolk had to use lanterns to search for him. The lanterns now represent his kindness, which we should all emulate."

"Yes." Mom looked from the customer to Brendon. "And it's an example of how we don't do kind things in order to receive praise."

Brendon stood rigid as the customer thanked them and wandered away. It felt like Mom had just accused him of only donating to single moms in order to gain attention for himself. "I'm not trying to get praise."

Mom pulled out a couple of paper lantern kits for them to make. She set one on the counter in front of him. "Then why does it bother you if Lacey Foster doesn't praise you?"

He jerked like he'd been slapped. "She doesn't have to praise me. I just thought she'd be grateful I want to help."

Mom unfolded the four sides of her lantern and studied its 3D shape before cutting out pieces like it was a paper snowflake. "Did she ask for help?"

"No." He shrugged, bewildered that he was even having this conversation. Every year he received so many requests for donations that he had to turn some down. Never had anyone rejected his donation. "She's not the type of person to ask for help. I just know from helping you how much work it is to be a single mom. Isn't that what the Bible calls pure religion? To help widows and orphans?"

Mom stuck a battery-operated votive inside her lantern and offered a magnanimous smile in the flickering glow. "James 1:27 also says not to let the world corrupt you."

Brendon held his hands wide. If giving to the needy was the worst thing he ever did, she had a pretty good kid. "How is the world corrupting me? I'm simply trying to do a good deed. To be kind."

Mom turned to face him, her head tilting, as if in compassion. "Good deeds don't get you into heaven. God doesn't need you. Whether you sell everything you have and give it to the poor or not, God is going to provide for them."

Brendon sucked in a deep breath, and the admonition stung like eucalyptus oil to his sinuses. He was willing to sell all he had—that wasn't the issue. But wouldn't he be able to give more to the needy if he used what he had to bring in a profit? There was literally a parable about Jesus telling servants to use their talents wisely. "If God doesn't need me to support others financially with my earnings, then what is my purpose?"

"Hon." She used the term of endearment that had slipped out when he'd been talking to Lacey the other day. That was where it came from. "God doesn't need you—He wants you. He's inviting you to share the wealth He's given you so you can experience the joy of giving. That joy of giving isn't going to come from man's praise. It's going to come in spite of how the world treats you. Pure love is the only love that doesn't require anything in return. St. Martin knew that."

Brendon rubbed a hand over his face. He'd grown up with the story of St. Martin, but he'd missed the whole point. All the while he'd been trying to fix things for Lacey, it wasn't his help she needed. "I have to go apologize."

"Good." Mom opened his lantern, which he hadn't touched, and stuck the second LED candle inside. "Take her my lantern so she can walk in the parade with you. My feet ache from standing all day, so I'm going to skip it."

Brendon frowned down at the handles on the lanterns. He'd love to walk with Lacey in the parade, but he doubted she could get there in time. The parking lot had been pretty much full when he'd arrived anyway. "I think we would have had to plan ahead for her to walk in the parade with me."

Mom sent him a sly smile, then nodded toward the petting zoo. "It looks like God was planning ahead."

Brendon's pulse surged with wonder. He looked in the direction Mom motioned. Across the walkway stood a tall woman with long dark-blond hair. She had her back to him as she tried to feed sheep while avoiding a camel's attempts at stealing the snack. Brendon wanted to believe the woman was Lacey. Who else would wear a dress outside in these temperatures? But she was stick skinny. Definitely not pregnant.

Having Lacey just show up here when he wanted her to would

have been too much of a coincidence. If he wanted something, he had to work for it. God didn't just drop gifts in his lap like that. "Mom, that woman is . . ."

The woman turned, her stomach sticking out in a way that would rival Santa's. Whoa. How did Lacey stay balanced?

"She's what?" Mom asked.

She wasn't who he'd thought she was at first. While he'd expected her to need his help, she'd actually been what he needed. She'd challenged his mindset and forced him to see how he'd become prideful about giving. That made her worth waiting for.

"If she ever goes out with me, I'll consider her—and her child—a gift from heaven."

⁓⚜⁓

Lacey shivered and crossed her arms above her belly. She wished she hadn't promised Gemma she'd stick around to watch the parade. If she had to wait much longer, she'd give in and buy a second apple strudel. Her little nugget loved apples, and the dessert had been the perfect blend of sweet and tart. Not to mention the flaky crust that was almost rich enough to make up for the rich man who'd turned her stomach sour earlier.

"Lacey?"

She shook her head to get his voice out of her mind.

"Miss Foster?"

The use of her surname stopped her. She wouldn't have imagined anyone referring to her so properly.

She whirled away from the camel to find Brendon holding two paper lanterns that splashed golden light across his sharp features. In spite of his youthful appearance, the wisdom of age flickered in his eyes.

"I owe you an apology," he said.

She inhaled in surprise and was hit with the ripe scent of petting zoo. Definitely not a smell Brendon would ever want in one of his oils. She exhaled slowly, taking time to gather her thoughts.

Earlier she'd been lamenting how Brendon hadn't followed her, but she'd never expected him to show up at Christkindlmarkt. Of course, Oil of Joy had a booth here.

So he hadn't followed her. They were both at the market out of mere coincidence. Was he really sorry or simply doing damage control?

"What are you apologizing for?" she asked.

He studied her. His chest rose and fell. "I assumed you needed my help. You don't. That was arrogant and insensitive of me."

She wanted to believe him, but was his pride something he'd ever be able to see on his own, or would he always need someone to point it out to him? At least he'd admitted it, whereas Scott never could. "Thank you."

"I wanted to follow you when you left earlier, but Hallie suggested I redo my interview with Melanie while I had the chance. I hoped that if I fixed the news segment, then you'd be more likely to believe me when I said I was sorry."

She trembled, though with the way her heart also seemed to shiver, it was more than the cold that made her shaky. This moment, this apology, wasn't only about him. It was about the panic that rang warning sirens inside at the thought of depending on somebody else ever again. Only because she hadn't depended on Brendon did it not devastate when he let her down. She'd keep it that way. "I forgive you."

His shoulders sagged. "You don't know how much that means."

Really? She hugged herself tighter.

"I don't presume to be in a place where I can ask you on a date again, but I do want to be your friend."

Okay, that word *friend* was the white flag she'd been waiting for. Friends were on equal ground. They had something to offer each other. "I'd like that."

He held up a lantern. "I brought you a lantern, if you want to join me in the parade."

She faltered. "You need to stop giving me things."

Brendon took a step back and swung one lamp wide as if pointing across the street. "This isn't from me. My mom told me to give it to you. Her feet hurt too much to walk in the parade."

Lacey glanced in the direction he was pointing to find the older woman polka dancing outside her booth with some young guy in lederhosen. "Are you sure about that?"

Brendon did a double take. "That's what she told me, anyway. I can see why you might have questions."

Lacey let a laugh escape. "Brendon, when I left your campus earlier, it wasn't because I didn't want to talk to you. It was because I didn't want to talk to you in front of a camera."

"I was an idiot." He sighed. "For some reason I thought you would be honored to know you inspired my choice of charity for the year. It was supposed to be a show of respect."

She liked the word *respect*. He was saying all the right things. Was it possible his heart could be in the right place? "I love that you want to donate your funds to single moms, but know I'm not going to be one of them."

He hesitated, then nodded.

"Brendon . . ." She used a warning tone that made her already sound like a mom with a toddler.

He set his jaw. "Sorry. It's just that I was raised by a single mother and understand how hard it can be. Not only for single mothers but for lots of families. I can offer your child things that you might not be able to, and I want you to be able to ask me for help anytime."

Her heart hitched. He couldn't be her safety net. "I'm not going to ask."

"Okay, but—"

She stopped him with a look that matched her earlier warning tone. If he didn't accept her boundary, then she would still feel like a charity case.

He pressed his lips together.

"Thank you."

With his mouth still pinched shut, he offered a lantern and lifted his eyebrows. As adorable as his expression was, he could make that face and get away with anything. It wasn't the kind of rugged, sexy smolder that had once attracted her to Scott. It was more a contagious enthusiasm for life. Definitely hard to resist, which scared her.

She took the lantern with a huff. "I'm only taking this because it's from your mom." A gift from one single mom to another. She'd pay it forward after her baby was born and started his or her own Fortune 500 company.

The polka music came to a finale with the screeching drawl of a trombone. Then the hum from multiple conversations merged into a haunting rendition of "We Three Kings." A river of lanterns poured onto the street, led by two Fräuleins holding a long banner between them. Gemma waved from the far side of the banner, staring longer than she should have at Brendon. Behind her, families, groups of teenagers, and elderly couples bumped and jostled along, their voices united in song, their lights shining in guidance like the star of Bethlehem.

Brendon turned to stand beside Lacey, shoulder to shoulder. "Shall we?"

Joy wrapped itself around her, insulating her from the cold. There she found the peace of community with strangers. The beauty of swinging lanterns under a navy sky. The hope of ancient mysteries that meant the God of old still loved her today. And in that moment there was honestly no place else she'd rather be.

She didn't even have to answer Brendon with words but joined in step and song. Together they became part of a world that she wanted to introduce her child to. A world that built up rather than tore down. A world that gave more than it took. Her child wouldn't get that from her ex, but it existed when people took the time to create it.

Lacey's eyes met Brendon's, and her vision blurred, a kaleidoscope of lantern lights. She blinked and looked away. She wasn't going to ruin this perfect moment with tears.

All too soon they ran out of road, and the parade faded with extinguished candles and broken melodies. Night had fallen without her permission. "I wish the parade could have gone on forever."

Brendon turned to face her again. Their lanterns flickered between them, casting shadows that she hoped hid her regret at having to leave him.

"I can't offer you an infinite parade, but we do have a candle-lighting service at our church the afternoon of Christmas Eve."

Now she wished for a little more light to reveal secrets only Brendon's expression could tell. She'd said she wasn't dating, and she'd already turned Brendon down twice, but he seemed the determined sort. "Are you asking me out?"

"No."

That was okay. She wasn't dating, so it would be silly to feel disappointed by his response. *Baby, not butterflies.*

"I'm inviting you whether you ever want to see me again or not. I think you'd enjoy it."

She nodded. She definitely wanted more of what she'd just experienced.

Apparently encouraged by her nod, Brendon continued. "If in the meantime we start texting each other or, you know, talking on the phone, you're welcome to sit by me at the service. Just because I'll be there too. And it's nice to sit with a friend."

Oh baby, those were butterflies.

Chapter Eight

Brendon: Did you see
the real-life gingerbread
house in Yalecrest?

Lacey: Yes! I used to live
in that neighborhood, and
I know the homeowner.
She's an interior designer,
and she made all the
decorations herself. Cute
enough to eat.

Brendon: Pregnancy
cravings?

Lacey: I crave apples and
potatoes.

Brendon: They ARE
ap-peal-ing.

Lacey: Nice dad joke.

December 13

Brendon: I saw a family at the living nativity last night. The youngest son pointed and said, "There's baby Jesus!" Then the older son said, "He's just a prophet, right, Dad?" It made me sad they are missing the true gift of Christmas but also glad that we were able to put up a living nativity.

Lacey: I'm glad too. It breaks my heart that people miss who Jesus is and what he's done. It's got to be a burden to try to earn salvation on your own.

Brendon: Been there.

Lacey: We all have. But it's not about us.

Brendon: Wise men still seek him.

Lacey: You would know. ●

December 14

Brendon: I asked the owner of the petting zoo if she would want to offer camel rides at Christmas of Joy next year. She said yes.

Lacey: Who wants to ride a camel?

Brendon: Me.

Lacey: I take back what I said about you being a wise man.

Brendon: You realize wise men are literally known for riding camels, right?

Lacey: I'm still stuck on the fact that Mary rode a donkey while pregnant without puking.

Brendon: She could have puked. We don't know. The Gospels might've kindly omitted that part.

Lacey: And the part where Joseph was like, "What have I gotten myself into?"

Brendon: Joseph wanted to be there for her. That part was clear.

December 15

Lacey: My church threw me a baby shower today. It made me wish I'd found out my baby's gender. Because now whether I have a boy or girl, the poor kid is going to be wearing nothing but yellow for the first year of life.

Brendon: Am I allowed to get your baby gifts? Because I could fix that.

Lacey: No.

Brendon: Didn't think so. Besides clothes that aren't yellow, do you have everything else you need?

Lacey: Yes. I decorated the nursery with stars. I

tell people the theme is
for "Twinkle Twinkle Little
Star," but secretly it's in
honor of the Christmas
star.

Brendon: Your secrets are
safe with me.

December 16

Brendon: I got your
Christmas card. Very
creative how you put
the bow on your belly
with a "Do not open until
Christmas" tag. Is that
your due date?

Lacey: Yes. Though I'd be
okay if my nugget came
sooner. I'm so over this
heartburn and back pain.

Brendon: Do you have
names picked out?

Lacey: I'm probably
going to use one of my
grandparents' names.

Brendon: Chuck and
Gladys?

Lacey: How'd you know?

December 17

Lacey: When did you first find out Santa isn't real? I'm trying to decide how to tell Gladys.

Brendon: My uncle dressed up as Santa when I was five, and I recognized him. I'd had my suspicions, so I pulled down his beard.

Lacey: Shrewd. I was a little older. I asked my mom if he was real, and she said, "What do you think?" Finally I was like, "I think if he was real, you'd say so."

Brendon: Sounds like a smart way to go with Gladys.

December 18

Lacey: One week!!!

Brendon: Until you see me at the Christmas Eve service? I didn't realize you missed me so much.

Lacey: No. Until Chuck is due and I get to dress him in yellow. I see you in six days . . . if I decide to sit with you. I mean, you said we'd sit together after we got to know each other better through texts and phone calls, but you've never called.

Brendon: I wasn't sure if you'd answer. Calling now.

December 19

Brendon: Just a reminder that I'm taking a quick business trip to New York today, so I won't be able to call from the plane, and my time will be ahead of yours by two hours. If we don't get a chance to connect, I apologize. I'd much rather talk to you than my advertising agency.

Lacey: You're going to try to get them to plan a campaign around you riding a camel and giving out myrrh, huh?

Brendon: Genius. Can I
fire them and hire you?

Lacey: You know how I
feel about camels.

Brendon: You're going to
have to remind me. Over
dinner tomorrow night?

Lacey: Are you asking me
out?

Brendon: I know better.
This is strictly business.

Lacey: I'm taking the
month off from work, but
I suppose I could make an
exception.

December 20

Brendon: I'm stuck at
JFK. Flights have been
grounded due to snow.

Lacey: I usually love snow,
but I hate it when it ruins
my business dinners. Do
you have a place to stay
tonight?

Brendon: I'm in a taxi on

the way to my hotel. Call
you when I get there.

December 21

Lacey: Let me know when
you land so I know you're
home safe. I might not
message back right away
because I'm going with
Gemma to a production of
A Christmas Carol.

Brendon: I'm home. "God
bless us everyone."

Lacey: I just got out of the
show. Are you still awake?

Lacey: Good night.

December 22

Brendon: I'm canceling a
less important business
dinner so I can do
business with you this
evening.

Lacey: I'm sick. Not sure
if I overdid it yesterday
or I caught the bug going
around. Just gonna sleep
all day.

Brendon: I'm sending over
chicken noodle soup.

Lacey: Don't you dare.

Brendon: I do it for all my
business associates.

Lacey: Liar.

Brendon: You didn't let
me finish. I do it for all my
business associates who
are pregnant with babies
named Chuck or Gladys.

Lacey: If I feel this bad
with a little cold, how am
I going to make it through
labor?

Brendon: You're not going
to do it alone.

December 23

Brendon: You feeling any
better?

Lacey: Physically, yes.
Emotionally, I'm a wreck.
What am I going to do
when I have a baby and
get sick? I can't sleep
all day. And I'll probably

make my baby sick. I
don't know how to take
care of a sick baby. I don't
even know how to take
care of a healthy baby.

Brendon: You could ask
for help.

Brendon: Lacey?

Brendon: You don't have
to ask me for help, but I'm
here for you. As are a lot
of other people.

Brendon: I hope to see
you tomorrow.

Chapter Nine

Lacey wanted to see Brendon so badly it scared her, which was why she considered not going to the Christmas Eve service. In the end she had nothing else to distract her until her parents arrived that night, so she put on her green crushed-velvet wrap dress and drove through the slushy streets to a church much smaller than she'd expected the mogul to attend. If he was tithing 10 percent of his income, they must have been using it for mission work.

The interior of the mid-century-modern building was just as clean and simple. A coffee bar in the corner smelled of French roast, and a Christmas tree between two sets of double doors held ornaments that were also gift tags. She twisted a tag around to better read it.

Boy, age 7. Tonka truck.

Her heart went out to that kid. What kind of situation did he have to be in where his parents couldn't afford to buy him a toy? She hoped somebody had, though the fact that the tag remained on the tree on Christmas Eve didn't bode well.

A figure stepped beside her, and she knew it was Brendon before she even looked. His energy made her both comfortable and agitated in his presence—agitated mostly by how comfortable she felt with him.

He nodded to the tags on the tree. "They're all coming to Christmas of Joy tonight to receive their gifts. We sponsor families, and I hung the tags so other people in the church could pick one or two and go shopping, but I'll take care of the rest that are left."

Lacey's heart warmed. "Is it too late for me to buy this Tonka truck?"

Brendon's eyes searched hers—for what she didn't know. "You're going to be a great mom."

Her throat clogged. Those might have been the words she'd needed to hear, but they didn't answer her question. She sniffed away her sentiment. "Thanks. Is it too late to get this gift?"

"Not if you want to go shopping with me after the service."

She laughed and looked away. "You don't give up easily, do you?"

"No, but you have to understand that I didn't know if you were going to come today or not. I didn't know if I'd ever see you again or if you'd even respond to any more messages. So forgive me if I don't want to let you out of my sight." One corner of his lips curved up. "But also, if you're going shopping, you might as well go with me."

Had anyone ever pursued her so fiercely while being completely respectful of her boundaries? It had her questioning whether she needed boundaries or not. Which made her want to build walls. "Mr. Wise . . ."

"It's just shopping, Lacey."

He'd refused to revert to the more formal address the way he always had before, and the use of her given name sent her pulse galloping. Because they both knew it was practically a date.

"And right now we're simply going to sit in a church service. You don't even have to sit with me if you don't want."

She wanted so much more than that. "I'll sit with you."

His smile lit fully this time, like the star on top of the tree after missing bulbs had been replaced. "Mom saved us a table."

Lacey closed her eyes. She should have expected as much since it was Christmas Eve, but meeting Brendon's family seemed too personal. Intimate.

"Are you coming, or should I take your hand to guide you?"

Lacey's eyes flew wide. She clutched her fingers together below her belly. "Are you trying to start a scandal?"

Brendon looked around at the families in their holiday best. "I was thinking of you, not them, but, hey . . ." His amused gaze returned to her, and he shrugged. "Could be fun."

In a city where image was everything, the man needed his assistant here to keep him out of trouble.

Lacey sighed, trying to refocus on her reason for being at church. *Baby Jesus, not butterflies.* "I'm coming."

She followed Brendon into the dimly lit sanctuary. The room had been filled with round tables rather than rows of seats that she assumed regularly held parishioners. White twinkle lights decorated the garland and trees along the walls, while each table held a plate of Christmas cookies, coloring sheets for kids, and unlit taper candles with round cardboard drip protectors around their centers. She'd come because of those candles, but she loved everything else the service seemed to offer.

"Lacey, meet my mom, Elizabeth."

The woman had Brendon's coloring, though she painted her small mouth a shade much darker.

Lacey shook her strong hand. "Nice to meet you. Thank you for letting me carry your lantern in the parade the other day. I loved it."

"You're welcome, hon." Elizabeth pointed to the plate of cookies. "I also made you my favorite apple cinnamon oatmeal cookies with cream cheese frosting."

Lacey's eyes widened, and she glanced toward the cookies in shock. Not only had Brendon told his mom about her pregnancy cravings, but the woman had made a dessert specifically to satisfy. The two of them had never met. Lacey had never even gone out with Brendon. She was carrying another man's child. It was too much.

"Try them," Elizabeth encouraged.

At least if Lacey's mouth was full, she wouldn't have to think of anything to say. She reached for a crumbly cookie and took a sweet bite. Okay, she'd amend her rule about accepting gifts from Brendon's family. Cookies were acceptable. "So good."

A strum of the guitar onstage led them into worship through Christmas carols.

Lacey set her cookie on a napkin and swallowed to join in. This was the peace she needed after yesterday's meltdown. It wasn't about the impending pain of childbirth or single parenting. It wasn't about fear over trying to balance a career with a kid. It wasn't the lonely ache inside that disappeared whenever she talked with Brendon but then intensified whenever they were apart. It was about the way God came to earth and experienced pain, fear, and loneliness for Himself. He did all of that for her. He was the only One who wouldn't let her down. He was all she needed.

As the music faded away, Pastor Dirk carried a chair to the stage and invited all the kids to join him for reading the Christmas story. Children of all ages giggled, shouted, and stomped their way up to the front. It was loud and irreverent and one of the most beautiful things Lacey had ever seen.

She rubbed her belly. She might not have enjoyed pregnancy, but it was her chance to be part of a miracle. Soon the life inside her would be one of those loud, irreverent children who wiggled in their spots on the stage.

The pastor opened his Bible. "Who likes presents?" he asked the kids.

Pandemonium from the peanut gallery.

Brendon smirked at Lacey.

She smirked right back. She didn't want presents from him, but she did want to kiss him. At the most inappropriate moment possible, she wondered how kissing would work with her huge stomach in the way.

God had to see her like the pastor saw all those kids on the stage. Loud, irreverent, and beautiful.

Sorry, Lord. Help me focus on what You have for me.

"Today we're going to talk about the presents the wise men brought Jesus."

She glanced at Brendon with that one. He was a Wise man who'd made his money off essential oils like myrrh. Not that she really knew what myrrh was. She listened to see if the pastor would explain its meaning.

First, he brought up gold, which the children seemed to enjoy talking about as much as presents. Frankincense was a little less relatable and included more of the kids joking about Frankenstein than anything. Impatient, she tucked her phone into the folds of her skirt and googled.

Myrrh came up in multiple passages, not only in the Gospels. She clicked on one. *My beloved is to me a sachet of myrrh resting between my breasts (Song of Songs 1:13).*

Her face warmed. This probably wasn't a reference the pastor would be using today, if ever. It had been a long time since she'd read Song of Songs, and she'd forgotten how steamy it was. Of course, she'd been married at the time, and it had hit differently. Now the verse felt like a reprimand. She'd had her chance at love, and she'd chosen a cheap knockoff. Brendon deserved the real thing.

She tilted her phone to make sure he couldn't read it. No use them both being distracted.

I'm trying, Lord.

Pastor Dirk leaned toward the kids. "My favorite of the gifts is actually myrrh."

Lacey arched her eyebrows. She doubted the pastor appreciated it for its history of perfume in the bedroom, so what did he find so appealing?

"While the gold represented Jesus as our King, and frankincense represented Him as our Priest, the myrrh represented Him as our Savior. See, myrrh is used in embalming. It was mixed in the wine Jesus was given during His crucifixion to help ease His pain, and it was used when He was entombed. That makes it the strangest gift to give a baby."

Little Chuck or Gladys rolled, pushing against Lacey's ribs. She pressed a palm to the spot, wondering how she would have reacted if someone had given her a casket or burial plot at her baby shower. Perhaps with horror? A parent should never outlive their child. So why did Pastor Dirk like the gift of myrrh so much?

"Here's the thing. God already had a plan for Jesus's resurrection.

In the same way, when your dreams die, He has a plan to resurrect them."

The words pushed Lacey's spine against her seat. Her dream had been for a happy family, but her child's father had remarried someone else. Her dream had been laid to rest. It couldn't be resurrected.

As her thoughts darkened, so did the lighting, including the decorative white Christmas lights on greenery around the room. Only a wreath with four taper candles flickered from onstage.

The children oohed, then their gentle voices joined in practiced harmony to lead the congregation in singing "O Holy Night." As the song grew stronger, the pastor lifted a candle from the wreath, and his dot of light traveled down the stairs to the table nearest the stage.

From candle to candle, the warm glow spread her way, lighting faces and offering warmth. Brendon twisted and extended an arm to light his candle from the gentleman sitting at the table next to theirs. Lacey reached for her own taper, then held it out for Brendon to light.

She couldn't help remembering the candle lighting at her wedding ceremony, representing two flames becoming one. Sadly, their fire had been snuffed out, but this new light was symbolic of God's continuing love for her in spite of the way her wick had been extinguished.

Her gaze lifted to Brendon's, and a thrill of hope shivered down her spine.

No. She squared her shoulders and closed her eyes.

Brendon may have been a wise man, but Jesus was the King of Kings. He was born to save her. He was all she needed.

Her mistake in marrying Scott had been depending on a man when she should only have depended on God. That was a mistake she'd never make again.

Chapter Ten

BRENDON WRAPPED THE last of the gifts. He always enjoyed shopping for presents to give the families sponsored by Oil of Joy, but he'd never enjoyed it this much. Lacey's presence made everything about the holidays brighter. And Dirk's sermon had been exactly what he'd needed.

He'd thought he had to lay his dream of spending the rest of his life with Lacey to rest, but God had resurrected it. Somehow, through just texts and phone calls, they'd grown closer over the last couple of weeks than he'd ever been with another woman. And though she'd expertly avoided any talk about dating, she seemed to like being with him as much as he did with her.

She looked up from the festive package with her Tonka truck inside. Her light-brown eyes met his, and if the effect it had on his body could have been bottled, it would have been the most expensive essential oil ever sold.

Her eyes widened. "Oh . . ."

So she was finally going to admit she felt it too?

She pointed past him, out the window of the fifth-floor boardroom. "It's snowing."

Okay, he'd have to keep waiting. He turned to watch the white flakes float through twinkling light toward the earth below. It was barely past five o'clock, but the sun had already set, and the campus was lit by bright decorations. Maybe the snow would stick this time and he'd actually get the winter wonderland he'd been asking God for.

Lacey walked to the window to enjoy the beauty, and he joined her, hoping this would be the first of many Christmases together.

"Are you staying?" As his words came out, he realized the question had double meaning.

She sighed in contentment. "Oh yes. I want to see the boy who gets the truck I bought. I invited my parents to drive here when they arrive in town."

Brendon would get to meet her parents too then. He studied her, wondering if she also felt the largeness of this thing between them or if it would have to be revealed to her slowly.

Her gaze snagged on his and grew hard with wariness, as if she realized how close she was standing to him. Close enough for him to smell her lavender scent. "What?" she asked.

How much could he share without scaring her off? "I was thinking about the message today. About how you called me out on my pride and how I used to feel like I had to do good deeds because God needed me."

She chuckled but glanced down. Perhaps to sever their electric connection like she had during the candle-lighting ceremony. "Now what do you believe?"

"I do believe being generous is God's will, but I think it has more to do with dreams like Dirk was talking about. When we don't follow God's will, that's when dreams die. For example, it would have been God's will for your husband to stay committed to you."

Lacey shifted. Turned her head.

"However, when we follow God's will, dreams are restored. It's not about God needing me. It's about me needing Him."

Lacey refused to meet his gaze. "It's too late for my dream to be restored."

Okay, he'd said too much. His pulse thrummed. He motioned in the direction she was looking to the painting of Jesus with Mary and Joseph. "You can still have a family, Lacey. You can remarry. Your child can be adopted by another man."

"Brendon." Her tone dropped like her expression, but at least she hadn't called him Mr. Wise this time. She turned to face him. "I married Scott because I took what I wanted rather than wait for God to give me what I needed. That was me not following God's will. And now I know not to depend on anyone other than God."

So that was why she'd been so upset by charity. That was why she refused to accept gifts. She thought she'd brought single parenthood on herself. It wasn't pride like his that kept her from receiving—it was the flip side of the coin. She thought she'd failed to earn good things. And if she didn't think she'd earned good things, then the two of them could never have a good relationship.

"Hon." There was that word again. Well, if he was going to reveal his feelings with a term of endearment, he might as well reach for her hand. He hooked her cool palm with his fingers, reminding him of their first handshake when he'd wanted to warm her.

She pulled her hand away and tucked it behind her back. She averted her eyes once again.

His chest constricted. "Hon," he repeated, because she really was dear to him. "Yes, God is here for us when others fail. But sometimes He gives good gifts through people too. Like how my oils helped your headaches. And the gold, frankincense, and myrrh would have helped Joseph and Mary. God created us to be here for each other. There is joy in giving but also in receiving."

She didn't look up, but her chest rose and fell. She'd heard. But had she listened?

The tap of high heels grew louder. The door whooshed open behind him. "Mr. Wise. Your . . . uh . . . delivery is here."

He looked at his watch. Right on time. If only he'd known Lacey was going to be here as well. That she was going to need him.

Scratch that. She didn't need him. As much as he hated to admit it, she would be fine without him. God would bless her whether they ended up together or not.

"Thank you, Hallie. I'll be down in a minute."

She glanced at Lacey, nodded, and backed out. The door thunked closed.

Now what? He had to go, but like when Lacey wasn't answering his texts, he didn't know if he was going to see her again. He wanted to lift her chin and press his lips against hers because it could be his last chance to kiss her, but he knew that wasn't the best way to show his love.

"The thing about gifts is, they can't be earned." He strode to the table of presents by the door. He'd planned to give her the small package when he was handing out the rest of the gifts because then it would be harder for her to turn it down, but she might not stick around that long. He retrieved a box the size of a double deck of cards wrapped in shiny gold paper. "Don't worry—this isn't for you. It's for your baby. I know what it's like to be the only child of a single mom in a city of large families. God had to be my Father and fill the voids. And whether you give me a chance or not . . ." His throat pinched tight, cutting off his words. He had to swallow his fears to finish. "I want God's best for you both."

She blinked watery eyes at him, not moving, not saying anything. She wasn't making this easy.

"I want God's best for you too," she finally whispered.

The relief that came with her words only lasted a moment before he realized that was her way of saying goodbye. "Then please stay. Stay for the boy with the Tonka truck. Stay for me."

She made no promises. No move to take his gift.

He set it on the table. "I have to go give out a lot more presents now, but just know this gift means more to me than any of them."

Lacey waited for Brendon's retreating footsteps to fade completely before she let herself reach for the package. She'd wanted to spend time with Brendon, but she hadn't wanted to lead him on. Now she'd come to the Y in the road. Either she had to be open to having a relationship or say goodbye forever. But why did it have to happen on Christmas Eve? Right before her nugget was due? Now every Christmas she'd think of Brendon. Every time she celebrated her baby's birthday, she'd think of him. She'd wish he was there with them.

His suggestion of friendship had seemed a good compromise until that friendship had been set on fire. There was no denying her attraction, and pretending it didn't exist wasn't fair to him.

She picked up the gift he'd left. It didn't weigh much, but it was too solid to be jewelry, thank goodness. She didn't need another reminder of all she was giving up.

His words about not being able to earn a gift rammed at the walls around her heart. She knew the fact in her head, but she didn't feel it.

In her experience gifts were given to hold the recipient down in order to make the giver feel better about himself. They were a form of manipulation.

In return for all Scott's care, she'd had to depend on him the way people should only depend on God. When she'd found healing and put God back in place as her provider, Scott had withdrawn all gifts. So maybe it wasn't that she didn't think she'd earned good things, but that she didn't want to be in debt to the giver. The thought of opening this gift from Brendon felt like taking out a loan.

Still undecided, she pulled on her coat. She'd carry the package down to the nativity and watch everyone else open their presents.

The crisp air stung her nose and cheeks as she walked out to the amphitheater. Snow dotted her shoulders and hair and caught in her eyelashes. The campus was just as festive as always with its bridges and tunnels of Christmas lights, but the night was quieter. The skaters and carolers were all at home with their families, and they'd left silence behind. Lacey could even hear the water in the pond trickling over rocks.

Only a few groupings of families huddled around burn barrels dotting the amphitheater, but the falling snow had muffled their voices until she arrived at the stable. They joked with each other, anticipating Brendon like Santa. She wasn't part of their worlds, so she took a seat at the manger. Not to mention, the pressure of standing made her lower back feel like she'd been lying on rocks.

"Yikes!" A little boy shouted. "Is that a camel?"

Lacey glanced toward the kid's voice to see if he would point her in the direction of said camel. Because she knew without a doubt that the answer to his question was yes. Brendon was getting his camel ride. And he was doing it to deliver gifts like the magi had. Move over, St. Nick.

The little boy didn't only point toward Brendon. He took off running down the hill.

"Wait, baby," his mom called.

"It's okay." Brendon pulled on the camel's reins to stop the beast. He sat regally between humps, a bag of gifts over his shoulder. "I've brought him a present."

Lacey's heart hammered in her chest. First because of Brendon's presence. He was larger than life. Yes, ridiculous, but in all the best ways. Secondly, because he handed the kid her package.

"Look, Mom," yelled the boy. He didn't even wait for his mother to catch up before he ripped off the paper. "Whoa . . ." He held up the box with the truck inside like it was a trophy. Only it wasn't something he'd earned. It was a gift.

"Wow." His mom caught up. "It's just what you wanted. Somebody must be looking out for you."

Emotion clogged Lacey's throat. She'd bought the toy that day. It hadn't cost her much, but there was nothing the kid could have done to earn it. More importantly, there was nothing she wanted in return. Blessing the boy had been enough. Seeing his joy brought her joy.

Really, being part of God's bigger plan was what had brought her joy. On her own she didn't know the child or what he wanted. She'd simply been in a place to give, and what a beautiful place that was.

She watched Brendon climb from his camel and continue to hand out gifts. Each package came with a tag of what had been requested. In that way each package represented a dream. The families hadn't been able to buy the gifts themselves, but God cared about even their smallest desire. He brought their dreams back to life.

Lacey looked down at the package in her gloved hands. She hadn't put any tags on the tree, so what might have Brendon given her? What dream did God want to restore for her?

With a deep breath of icy air, she slid a finger underneath the fold and pulled. The package didn't hold one box, but two—one pink, one blue. They contained little New Testaments. Baby's first Bible.

Her heart swelled. This was what it meant to be loved.

She leaned forward to set the boxes in the manger and tugged off her gloves so she could pry off the top. Underneath the baby blue lid, she found the baby blue leather book. And on the bottom right corner, the name Chuck Foster had been engraved in gold.

With a laugh, she ripped open the pink box. Gladys Foster.

Not really the names of her grandparents and definitely not names she would give her child, but it wasn't the name that mattered. For she'd married into the Foster name, and Scott Foster had disowned them all. What mattered was relationship to the baby. The baby was hers. The baby was God's.

She looked toward Brendon in wonder to find him watching her from afar. From the center of a group all ripping into their own gifts. He was offering her everything she'd ever wanted. All she had to do was accept.

Chapter Eleven

"Lacey. There you are." The light voice belonged to Mom.

"Merry Christmas!" Dad boomed.

She looked up to find her parents circling the side of the stable. Mom ran with arms outstretched. Dad appraised the grounds around them.

"You did all this?" he asked. "Incredible."

Lacey felt their pride. Not the kind of pride that made someone think they had to rescue others or the kind of pride that kept the other person from wanting to be rescued, but the kind of pride she had in her own child. This was healthy pride. Satisfaction. Contentment in existence.

She stood to hug her parents, soon to be grandparents. Dad's bald head gave him the appearance of a grandpa, but Mom's long, wavy hair made her seem at least a decade younger. Looking at them now, nobody would know how much her recent divorce had aged them.

Mom wrapped her in a warm side hug, and Lacey groaned with both relief of having family in town and from the cramping of her stomach. She'd take a warm bath when she got home. But first she wanted to introduce her folks to Brendon.

Her belly fluttered in excitement. Even though she'd just opened her heart to the possibility of romance, she already knew this was the man she was going to marry. Brendon was her dream come back to life. More than she deserved. Where was he? She couldn't see him with all the people crowded around.

Mom pulled away to let Dad have his turn enveloping her. Big, solid, protective Dad. He'd test Brendon's dedication more than she had, so it was a good sign that her father was already impressed by the younger man's campus.

"What's this?" Mom held up the Bibles. "Are these the names you picked out for my grandbaby?"

Dad released her to turn and look. "What names?"

"Chuck and Gladys."

"Who names a kid Chuck?"

Laughter rocked Lacey, cramping her stomach even more. "No." She intended to appease them, but pain fisted beneath her belly button. "Oh . . ."

"What's wrong?" Mom returned to her side.

The pain subsided. Lacey took a breath. "It's not . . ." The tickle of warm water ran down her inner thigh.

～⁂～

Brendon waved goodbye to the last of the families he'd been able to bless, then handed off the camel to its owner.

When he'd left Lacey, he'd been nervous he wouldn't see her again, but she'd come to the stable. She'd opened his gifts. And for the first time, she'd looked at him without reservation. His chest still itched from that look.

He jogged across the courtyard, overflowing with thankfulness at the opportunity he'd had to share God's love as well as the expectation of finally finding a love of his own. He fought the goofy grin that probably made him look more foolish than wise but then gave in to the absolute pleasure of it. He'd be a fool for Lacey. With one giant puff of crystallized breath, he looked up at the seat where he'd last seen her. The rickety wooden chair sat empty.

His eyes roved the stable. All that remained from the woman's presence were the pink and blue Bibles resting in the manger.

She'd left. Lacey had left him after all.

He sank down in the spot she'd vacated, his heart heavy. There wasn't an essential oil to soothe this ache.

He'd tried to prepare himself for such a response to his gift. In fact, he thought he'd been prepared. He'd chosen to love Lacey whether she accepted his love or not.

But then she'd followed him down to the amphitheater. They'd shared a raw moment from across the pavers. Visions of mistletoe had danced in his head. Freezing snowflakes replaced that vision.

He bent forward, forearms on his thighs, and stared at the manger. It represented the hope on earth. Right now hope was empty.

Not all dreams came true, did they? Some died. Like Brendon's dad had. Like Lacey's marriage had.

Bad things happened. Even the magi who'd brought gifts had triggered events that led to the death of all the baby boys in Bethlehem. There was happiness. There was sadness. Then there was Jesus. In moments like this, Jesus had to be enough. He was the meaning of "joy to the world."

Brendon folded his hands and dropped his chin. "Thank You, Lord, for Lacey. Thank You for her baby. Be with them. Love them. Provide more for them than I ever could."

"Brendon Wise?" a voice boomed, unfamiliar.

His name echoed through the night. Brendon frowned up at a bald man standing at the edge of the stable with hands in his pockets and one foot planted wide. "Yes?"

"My daughter is in labor at the hospital. She asked me to come find you."

⁂

Lacey hugged her baby to her. The little nugget had a squished pink face, adorable little nose, wrinkles for eyes, and what looked like a really bad toupee of dark-brown hair. "Merry Christmas," she whispered.

Giving birth probably felt similar to how the Grinch's dog, Max, felt when he'd had to pull the whole sleigh up a mountain by himself. To quote his green master, "We're gonna die, we're gonna die, I'm going to throw up and then I'm gonna die." Somehow, Lacey had survived to become as happy as a Who in Whoville.

Everything she'd been through—her headaches, her pathetic attempt at marriage, her divorce—was all worth it for this child. For this moment. None of it defined her anymore. And none of it ever should have.

"Congratulations." The voice belonged to the man she'd sent her dad to hunt down.

She hadn't wanted Brendon to think she'd abandoned him. But she didn't expect him to sit in the waiting room for her eleven hours of labor. It was Christmas morning. He should be drinking cocoa with peppermint oil in front of a cozy fireplace. He was almost too good to be true.

In her dazed state, she recalled their conversation over the existence of Santa. "Are you real?" She held her breath.

He strode over, pink and blue Bibles in hand. "What do you think?"

"I think if you were real, you'd tell me."

"I'm real." He smoothed her hair from her face. Soothed the doubt from her soul. "This is real."

It still felt a dream. She nodded down at her baby. "Is she real?"

"No, she's unreal. Beyond belief. Extraordinary." He held up the pink Bible. "I take it from the little red bow glued to her head, this is Gladys."

Lacey leaned her head back against the pillow with a weak but delighted laugh. "My grandmother's name wasn't really Gladys."

"That's too bad, because the name has grown on me." Brendon set the Bibles on the side table.

"You, maybe. My dad, not so much." Lacey gave a little snort at her parents' reactions to the names engraved on the pink and blue New Testaments.

"Well, as I'm also fond of your folks now, it's probably good you picked another name." He rubbed a finger over the infant's cheek. "Want to introduce me?"

Lacey's heart warmed. She hadn't had the chance to introduce Brendon to her parents, but it sounded like he'd taken care of that himself. So she'd introduce him to her daughter. "Brendon, meet Joy."

His multicolored eyes jumped to hers. They shimmered with unshed tears. He shook his head and took a moment to swallow. "That's beautiful. I'll have her name engraved on another Bible."

She smiled softly. She hadn't thanked him for his gifts yet. She hadn't told him how much they meant to her. The good news was that God offered redemption, and she'd have a whole lifetime to come up with the right words.

At the moment, she only had the energy to offer, "I think that would be wise." And, of course, for the sweet peppermint kiss that followed.

Author's Note

DEAR READER,

When I first asked my editor if I could have a pregnant heroine, she questioned how the character had gotten pregnant. I responded, "Yada, yada, yada." After my editor clarified she knew *how* my character conceived, she requested a backstory that would allow the heroine to enter into a healthy relationship with the hero. It's this question that makes redemption even sweeter. Because my heroine also believed her condition excluded her from having the family of her dreams, her happily-ever-after becomes more about the joy of the Lord.

As for my hero, I didn't want him to be your typical millionaire. He's shorter. He has a baby face. But he also has this natural energy that makes him a little quirky and a whole lot authentic. His toxic trait is that he prides himself on doing good, which only makes me want to pinch his adorably smooth cheeks even more.

The German family heritage of the Weise clan played perfectly into my story's message. Christkindlmarkt SLC is a real festival. The lantern parade is based on real folklore. Some stuff you can't make up.

As for Oil of Joy, I based the company on Scentsy here in Idaho. If you haven't heard of it, Scentsy sells electric candle warmers, and their beautiful campus becomes a destination for families during the holidays. It makes for a magical meet-cute.

Happily ever after is more than anyone deserves. And that's where the good news comes in. That's why the birth of Jesus brought joy to the world. The gift of joy is for all.

C. S. Lewis said it best. "Joy is the serious business of heaven."* And that's what I want to wish you this holiday season. Wherever you're at and whatever you believe, you are loved.

Joyfully,
Angela

---

* C. S. Lewis, *Letters to Malcolm: Chiefly on Prayer* (San Diego: Harvest, 1964), 92–93.

Acknowledgments

Crystal Caudill

No book is completed in solitude. All thanks and glory go first to Jesus Christ; without Him there would be no story. Thank you to my family, especially my husband, Travis, for all your support and patience. You guys always cheer me on and make it possible for me to get the writing done. Thank you to my group of besties. I don't know what I'd do without you. As always, thank you to my agent Tamela Hancock Murray and the amazing Kregel team—in particular Janyre Tromp, Dori Harrell, and Rachel Kirsch. Thank you for all your editing prowess and teaching. This story is all the better because of you. And thank you, readers, for picking up this collection and blessing me with your precious time to read it.

Cara Putman

It was a thrill to get the email from Catherine DeVries with an offer to write a novella in this collection. My smile couldn't have been bigger when I saw I would get to return to the world of World War II and Europe. There are so very many stories worth telling from that time period, and it was so much fun to brainstorm with my coauthors Crystal Caudill and Angela Ruth Strong along with our editor Janyre Tromp about how this family collection could align across time. I love working with other authors on stories that connect and hope you enjoy every page. This was my first book with Kregel, and it was so fun to work with Catherine, Janyre, Katherine Chappell, Rachel Kirsch, and the rest of the team. Thanks for making it such a great experience.

This was my first book with Rachelle Gardner as my agent. I'm excited to see what the future holds. Thanks for cheerleading me in this season.

Thanks also to Andrea Cox and Hannah Grindly for serving as beta readers on this story. You were great encouragers that this story was worth telling when I began to wonder. I always say a book isn't really a book until someone reads it, so thank you for reading the early version of these words.

My family has taken this crazy journey with me almost forty times—y'all are amazing. Eric, thanks for always believing I can do it again. Abigail, Jonathan, Rebecca, and Daniel, thank you for thinking it's kind of cool that Mom writes, but even more for being patient with me when I lose track of time and ask for five more minutes that morph into twenty or thirty.

And to everyone who makes time to read these words. Thank you. I don't take that gift lightly.

Angela Ruth Strong

I have a vivid memory of being crammed into a car with my parents, grandmother, and daughter as we drove back to Grandma's house in the dark after dinner in Sedona, and they listened to me tell this story. When Dad asked what book I was currently working on, he probably hadn't expected a full synopsis of Brendon and Lacey's romance, complete with hand gestures, laughter, and tears. But it does a storyteller's heart good to have a captive audience, and I never would have become a storyteller if my family hadn't been willing to listen in the first place.

So thank you to all those grandparents who believe in their grandchildren when they forget how to believe in themselves. Thank you to the parents who really care what their kids have to say. Thank you to the children who can't stand Hallmark-type love stories but will attend their mother's movie premiere, even if it means missing the concert they'd wanted to attend. Thank you to the husbands who want to see their wives fly, even if they can't join the trip. Thank you to the publishing professionals who make each story better and get it to its audience.

And thank you to my audience. You do my heart good, and I hope "Perfect Light" makes your day just a little brighter, as well.

CRYSTAL CAUDILL is the author of "dangerously good historical romance," with her work garnering awards from Romance Writers of America and ACFW. She is a stay-at-home mom and caregiver, and when she isn't writing, Crystal can be found playing board games with her family, drinking hot tea, or reading great books at her home outside Cincinnati, Ohio. Find out more and sign up for her newsletter at crystalcaudill.com.

To read more about some of the characters from "Star of Wonder," check out the other titles in Crystal's Hidden Hearts of the Gilded Age series, *Counterfeit Love*, *Counterfeit Hope*, and *Counterfeit Faith*.

CARA PUTMAN is a born storyteller. Whether she's teaching in a classroom at a Big Ten university or writing award-winning, best-selling novels, she's engaging with others through the power of story. She's also passionate about her family, faith, and building relationships. You'll often find her connecting with students, friends, and colleagues at various coffeeshops in her hometown. She also loves to explore, so ask her about her favorite places to travel—but make sure you have time! She just might share pictures. Join in on her adventures at caraputman.com

ANGELA RUTH STRONG sold her first Christian romance novel in 2009. Her books have since earned honors such as Top Pick in *Romantic Times*, winner of the Cascade Award, nominee for a Christy Award, and becoming Amazon bestsellers. Her book *Finding Love in Big Sky* was made into a movie and aired on UPtv in 2022. To help aspiring authors in her home state of Idaho, she started Idahope Writers. She also blogs regularly for My Book Therapy. She'd love to have you stop by for a visit at angelaruthstrong.com.

To read more about some of the characters from "Perfect Light," check out the other titles in Angela's Love Off Script series, *Husband Auditions*, *Hero Debut*, and *Fiancé Finale*.

HIDDEN HEARTS
OF THE GILDED AGE
SERIES

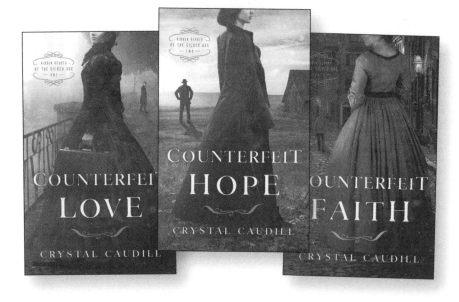

"This series has been perfection from book one! . . . Caudill creates characters that are easy to love. . . . Fabulously entertaining and grace-filled."

—CARRIE SCHMIDT, blogger at ReadingIsMySuperPower.org and author of *Getting Past the Publishing Gatekeepers*

KREGEL
PUBLICATIONS

Looking for more romance with a Christmas twist? Look no further!

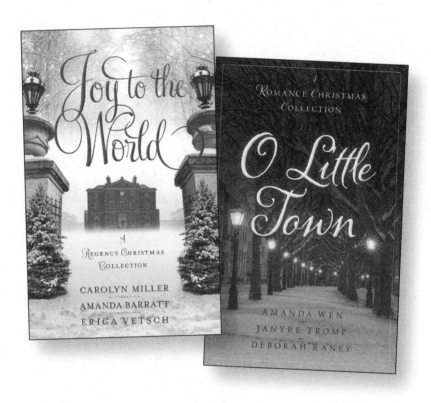

"You'll want to grab a cup of hot cocoa and soak in these unique tales."
—Amanda Cox, author of *The Edge of Belonging*